A Shot Heard 'Round

By

Kevin M. Prochaska

ISBN: 1-4107-2272-4 (e-book)
ISBN: 1-4107-2273-2 (Paperback)
ISBN: 1-4107-3938-4 (Dust Jacket)

Library of Congress Control Number: 2003091084

This book is printed on acid free paper.

Printed in the United States of America
Bloomington, IN

1st Books - rev. 04/07/03

Table of Contents

1   A Shot Rings Out

Sheriff Everett Hiram heard the shot just about the time the office door flew open and slammed against the inside wall, rattling the wood-framed photograph of Governor Harold E. Hughes. Old Duke, his sixty-two year old use-only-when-desperate deputy, dove headlong into the room and splashed on the floor in front of his desk.

"They're at it again, Everett!" he shouted, picking his starved, one hundred forty pound, chicken-like body from the floor. "It's them damn Petler brothers, Sheriff. They're drunk again and they're shooting up the town."

Through the French glass window facing Main Street, Sheriff Hiram observed the results of the gunfire. Everett shook his head in disbelief as he leaned forward to watch the hoopla outside. Scurrying past the window, away from the gunfire, were three of the town's finest citizens, if a town of five hundred could be said to have such people. One of the fleeing trio turned toward the window and stared with horror-filled eyes at the sheriff, pointing back from where he had run. Two other men ran east, down the middle of the street and dropped prone on the pavement, covering their heads when a second shot rang out.

The town dog pack, comprised of a distinguished array of the filthiest mongrels Corwith County had to offer, was also on the move. Every shape and size of confused canine ran together as a single body of bedlam. Some of these curs had felt the sting of number six shotgun pellets more than once on one of their nightly forays through the surrounding farms and knew to run at the sound of the thunder. The remaining pack ran just because every other dog around was running, and it just appeared to be the proper thing to do at the time.

Bringing up the rear of the pack, Merle Oaken's guide dog loped with long strides, eyes peering beyond his long nose, as if searching for some unseen prize ahead. The dog's tongue dangled over the right side of his jowl, slopping frothy bubbles of saliva on the pavement

2

each time the dog's enormous paws slammed against the concrete. Galloping along the north side of Main Street, the pack turned headlong into an alley, the lead dog falling, to be trampled by the rest. Through the rising dust the dog's feet shot toward the sky like the legs of an overturned table. The mongrel attempted to correct its predicament by twisting his body to right itself, pushing its nose against the dirt for leverage. The dog rose, confused by the dust, and ran in the opposite direction of the pack, until his instincts, or perhaps just plain dog-sense, informed his legs that the pack was now behind him and running the other way. The dog turned around clumsily and retraced its path, running down the alley in a valiant attempt to catch up with the stampeding pack.

Viola Vanderhoff, moving swiftly along the sidewalk in front of Everett's office, glanced back toward the shooting sounds behind her, ramming violently into the unsuspecting Amy Flanigan. Mrs. Flanigan, carrying two brim-filled bags from Merle's Grocery, had been watching the brilliant colors of the setting sun bouncing off the low clouds in the western sky, and not the least bit concerned about anyone running toward her at that particular moment, since she thought the shots were just thunder. Through the window Everett observed apples, vegetables, and other assorted items flung into the air as the flimsy brown grocery bags exploded between the women. Among the items gaining altitude were Mrs. Flanigan's glasses, spiraling upward in a circle, as if a pinwheel caught by the wind. Everett felt tremors in the wooden floor of his office as the amply rotund Vanderhoff woman crashed to the sidewalk like a wrecking ball.

It was about that time when Everett figured he'd better get up from his chair.

Before the gunfire erupted, the late afternoon was dimming to a typical Friday night in Apology, the September weather cooling the small Iowa town, signaling the end of the summer of 1965. The town's high school students had gotten home safely, after being bussed to Renoir, twenty miles away, where the population was big enough to have argued for a school years ago. Now, many of the town's residents were preparing to travel back to Renoir for a football game. It would be a clear, cool night for the event.

A brown leaf floated by the window, as summer turned another page to autumn.

"Well, get out of the way, Duke!" Everett grumbled, grabbing his Stetson. "I'd better get out there before the whole damn town kills themselves."

Everett grunted as his boot kicked the leg of the desk, pushing his chair away from the worn piece of furniture. He stood, wiping the face of his left sleeve across his brow before dropping his cream-colored Stetson on his head. Everett, a man of medium build, was proud of his physique at age forty-four. His stomach protruded only slightly over his belt, and his sandy brown hair had yet to show a hint of gray. While in uniform he was neat as a pin, even though he liked to joke that he was an unconfirmed bachelor. Everett often told the boys at Duffy's Tavern that a wife would be OK to have, just as long as she didn't interfere with his hunting and fishing plans.

Old Duke, sensing the sheriff's displeasure, wisely rolled to the side, away from the door. Everett slid his right hand down along his side, feeling his gun belt, and lightly tickled the butt of his pistol with his fingertips. Grabbing the gun belt firmly with both hands, he jerked the leather band upward two inches and strode through the open door. The office door slammed behind him, and Everett knew Old Duke had closed the gates to the fort.

The two dazed women lay amid the rubble that had been a week's worth of groceries. The leaf Everett had seen floating by his window rested on the concrete between them.

"You ladies, OK?" he asked, extending a hand to Mrs. Flanigan, closest to the door.

Amy Flanigan, her long brown hair now in complete disarray, swiveled her head robotically side to side, surveying the wreckage surrounding her. Her slim, thirty-two year old body had been no match for Viola's mass when the two had collided. Since Amy was roughly half the size of Mrs. Vanderhoff, Everett figured he'd help her up first, to kinda warm up his back for the real work that would come when he turned his attention to Viola.

"OK!" Viola huffed, her massive body spread around her on the sidewalk, the spacious yellow dress she'd worn to diminish her volume now giving her the appearance of an oversized pineapple, "Does this look like I'm OK, Sheriff?"

Viola Vanderhoff had been plump all her life and had gotten used to the childhood nicknames she'd endured. But she'd never been privy to the really good ones her classmates had come up with, the ones they dared not utter in her presence. For being big had one advantage for Viola during her school days, and that had been intimidation. Not even the toughest of schoolboys dared challenge Viola's sharp tongue when that forked darling flapped in the winds of tirade. Viola took up so much earthly space that when she had eventually married and become in the family way, most of the townsfolk hadn't even noticed that she was carrying a child. Some of the townsfolk who did take note joked that Viola's baby had something in common with Cinderella, in that, for a short period of their lives, both of them got to ride around in a pumpkin.

"Hey!" Mrs. Flanigan blurted, "look at me. This fat petunia ran into me. Look at this mess!"

It did appear to be a mess, Everett agreed, as he scanned half a dozen apples rolling across the street. The grape juice running down the front of Mrs. Flanigan's white blouse added a nice tie-dyed touch to her ensemble, but Everett thought it best not to bring that observation up at the moment.

"Don't you be calling me no fat petunia!" Mrs. Vanderhoff shot back, the red vessels in her widening eyes gorging to flames. "You know I got a glandular disorder that I've been fighting all my life."

The glandular disorder, Everett had always secretly maintained, most likely resulted from Viola's love affair, over the space of fifty-two years, with anything chocolate. But that was just a speculative guess.

"I don't give one hooty-hoo about your dang glandular problem," Mrs. Flanigan retorted. "Oh, look at my shirt. Look at this mess!"

Uh-oh, Everett thought. Perhaps just a tad too much purple.

"You're gonna pay for this shirt," Mrs. Flanigan declared. "If I'da wanted my shirt to be purple, I'd bought it that way."

"Now, Amy," Everett cut in, "it was an accident."

Everett stopped, and the trio turned as a shot rang out down the street. Everett instinctively crouched.

"But my shirt!"

Everett watched Mrs. Vanderhoff's eyes, a glazed look forming over them. During the initial collision between the two women, five pounds of canned ham had launched itself from Amy's grocery bag, and had given Amy's glasses a pretty fair race upward. The glasses won the contest, but the shock of the ham's abrupt orbital reentry onto the fat women's bouffant crown was beginning to set in.

Through the office window, Old Duke cautiously watched the events unfolding on the opposite side of the glass. He caught Everett's glance and slid along the wall to the safety of anonymity.

"I'll tell you what, Amy," Everett offered. "Since the accident happened on town property, why don't we let the town buy you a new shirt? I tell you what—why don't you just go on over to Rutland's General Store and—"

"Why should the town pay for my shirt?" she snorted, pointing at Mrs. Vanderhoff. "She ruined it. People's complaining already about how the town council spends our money. And now you want to use some to buy a shirt."

Mrs. Vanderhoff's bulky frame leaned against a pole that held up one side of a small porch protecting the front door of the sheriff's office. Everett pointed to the ground, to a gaping crack in the cement sidewalk that began where the pole went into the ground.

"You know, Amy, I saw the whole thing from my office. Poor Mrs. Vanderhoff was just minding her own business when the Petlers started shooting. Why, she was so frightened, she ran and tripped right over that crack, she sure did."

Another shot interrupted the conversation. Everett instinctively hunched down once more and straightened up when he felt the danger had passed. Old Duke, slithering along the wall once more for a better view, retreated at the sound.

"So you see, Amy, it's simple. It was the sidewalk that caused poor Viola here to smash into you. Hell, she was going down anyway, and you just broke her fall. Now don't you feel better that you saved Viola from falling on those poor, weak knees of hers? Just imagine her, laid up in the hospital, her legs dangling all helpless from a sling."

He could tell by the look in Amy's eyes that the woman saw the image of Viola Vanderhoff's near plight in her mind.

"Why, you may have even saved her life," he added.

Mulling over what Everett said Amy stared over at the dazed woman on the sidewalk. She touched the stain on her shirt, rubbing purple liquid between her thumb and finger.

"You know what I'm going to do for you, Amy?" Everett continued. "I'm going right down to Rutland's first thing tomorrow morning and tell them to give you a line of credit for one hundred dollars to spend on whatever you want–compliments of the town of Apology for an act of bravery and kindness."

"A hundred dollars!"

"That's right. A hundred dollars. I'll even make sure this gets in the newspaper."

"We don't have a newspaper."

She had him there, he realized. Sometimes, he reminded himself, he had to tighten the reins on his overflowing optimism.

"Oh, I'm thinking about having the town start one. And you'd be the first story."

That should get him out of that mess, he thought. For now.

"So, what do you say, Amy?"

She eyed him suspiciously.

"Everett Hiram, if you ain't a twin-tailed skunk swimming in the toilet water. OK, I'll take you up on that offer. But if you can't make good–"

"Then I'll pay it out of my own pocket," he declared.

He'd caught her one step behind, and the woman fell silent, beaten by the fast-thinking lawman. She held her hand out to Mrs. Vanderhoff.

"Well, come on, Viola," she grunted. "We ain't plant holders. Let's get off this sidewalk before the sun goes down."

Mrs. Vanderhoff got up slowly, propped between the sheriff and her collision mate. She stood up, grateful, and smiled weakly.

"We'll pick up here, Sheriff," Mrs. Flanigan said in a subdued voice. "But you'd just better go and see to those dang Petler boys."

Everett spotted Old Duke's face through the glass, partially hidden by the window frame. An approving smile, like a slumbering crescent moon, split his weathered face in half.

"You're right, Amy," Everett answered. "I'll attend to that right now."

He really should go see the Petlers, Everett thought as he walked away from the debris-strewn sidewalk. After all, they might actually fool around and hit something for once.

Kevin M. Prochaska

2   Rooster in the Corn

Everett began walking west down Main Street. He didn't have much choice about the walking part because his patrol car was on a hoist in Plit Butler's Garage, getting new tires. To any other lawman in this part of the country, having to walk eight blocks would have been embarrassing. But not to Everett Hiram, for he knew he'd soon have company as he strolled along the pavement toward the Petler place, just beyond the city limits.

Apology had sprung from the fertile black soil of the flatlands of Iowa, a human plant out of place among the natural greenery. The existence of the community, built one hundred years before, seemed ironic, for the town's original purpose had been to cater to people who would never live within its borders. The town was a typical Iowa

15

farming community, begun when horse and buggy transportation made traveling great distances a cumbersome and time-consuming bother. Because of these constraints, many small towns sprang up to support the growing armies of farmers and farm families within a five to ten mile radius. Farmers needed supplies–building wood, tools, fertilizers, and other goods, and the small towns provided them, all at a central location. All over the farm country hundreds of small towns like Apology were spaced with checkerboard uniformity of both distance and size. The towns formed small hubs where north-south and east-west running dirt roads intersected perpendicularly, and between the towns, less traveled roads divided the land into large squares of individual farms. Eventually the main roads were covered in blacktop, and the secondary roads were graveled to provide more stability for farm machinery and cars.

From the air, the land was rich in symmetry, with the roads dividing the countryside into sections of land a square mile in area. The sections were divided into individual farms, separated by long lines of fence. Each farm was a small town unto itself, with the main house, barn, machine shed, corncrib, and other buildings clustered together, usually bordered on the north by a small grove of trees to hold back the raging winter snows. Surrounding the main farm, the land was divided further into fields of grain growing in arrow-straight rows, a point of tremendous pride for the farmers who planted them. Miles of fence lines bordered the fields, the fence wire fastened to posts spaced at intervals of exactly the same distance between each post. In the summer, weeds sprouted among the soybeans and rose above the crop. Although farmers contended that the presence of these weeds complicated the harvesting process, it was perhaps a greater crime that these interlopers interfered with the rigid order of the field. Armies of bean walkers were conscripted to march through the fields in the stifling heat, and like skirmishers on line, they stretched across the rows with paper-doll uniformity, moving forward as one. Under the command of the farmer, these mercenaries brandished corn knives and slew the upstart weeds, restoring symmetry to the land, and by doing so, reaffirmed the pride of the land masters. In such a land of rigid order, the reality of basic right and wrong was never an issue, although some, burdened by their human frailties, occasionally sought to stir the mud resting deep in the lake of common sense.

Some towns, like Apology, had railroad tracks running diagonally through them, connecting the towns by a second means of transportation. Long trains of open railcars passed through these towns, a metallic rectangular of snake, the sound of their heavy steel wheels changing in tone at spots where they rolled over a rotting tie or loose rail. Schoolboys would sit on a rise near the tracks, hypnotized by the endless rows of cars that blurred into one, and lulled by the cla-clack-cla-clack-cla-clack of the slow moving train. Some of the trains stopped beneath the grain elevator. There each open railcar waited its turn below a feeder pipe used to transfer the stored grain from the elevator to the railcar. When the feeder pipe swung over the tracks, the grain flowed through the pipe like water over a falls, and each railcar gorged its square belly with tons of golden corn or cream-colored soybeans collected from local farmers, who, for weeks, had brought their offerings to the elevator god. And from practically any small town in Iowa, one could look across the open countryside and find a half dozen or more elevators rising from the ground as enormous white cylindrical monuments to progress.

Many of the small towns had been started by different groups of European immigrants, migrating into the state in clusters of ethnic origin. Irish, Czechs, Swedes, Germans, and many other nationalities had dominated separate towns at first, each comfortably clustered within their own familiar cultures. Over the years these distinctions had become less important as native languages and accents disappeared with the merging of nationalities. Apology had a mixture of Irish, Czechs, and Germans, with the predominate religion being Catholic. There was only one church in town, St. John's Catholic Church, but other towns in the area catered to various other religions, mainly Lutheran.

The business district of Apology was a mere four blocks long, and Everett quickly found himself west of it, walking among the odd array of houses that lined Main Street. The town of Apology had been aptly named, a visitor once said, because someone should apologize to God for making a mess like this on His good green earth.

None of the houses standing side by side had much in common with one another in an architectural sense other than they all had a roof and were small. Some houses had slate-shingle siding, and some of the shingles at the bottom of the houses dangling at odd angles. Over the years, the impact of children bouncing balls against the side of the houses had popped the nails. Other houses had wooden siding, with paint peeling off in large bubbles. On the few pieces of board where the bubbles were absent, the smooth siding trapped shallow depressions where paint had peeled repeatedly, and where the wood had been painted over on numerous occasions during the life of the house. Several houses had makeshift additions built over the years, none of which matched the architecture or material or even the color of the original structure.

The front lawns along Main Street were small and varying. Some lawns were neat, with birdbaths and ornaments, while others were littered or badly in need of mowing. One lawn had been almost entirely converted into a rock garden, the bright pink quartz capping the rock wall curiously out of place above the predominantly brown sandstone to which it had been cemented, and the whole menagerie rising quite irregularly from the flatlands on which it had been built. The rock garden was separated from the sidewalk by a white picket fence that leaned toward the road, as if it were intoxicated.

The backyards of most of the houses were littered and unkempt, some serving as the final resting place for automobiles long past their prime. People talked seriously about how the old Chevy in Moog Raymond's back yard ought to have one of those identification numbers that the FAA required on airplanes, because the vehicle had been up in the air for years, resting on jacks, and wasn't scheduled to land anytime soon.

But then, it really wasn't entirely Moog's fault that his car was sitting in the air like that. For Moog had tried to get the car fixed, that is, the leaky gas tank causing the problem in the first place. Moog toiled and swore half a day trying to remove the rusty bolts holding the gas tank to the undercarriage, only to discover that the hole in the tank was larger than he'd at first thought. Moog then phoned Jacob Witt, the town handyman, to see what he could do about fixing the leak in the tank. In hindsight, it probably wasn't the wisest decision Jacob Witt ever made when he fired up the acetylene torch and attempted to weld the hole shut. For the long tail of flame touched off the gasoline fumes trapped inside the tank. Etta Ivy, next door, still told anyone who cared to listen about Jacob's glorious flight south into the blackberry bushes as the explosion propelled the man, welding mask and all, through the air, his rubber apron flapping around him like the wings of a blackbird.

After news of his unfortunate incident got out, some of the town folks just referred to Jacob as Nitt Witt for a week or so. But lucky for Jacob, the burns healed, so that tag didn't stick.

As Everett walked he spotted minute, gleaming brass objects on the road ahead. The Petler brothers had been in the vicinity all right. Stooping down to pick up one of the objects, Everett felt the warmth against his palm. The powder inside the shell casing had been fired very recently. A total of six brass casings littered the street. Everett was surprised. The Petler brothers always shot on their own property when they were feeling drunk and ornery. They were known for making a lot of noise, but, until now, had never ventured into town when they were drinking and shooting.

"You goin' after them Petler boys, Everett?" a coarse voice behind him asked.

Everett turned around slowly, as he always did. For he wasn't too afraid of anybody in Apology doing much damage to him, with him being the sheriff and all. Olaf Clancy stood on the crumbling sidewalk, his hands buried deeply inside the pockets of the man's ragged blue and white pinstriped bib overalls.

"Looks like I'm gonna have to," Everett replied, fondling the shell casings clinking in his hand. "Those boys done come into town this time."

"Good, Sheriff," Olaf replied. "Mind if I walk with you?"

"Sure, Olaf. Come on along."

Olaf could use the company, now that half the town didn't talk to him anymore. It was that pesky incident with his wife that had done him in with some of the good people of Apology.

Olaf always insisted that his nagging wife had died of natural causes, and the talk around Duffy's Tavern pretty much supported the man. But Duffy's was the watering hole for most of the men who thought they were being unduly nagged, so it seemed just decent that they supported him in that regard. Olaf contended that a person conked on the head with a two-by-four would just naturally die if you swung the board hard enough, and the boys at Duffy's agreed. The fact that the jury had hung just re-enforced his contention. And Everett, being the lawman, had no problem with that logic. After all, he had known Zelda, even incurring the wrath of her sharp tongue on more than one occasion. And the fact that Olaf had won in court—well, that had been good enough for the town sheriff. Besides, anyone who could argue with a judge and get his two-by-four back must have something going for him, Everett figured. Olaf had cut the two-by-four in half and propped up the north window of his bedroom, the very reason, it was said, that he had conked the air conditioning-loving Zelda on the noggin in the first place.

Olaf must have figured what the sheriff was thinking, for he caught Everett glancing toward the upstairs of his house.

"God, I love this weather," Olaf said, grinning. "These cool nights are so nice for sleeping."

Olaf was in his late thirties, but could have been ten years older to look at him. The man worked at the grain elevator in Apology. He wore a soiled, frayed T-shirt beneath worn bib overalls, the white cotton long since yellowed around the armpits. Some of the yellowed cloth had rotted away, and thick hair grew from the holes around Olaf's armpits, like the unwanted rye grass that had attempted to strangle the soybeans all summer. Olaf's white, over-sized sweat socks flowed through slits in his paint-splattered leather sandals, as if attempting to escape the smell of his feet. Although Olaf's armpits had been blessed with a bountiful harvest of hair, his head hadn't, and his balding pate sat like a small plum on his portly body. He was a short man, and in a brown robe, might have passed for a monk.

As they strolled toward the end of town, Everett saw curtains fluttering inside breezeless houses, and he knew that they were being watched. Doris Donahue exposed her face to the two men when she unwittingly pulled the wrong string on the drapes. She stared at them, the initial caught-in-the-cookie-jar look on her face quickly turning to disgust. Zelda Clancy had been her second cousin. And, though the two cousins had never been close, Doris declared that it had been her two-by-four that Olaf had claimed in court, and she by God wanted it back.

In the distance Everett could see the Petler place, an eyesore conglomeration of chicken coops and animal pens surrounding a white house badly in need of paint and repair work. Rabbit skins hung from a number of trees, some of the skins having resided in that position for several years. Where an immaculate lawn had once stood when Birdy Petler was alive and running the show, swaths of weeds now sprung up sporadically, and patches of bare, dry ground could easily be seen from the road. Some of the bare patches had resulted from spilled motor oil killing the grass.

Chickens surrounded the house, pecking nervously at the ground as they kept one eye on the approaching strangers. The Petlers' dog, usually confronting visitors with bared fangs, had taken flight with the dog pack, and was presumably halfway to Renoir by now. At least, Everett realized, with the dog out of the way, he wouldn't have to kick his way onto the property for once.

In front of the house, a crooked white board fence badly in need of painting paralleled the main road running east into Apology. The house was surrounded on the remaining three sides by a wire fence that kept the chickens and whatnot contained on the property, and the east fence, facing the town, contained a rickety wire gate. Everett lifted the rusting latch and pushed the gate open, brushing his hands together to shake off the brown crusty flakes of iron. As he entered the property, followed by Olaf, the top hinge pulled loose from the wooden post and the gate flailed to the ground at an odd angle.

From the rear of the house, out of view, Everett heard five shots fired in rapid succession. He could tell by the shadows on the ground that Olaf had stepped directly behind him, shielding his body from the unseen gunman. Everett stopped, his hand instinctively reaching toward his own weapon on his right hip.

Around the side of the house a scraggly rooster suddenly appeared at a dead run, dirt kicking up from around the bird as ruffled feathers flew from his body. The rooster's feathers were comprised of various mixtures of red colors along the length of his body, abruptly changing to deeper reds and brilliant oranges in the plumage of the long tail feathers. Everett heard more shots coming from the back of the house as more dirt kicked up around the escaping bird, the bullets keeping the rooster in full flight. Emerging from the back of the house, Deke

Petler's attentions and pistol sight were focused on the tail feathers moving through the grass.

"Ya damned crowin' fool!" he shouted, his reddish hair flaming in the sun. "Ya ain't supposed to crow at sunset! Ya suppose to crow at dawn!"

He halted, drew a bead on the rooster, and fired, killing a duck splashing in a water puddle twenty feet beyond the scurrying bird. Deke's eyes caught the twinkle of Sheriff Hiram's badge and he looked up, amazed to find Everett and Olaf watching him. The rooster fled into the tall weeds, the bright orange tail looking like a cattail shaking in the breeze.

"Ah, hell," Deke said disgustedly as he strolled around the edge of the puddle to retrieve the duck. "And I wanted chicken for supper."

Deke was a piece of work, as was his brother Durham. Both of the brothers were in their early forties and had similar facial features, low brows and elongate noses. Durham was two years older than Deke and slightly taller. From a distance the two might have been mistaken for one another if their hair color hadn't set them so far apart. Deke had a nest of wild red hair and Durham's was a dull-as-dust brown.

The brothers usually wore blue jeans and some sort of T-shirt, most of the time soiled. However, when the brothers showed up for Sunday Mass, they wore clean, plaid-patterned shirts and pressed trousers, and even shined their shoes beforehand. On Sundays their pewmates got to smell the strong tonic they slapped on to slick their hair down close to their scalps, the smell of the tonic trailing them until the following Tuesday.

Deke recognized Olaf and turned to Everett.

"Hey, Sheriff," he laughed, a thick smell of alcohol escaping from his throat, "what are you doing with that killer?"

Being called a killer didn't bother Olaf much anymore, for he had heard it often enough since the trial almost two years ago.

"Taking a stroll, Deke," Everett answered. "Where's Durham?"

"Last I saw Durham, he was chasing that damn rooster towards town. He didn't get him, either."

Everett knew that Durham couldn't chase anything very far. For, most of the time, Durham walked with a slight limp, favoring his right leg. In his ornerier days Durham had lost a bet—missing a fly on his big toe–but by no more than the width of a bullet, he claimed later. And Durham, at one time, had been considered the smarter of the two.

"So Durham's the one shooting up the town then?" Everett asked.

A look of guilt came over Deke's face, vanishing as quickly as it had appeared. For a drinking man in the midst of his trade has no need for conscience.

"Hell, yes, he was!" Deke shouted, proud of his brother's accomplishment. "And he'd a got that bird if'n we had started drinking at our regular Friday time. But we decided to celebrate the big win tonight, and we didn't want to wait that long."

"Big win?" Olaf asked.

"Yea, Killer," Deke replied. "The win over Eagle Nest."

"Win?" Everett asked, turning his wrist to look at his watch. "The game don't start for two hours, Deke. And then it'll be two more hours before it's done."

The Petlers had performed this feat before. Why let a little thing like a final score, or for that matter, the game itself, get in the way of some serious celebrating?

"Hey, there's Durham!" Deke yelled, waving his pistol back and forth above his head to signal his brother.

Across the road from the Petler place stood a vast field of golden soybeans, separated from a cornfield to the east by a wire fence. The cornfield field extended to the north and east, butting against the northern boundary of the town. The corn was in the final stages of growth, drying and turning yellow for harvest. Durham Petler walked out of the cornfield, white-faced and tired. Durham held the pistol low, and it seemed to pull at his arm as if it weighed a ton. His face had been cut in several places by the razor sharp edges of corn leaves, and numerous prickly cockle burrs stuck to his clothes. Sweat poured from his head, the salty drops stinging as they flowed into the thin cuts from the corn leaves. He approached the group, grumbling as he wiped away the irritating sweat from his face. Passing through the opening in the fence, he noticed the rusted gate on the ground, but said nothing about it.

"That damn rooster ran into the cornfield," he complained. "Got clean away."

He surveyed the group, moving slowly to allow his strength to build, and then turned to his brother.

"What are you doing with that duck, Deke?"

Deke grinned.

"I shot it, see, right here."

He pointed at the red stain on the duck's white back.

"We were supposed to be killin' that noisy old rooster."

Everett and Olaf watched as the pair talked, enthralled by the prospect of where this all was leading. Durham glanced toward Olaf.

"Oh, hi, Killer," he said, then turned back to Deke. "Well, let me just see now–last time we talked, we were going to shoot that cackle-beaked old feather bag and have him for supper. Now when did we decide on duck?"

"When you disappeared into town, chasin' him and shootin'," Deke replied. "I thought you was never comin' back. Hell, the rooster's been back for twenty minutes. So while you were gone I decided on duck instead. You were so danged fired up about shootin' somethin' and gone so long that I thought you mighta even shot yourself. And I was getting mighty hungry."

32

"Now why would I do a stupid thing like shootin' myself?" Durham asked sarcastically.

Deke pointed to Durham's right foot, the one with the missing big toe.

"Well, it's not like you haven't never done it before, Durham."

Deke held the duck up, his arm extended straight away from his body. Clenching the duck's legs in his fist, he shook the bird. The duck's limp head swung back and forth upside down, like a pendulum.

"So, duck it is, thought I."

"Oh, how short's our memory," Durham wailed, reciting lines from a bit part in a high school play twenty years ago. "How fickle our brothers."

Everett thought this was just about as good a time to jump into things as he was going to get.

"So it was you who was shooting up the town, Durham?" he asked.

"I wasn't shootin' up the town, Sheriff," Durham defended, his voice soft but with a tone of hurt. "I was tryin' to shoot up a rooster. Can I help it if the town got in the way?"

Everett had to remind himself once again that Durham was once thought of as the smart one.

"Now Durham," Everett scolded, "you can't do that anymore. We got a law that say's there's no shooting inside the city limits. You know that."

"And I don't shoot in town, Sheriff," he defended, "except when I'm huntin' roosters. And since we're talkin' about law, isn't there a law about disturbin' the peace? That there rooster's been disturbin' my peace for years. Arrest him if you want to."

"Well, let's make sure that you don't go hunting any roosters for the next few days, OK?" Everett said, extending his hand. "Let's have the pistol."

Durham turned the pistol sideways in his hand, looking down at the gleaming chrome barrel.

"Ah, Sheriff, you wouldn't take my pistol away from me, would you? Over a chicken? That got away? That just don't seem fair."

"Now, Durham, it's only for a few days," Everett explained. "Think about what kind of a position you've put me in. What would the townsfolk say if I walked all the way out here and at least didn't take your gun away for a while? They'd just up and run me off and might even get a new sheriff–"

"Oh, they don't need to do that, Sheriff," Durham replied, raising his hands and waving them at Everett.

Durham wasn't the brightest star in the heavens, but even he knew a good thing when he had it. He handed the dirt-covered pistol reluctantly to Everett.

"Clean it for me, Sheriff?"

"Sure, Durham. But you'll have to give me a ride back uptown. My car's in the shop."

"Let me drive ya, Sheriff," Deke offered.

Five minutes later, Deke braked the Petler's rusty brown Chevy pickup in front of the Sheriff's Office. Everett opened the door and got out, holding Durham's dirt-encrusted pistol. The door protested with a metallic creaking as he shut it. He leaned through the window of the shotgun side, resting an arm on the open window.

"Appreciate the ride, Deke."

Deke grinned, the smell of whiskey strong in the cab.

"One other thing, though," Everett warned. "I'll let you off this time, understand, but don't ever let me catch you driving drunk like this in town again."

3   Barbershop Justice

Shilling's Barbershop had been a beehive of activity for a good part of the morning. Saturday usually brought a couple of dozen or so of the townsfolk, as well as farmers from the surrounding countryside, into the shop. Two events of the prior evening provided more reason for idle chatter than the town had experienced in a good while, some said, even since Olaf Clancy's trial.

The shop, located on the north side of Main Street, was marked in front by a long, vertical barber pole. The pole was painted in thick, downward spiraling red and white stripes and looked like an oversized candy cane, which it was passed off as during the Christmas season. When Everett stood at his office window, he could easily see the shop's storefront across the street, several buildings east of his office. Behind the shop, several blocks north, the town's grain elevator rose above the downtown. Everett sat at his desk, with Durham Petler's disassembled pistol spread out before him as he rubbed the barrel with gun oil and a white cotton cloth.

The barbershop actually constituted the last building of the business section on the eastern end of Main Street, where men would gather on Saturday while the women talked and shopped in Merle Oaken's Grocery Store. If a man wanted a quick piece of news, he'd visit the post office at the west end of the downtown area. But if he wanted some serious jowling, he'd saunter on up a few blocks to the east side, to the barbershop.

Earl Shilling had been the town barber for as long as anyone could remember. Some said he just wandered into Iowa one day and sat down on the road until the town of Apology had sprung up around him. Although he was not an educated man, he attracted attention because of his lucidity. He was the last to take sides on most issues, preferring, unlike most, to wait for all pertinent facts to be known. It was this quality in the man that caught the attention of those not always in need of haircuts. They visited Earl if they had a problem and couldn't ask Father Coleman. Earl was the layman's spiritual advisor, confidante, and ears for the distressed. And he rather reveled in the role. Earl was average looking, fifty, and a confirmed bachelor. His jet-black hair was perpetually greased and combed back, and the top of his forehead near the hairline always shone from the excess hair oil.

Two pieces of brand-spanking new gossip buzzed through Shilling's this Saturday morning, intertwining in mixed conversations as men in the waiting chairs hashed and rehashed the facts, assumed or otherwise, while customers came and went via the squeaky front door.

The first topic of conversation was the Friday night football game, or rather, lack of one. The school bus carrying the opposing football team to Renoir had broken down six miles south of Eagle Nest, on a gravel road the driver had used as a short cut. The coach had tried to walk back into town for help but suffered a mild heart attack after walking three miles. A farmer, driving a tractor pulling a trailer full of hay bales, had spotted the man sprawled next to the road, unfortunately not until after running over the man's legs. By the time the tractor got to town to summon help for the coach, and the bus had been found, it was an hour past game time. And it would have been a tough game to play anyway, for the Eagle Nest football coach was in the hospital in Renoir, his broken legs sealed tightly in plaster casts.

Quizzy Boxliter, still burly from his football playing days, was quick to anger. The man's son quarterbacked for the Renoir Cornbender's and Quizzy served as one of the assistant coaches. Quizzy was seething because his son Dirk hadn't been able to play.

"What kind of a stupid bus driver would take a gravel road when there was perfectly good two-lane blacktop to use," he argued. "Here we go spending all this money on making nice roads and some ying yang bus driver can't tell the difference between loose brown gravel and hard black top."

"What kind of an idiot coach have they got running that Eagle Nest team anyhow?" Jim Hissy asked, directing his attention to Quizzy. "I mean, the guy's got a busload full of perfectly healthy athletes, any of whom could have sprinted down that road, gravel just a flying from beneath their shoes. But did he send any of them for

41

help like any sane man would do? No, he waddles up the road with that big old beer gut pouring over his belt and look what happens."

Of course, Jim had been forced to listen to his wife, Stella, for an hour the previous evening as they sat in the stands waiting for the team to show, going on about how the fried chicken she carefully prepared and brought to the game had gotten cold and greasy tasting. This was especially disastrous in light of the fact that Stella had just won a blue ribbon the month before at the Iowa State Fair for her chicken recipe, and intended to pass portions of her award-winning entree out to her friends as they watched the game.

Evander Carlson, always the diplomat, spoke.

"You know what I think, boys?" he asked. "I think that this whole affair was just a ploy by Eagle Nest."

"How's that?" Quizzy asked.

"They got to know over there about the Cornbenders by now," Evander continued, raising his hands for effect. "I mean, they *do* read the Renoir Gazette in Eagle Nest, don't they? They get it on Saturday, same as us, so they got to know our team's record. The way I figure it is they just plain got scared out. Can you imagine how those Eagle

Nest coaches would feel if we whipped up on them as bad as all you damn well know we would have, and then having to read about it in the Gazette the next day?"

"By golly, Evander," Jim Hissy said, "I believe you might have something there."

Evander's conclusions were greeted warmly as gospel from the general population inside the shop because, after all, a man who could manage the many responsibilities of running a grain elevator, while keeping in his employment the killer Olaf Clancy, must have something going for him in the way of intelligent thinking. On any given Saturday in Earl Shilling's barbershop, rarely did all heads nod together in agreement, mainly because mutual agreement brought with it the nasty vice of dampening the lively conversation peppering the air. But once in awhile, as was the case now, the logic embedded in Evander Carlson's words was sound, and only a fool would mount an objection against their own.

The second subject in the shop that morning was the Petler brothers, and the ruckus Durham had caused within the city limits by chasing the rooster up the street, blasting away at it with his pistol.

43

And Moog Raymond had been patiently waiting, knowing it was just a matter of time until the conversation rolled around to him.

"Come on, Moog," Quizzy Boxliter urged, "Tell us what the heck went on out there yesterday."

"Yea," Jim Hissy added, "What's with those Petler boys, anyhow?"

Moog Raymond beamed, and with a voice like a politician pulling in voters, began a detailed account of how he had watched the entire incident unfold.

"Well," he replied, taking a deep breath and looking around, "I'll see if I can remember. It all happened so fast, you know."

In reality it had all happened real slow, as most events did in Apology, but Moog's comment served to ensure that all eyes and ears were focused on him as he began his story.

Earl Shilling could always tell when a storyteller in his shop had the crowd's attention. Over the years Earl had observed that, the more interesting the story, the further the listeners bent forward, away from the wooden-slatted backs of the worn captain's chairs that served as comfort stations to those who waited patiently for an open barber

44

chair. Earl noticed now that, as Moog began his story, the crowd was inching, one by one, toward the edge of their seats.

"Well, I was upstairs, fixing Ellen's hairdryer," Moog began. "You know she dropped it a while back when she was waving a bee away from her face–I don't know how many times I've told that woman to keep that bathroom window shut until I can put a screen on it, and look what finally happened. Anyway something must have shook loose when that hairdryer hit the floor–you know how shoddy those things are made. Doesn't surprise me one bit. So I got my tools and was taking the darn thing apart when I thought I heard a shot. I knew darn well it wasn't coming from inside the house so I stuck my head out the north window and looked east toward downtown. Didn't see nothing so I turned my head and looked the other way down Main Street, to the west."

Moog paused, making sure all the barbershop patrons were up to speed with him so far.

"So I was looking west, towards out of town, to the Petler place. And there they were, four blocks away, the Petler boys, standing in their back yard. Both of them, Deke and Durham, were holding pistols over their heads, waving them around like those guns were fans and they were just shooing away the flies. And, if that wasn't bad enough, Deke was sucking on a whiskey bottle while he was waving that gun of his around. Didn't seem to be paying any heed to where he was pointing that thing, either."

"Ooh," Jim Hissy grimaced, "Whiskey and guns–that's a dangerous mix."

"What's more," Moog continued, "they must have been having some sort of row over whose turn it was to take a pull, because as Deke was holding the bottle over his head, just a sucking away like a spring calf. Durham reached up to grab the whiskey bottle from Deke's hand. I could see right away that that didn't sit too well with Deke because he twisted his body away from Durham to protect the bottle. Then the two got to arguing–I couldn't hear what they were saying–but I'm sure it wasn't anywhere near something Father Coleman would be wanting to be hearing."

Moog stopped, hearing chuckles from the crowd. Seeing their smiles, he grinned broadly, raised his hands and slapped them hard against his thighs. Leaning forward slightly in his chair, he continued.

"So they're out arguing in their back yard, with Deke holding the bottle up high while he was backing away from Durham while Durham was moving toward Deke, trying to figure a way to get the bottle. While this all was going on, that flock of scraggly chickens they got penned up out there surrounded the two, probably thinking that with all that waving going on that one of those two yahoos was bound to be holding some corn to throw their way. So there they were, the two of them, circling each other in the yard, looking like they're doing some kind of voodoo dance, and followed around by a bunch of chickens with just about as much common sense as either one of those boys have got."

"Then what happened, Moog?" Quizzy asked.

"About that time Durham must have got a bit short with old Deke," Moog continued, "and he just up and shoved him backwards. Then Deke shoved Durham. And remember, they both are still holding their guns. Then they started shoving each other all over the yard until finally Deke backs over a log and falls down. That's when Deke's gun went off, when his butt hit the ground. At first I thought that big old red rooster of theirs took a bullet–you know the bird I'm talking about–that bird that don't know what time zone he's in, cackling at dusk or any other time that seems to suit him–but then I saw that the bird had just jumped in the air and came back down, probably just spooked by the gunshot, I suppose. Now when Deke hit the ground some of that whiskey must have splashed out of the bottle and landed on his belly. And all those chickens who'd been just waiting for something to be thrown their way took notice and ran to Deke, where they commenced to pecking at the spot where the booze dropped until Deke shooed them away by trying to knock 'em in the head with his gun butt. I don't suppose he was too happy that his birds thought he was nothing more than chicken feed."

"So then what happened?" Evander asked.

"Then, not to be left out of all the excitement, that rooster of theirs just took off running," Moog explained. "That bird must have figured the boys were shooting at him and didn't want any part of what was to come. And seeing the rooster on the run must have set Deke and Durham to thinking that it was about high time they did away with that scraggly old bird that couldn't tell what time of day to crow and always was disturbing their sleep. Then I saw Deke sit up and look at

Durham. Then they both looked at the rooster who was running away for no reason at all. Both of them boys must have come up with the same idea about that time; that it was about time to settle things with that bird."

"So that's when all hell broke loose?" Quizzy asked.

"It sure enough did," Moog answered. "And fast. Both those boys raised their guns at the same time and began unloading lead at that poor bird, who by now was just standing still near the trunk of that big old oak tree in the back yard. Even from where I was watching I could see pieces of bark flying from the tree as the bullets hit the trunk. But when they got done shooting all those bullets, there stood the rooster, not a feather touched on his body."

"They *both* missed?" Evander asked. "That's not like them. I bet that really raised their dander."

"Now you know as well as I do that either of those boys would have nailed that bird with the first shot if whiskey wasn't involved," Moog explained. "But I'm sure that the fact that they both missed a target that size from less than thirty feet must have really raised their hackles. Durham must have had some more bullets on him, for I saw

49

him pulling something from his pocket and just about that time the rooster got a good run up and flew over the fence. When he cleared the fence he flapped for about fifty feet and lit on the pavement. Then that bird just started running toward the downtown. And I tell ya, he was running hard, and those little bandy legs of his was stretched to wide open, like he was the guest of honor at a taffy pull."

"And that's when Durham headed after him, I suppose?" Jim Hissy asked.

"That's right," Moog said. "Durham came charging through that east gate and went after him. Durham wasn't moving near as fast as the rooster, ya know, the rooster being the more sober of the two–"

He paused for a moment as the crowd laughed.

"–so Durham took a shot at him from about a hundred feet away. I saw the bullet hit the road about fifty feet short, then I saw it ricochet off the pavement and heard it whizzing right by me and on up Main Street. That chicken ran about fifty feet further and stopped right in front of my house."

He stopped, as if thinking, and then grinned.

"Maybe that bird was just taking a breather."

"Or maybe he was just giving old Durham a chance to catch up," Jim Hissy offered with a smirk, his comment adding to the amusement of the crowd. Moog continued.

"Durham kept on coming on up the street, limping all the way and gaining ground on the bird. He stopped and fired again, and this time hit the pavement in front of the rooster. This must have scared that rooster even more because that bird turned north and made tracks between Yig Digler's house and garage and on out into the cornfield, all the while with Durham still blasting away at its tail."

"So he still hadn't hit anything?" Evander asked.

"So far, just the road," Moog answered. "But I think I saw an ear of corn flying off a cornstalk from where a bullet hit it. But I ain't sure–it was in about two rows, ya know."

"Then what'd old Durham do next?" Quizzy asked.

"Then Durham stopped in the middle of Main Street and opened the cylinder of his gun and emptied the spent casings into his hand," Moog answered. "That wasn't too smart, because all that heat from all that brass burned his palm. I heard him cursing up a storm, and he bunched up his fist and slammed those the shells to the street, where they scattered in all directions and rolled along the pavement, making this sort of clinkering sound."

"Did Durham see you watching him?" Quizzy asked. "I mean, he did have a gun and he was drunk."

"Nope, never saw me," Moog answered. "He was too busy trying to reload as he was licking his burned hand. But I watched him chase that rooster into the cornfield and I'll be damned if that bird didn't lead old Durham smack into this big old patch of cockle burrs growing with the corn. I saw Durham fall down real hard. You should have seen it–he planted his face in that dirt better than any farmer could pop a soybean in the ground, and when his face stopped his feet was still moving and they just flopped up in the air behind him and then dropped down."

Moog saw that everyone was grinning at the scene he had described, and not being one to miss such a plum of opportunity, he repeated it.

"Yep, you should have seen old Durham kicking up his heels in the back while his face was talking weather with the night crawlers," he chuckled. "And he stayed down there a goodly while. I thought about going over and checking on him, but then I thought, what the hell, he's in the shade and he'll come to eventually. And he did, too. But by that time the rooster was long gone. He'd turned west and back south and I saw him cross back over the road and head for home while Durham was still plowing up the field with his nose. Then a few minutes later I saw Everett coming down the street. He picked up Olaf Clancy and headed on down to the Petler place."

"Olaf?" Jim Hissy asked. "Olaf was with him?"

"That's right," Moog replied, "Olaf."

The room went silent, each man digesting his own thoughts regarding the appearance of Olaf Clancy with the town sheriff.

"By golly," Quizzy declared, "those danged Petler brother have been a nuisance since their dear old ma died five years ago. I wish she was still with us, the poor old soul, just so she could thump them boys in the head about twice every Thursday."

"Poor Birdy," Jim Hissy said thoughtfully. "She was a God-loving saint, that woman was. Just to keep those two boys in line was a full time job."

Jim used God's name a lot, out of habit, for he sometimes helped Father Coleman write his sermons. Jim would often wear a suit when he stood before the congregation at St. John's on Sunday, doing the readings that came just prior to the gospel, and once in a while, especially during the cold season, when the good priest found his throat sore, Jim stepped in to read the sermon Father Coleman had written.

"Yea," Evander Carlson added, "she was a sweet woman. Remember how pretty the place used to be–petunias and roses growing right outside the fence next to the road. Fence painted nice and white. Lawn mowed. Chickens penned up. I remember a salesman I met at the post office telling me how he'd detour his route and pass through Apology just so he could gaze for a few seconds at Birdy Petler's beautiful garden."

"I remember how fond Birdy was of that garden," Moog said. "Remember how straight the rows were, almost like green lines painted in the dirt. And every year she planted the same pattern– tomatoes on the east row to catch the sun all day. Corn on the west row. Peas and beans next to the tomatoes for shade against the morning sun. And everything else next to the corn. Always had a nice stand of sweet corn, she did."

Moog worked at a hardware store in Renoir and often got sentimental when he spoke. At one time he'd intended to join the Peace Corps until he met Ellen. The thought of living in a jungle somewhere and building a bridge that would probably wash out anyway with the next hard rain didn't sound near as exciting as it had after he'd caught a flash of Ellen's white satin and lace slip while he twirled her around at a dance one Saturday night.

"It was a gardener's dream," Quizzy remembered fondly, almost moved to tears. "And she was a saint with a green thumb."

"I miss those vegetables," Earl Shilling said. "I remember when Deke and Durham used to come into the shop and swap fresh produce for haircuts. I don't think Birdy ever knew, and I suspect the money they most likely borrowed from her for their cuts was diverted to liquor."

"And now look what's happened out there," Quizzy complained. "Just look at the mess those Petler boys have made. Why, folks coming into our town get a bad idea right from the get go about us, just seeing that trash pit outside of town. It's just a damn shame, it is."

"But I don't see anything we can do about it," Jim Hissy replied. "After all, it's their property."

"What do you think, Earl?" Quizzy asked.

All eyes were now on the barber, his fingers buried beneath the fine strands on Tiny Fremont's sparse nest of hair. Tiny's huge body filled the entire barber chair, and rolls of fat around his waist flowed through the square formed by the intersection of the arm rest and the seat. Hearing his name, Earl stopped in mid-clip. He thought for a moment–he always did–and then replied.

"I've seen the mess out there. And it isn't the kind of activity that Birdy would have condoned. But, it is their property and they can do with it what they want. Now, if it were in town, it would be a different matter. We could make them clean it up a bit. But I'm no lawyer, either. I think the prudent thing to do in this case is to seek the advice of our sheriff, Everett Hiram."

"Everett Hiram!" Evander Carlson shouted. "He's a rogue first and a sheriff later. Hell, wasn't he walking around with Olaf Clancy just yesterday? And who gave our good sheriff a ride back to his

office after he went out to lay down the law to those two out there?

I'll tell you who. It was Deke Petler, driving drunk in that beat up

truck of his. Now why should we seek the advice of that man?"

4 Everett Takes on the Mob

Everett balanced the freshly oiled pistol in his hand, feeling the heft of the assortment of various metals and wood that made up the weapon. It was a fine piece, he concluded, well constructed and balanced. No wonder Durham Petler had been reluctant to give it up. With a little oil and some rubbing, all the chromed-steel gleamed once more. It had taken Everett some time to clean the cylinder, for when Durham had tumbled into the cockle burr patch, the pistol had flown from his hand, plunging into the moist, black topsoil. Now the weapon shown so brightly that Everett was able to see the curved reflection of Old Duke wrapped around the barrel.

Old Duke was sweeping the hardwood floor, or at least attempting to. Duke liked to make himself look busy in front of the sheriff so he had an excuse to stay and hold the fort if Everett actually was called out to do something that might involve a little danger. Watching Old Duke's scrawny frame, smaller in the shine of the barrel, Everett was reminded of the event that had turned Old Duke into sort of an icon in Apology.

For Old Duke had been witness to the now infamous Dwivel-Othoco battle that had happened over fifty years ago, a piece of nostalgic history still forged on the pages of certain Iowa textbooks. And every time Old Duke told the story of that event, it was like he was telling it for the first time. His eyes twinkled, and his voice took on a pride-filled clarity not normally heard in the man.

When Old Duke was a child, he lived with his parents in the small Iowa town of Dwivel on the Iowa-Minnesota border. Two miles to the north, just inside the Minnesota state line, sat the equally small town of Othoco. Now, in the winter months, with the crops out of the fields, things apparently got very uneventful in the area, and after a round at a tavern one evening, some of the farmers living near Dwivel put up a billboard on the northern outskirts of town. The billboard proudly read, "We feed the Nation." The crowd hoisted the sign at the top of a hill, taking great pains to make sure that the sign could be read by those Norwegian squatters who'd invaded Othoco a century or so before. Word of the billboard's presence quickly got around Othoco, and the talk at the local tavern was like that coming from a jealous woman. So some of the farmers from around Othoco banded together two days later and made their own sign. The sign faced south, toward Dwivel, and read, "We feed the World."

Now the farmers from Dwivel never really intended to start anything with their good neighbors across the state line, but when they read Othoco's billboard, they took it as a challenge to their town and to the great state of Iowa. The next afternoon a large crowd gathered below the Dwivel sign and cheered as some of the farmers changed the sign to read, "We grow the largest cattle." And, as Old Duke told it, that was true. And that, Old Duke said, was why Othoco, to the cheers of its large crowd, countered with another sign that read, "We have more hogs." Oh, whiskey is an evil-doer on the night prairie in winter, and the Iowa-Minnesota Billboard War, as it was later called, really got interesting when some bottle bravery from Dwivel came up with an idea for the next sign, something that was bound to silence that Norwegian crowd from Othoco. The next day Dwivel countered Othoco's sign with one that read, "We know. We've seen your women."

Now it was pretty much agreed by all parties after the brawl in downtown Dwivel that the sign had been just a tad too blunt and shouldn't have been put up in the first place. But to their credit, Old Duke said, not a man who rolled in the snow with his neighbor that day long ago ever regretted participating in the battle. And for the most part, the only scars acquired by any of the combatants came not during the brawl, but at the big kiss-and-make-up party thrown on the lake later that day. People were so busy patting each other on the back and saying what a hell of a battle it had been that they forgot one little detail. And that was just about the time the ice gave way beneath the bonfire.

The door to the sheriff's office opened just as Everett pulled out the top draw of his desk to put his gun-cleaning equipment away. Everett looked up from his work to discover that his visitor was Owen Fuller, the mayor of Apology. Owen was a short, portly man, and people often said he took his job as mayor much too seriously.

Unfortunately for Owen, from a distance he looked a little like Olaf Clancy. Before Olaf had bashed Zelda with a two-by-four, this had been a joke around town, with people sometimes referring to Owen as Mayor Olaf. Now, the hair on the back of his neck bristled when someone would accidentally call out Olaf's name, attempting to get Owen's attention when they saw him from afar.

Owen was an insurance salesman by trade, and was very sensitive about his personal appearance. The man always wore shined shoes and new clothing, and meticulously groomed his hair, so much so that, when he visited Shilling's Barbershop, other customers would tease him about how much time Owen spent in the chair, making certain Earl had every hair arranged just so. Two years ago, shortly after Olaf's trial, Owen changed his hairstyle. Now, out of Owen's earshot, some whispered how it sure took a lot of money to not look like Olaf Clancy.

Owen's rise to the position of mayor had been quite uneventful, since no one else in Apology really wanted the job. But Owen had seen it as an opportunity to expand his insurance business, and because Owen's wife, Bonnie, liked to know what was going on in town, she'd encouraged him to accept the job. Bonnie was both nervous and energetic, and Owen's life was always less complicated when Bonnie was busy doing something that didn't include bothering him. Bonnie was proud of her gleaming blond hair, always tucked neatly on her head and always wore brightly colored clothes that looked like they'd come right from the dry cleaners. Bonnie had volunteered to be Owen's campaign manager when he'd run for mayor.

"My Owen will do this for you if he's voted in as mayor," she'd promised her friends, unbeknownst to her husband, or, "my husband will fix that problem."

A goodly amount of promises had been made by Bonnie to secure her husband's election, but since Owen had run unopposed, the victory was somewhat diminished, although this fact never seemed to bother the woman in the least.

Into their lives had stampeded three free-for-all sons, Arnold, Bull, and Fuller. Some of the women in town had commented on the wisdom of naming an offspring Fuller, when the poor child already had that as his family name, but that talk had eventually died down, and only surfaced once in a while when other gossip was sparse. They were fine boys, but a handful, even for the saint Bonnie imagined herself to be.

Noticing the stern look on Owen's face, Everett figured that something was bothering the mayor.

"Morning, Owen," he said, shutting the door to his desk.

Owen looked at the freshly oiled pistol on the desk.

"Buy a new gun, did you, Sheriff?"

"No, Owen," Everett replied, glancing at Durham's gun. "I just borrowed it to practice with."

"Oh," Owen said, unimpressed by the explanation, "what's the matter with your own gun?"

"Nothing. Just wanted to try out this fine piece."

"Where'd you get it?"

Everett hesitated, then answered.

"Took it from Durham Petler yesterday."

Owen's face took on a look of disgust.

"I heard about what those danged Petler boys was up to yesterday, Everett. And I ain't too happy about it. Shooting in the streets and all. It's just downright dangerous to be doing something like that."

At one time, Owen had prided himself on his correct use of the English language, free of slang and ignorant talk. But living with those who misused the language had also caused Owen to sometimes stumble, as much as he tried to do otherwise.

"I had a talk with Durham about that very thing, and then I took away his gun," Everett explained. "That's about all I can do. You know they live outside the city limits."

"But wasn't Durham shooting inside of the city?"

"He was, that's a fact. But he didn't harm no one, and he promised not to do it again. He was trying to hunt a chicken and it ran up Main Street. In all the excitement, Durham just kinda forgot where he was."

As sheriff, Everett often found it prudent to lightly polish the rough-hewn wood when need be, that is, to keep simple problems simple, and not let them get complex by overworking the facts. That way the solution would be no more involved than the problem. And over the years Everett had found this logic worked most of the time in

dealing with the day-to-day life in the town of Apology.

"What happened to the chicken?" Owen asked.

"Oh, it got away," Everett explained.

Owen knew that the Petler boys were good shots, and they only

missed their mark for one reason.

"So Durham was not only shooting in town, but he was shooting

drunk, is that it?"

"That's about right, Owen. But I got him all straightened out."

Everett leaned to his right, looking around Owen and through the

spacious glass window. A small, stern-looking crowd was on the

march. Leaving the porch of Earl Shilling's Barbershop, they crossed

Main Street as a jumbled mass, steering for the sheriff's front door.

Owen, curious about Everett's action, turned and spotted the crowd

also.

"I wonder what they want?" Owen asked.

"I expect we'll find out real quick," Everett replied calmly. "But

you can bet it ain't about last night's football game."

It was like a small parade, and it didn't take much of parade to fill up the business district of Apology. Heading west along Main Street, the group crossed the road in a long diagonal line from the barbershop to the sheriff's office. Everett saw Evander Carlson out in front of the crowd, the man's gait fast but each step deliberate. Evander's arms hugged his hips, swinging back and forth like those of a marching soldier. Trailing Evander were Moog Raymond, Quizzy Boxliter and Jim Hissy, each man attempting to conform to Evander's rapid pace, but in doing so, appearing clumsy in own their steps.

From up the street, Stella Hissy spotted the crowd heading toward the sheriff's office, and moved to join them, figuring she could use some ammunition to hip shoot from her gossip gun. Stella, one of her hallmark plain-colored dresses hanging from her body with all the erotic thrill of drab linen slung over a dining room table, looked herself over before joining the crowd, finding, to her chagrin, that the bottom of her dress was bunched up with static near the hemline. Grabbing the hem firmly at the bottom she yanked the front of her dress downward to cover her knees. Her face screwed to prudish, eyes scouring the surrounding area for any male who'd dared gaze upon those four inches of pink thigh exposed briefly above that knee, and intent upon delivering the evil eye of righteousness to any of that species who'd seen that square of private flesh, inadvertently or otherwise.

Over the heads of the crowd, Everett spotted Earl Shilling closing the front door of the barbershop, leaving Tiny Fremont in charge. Through the narrowing crack of the barbershop door, Everett could see Tiny's massive form attempting to pry itself from the barber chair. Earl pulled the door closed, appearing reluctant to let go of the knob as he stared at the crowd now distancing itself from him. Earl's hand dropped away from the knob, and the man stepped into the street.

"Better open the door a crack, Duke," Everett ordered, "before they run over it."

Duke's nervous eyes barely glanced at the sheriff, but Duke did as he was told, pulling on the door to expose a four-inch crack to the outside. The door creaked open further as a puff of wind pushed it from outside, the door's movement aided by an out of kilter doorframe that forced the door to creak open ghost-like, even in the absence of a stirring breeze. Glancing through the opening, Duke sensed trouble, and in line with his self-preserving character, furiously swept his way into the back room and out of sight.

Everett lost his view of the crowd as they neared the building, but heard the pounding of their footsteps as they moved onto the sidewalk. The crowd reappeared at the threshold of the open door. Owen turned to look at them and stepped away from the desk, allowing them to direct their attention toward Everett.

"We've come to talk to you, Everett," Evander Carlson, began, his voice solemn and direct.

Evander was a stern-looking man when he wanted to be, for when things had to be done around the grain elevator, he had to sometimes turn from hot to cold to make sure his words were understood by the employees. It didn't bother Evander at all to speak before a crowd, like he was now doing.

Owen squeezed a few more steps away from the desk, out of the line of fire his instincts warned might be coming. Everett remained calm, unruffled by the appearance of the stern-faced crowd.

"Well, come on in, good people of Apology," he said. "I'm always willing to listen to concerns of the citizens of my town."

Owen attempted to hide his look of disbelief. His reaction stemmed partially from what Everett had told the crowd, but also because, deep down, Owen knew that Everett could sometimes lay it down thicker than any manure spreader within a ten-mile radius of Apology.

If Evander was surprised by Everett's invitation, he didn't show it. Instead, he stepped boldly inside the door. Moog Raymond, Jim Hissy, and Quizzy Boxliter followed his example, each stepping gingerly over the threshold separating their world from that of Sheriff Everett Hiram. Stella Hissy eased through the doorway and stood partially hidden behind the four men. Spotting Owen Fuller, Stella stared with disgust at Owen's downcast eyes as she pulled once more at her hem, convinced that Owen was sneaking a peek near the pull, when, in actuality, all Owen was trying to do was avoid eye contact with the crowd. The small floor space between the door and Everett's desk was now crowded with people representing a cross section of Apology's citizens.

"We've come to register a complaint, Sheriff," Quizzy Boxliter said firmly. Evander Carlson jerked his head toward Quizzy, surprised, for the man had stolen his opening salvo right from Evander's mouth. Over the years, Quizzy had often used his football burliness as a means of intimidation when needed and hoped to get the jump on the sheriff. But that trick had never worked with Everett Hiram. Everett reached into the top drawer of his desk and pulled out a sheet of paper. Evander raised his hand, shaking an open palm toward the sheriff.

"No, Everett, we won't be filling out no forms today."

"Well, tell me what I can do for you people, then," Everett said, "for I am a bit confused by what you want."

"You know darn well what we want, Everett," Jim Hissy said curtly. "You know we've come to see you about the Petler boys."

"I have no idea what you want, friends," Everett lied. "And what's this about the Petler boys?"

"Don't act stupid, Everett," Moog Raymond said. "You know darned well what we're talking about."

Everett realized that the crowd was, indeed, a bit worked up. This had happened to him on more than one occasion over his years as a lawman, and most of the time, not surprisingly, on a Saturday. People had a tendency to get worked up about something when they got together at the barbershop, their collective tempers boiling over like an overcooking stewpot.

"Oh, you mean that little incident with the shooting," Everett said innocently.

Even Owen Fuller cringed upon hearing the part about "little incident."

"Yes, that's exactly what we mean," Quizzy said, puffing his body in an attempt to make himself appear larger. "And it's just not a little incident. Those Petler boys coulda killed someone yesterday with all that damn shooting. Surely, even you could see that, Everett."

Everett leaned back in his chair seat, putting some distance between him and the crowd.

"In the first place," he began, "you don't seem to realize that I rushed down to the Petler place right after I heard those gunshots yesterday. I was in the street and there wasn't anybody around after the first shot or so to get shot. So, if no one was around, you tell me how someone was going to get killed. Your math just ain't adding the way my numbers are."

Everett thought he had the crowd on the run until Moog Raymond spoke.

"Wait a minute, Everett," he said, "I saw you going down the street and it didn't appear to me that you were rushing anywhere. More like strolling along is what I saw."

Everett forced a look of anger on his face. When he needed to, he could really make his anger quite believable, and even amused himself by practicing an assortment of expressions now and again before the mirror as he enjoyed his morning shave.

"Wait a minute, Moog," he explained. "You don't know the whole story. Just tell me how far it is from my office to the front of your house."

"You know that just as well as I do, Everett," Moog defended.

"Well, for the sake of these good people," Everett said, sweeping his hand toward the rest of the crowd, "tell me."

"Four blocks," Moog replied.

"So you didn't see me run the four blocks before I stopped in front of your house to catch my breath, did you? You didn't know that my car was getting new tires, long overdue I might add, so I can

73

perform my duties to the town. If I had more money in my budget, I mighta been able to get those tires changed a couple of months ago and then I could have driven to the Petler place and got there faster–maybe even before Durham got on the loose and into town. But remember, it was you people who decided to cut my budget, leaving me to scrounge for equipment. So if you've got a gripe about how I perform my duties, why don't you take it up at the next meeting of the town council."

What Everett said about the town council cutting his budget was true. Although the town had ample funds at the time, one of the councilmen had vehemently argued for the cut, citing alleged flaws in Everett's own budget data as reason for the decrease in funding. Two weeks after the vote was cast to cut funds from the sheriff's budget, the real reason surfaced. A week before the monthly town council meeting, Everett's had issued a speeding ticket to that particular councilman's teenage son, an act that infuriated the councilman because he felt, due his position on the council, that the sheriff should have let his teenager off with just a warning. Unfortunately, it was the third ticket Everett had given to the youth in ten months. As a result, the man had received a call from Owen Fuller, his insurance agent, notifying him of a sharp increase in premiums. By the time this information surfaced, the damage had been done, and though embarrassed by this disclosure, the town council concluded that returning the sheriff's funds would make them all look inept, and Everett's budget remained as it had been changed.

Owen Fuller surveyed the stunned faces of the crowd, absolutely amazed by how Everett had silenced all the bantering with one well-placed volley. Only Stella Hissy remained unimpressed. The dull brown purse hanging limply from her right arm looked a little like a fodder bag, swinging back and forth as she shifted her weight to confront the sheriff.

"Well, what were you doing running around with Olaf Clancy, then?" she demanded smugly.

Everett had purposely left the part about Olaf Clancy out of his explanation, figuring he'd let someone else bring that up. That way it wouldn't look too evident that he'd salted the meat, so to speak.

"Were you out there helping me yesterday, Stella?" he asked her curtly.

His comment caught her as flatfooted as a right cross would a drunken man. Backing away from Everett she gasped, covering her heart with one hand, the handbag falling against her shocked body.

"Me?" she shouted incredulously. "What? Why, I'm a woman!"

As Stella's face flushed red, Everett directed his words to the three men.

"How about it boys" he asked. "Were any of you out there? I know damn well you was watching was going on yesterday, Moog. Where were you?"

Rocked by Everett's directness, Moog attempted a reply, unfortunately with very little thought involved in his answer.

"Wh-h-yy, wh-y-y, tha-a-t's that's not e-eeven, even my–my job," he sputtered.

"How about you, Quizzy?" Everett asked. "You used to play football, didn't you? I could have used that muscle of yours yesterday."

"I was working," Quizzy defended. "I didn't even know about it until it was all over."

"Point well taken," Everett replied, turning to Evander. "How about you, Evander? You were at the elevator, working. I know you were."

"Come on, Everett," Evander answered. "I didn't know what was happening, either, until it was over. Give me a break, will you?"

"It seems that I'm the one that's in need of a break here," Everett pressed.

He stared up at Evander.

"Do I tell you how to run your elevator, Evander?"

"Well," Evander replied, "not exactly."

Everett turned to Moog.

"And do I come over to Renoir and tell you how to run the hardware store?"

Moog shook his head, afraid to speak.

"And, Quizzy, do I interfere with that great football team you coaches seem to have put together this year? The one that'll probably go undefeated?"

Quizzy perked at the compliment.

"No, Sheriff. Of course you don't"

Everett turned his attention to Stella Hissy, who he'd saved for last.

"And Stella," he smiled, "when you're cooking that Iowa State Fair First Prize Blue Ribbon chicken of yours, am I in your kitchen telling you how to fry it up?"

Stella hesitated before answering.

"No," she admitted begrudgingly.

"Then why oh why do you people come into my office and try to tell me how to do my job?" he asked. "One, I might add, I've been doing in this town for well over ten years."

Everett leaned forward, resting his arms on the desktop. He glanced at Stella.

"OK, you wanna talk about Olaf Clancy, do you?" he asked. "I wasn't going to bring it up myself but now that the issue's on the table, let's talk about Olaf and what he did for this town not more than twenty-four hours ago. Remember when the shooting started? How many people in town heard it? Ten? Twenty? I don't know, but I do know some did. How many is really not important. But nobody came to me offering to help. Everybody just ran. And I can't say that I blame them. Believe me, if I weren't the sheriff, I would have had second thoughts about going onto the Petler property, where two expert pistol shooters were drinking and shooting."

He directed his next words to Stella.

"To answer you question about hanging around with Olaf Clancy, Stella, the answer is, I wasn't. Olaf Clancy stepped out onto the streets as a concerned citizen and offered to come with me."

He looked toward the three men.

"And if that's the best man the town can offer when a crisis arises, so be it–I'll use him."

Everett knew that he had humiliated them with his comment about Olaf Clancy. He'd made Olaf into somewhat of a hero, and set everyone else to wondering if they were cowards.

"But, you didn't ask anybody," Quizzy protested weakly.

Everett noted that some of puffiness in Quizzy's body had deflated, and the man didn't look quite like a bloated pincushion.

"I didn't ask Olaf, either," Everett countered. "But he came into the street, knowing that he might just take a bullet."

Everett let them absorb what he had just said, noting that Earl Shilling, who'd been listening from outside, had stepped into the office. Everett played his final card.

"Now I know it's been said that I let Deke Petler give me a ride home yesterday. And the word is that he was driving drunk when he did. But actually, the real reason I let Deke give me a ride home was to test to see if he actually was drunk. For you all know that Deke and Durham might have been heading for the football game in Renoir, and I had to see if Deke was too drunk to drive. I suspected he was, and after he gave me a ride back to the office, I made him promise to go home and stay there for the night, and not endanger anyone else going to the game. And that's just what he did. Drove those eight blocks and parked it. If any of you had taken the time to notice, you'd have seen that their truck has been sitting in their driveway for almost a day now and hasn't moved."

Everett could tell by their faces that they all agreed with his logic, although if they'd have thought for a moment, they would have realized that Deke and Durham hadn't been to a football game since they had graduated from high school over twenty years ago. And that graduated part was kind of misleading, for it is said that the school just gave them diplomas to get rid of them. But Everett also knew he had the crowd on the run, and wasn't about to give them any time to think things over.

"Well, since you put it that way," Stella Hissy admitted, "I guess you had a reason to do what you did."

Stella's lips twitched uncontrollably as they pressed tightly together, as if trying to hold back other words she wanted to say.

"Yes," Moog agreed, "you did. We were wrong about how we thought you handled things, Everett. You know your job, Sheriff, we know that."

"Sorry we doubted you, Everett," Jim Hissy said, extending his hand toward Everett. As the two shook hands, he continued, "And don't worry about your budget. You can just bet that at the next meeting of the town council, I'll see what I can do about getting some more money funneled into your department."

"I'll second what Jim just said, Everett," Evander added.

Evander also held a spot on the town council and had a say in how the town's taxes were spent.

"I would greatly appreciate that," Everett replied.

Owen Fuller watched as the group glanced toward each other, each person trying to figure out a way to exit gracefully. Stella Hissy, lips pursed tightly, was still confused about the quick turn of events. But with nothing to argue about, and no one to back her, she remained silent and eased out the door with the rest, but not before giving Owen a hard stare for the thigh peep that never happened.

"Close that door, Stella darling," Everett said nonchalantly as the woman crossed the threshold, "Will ya please?"

Stella turned back toward Everett and eyed the man before grabbing the knob.

"I got the heat on," Everett said, pointing to the space heater near his desk. "And it costs the town money to run this, ya know."

Stella's lips pressed together tighter, whitening the area below her nose. She shot Everett a cold look and shut the door behind her. Through the window he could see her icy tongue lashing out at her husband. Owen Fuller watched Everett rise from his desk and step toward the window to observe Jim catching the brunt of Stella's wrath, an evil smile delightedly creeping across the sheriff's face. The words Stella was giving Jim probably wouldn't make it into Father Coleman's sermon the following Sunday.

From the back room, a dull crashing sound interrupted the men. Owen and Everett turned to see a stream of water racing into the room through the doorway to the back room. Everett sidestepped the growing puddle and peeked through the doorway.

"Damn it, Duke!" he shouted, "if you're gonna eavesdrop, you gotta watch where you're walking."

On the floor of the small room, in a puddle of soapy water sat Duke, somewhat bewildered by what had just happened. Duke had been listening to the events transpiring in the next room, and when the crowd had departed, forgot just where he was and tripped over the mop bucket he had filled prior to the crowd's arrival. The butt of his light brown pants turned dark as the mop water absorbed into the fabric.

"Duke!" Everett shouted, "What the hell are you doing back here?"

Now Everett knew exactly what Duke had been doing, sneaking around in back, getting an ear full of news to take back to Duffy's

Tavern with him later, knowing this news would make him look important to the patrons at the bar. Everett liked to jump on his deputy once in a while, just because it kept Duke on his toes. And Duke's doing something stupid was just the kind of opportunity that sat well with Everett. It only helped the situation that the mayor of Apology was standing behind Everett, watching the scene unfold.

"You're supposed to mop the floor with a mop," Everett continued, "not with your butt."

Everett pointed to the mop leaning against the wall. Duke wanted to say something, but couldn't figure out exactly what. So he remained silent.

"Duke, you're gonna have to go home and change those pants," Everett said sternly, remaining less than sympathetic about his deputy's predicament.

Duke got up slowly and stood before Everett, water dripping from his pants.

"I think I'll just go home and change them," he said sheepishly, shooting a glance at Owen Fuller.

With that he eased away and disappeared through the back door.

"Being kinda hard on the guy, aren't you?" Owen asked, eyeing the water continuing to spread over the floor.

"He knew it was coming," Everett replied. "Besides, that's nothing compared to what that she-devil of a wife of his used to say to him when she was living. Blanch used to give him the dickens on a regular basis. Maybe that's why he's so fond of that pet coon he keeps. It kinda looks like old Blanch did when she was still around. And to tell you the truth, I think he has dearly missed those tongue-lashings since she passed on. So, in a way, I'm kinda doing the guy a favor."

Everett returned to his desk and sat down. Owen took a seat near the desk.

"Well, Everett," Owen began, "just what kind of favor do you intend for Durham and Deke Petler?"

Everett raised his eyebrows.

"What do you expect me to do about them, Owen? They're outside of town so they can fire off their guns anytime they damn well please. You know that as well as I."

Owen breathed deeply, his chest rising and falling as he did.

"I know it, Everett. But I wish sometimes they'd act a little more like civil human beings and less like half-educated moonshiners. Since Birdy died that place has gone to the dogs and it's become a real eyesore for the town. I sure wish we could do something about straightening them two boys up."

Everett thought about correcting Owen's remark about the Petler place going to the dogs. In reality the place had gone to the chickens, but Everett kept that observation to himself, certain Owen wouldn't find that tidbit of information amusing.

"Well, Owen, I suspect they aren't near as much of a pain as most people make them out to be. Aside from their drinking and shooting on their property, they've never bothered anyone in town. They're sure not bullies. Remember when Durham went over and helped poor Anita Biningham harvest her tomatoes when she wrenched her back last year?"

"What I remember about that, Everett, was that Anita came to me complaining that Durham ate twice as many tomatoes as he picked when her back was turned, and she wanted him to pay for his thievery."

"Well, whatever she ended up getting is more that she would have canned if they'd rotted on the vine. That's for sure."

Owen watched the sheriff toying with Durham's pistol.

"You sure like to stick up for them, Everett."

Everett hung the long pistol barrel over his wrist and peered across the sight to the window.

"Think so, Owen?"

"Well, some people say that."

Everett pulled the pistol back and leaned against the back of his chair.

"Well, what do you say, Owen?"

Owen knew that Everett was trying to test him.

"You're the one that's supposed to be answering the questions, Everett."

Everett leaned forward, resting his arms against the desk.

"Good," he said. "Then let me tell you. It may seem that I stick up for the Petlers, and maybe that's true. But I stick up for everyone unless they give me reason not to. Look, Owen, this is a small town. Everyone knows everyone else and when they do their laundry. We

87

need to get along because we're all each other has and might ever have. Sure, I cut Deke and Durham some slack. But I do that for lots of people. I didn't raise a big stink when Tiny Fremont snuck over three nights in a row, stealing the milk right out of Irk Hickenlooper's cow—"

"But remember what happened after that," Owen cut in. "Irk got so mad at that cow for being stubborn about giving up her milk that poor Irk didn't know had already been taken from her that he sent her off to be butchered. And when he finally found that his milk was soaking Tiny's morning cereal, it dawned on him that his prize milker was in his freezer, wrapped in butcher paper when it should have had two more good milking years left."

"But it wasn't Tiny's fault that Irk butchered his cow," Everett said. "And besides, Tiny agreed to pay the butchering fees."

"I'm sure that soothed Irk, knowing all that money his prize cow's milk would have brought in over the next two years was gone."

"But you see, Owen," Everett said, "we were talking about treating everyone the same. And I dealt with the Petlers the same way I deal with everyone else. Including Tiny Fremont."

"Ah, the Petlers," Owen said. "It's too bad we couldn't move them about two miles west of town."

5   A Few in Town

The weekend came and went as the town of Apology digested the recent events, hammering out their conclusions after the Sunday morning service at St. John's. Forming near the doors just outside the church, separate groups, talking in hushed tones so Father Coleman wouldn't hear, gave their opinions once more regarding the fate of the unplayed football game, and from there jumped to the shooting incident involving the Petler brothers. Viola Vanderhoff picked the ripest plumb, discovering, to her amazement, that Anita Biningham hadn't heard about either incident yet. Anita, who owned and operated Anita's Cafe in downtown Apology, usually knew everything, because all gossip worth noting flowed through her eating establishment during lunchtime. But Anita had been away visiting relatives, and had just returned to town late the night before. And in Viola's way of thinking, fresh gossip was just about as much fun for the spreader as for the listener, especially when everyone else already knew, and Anita and Viola soon found themselves isolated from the crowd, whispering out of earshot beneath the dark, elongate shadow thrown by the spire of St. John's Church. There they stood, Viola's tongue wagging like the tail of a happy dog chewing on week-old rabbit carcass, with Anita's hand occasionally pressed to her lips, amazed by the story she had nearly missed.

Monday morning arrived, and Everett drove his patrol car down Main Street, the shiny new black wheels standing out against the dim gray of the pavement. The car rode much smoother, Everett noticed, and the road beneath him seemed to hum after he'd endured months of the bumpity-bump of the old tires.

About ten in the morning Everett had driven west out of town and past the Petler place. He saw no activity at that hour, for the Petlers were not early risers. One reason for that, of course, was that their rooster only crowed at dusk. And, in trying to alleviate that problem, the brothers had gotten only a duck supper and a confiscated, but well-oiled pistol.

Three miles past the town limits, Everett spotted a truck parked in the ditch. He knew surveyors were active west of town, working along the road as part of project aimed at deepening some of the ditches. During the long Iowa winters, snow would accumulate along certain spots where the ditches were too shallow to accommodate all the snowfall, and the road continually clogged by the sweeping white drifts pushed from the ditch by a cold northern wind.

Bert Kestral lived in Apology and worked for the county, keeping the many routes of travel passable by dumping generous amounts of gravel on the washboard roads surrounding the town. Bert had the same size and build as Earl Shilling, but had dull brown hair instead of the shiny black hair adorning the barber. The skin covering Bert's hands was hard and dry by hard labor, and when people shook Bert's hand it was like grabbing onto a piece of dead elephant hide. Bert was a no nonsense, get-things-done-right-now kind of guy, and it showed in his work ethic.

During the winters Bert drove one of the county snowplows, keeping the roads around Apology clear of drifts. Bert had grown pretty tired over the years of getting phone calls about the road west of town being blocked with snow only an hour after he'd plowed through it. The ditch had a high spot, and it seemed, every snowflake in the state of Iowa wanted to gravitate to it. Bert, fed up finally, had convinced the county engineer to deepen the ditch to accommodate more snow so he could get a full night's rest during the winter months. But first a survey had to be completed by the county to make sure all property lines were in order along the road. And that had been going on for about a week now.

Everett waved at the survey crew as he watched them work. The surveyors had called Everett out the first day to put the three pesky Fuller boys on the run so they could work in peace. Everett could see the town in his rear view mirror, the bulb-shaped water tower rising over the rooftops like some gawky, four-legged spider from a science-fiction movie, about to consume the unfortunate victims in its path. The sight of the water tower reminded Everett of a piece of pending business for the town council, a problem that was actually created by some less than brilliant decision-making by certain individuals on the town council; the results of which had created quite a stir in town, and whose impact was still being felt. He grinned as he remembered the event that created the problem, as well as the consequences that followed.

Everyone raved about the new silver paint job on the exterior of the steel water tower. The structure shone brightly during the day, and when the setting sun awakened elongate shadows, the tower gleamed even more above the darkening earth. Many residents were concerned, however about the town's name painted on the face of the tower. The man who painted the bold black letters on the silver tower had come down from Minnesota, he said, and did a fine job of carefully stenciling the letters on the rounded steel. He had been in a hurry to get back to Minnesota, and finished up the job two hours past sunset. The town council, looking up at the lettering in the dark, was very pleased by what they saw. They paid the man in cash, and satisfied, the painter went on his way back to Minnesota. The next morning, as the sun rose on the fresh paint job eighty feet in the air, some of the early risers of the town looked up to see that the painter had misspelled the name of the town. The second "O" had been left

from the name "APOLOGY" reading instead "APOLGY."

At a hastily convened town council meeting that night, all sorts of

finger pointing went on. No one seemed to know who hired the

mysterious Minnesota water tower painter, or even who paid him.

Amy Flanigan berated the town council for not having the brains to

check the man's work before paying him. Quizzy Boxliter demanded

to know who the fool was who'd hired the man in the first place, but

nobody would own up to it. Moog Raymond wanted to know how

they were going to fix the mistake, and that it was a blight on the

good people of the town to have the water tower hanging in the air

like a sign of ignorance. Jacob Witt threw in the comment that one

should never trust a Swede to do anything right. Irk Hickenlooper

observed that the mistake wasn't all that bad–he couldn't read it from

his farm three miles away. And of course, Deke Petler didn't want to

be left out of the ruckus. He suggested that if you really thought hard

about it, it wasn't that big a deal because, if you said the town's name

real fast, you wouldn't even miss that second "O" anyway. There was

some under-the-breath speculation from the back of the room that the reason Deke didn't miss the letter was because he had no idea it was there in the first place. Not to be outdone by his brother, Durham Petler explained that the problem went after sunset, and therefore was only a concern half the time, except during the winter, when the shorter days diminished the problem even further.

That had all happened last fall, and the tower remained in error for almost a year now. Some people were getting used to the idea, and once in a while some mail would arrive with the town's name spelled just like it was on the water tower. And when that happened, it only confirmed to Deke Petler that he had been right all along, and to just leave it go at that. But whatever one's thought on the matter, one would have to admit that the dilemma of the water tower sure made for interesting conjecture at the barbershop when topics of conversation grew sparse.

Everett turned the car around and headed back into town, driving past the Petler place once more. He drove east and noticed some clouds hanging low in the northern sky. As he lowered his eyes, a blur shot in front of his bumper. He grimaced at the head of a small child, expecting the dull thud he couldn't avoid. Everett slammed on the brakes, his new tires digging hard into the pavement. As his Stetson slid over his eyes, the child's head became Merle Oaken's guide dog, on the loose and trotting across the road. Everett was furious, for he could see the fresh rubber from his brand new tires on the road behind him, and the vision of a small child standing helplessly before his patrol car was fresh in his mind.

There was just something about having brand new tires, and he wanted them to stay nice for a little while at least. And now a dog had forced him to put some unnecessary wear on all that new tread. It was like getting the first ding on a new paint job.

"Go home, you damn mutt!" he shouted, sticking his head out the window. "I oughta shoot ya!"

The dog casually glanced toward the bumper eighteen inches from its left shoulder, but continued along at a trot, not at all concerned by the squealing of tires or the shouting. He'd heard it before, and assumed it was just part of the natural order of things.

Any other time Everett just might have shot the dog. He was the sheriff, and he had every right to shoot any stray dog wandering through town. But he didn't have the heart to shoot a guide dog.

The dog's name was Rooney, a gray, loose-haired mongrel if ever there was one, and he ran the fields around Apology at night with the rest of the pack, chasing farm animals around for fun. The pack had incurred the wrath of many a local farmer who stormed through their screen door late at night, brandishing rusting shotguns and firing blindly into the night as the dogs fled, the flames from the muzzle tearing holes in the darkness.

Rooney wasn't much of a dog, but Merle Oaken didn't care–he'd gotten a real good deal when he'd bought the animal near the stockyards at Renoir. And to Merle, saving a buck or two was a lot more important than just about anything else in life. The fact that, when Merle had purchased the dog, the animal had no idea about how to guide anything seemed immaterial to Merle, for he had in mind to teach the dog what he needed to know. After all, the dog was the right height.

You see, Merle Oaken wasn't blind at all. He could see very well, as a matter of fact, including being able to read the misspelled letters on the water tower from Irk Hickenlooper's farm. But Merle's father had gone blind in the twilight of his years, and to Merle's way of thinking it just seemed like a matter of time until he would suffer the same fate. Every now and then Merle was seen around town, dragging his reluctant guide dog down the street. Each time the dog would attempt to sit down on the sidewalk, Merle would give the leash a hard pull, and the choke chain tightening around Rooney's neck would let the dog know that training time wasn't the proper time to sit down.

"Whatcha doin', Merle?" people would shout from their cars.

"Just practicing for when I go blind!" Merle would holler back. And sometimes he'd add, "Peas are on special this week" or, "Got some good rump roast just in" because he also owned Merle's Grocery Store, where Rooney spent most of his time lounging when not in training or running loose with the pack. Perhaps it was because he worked in the grocery store business, and was always walking the fine line between red and black ink, that Merle had become a bit of a miser over the years. Merle stood just over five feet tall and had a body like a pear. He carefully groomed his remaining hair, letting it grow long on top and draping it across his head to hide the pink scalp on top. There was also some talk around town about how the crow's feet around Merle's eyes were starting to become more pronounced because Merle was spending so much time with his eyes squeezed shut, pretending to be blind as Rooney pulled on the leash ahead of him.

A few months before, Rooney had nearly run Merle into an oak tree while they were training at the park. In hindsight, it might have been better for everyone involved if Merle had hit the tree. Instead, Rooney had accidentally caused Merle's head to bump into a hornet's nest hanging from a dead limb. As the hornets swarmed from their hive, Merle had headed north and Rooney south, leash in tow. Merle was seen later, back at the house, chasing the dog around the front lawn, a bunch of orange Mercurochrome spots dotting his face. Training was suspended for about a week or so after that when Merle sprained his ankle. That was because Rooney jumped to the east while Merle kicked to the west, and Merle's foot found the old tree stump he'd been meaning to clear out since he'd moved onto the property a few years before.

Everett watched the dog depart, slinking between two houses like a snake's tail in the grass. It might not have been such a bad idea to send a shell behind the dog after all, he thought, watching Rooney's tail disappear behind Yig Digler's abandoned burning barrel near the edge of a cornfield.

Everett continued his rounds, heading east to see what was happening at the opposite end of the town. He passed through the downtown business district, observing that some of the town's merchants were in the process of opening their stores for the day's business. His eyes caught a flash of sun bouncing from a store window, and Everett tapped his brakes, feeling foolish even as he did so. For the sheriff had reacted to a stoplight turning from green to a bright yellow, and the town had no stoplight–anymore, that is.

But, for a brief period of time the town did manage to erect a traffic signal–sort of. It was a beautiful light, rising ten feet in the air on a black cast iron pole that held one red, yellow, and green signal on each of its four sides. Some of the town fathers had approached Owen Fuller about getting it because they'd found out that Eagle Nest had just gotten one and they were afraid that Apology might be the only town in Corwith County that was missing out on the Age of Technology. The town council took it up at a meeting one night and voted to purchase the traffic light, to be placed somewhere on Main Street. At first that didn't seem to be a problem, for there weren't but three or four intersections of any significance on Main Street. But, as with everything involved when dealing with humans, there was a big whoop-dee-doo about where the light was going to be placed. The townsfolk naturally divided along geographic locations, with the west end of Apology, the most outspoken, reeling off the first shots. The east end of town organized and countered, arguing that they had just as much right to the traffic signal as the west end. Some of the businesses in the downtown area lobbied for the light, too. If they could somehow make cars slow down for a minute or so, the businessmen argued, the drivers of those cars might stop in and spend some money.

What started out as a simple traffic light location mushroomed to a major issue dividing the town. Three different petitions began circulating, each bearing the names of supporters for a particular location. Owen Fuller received numerous, annoying phone calls about where to put the light. He began receiving fancy desserts and entrees from women living at either the east or west end of town, who wanted the stoplight in their neighborhood. Gift certificates from the downtown businesses showed up in his mailbox. Owen finally solved the problem of location, more because he was putting on too much weight from all that food than because of anything else.

Owen got the solution from Everett, but took the credit himself. At a town meeting, with all three groups present, Owen happily announced that the traffic light the town had purchased was not to be cemented in place. The light would be moved to a new intersection every two weeks so everybody could enjoy it. The light would be placed at the west end of town first, move to the downtown area two weeks later, and two weeks following that, the east end would get it. And then the whole process would repeat itself. Everyone at the meeting said how brilliant the idea was and that it all made sense to do it this way.

This was all well and good until sections of the town started swapping turns with the light. Someone's cousin visited from Des Moines and one of the west end families wanted the light in their neighborhood that week, so they swapped turns with the east end. Then the town had their Crazy Daze Celebration and needed the light, so the business section swapped out with the east end. Thrown in amongst all the swapping, an electrical problem put the light out of commission for five days. When the west end wanted the light again the business section said it was their turn, and the east end argued, no, it was their turn. Then nobody knew whose turn it was. It got so a person driving into town wouldn't know where the light was going to be, not that it mattered all that much to the townsfolk. But to people from other towns driving through the Main Street of Apology every day on their way to work in Renoir, the traffic light became somewhat of a joke.

"Wonder where the stoplight's gonna be today?" they'd say. "Let's see, this is Monday and the wind's blowin' from the east so…"

That kind of teasing didn't set too well with the people of Apology. It was one thing to poke fun at your own town. When someone else did it, it was a scandal.

The problem was finally solved by, of all people, avid angler Flem Frederickson as he drove home from a fishing trip after dark one Friday evening. When Flem left Apology, heading east that morning for Tinker's Lake, the stoplight had been in the downtown area.

However, the east enders had moved the stoplight early that afternoon, and now the light was two blocks east of where it had been when Flem left on his fishing trip. Flem drove into Apology from the east, pulling his boat. Rain falling on the windshield blurred his vision, for Flem had failed to change the wiper blades, as Plit Butler had suggested during the last oil change, and the wiper blades merely smeared the wet dust across the glass in sweeping arcs. Flem's notoriously poor eyesight, combined with the smeared dirt, now created a problem for the man. In the distance, Flem saw the traffic light and remembered that it had stood in the business district when he left town that morning. Not knowing that the sign had been moved, and peering through a dirty windshield on a dark, rainy night, Flem miscalculated the distance to the light by two blocks and rammed the cast iron base with the bumper of his pickup at thirty-five miles an hour. The light tottered back and forth for just a moment, and then crashed on the roof of Flem's truck. As Everett pulled up to see what happened, he found that the town's brand new shiny stoplight was totally destroyed. The cast iron base had shattered and pieces of red, yellow and green glass lay scattered around the wheels of the Flem's pickup.

At first some of the townsfolk were noose-making angry with Flem for destroying their only stoplight. They talked of how the sheriff should pull Flem's license for being so stupid or make Flem pay for a new stoplight. But, after a week or so without the stoplight, people found they didn't really miss it, or the squabbles that the light had brought with it. People had grown tired of having to move the light so often or figure out who should get it next. What they'd really grown the most tired of was the comments from surrounding communities about how the town of Apology had a stoplight that wouldn't sit still.

A few months later someone suggested that the town install speed bumps. When Everett got wind of it, he'd quashed the idea real fast. Speed bumps were too hard to move around.

An hour later Everett drove west, heading for the Petler place. He pulled the big Pontiac into the Petler driveway and got out, Durham's cleaned pistol in his hand.

"Nice tires ya got there, Everett," Deke Petler drawled as Everett opened the recently repaired gate that opened into the Petler's yard.

Everett glanced back toward his patrol car, admiring the tires himself, even if they were now a week old and not quite as shiny black as they had been.

"Got them from Plit Butler," Everett answered. "Best he could get me."

"What can I do for you, Sheriff?" Deke asked.

Everett knew that Deke had been watching the patrol car as it passed through town and slowed in front of their driveway.

"Well, I'm looking for Durham, actually."

Deke looked down at Durham's pistol in the sheriff's hand. He grinned.

"You gonna give Durham his gun back, are ya?"

"Think I should, Deke?"

Deke rubbed his chin, thinking.

"Aw, go ahead and give the man his gun back, Sheriff. He's learned his lesson, I suspect. He's been missin' it something awful. Like he lost his best girl or somethin'."

"You mean Durham has a best girl?"

"No," Deke replied. "But I'm sure he's thought about gettin' one sometime."

A screen door slammed behind Deke. Durham walked toward them, yawning.

"Up awful early, aren't ya, Sheriff?" Durham asked.

He spotted the freshly oiled pistol in Everett's hand and smiled.

"Aw, Sheriff, you cleaned up my gun, didn't you?"

Everett handed Durham the weapon, the chrome of the barrel gleaming.

"You think you can behave yourself with this thing, Durham?"

Durham's eyes were on the gun.

"Sure, Sheriff," he replied. "I've learned my lesson. I won't shoot in town again."

"Good," Everett said. "See that you don't. A lot of people are mad about what you did, so I'd lay low for a while. But if this happens again, I'll have to keep your gun for more than a week, not like this time. Understand?"

"I do, Sheriff," Durham replied humbly.

"Then see that you do," Everett warned.

Everett glanced west, past the Petler house, to the white survey truck half a mile away.

"What are they doin' way out there, anyway?" Deke asked, turning his head to see what Everett was watching.

"Surveying," Everett answered. "They're gonna deepen the ditches along the road, especially in that low spot, so the snow won't block the road so badly during the winter."

"About time somethin' was done about this road," Durham said. "It must have been plugged up half of last winter."

"Could have been," Everett replied. "But it sure will please Bert Kestral when it gets done."

"Bet you'll be happy about that," Deke grinned.

More than you know, Everett thought. For Everett had had to endure the constant griping from Bert, even though the sheriff had little to do with the upkeep and maintenance of the county's roads.

"Looks like they're going to be surveying around your place tomorrow," Everett observed. "And right up to the city limits."

Everett knew the Petler boys well.

"So, you boys leave them alone and let them work, OK? Remember, Durham, I gave you your gun back when I probably should have kept it a little longer. So you do something for me and don't complicate my job by making me come down here listening to those surveyors complaining about you two harassing them."

"No, not us," Deke shot back. "We'll be saints in the makin'."

"See that you are," Everett said, glancing at Durham's pistol.

Durham was aware of just what Everett's glance meant.

"Hey, Sheriff," Durham said, his voice fresh with optimism, would you like some fresh pickles?"

"Dill pickles?" Everett asked.

"Dills," Durham grinned. "Sour. And crisp as corn flakes. Real good. Can I get you some? They're swimmin' in the brine right now."

Everett knew that one of the few things Deke and Durham ever took the time to learn from Birdy was the art of making very good pickles. Next to gardening, pickling had been one of Birdy's favorite past times, and over the years she had perfected her technique. The trick to making exceptional pickles, Birdy said, was to grow the cucumbers in your garden. That way, she said, you could watch their progress day by day. And that's exactly what Birdy did.

Every day during the growing season, Birdy dragged Deke and Durham out to the garden and checked the cukes to see how they were doing. Something must have clicked in the boys' minds, for they actually learned from Birdy how to know when the time was right to pick the cukes for pickling. Birdy taught the boys how to make the pickling brine. The brine needed to be salty, but not too salty. Birdy made the brine in a wooden barrel that sat in the basement, where the cooler climate aided the pickling process. Two iron bands on the outside of the barrel held the wooden slats together, and Birdy always made sure to fill the barrel to the second rim when she concocted the brine. Then the boys and she would dump in the cukes, where they would float in the brine for weeks. During that time, two inches of mold would grow on the surface as the brine transferred its magic to the cukes. When tasting time arrived, Birdy would plunge her hand through the green slime and pull one of the fat pickles from the brine. She would bite it as green slime rolled from the surface of the pickle, testing if the process was complete. The crisp sound escaping into the dampness of the basement was the first indication that the batch was ready. The boys would then plunge into the green slime to get their pickle, their faces puckering as they tasted the delightful dills.

When Stella Hissy would compete at the Iowa State Fair in August with her chicken recipe, Birdy Petler was at the other end of the building, winning first prize for her dill pickles. Apology had been the only town in Iowa one year to have had two blue ribbon winners to brag about, and Stella Hissy and Birdy Petler's picture had appeared on the front page of the Renoir Gazette.

"I believe I'd like a few of those dills," Everett said.

"You'll have them then," Durham replied.

Turning away, Durham limped toward the house, swinging the pistol in his hand. He turned back.

"Don't leave now!" he shouted. "I won't be but a minute."

"His foot's been actin' up a bit," Deke explained as they watched Durham favoring his right leg. "Since he tried to run down that fool rooster."

"How did the rooster come out on all of this?" Everett asked.

"The rooster is just fine," Deke replied.

Deke motioned to the bird half hidden in tall rye grass near the south end of the property. The bird was pecking at some unseen object hidden in the grass, unaware that it was being observed.

"Got 'em!" Durham yelled, limping back across the yard.

He carried a brown paper bag, dripping with brine.

"You know that bag's gonna break, Durham," Deke scolded, "and get all over the sheriff's car."

"It'll be OK," Everett said, grabbing the bag. "I'll get them to my office and put them in the refrigerator. They'll be fine."

Everett pulled one out of the bag and bit into it, chewing.

"Birdy would be proud of you boys," he said, smiling and holding up the half-eaten pickle. "Mighty proud."

Everett noted the pride welling up in their eyes. Rolling up the sack, he turned to go.

"Thanks for the dills, boys. And be kind to those surveyors when they come across your land."

6   The Boundary Hunters

Everett wiped the tattered rag across the front seat where the salty brine had sunk into the car seat, muttering as he worked. The smell of dill pickles had been strong at first but with a little lemon cleaner the aroma appeared to be subsiding. He would have been angry, but the pickles had been very tasty, and the fact that he had pickle smell in his patrol car was no one's fault but his. For he'd accepted the pickles in a brown paper sack from someone who, earlier in life, had shot off his own big toe.

Everett heard the banging sound and looked up to see Flem Frederickson driving by, pounding on the side of his truck door. Everett stopped his work and stood up, facing Main Street as Flem braked in front of the Sheriff's Office.

"Hey, Everett, why don't you come on over here and shine up the inside of this old Dodge?" Flem teased.

A jolly Norwegian, Flem never seemed to be too shaken by anything that happened. The man talked slowly, with a distinct Scandinavian accent that hit certain syllables hard, causing him pucker his lips and chop his sentences as he spoke. Flem's hair was a mass of blond and browns that mixed with the wind, and the man had easy-going eyes that matched his gentle disposition.

Everett leaned over and took a whiff of the inside of the truck, noticing a fish-shaped deodorizer hanging from the rear view mirror inside the cab.

"Whew," he replied, making a face. "Ain't nothing gonna help the inside of this old thing. You sure you ain't left a dead fish or something under the seat about six weeks back?"

Flem rolled his lower lip forward, thinking.

"Come to think of it," he said, "that was about the time I got back from tying into that mess of perch at Spirit Lake. Could be that one of them's still swimming under the seat somewhere."

Everett sniffed, long and deep, a repugnant look forming on his face, albeit only in jest.

"If he's still under there, he ain't doing much swimming," he said. "That's for sure."

"Then I'd better be going home," Flem shot back, "because he's about ready to chuck into Edith's frying pan."

As Flem pulled away Everett pinched his nose, shouting, while pointing below the seat of the truck.

"Better tell Edith to put some extra garlic and flour on that one–if you ever happen to find it."

It was well known by all serious anglers within a twenty mile radius of Apology that Flem Frederickson was not only the best fisherman around, but the man always seemed to have an ample supply of fat, lazy night crawlers nestled contentedly within two hundred pounds of cool soil in an old freezer unit stored in his basement. But that hadn't always been the case–for many years the man had been crawler starved. But fate had intervened and changed all that.

Flem liked to bragged that he'd found the perfect wife, and by accident, a flourishing business of selling night crawlers. Edith was a dark-haired woman, not much of a cook, and not much for looks, either. Perhaps that's why she was kind of a private individual, quite content to be by herself. Flem didn't seem to mind her looks, though– he had bad eyes. The woman's legs were spindly, so small in girth that one wondered if a good stiff wind wouldn't be enough to snap them off at the ankles. Some of the boys at Duffy's went so far as to ask Flem if they could borrow Edith and toss horseshoes at those skinny ankles in place of using a regular steel post. But Edith had a skill Flem hadn't even been looking for in a wife, because he thought it just wasn't possible for a woman to possess that kind of talent. You see, Flem was a die-hard fisherman, a trait passed to him from his Scandinavian ancestors. Gambling, drinking, and chasing women– they were all good clean fun, Flem agreed with the boys at Duffy's– but there was nothing like the thrill that came from a hard yank on the business end of a fishing pole.

Flem loved the single life, but on their third date Edith had shown him something that pushed this happy bachelor rapidly along the road

117

to the altar. It had been raining hard when Flem drove Edith home from the picture show at Renoir one Friday night in May. The rain had been so fierce that Flem had been forced to stop the Dodge pickup along the road to wait out the storm. It was still early when they got to Edith's house, so the couple took a stroll in the garden in back of the house. Flem had been talking nonsense, like most love-struck fools do, and suddenly he looked around to find that he was alone. He had been quite surprised when he discovered Edith kneeling on the ground beside him, her hands cupping around something hidden in the wet grass. When she stood up and opened her hands, Flem was dumbfounded by what he saw. Here was a woman who could not only catch night crawlers, but could find them in the pitch dark–and without having to use a flashlight! Edith casually handed the worm to Flem and dropped to her knees once more, her wet skirt clinging to the front of her legs. A few seconds later she stood again, holding another, fatter crawler. She repeated the task six more times, stopping only when the slimy worms began sliding through Flem's fingers and dropping to the ground. It was as if the woman been doing this all her life.

To the weak-eyed Flem, who always had trouble finding enough worms for his many fishing excursions, this discovery was a revelation from heaven. This was a talent he wanted in his family, by golly. He could only imagine the kind of children that would come from mixing his Scandinavian fishing blood with a worm-catching talent like Edith had. The very next day Flem high-tailed it to Renoir, scouting rental tuxedo costs, just in case Edith said yes when he asked for her hand. She did, and quickly, for Edith was a smart woman who knew she wouldn't have to go through Flem's stomach, like lesser women might, to arrive at the door to her man's heart. The last memory Everett had of their wedding day was Flem's truck leaving the parking lot of St. John's Church near sunset, Flem and Edith bunched in the cab, heading for their honeymoon at Spirit Lake. A stringer full of bullheads hanging from the back bumper followed the truck out of town.

As Flem pulled away, Everett grinned silently, recalling Apology's amusing stoplight fiasco and how Flem inadvertently put an end to that nonsense. Everett turned back to his patrol car and shut the door, lemon cleaner in hand. He scanned both ends of Main Street before stepping onto the sidewalk. The crack in the sidewalk where Viola Vanderhoff had fallen was now filled with a fresh patch of cement, compliments of handyman Jacob Witt. Everett grunted and shook his head as he remembered the recent collision of the two women. Everett glanced through his office window and found Old Duke, feet plopped on the sheriff's desk, snoring as he dozed comfortably in the sheriff's chair.

Everett didn't mind Old Duke sleeping in his office–it happened often. But Duke generally took a cot in the cell rather than snoozing in front of the large window where everyone in town could see him. Everett opened the door slowly and entered the office, taking great care not to wake his sleeping deputy. Before Duke settled in for a nap, he had been putting some marks on a land plat of the town, and Everett saw that, for some reason, Duke had been plotting the progress of the surveyors as they worked their way east to the city limits. Everett picked up a blue magic marker lying uncapped on the desk near Duke's feet. Duke had plotted several dots on the map, where the surveyors had ceased operations each day. Why Duke was so interested in the progress of the surveyors was a puzzle to the sheriff, but the deputy sometimes just needed something to do to fill up those annoying gaps between catnaps, Everett concluded, and the surveyors had given him that opportunity.

Everett pressed the point of the blue marker against his thumb and found that the pen still functioned even though the cap had been left off, exposing the marker tip to the open air. Everett examined the dark blue dot on his thumb and looked over at Duke, mouth open and head sagged back against the backrest of the chair. Creeping around the desk, Everett knelt on one knee next to the sleeping man. He stealthily raised the marker, inching the tip closer to Duke's face until the point made a minute depression in his cheek. Everett pulled the marker away, leaving a blue dot on the skin. Duke stirred in his sleep, snorting, and relaxed against the chair. Once again the marker left a dot his face, and again and again. When Everett put the marker back on the table five minutes later, Duke's cheeks were littered with blue dots. Everett stood on the opposite side of the desk, cocking his head as he admired his artwork.

Down the street marched Bonnie Fuller, and as the woman drew near the window, Everett spotted her and ducked behind the door, hidden from her view. Everett watched as Bonnie strode past the window, stopping when she spotted Old Duke sleeping in the chair, dark blue spots littering his face. Bonnie put one hand on her forehead to shield her eyes from the glare of the glass and pressed her nose closer to the window. Her expression turned from surprise to disgust as she studied the sleeping, blue-dotted Duke, feet propped on the desk. She turned and walked away in a huff. Everett peered after her, watching as her gait shifted up a gear. He puckered his lips, resting his hands on his waist as he swung his hips back and forth to mimic the woman's swaying motion. Bonnie, no doubt, was in a hurry to spill the beans to husband Owen that some sort of tomfoolery was taking place at the taxpayers' expense.

Everett spotted a white pickup truck driving through Main Street. He recognized the truck and its two occupants; the surveyors who'd been working west of town. Everett was surprised when they pulled in next to his patrol car and got out. The two men were small and wiry, and looked even more so as they stood next to the survey truck. Their gaunt faces were leathery and tanned from working in the sun all summer. Both men wore khaki shorts and brown shirts containing an abundance of pockets. Everett watched as the men exchanged some words and pulled a map from the cab of the truck. Everett placed the blue marker in Duke's palm and folded the man's hands together. He moved Duke's hands to rest on his stomach, as if his deputy were absorbed in silent prayer. That completed, Everett walked across the room and pulled open the second drawer of a filing cabinet, pretending to be occupied in paperwork as the doorknob turned.

The surveyors opened the door and stepped inside to find Old Duke sleeping, legs propped on the desk, his face dotted with blue marks. Everett placed a finger against his lips, motioning for the men to keep silent. Before the door could close, Mayor Owen Fuller entered the room and frowned at Duke. The presence of two strangers standing next to the sheriff didn't discourage the mayor from scowling at Everett, even though the scowl had originated with his wife, and therefore, had come to him second-handed. Owen slammed the door hard, causing Duke's feet to slide off the desk. Duke's legs, falling hard to the floor, yanked his body away from the back of the chair. His arms fell to his sides, but he instinctively raised them, attempting to balance himself in the chair. As he fought to right his body, he poked himself in the face with the magic marker, adding yet another dot to his cheek. Duke opened his eyes sleepily to find Mayor Owen Fuller, Everett, and two strangers looking down at him.

"Duke," Owen said, "what the hell are you doing sleeping in the Sheriff's Office?"

Owen turned to Everett.

"And what are you doing letting him use your office for a bedroom, Sheriff?"

He turned back to Duke.

"And what in God's name are you doing with those blue dots all over your face?"

Owen, as the mayor, was obviously embarrassed, especially finding visitors in Everett's office. He hadn't counted on anyone other than Duke and Everett being in the office, based on what Bonnie had told him. The two surveyors patiently watched the events unfold before them. Everett remained unfazed, unfurling an explanation born from years of practice.

"Let me explain, Mayor," he began, "right after I find out who these gentlemen are."

He ignored the red-faced mayor momentarily and turned his attention to the surveyors. In the chair, Duke rubbed his face and examined his fingertips, bewildered by the blue smudges he found.

"I'm Bill Trent, Sheriff," the older man said, addressing Everett. "We've talked before."

Everett nodded, for he had met the man previously when he'd visited them to put the run on Owen's three sons, who were making pests of themselves. Trent pointed to the other man.

"And this is Audry Cline."

"You're the surveyors who've been working west of town, aren't you?" Everett asked. "Nobody's been bothering you, I hope."

"No, Sheriff," Trent answered. "Not since you ran those boys off."

"Boys?" Owen asked. "What boys?"

"Just some farm kids," Everett fibbed, knowing that no good would come from informing the mayor that it had been his three kids the sheriff had corralled a few days before. "I've seen you men out there working every day. How's it going?"

"Extremely well, Sheriff," Trent replied. "The weather's been helping us a lot."

Everett figured that this was just as good a time as any to get both Old Duke and himself out of trouble with the mayor. He nodded toward Duke.

"My deputy, Old Duke, has been keeping a sharp eye on your progress. And you boys sure have been working up a storm out there."

Everett pointed to the plat on his desk.

"See," he said, tracing blue marker locations on the plat. "He's told me how quickly you've been working to get this piece of road surveyed."

Duke looked surprised by Everett's comment, but remained silent. Everett continued.

"See, Duke's been keeping track of your progress," he explained, eyeing the mayor, "just because he was amazed by how fast you two were getting the job done. And every day he marks how far you've surveyed. See all those marks on the county plat."

He saw their eyes focused on Duke's plat, and continued.

"Well, if he's so darn fired interested in marking on this map, how did he get those marks all over his face, unless there was some tomfoolery going on here?" Owen said, looking at Everett.

Everett directed his answer to Owen, aware that the two surveyors were just as interested in his reply.

"Very simple," Everett replied. "Duke usually updates his map every morning, just after he gets done with all his office chores. He's very thorough in his work, you know. And keeping track of the surveyors was just something he wanted to do. But you gotta remember, Owen, that this is the fall, and with all the harvesting that's been going on, there's a lot of grain dust and dirt in the air. You know as well as I do that Duke's sinuses can handle only so much dust, so Duke has to take medicine for it."

Everett pointed to a bottle on the top of the filing cabinet, making sure that the mayor saw it.

"Well, too much of that medicine makes a person drowsy."

Everett picked up the bottle.

"See, Owen," he pointed, "it says so right on the label. And with all the dust in the air lately, I guess Duke just took too much–poor soul, he's been suffering so. And with all the hard work he's been doing, trying to keep this office clean and answering the phone and sitting the desk so we can look good to visitors, I guess he musta just took a double dose that put him to sleep."

Everett knew that the mayor had to concede that possibility because he'd shown Owen the bottle.

"Well, what about all those dots on his face?" Owen demanded, unwilling to quit without some small victory.

"That's easy to explain, Owen," Everett replied. "You see, when Duke fell asleep he was working on that plat. And I suppose he had that marker in his hand, with the point sticking up. Now, if you've ever seen Duke in a deep sleep after he takes his medicine, you know that he stirs sometimes because this stuff makes him dream an awful lot. He usually sleeps with his head leaning back over the headrest, but sometimes it tilts forward, into his chin. Then he wakes up and pulls his head back. Only pretty soon it sags again. I've seen him do this lots of times–it's the medicine, you know."

"I know all about Duke's sleeping habits now," Owen snorted impatiently. "Yes, yes, sheriff. But that doesn't tell me about how is face is all marked up."

"Well, Mayor," Everett continued, "you saw for yourself that Duke had the marker in his hands when you came into the office and that the point was sticking up in the air. I think that every time his head sagged, it pressed against that tip and left a mark on his face. Sometimes even people who should know better about Duke's condition come by, looking through the window, maybe even tapping on the glass. That probably had something to do with disturbing Duke's rest, too. That's all that happened."

Everett knew that the mayor was now forced to remain quiet about how he'd found out about Duke's napping in the first place or risk exposing Bonnie as a busybody who ran to him tattling.

"Come to think of it," Duke interrupted, "I do remember kinda dreaming that something was prickling my face."

"You see, Mayor," Everett said calmly, "a simple explanation for a simple problem. Now Duke, why don't you just go and wash up your face?"

"Sure, Sheriff," Duke replied happily. "And thanks for telling me."

Duke stood up and disappeared into the back room, where the sound of running water was shortly heard. Everett, avoiding the mayor's stare, turned his attention to the two men.

"And now, since that's all cleared up, what can I do for you two gentlemen?" he asked. "Those Petler boys at the end of town giving you any problems?"

"Oh, no," Trent replied, "in fact, they've been more than helpful to us. Even gave us some rather tasty dill pickles."

"Well, that's nice to hear," Everett replied, throwing a sideways glance toward the mayor. "I've always said that those two boys were generally good folks down deep."

Trent held up the roll of maps.

"We've completed the survey, Sheriff, to the city limits," he said. "But we just need to clear up a little problem we have, and hope that you might be able to help us."

"What kind of problem?" Owen asked.

Duke reentered the room, his face scrubbed clean of dots.

"Well, if we could clear off someplace, I'll unroll this map and we'll talk from there," Trent offered.

"Fine," Everett replied.

The sheriff cleared a space on his desk. The map was unrolled and various knickknacks were placed on the corners, preventing the paper from curling inward. Trent pointed to a spot along the road, just east of the Petler property.

"This is just a minor error," Trent began, "but we thought we'd better tell someone. We've found this type of thing before and it's not uncommon to find. You can see where we've plotted the city limits of Apology, right here on this map–this pencil mark here. This is what the town has been using as its boundary for all these years."

He pointed to the spot on the map again, covering the faint pencil mark with a distinct red marker.

"You recognize the city limits here, about one hundred feet east of this last property."

"The Petler place," Everett said.

"That is correct."

"That's were the post is, marking the town limits on the west," Owen said. "And has been as long as I can remember."

Trent pointed to a second mark on the paper.

"This map, however, shows the original town site, the land area, I mean, when the town was incorporated. And if you compare this original western boundary with the one you've been using, you will see that there's a discrepancy of about two hundred and fifty feet. That is, the land originally set aside as the property incorporated into the town of Apology actually lies about fifty feet west of this Petler property here."

A look of concern turned Everett's face to stone.

"Are you sure about this?" he asked.

"We've checked our survey four different times," Trent explained. "And on the fourth time we found steel in the ground. We marked it with orange paint."

"Steel?" Owen asked.

"Yes," Trent replied. "A steel surveying marker. That's about as good a piece of evidence as we would need to prove that the town boundary was originally at the spot we've found. The boundary has apparently been moved to the east sometime since the town was incorporated."

"Are you trying to tell me," Owen said, "that we've had the city limit post in the wrong place for over thirty years?"

"At least thirty years," Trent answered. "Probably more than that. But we've seen this happen on numerous occasions when we've run surveys. It's really not a big deal."

Duke, who had been watching the group, spoke.

"Then that would mean," he said, "that the Petler property is really within the city limits of Apology."

"Do you know how long the Pelters have owned that property?" Trent asked. "Perhaps it was changed when the land was last sold."

Duke grinned.

"What's so funny, Duke?" Owen asked.

Duke's grin widened.

"Angus Petler," he said, "that's what's so funny."

"Birdy wouldn't want you making fun of her Angus," Everett cautioned, "even though they've both passed on."

133

"Don't make Birdy out to be no saint," Duke warned. "Especially if she knew what Angus had done. You see, before they paved this road through Apology, there were no signs marking the town boundaries. Angus put them up after the road was paved. I remember him saying that he wanted people to feel welcomed, and to know that they were entering the friendly town of Apology. I remember that he bought the signs and even dug the holes. And when they were in the ground, everyone talked about how nice it was that Angus Petler did that, and didn't charge the town a dime for doing it."

"What's so strange about that?" Owen asked.

"I was around at the time," Duke said. "And I recall that the town was assessed some money by the county to pay for a section of road paved within the city limits. The town would have to cough up some of the money, and that would mean higher taxes for everyone in town."

"And?" Owen probed.

Duke yelped.

"See what ol' Angus did? He was a sly one, he was. And wouldn't let go of a nickel if he didn't have to. That's why he didn't charge any

134

money to put up those posts. He shorted the boundary at the west end of town so he'd be outside of the city limits. Then he wouldn't have to pay any taxes for the new road. But he'd get all the enjoyment from it."

"Those are pretty slanderous words to be saying about someone," Owen cautioned.

"I spent plenty of late nights at Duffy's with Angus Petler," Duke said. "That is, when Birdy was off somewhere and wasn't keeping an eye on him. And I remember one time especially, when the snowplow knocked the boundary post down. Someone asked Angus if he was going to go out and put his fancy sign back into the ground so people wouldn't blink and miss the town."

"So what did he do?" Everett asked.

"I remember real good what old Angus did," Duke grinned. "He cackled out loud, which wasn't like him. And then he got up and left the tavern. He must've waded into the ditch in the dark, through all that snow. Next morning the sign was back up, arrow straight."

7 Where Do We Go From Here?

Like a spark plug awakening that first reluctant piston on a cold winter morning, the surveyors' news ignited a fire, churning up the motor of an already finely tuned rumor mill in the town of Apology. This was big news and traveled quickly by phone and word of mouth. The post office was unusually busy on Saturday, with farmers and townsfolk stopping in to buy stamps they didn't need or collecting mail that had already been delivered. A crowd of men formed outside Shilling's Barbershop around ten, because every worn chair inside creaked beneath the body of a man hungry for some news.

Everett had been busy since the word had gotten out, and had spent a good amount of time away from his office. Old Duke had manned the phone and sat at the desk, having been reminded by

Everett to stay awake and not invoke the wrath of the Mayor Owen Fuller twice in one week. The sheriff's absence had been planned, with good reason, to cut down on the visitors to his office. And on this Saturday morning, Everett peered through the window, watching the crowd form outside the barbershop. He checked himself, picking some lint from his shirtsleeve, and opened the office door and stepped outside.

As he strode down Main Street the crowd took notice, and Everett knew that all eyes were on him. It didn't escape his attention that some of these men had just gotten their hair cut the Saturday before and were a might early in showing up at the shop again. Everett crossed the street in a long diagonal walk, retracing the path taken by the crowd who'd confronted him the week before about the Petler brothers, taking his time as he walked. The downtown was alive with people. Someone in the barbershop crowd shouted at him.

"Hey, someone arrest that guy for jaywalking!"

As Everett stepped onto the sidewalk, he recognized the voice of Reef Langley. Reef leaned against the candy-striped barber pole, grinning broadly at him. A few black hairs dangled over his forehead as the sun shone on his boyish-looking face. Irk Hickenlooper stood close by.

Reef Langley had a set of choppers with jagged teeth looking like the business end of Paul Bunyan's saw. He hadn't come by his teeth naturally, however. They had been a gift of neglect, for Reef's parents hadn't been much on overseeing their son's oral hygiene. At one time Reef's teeth had been various shades of black, green, and yellow, and he let on like he cared little about what people said about him. But he was secretly ashamed of the appearance of a mouth that didn't dare smile because it would only show the world something ugly inside. There were some who said that Reef smiled only when he slept, and that was providing the moon was under a cloud. The sad state of his own choppers was more than likely the reason Reef would never let his kids have candy, except on special holidays. They ate plain cereal, with no sugar, and most of their food was seasoned only to ease the bland taste. Reef even made them brush their teeth with baking soda. Just how desperate Reef's kids were for sweets during those dry spells between holidays became evident the afternoon the Mulgoneys left town. Reef's two kids waited until the back door of the moving van slammed shut and was moving down the road before scampered through the back door of the vacant house. Everett, answering a call from Doris Donahue about kids in the house, checked the back door and found the kids sucking the toothpaste out of the nail holes with soda straws just for the sweet taste.

Everett faced Reef and grinned back at him.

"Yea, these damn jaywalkers."

"Gonna give yourself a ticket, Sheriff?" Reef teased.

"Well, I would," Everett answered, "but I forgot to bring my ticket book. So I guess I'll have to owe you one."

Reef's face lit up and he grinned back at the sheriff, showing off the brilliant whites of his teeth. Reef was still learning how to smile in public and showed off his recently cleaned teeth to anyone who happened to look his way. Their jagged points still looked like the teeth of a rough cut saw, but that seemed unimportant now. And it had been because of Everett's intervention that Reef's teeth now shone in all their God-given brilliance.

A few months before, Reef's wife Annie had phoned the sheriff and asked to come and see him about a problem she said couldn't be discussed over the phone. About ten o'clock that morning Annie arrived at the Sheriff's Office, and Everett, as agreed, sent Old Duke on an errand while he and Annie talked. Annie first began by telling Everett what a good man and husband Reef was, and how he was so kind to their two children. That was all well and good, Everett had told her, but what was it that he could do for her?

"Well, Sheriff," she began, "it's about his teeth. Well, you know."

"He does have a colorful set of choppers," Everett told her. "But you knew that when you married him, didn't you?"

"I did," she admitted. "But there's more to the man than teeth. He's a good man. But I wanna make him a better one."

"You've been married over ten years," Everett reminded her. "Why is it so important now?"

"Well," she began, almost apologetically, "I've been thinking about Reef for a while. You know I love him, Sheriff, that's a fact."

"He ain't found a girl in Renoir, has he?" Everett asked.

"Oh, no, Sheriff," she answered quickly. "Nothing like that."

"Well, Annie," he said. "You're gonna have to spit it out because I don't know what you want."

"Well," she began sheepishly, "it might seem like a small thing to you, but it's Reef's teeth. Actually, it's his mouth. You and I know he's always had bad teeth, but I put up with it because that's just the way it is. But lately his breath has taken on a real bad smell. And it's been getting worse."

"That would be a problem, I can see," Everett replied, silently grateful that the problem was not another woman. "Why don't you just tell him?"

"I just can't," she said. "You see, he's a good man, and honestly, Sheriff, I just ain't got the heart inside of me to tell him."

Everett could understand her thinking. Regardless of how she felt, Flem was her man, and loyalty sometimes meant accepting things one didn't necessary like or agree with.

"That's not all, Sheriff," she continued. "We're getting ready to go to a big wedding in Des Moines, and it will be the first time that I'll be able to show off Reef to some of my side of the family. And–"

"And you want to make a good impression?"

"Not only that, Sheriff, but I'm getting so I can't stand to be in the same bed with him. His breath smells like bleu cheese that's laid in the sun for about a week. I've taken to kissing his cheek, but I still dread it. And I know if word of this starts getting around town I won't be able to show myself for shame."

She looked at Everett, her eyes so mournful he pitied her.

"You just let me handle it, Annie," Everett replied. "It's good you came to me."

Everett recognized the delicacy of the matter, and when Annie left he picked up the phone and called Dr. Leonard McCain, his own dentist in Renoir. Two days later Reef Langley was pulled over by a friend of Everett's, an Iowa Highway patrolman, and arrested four miles east of Apology for driving without a license. As part of the conspiracy, Everett had instructed Annie to remove Reef's wallet from his pants so the arrest would be valid. Reef, having no money on him, couldn't post bail. For the sake of convenience, Reef had been taken to Apology and placed in Everett's custody. When Reef phoned Annie for bail money, no one had been home to take the call. It had taken Everett a while to convince Annie that this plan would work if she did her part, which was to be away from the house when the phone rang. Everett made sure before Reef entered the jail cell that the small, barred room was plenty hot, and generously supplied Reef with cold water laced with a strong sleeping potion.

Two hours after entering the cell, Reef's unconscious body leaned against the back of a chair, his mouth propped open with a stick. Dr. McCain worked for over an hour grinding and picking away at Reef's teeth, stopping only once when he got faint from the odor.

When Reef awoke in the jail cell Annie was at his side, telling him how the quick-thinking sheriff had saved his life when he'd had a seizure from the heat. Everett had phoned for a doctor as his condition deteriorated, Reef was told. The highly infectious bacteria would move rapidly into Reef's bloodstream if left untreated, the doctor warned upon examining the man. Annie approved the treatment, which called for extensive bacterial eradication, particularly from Reef's teeth and gums, where the bacteria had concentrated. Before Reef had too much time to think about the events transpiring while he'd been out cold, Annie placed a mirror before him. As Reef admired his gleaming white teeth, Annie happily told him that she'd found his wallet by the bed, and they were free to go. If Reef suspected a conspiracy, he'd never brought it up, for it was he who'd come out for the better. And for several nights following Reef's exit from Everett's jail, bedroom curtains in the Langley home fluttered back and forth with a vengeance, even in the absence of a breeze.

Reef popped a breath mint in his mouth as Everett watched.

"Winter Green," he said, holding up the roll.

Reef had certainly swung the other way since the incident, Everett thought. The man now took great care in the cleanliness of his teeth and the freshness of his breath.

"What brings you all down to the barbershop?" Reef asked.

"What do you think, Sheriff?" Irk Hickenlooper asked. "We all heard about the surveyors. What's gonna happen now?"

Irk stood next to Reef, hooking his thumbs under the straps of his bib overalls, the attire of choice for farmers in the area. Irk carried a pouch of chewing tobacco in the front pocket of his overalls, but rarely indulged, preferring to munch on a straw. But Irk smelled like pipe smoke anyway, because of the aroma given off by the tobacco he carried. During the summer months a knife-edge line formed across the middle of Irk's forehead, the separation point between the tanned skin on the lower part of his face and the fair skin protected by his cap. Irk was quick to make decisions, for he was a farmer, and his own boss, and had been for over thirty years. When Irk woke up each morning, his eyes peered across his fields, over the land on which his word was law.

It seemed strange to Everett that Irk, who didn't even live in Apology, or pay city taxes, was so concerned about the issue of the city's boundary. Irk, no doubt, had just caught up with the rest of the town, and felt compelled to say something.

"I guess we'll just have to wait and see," Everett said, shrugging off Irk's question and moving to the barbershop door.

Irk Hickenlooper seemed quite willing to get involved in the town's problems when they arose. Irk's contention was that he put his money into the town's barbershop, grocery, and general store, so therefore, any town business was his also. And no one seemed to argue the point.

The small crowd of men parted like wind blowing through a wheat field as Everett passed through them and entered the barbershop. When he saw the crowd inside, he was glad he'd picked that piece of lint from his freshly laundered shirt. As the door creaked open, Earl Shilling stopped his scissors in mid-clip, the instrument wavering in the air above Zippy Martin's head when the barber spotted the town sheriff. There was such an abundance of bodies squeezed inside the shop that when Everett swung open the door, it banged against a chair pushed close to the entrance, on which sat Taylor Cantrell. Taylor, a veterinarian, lived on five acres of pasture two miles south of Apology. Seeing Taylor, Everett instinctively thought about the half-moon dent of a deer hoof in the chrome above the windshield of his patrol car.

"Oh, sorry, Taylor," he said.

The air around the veterinarian always smelled like something septic or like pig manure, depending on what the man had been doing last. Slightly bulky, Taylor's frame was unusually solid for a man in his late forties. An amateur taxidermist, Taylor's house was constantly cluttered with an assortment of birds and animals in various stages of being mounted.

Taylor looked up at Everett.

"That's OK, Sheriff. It's a pretty tight squeeze in here this morning, as you can see."

"Looks that way," Everett said, looking around the room.

Earl Shilling waved the scissors in the air above Zippy Martin's head.

Zippy Martin usually delivered mail this time of morning, but he'd quick-stepped his route to finish early so he'd make it to the barbershop to join the crowd he figured would be there. He sat in the chair, knowing he was the center of attention until the cutting was complete. Zippy had strong legs and was often teased that he walked at a slant from carrying the heavy mailbag on his right shoulder all day.

"Come on in, Sheriff," Earl motioned, moving the scissors through the air, close to Zippy's ear. "I'll fit you in next."

"No rush, Earl," Everett said, closing the door. "Nothing pressing this morning."

For a few moments all eyes were on Earl Shilling, clipping away at the top of Zippy's head. The silence was almost deafening, an unusual circumstance for the inside of the barbershop, especially on a Saturday. It was as if someone were waiting for the sheriff to tip his hand.

"Hey, Sheriff," Earl said finally, "I had one of those surveyors in here for a cut the other day, just before they left town."

"Is that a fact?" Everett asked.

"Sure is," Earl replied. "They said they were done with their work and were packing it in for the week."

"Say," Merle Oaken said, directing his words toward Everett, "didn't I see their truck parked in front of your office yesterday?"

"Yes you did," Everett replied. "They stopped by to tell me that they were done."

"So everything's done now, I mean with the survey and all?" Jim Hissy asked.

"All done," Everett answered.

Bert Kestral spoke up, trying to get the conversation turned in the direction everyone had been wanting it to go.

"Say, Sheriff," he began, "I hear those surveyors found some sort of mistake when they were working. Is that right?"

Everett knew, of course, that by now the whole town had been informed about what the surveyors had found, but were just waiting for his blessing to begin talking publicly about it.

"It looks as if there's a problem with the position of the west city limit, Bert. But it shouldn't hold up the work the county is planning for the road."

Moog Raymond cut right to the chase.

"I hear the sign is wrong," Moog said. "At least that's what Ellen heard over at Merle's Grocery."

"I believe Ellen got it right," Everett explained, knowing that the men were thirsty for the knowledge he held. "It appears that some time in the past the western boundary of the town was moved about two hundred feet or so to the east."

"I hear tell that old Angus Petler was responsible for that," Tiny Fremont offered. "And that it was just his way of getting out of paying his fair due to the town."

"I wouldn't judge Angus too harshly," Everett cautioned. "Anyway, he's dead and we'll never know for sure how it happened. But we know that we'll have to move the boundary out a little, that's all."

"West of the Petler place, right?" Moog asked.

"That's right," Everett answered.

Earl Shilling stopped snipping Zippy's hair and spoke.

"What you're saying, Sheriff, is that the Petler place is now going to be part of the town."

"That is correct."

Moog cut in.

"And Deke and Durham are now going to be citizens of Apology."

"That would be right."

Tiny Fremont spoke, his big belly jiggling as the words came out.

"So the first thing people coming into town from the west are going to see, after the 'Apology City Limit' sign is that broken down trash pit Deke and Durham have managed to create after Birdy died."

"That sure doesn't speak well for the town," Moog complained. "It hasn't been so bad for the town, since we didn't have to claim them until now. But what will people think when they drive by our town sign and the first thing they see is that mess?"

"I got an idea," Taylor Cantrell suggested. "Why do we have to move the sign in the first place? Let's leave it right where it is and no one will be the wiser. After all, who's gonna raise a stink about one

little measly old sign?"

Kevin M. Prochaska

8   A Meeting of the Minds – Sort Of

Eunice Boxliter sat her square-shouldered body in the front row of the Apology town hall meeting room the following Monday evening, pressed against Viola Vanderhoff's immense mass, although a good six inches of air separated the two chairs. Viola's bulky frame tested the engineering limits of the flimsy wooden folding chair on which she perched. Around the two women, various groups of people murmured, attempting to keep their conversations private.

Eunice Boxliter wore a lot of talcum powder and sometimes one could see a cloud around her when the powder was freshly strewn. From a distance, some who didn't know her well might have assumed that a swarm of gnats had surrounded the woman, waiting for the opportunity to land. Some would even go so far as to say–there goes Eunice, crop dusting again. When she greeted people and struck up a conversation, Eunice became very theatrical in her movements, and this merely made the powder roll out in more energized clouds.

Taylor Cantrell's question about who would raise a stink about one measly old sign had turned from a small breeze to a squall in front of the Apology post office when Eunice and Viola had caught wind of what had gone on in the barbershop earlier that day. Word had gotten out that the sign was staying where it was, and although neither Eunice nor Viola had anything to gain or lose in the matter of the town's western boundary, the two women had demanded a town meeting, more out of prying than from anything else. Eunice and Viola had stormed into Mayor Owen Fuller's office that very afternoon to make sure a town meeting was called as soon as possible.

Everett rested his back against a wall, scanning the room as he waited for Owen to make his appearance before the crowd. Everett had been surprised at how the flames of gossip had blown the problem of the sign entirely out of proportion. To call a town meeting just to talk about a sign seemed ridiculous, he thought. He stood away from the wall and faced the crowd, surveying their mood.

Six rows behind Viola Vanderhoff, seated on the end chair next to the wall, Everett spotted Phil Granger, shaking like a naked Eskimo. At sixty-seven years of age, Phil appeared extremely frail. He walked bent over, using a cane, and had a yellow tinge to his skin from smoking cigarettes for forty years. Phil hadn't smoked for ten years now, not because he didn't want to, but because he couldn't. The man had been an exterminator for three decades and had absorbed all types of toxic chemicals meant to kill off any of the various types of pesky bugs infesting the houses of Apology and the surrounding farms, while the homeowners waited outside, breathing clean air and complaining about the bill when he was through spraying. He had not expected much from life, only fair treatment, and was still trying to decide if he had ever gotten it from anyone.

He still enjoyed the smell of burning tobacco but was unable to hold a cigarette in his hand, for the man shook so badly at times that, on several occasions he'd started his shirt on fire by dropping his cigarette on his lap and was unable to pick it up. Ten years ago Everett had driven him to the hospital in Renoir with burns on his leg, and the doctor warned Phil in no uncertain words that he needed to give up smoking, unless it was his intention to perform his own cremation.

Phil never ventured far from his house because he was conscious of his bouts of shaking and embarrassed by how it was perceived. Other exterminators he'd met at conventions used to visit his house, but they had all eventually died, victims of their years of exposure to DDT. Phil's yellow skin still smelled a little like the chemicals he'd used, even though he'd been retired for more than a decade. In the summertime, when the heat warmed his body, the smell of the chemicals trapped in his skin became even more pronounced.

As the years rolled by Phil had trouble finding a good night's rest. His sleep, continually broken by his abrupt bouts of shaking, would come and go at odd times. Some days he ventured into downtown Apology, his cane poking at the sidewalk before him. He didn't seek pity by traveling, just a relief from boredom, and a little conversation.

The chairs around Phil were empty, and Everett knew, would remain so throughout the meeting.

People continued to trickle into the room, gathering in groups of two or three. Amy Flanigan entered and gave Viola Vanderhoff the once-over, frowning as the memory of their recent collision came to mind. Behind her came Mayor Owen Fuller, greeting people as he made his way to the front of the room. Everett saw that everyone had begun to look up from their conversations, aware that the presence of the mayor meant the meeting would start soon. Quizzy Boxliter caught Eunice's pointed stare, realizing that he was speaking with Taylor Cantrell. Quizzy was well aware that Eunice was outraged that Taylor would poo-poo such an important issue as the proper placement of the town's boundary sign. Everett watched as Eunice signaled Quizzy half a dozen times via facial expressions, grinning as Quizzy attempted to reply with hand gestures while trying to maintain his conversation with Taylor. Quizzy finally gave up, excusing himself, and sat down in the front row next to Eunice and Viola.

Most of the crowd of fifty or so settled into their seats, in clusters of two or three. As Everett predicted, Phil Granger sat by himself, the chair in front and behind him also vacant. One of the last to enter was Earl Shilling, who had come directly from his barbershop. The mayor seated himself at a long table in the front, facing the crowd. Owen was not a big man, and the fact that he was alone behind the table made him look smaller than he intended. He raised a hand to quiet the crowd but froze open-mouthed as Viola shifted her weight, her chair creaking loudly as two boards squeezed together in protest of the load they carried. Owen stared at her, his voice silent, but his mind saying, "Good Lord, lady, have a little mercy on that chair."

"Good evening, ladies and gentlemen," Owen began. "I'm sorry to call you out tonight, but I have received some important news regarding the town and a decision which must be reached by us citizens. As most of you know, a survey team has been working the road west of town so the county can come in and fix some parts along it where the snow blows the road shut during the winter."

Owen pointed to Bert Kestral.

"And we owe the fact that the work is being done to Bert Kestral. Thank you, Bert. We all owe Bert a word of thanks for getting the ball rolling on this. Now when the road is fixed, we won't have to worry so much in the winter when we want to use it. It will be as clear as the rest of the roads around here."

Owen saw several heads nodding with approval. He spotted Phil Granger's head shaking as well, and took that as a blessing from Phil, even though he couldn't really be sure.

"We have been informed by the surveyors that the western end of the town's boundary has been marked incorrectly. We don't know when this happened, but we know it did. The surveyors found the original marker stake, so we are quite sure where the western boundary should be."

Owen was being diplomatic. By now, Old Duke had blabbed the news of what Angus Petler had done all over town. But it was still a rumor. Owen had no proof that Angus had moved the sign, and as mayor of Apology, was not going to condemn the actions of the man, who, hopefully, was enjoying his eternal reward. It wasn't that Owen thought Angus didn't move the sign. He had known sweet Birdy, and preserving her innocence was far more important than dwelling on Angus' guilt.

Owen continued.

"It seems that the town's boundary on the west end extends about two hundred and fifty feet further west from where the sign sits now.

The surveyors tell me that they've found this before, in other towns. I have been asked to bring you together tonight to tell you this and to determine what, if anything, we should do."

Eunice Boxliter spoke up, asking a question, the answer of which she already knew.

"Where is the boundary supposed to be, Owen?"

"Just past the Petler property, Eunice."

Owen spoke to Eunice, aware that everyone wanted to hear. He raised his voice to answer.

"Does that mean Deke and Durham are in town now?" Viola asked, her voice betraying distastefulness.

"I suppose," Owen answered. If the town boundary is west of the Petler place, yes, they're in town now."

"Oh, goody," Taylor Cantrell complained. "Just the kind of people I'd like to see move into Apology. That place of theirs is an eyesore. And now it's going to be part of our town."

"Can't we just leave the sign where it is?"

Everyone in the room turned to look at Phil Granger, who'd asked the question. Phil rarely said anything in a crowd, and his appearance at the meeting had come as a surprise.

"Leave it as it is?" Viola asked indignantly. "What for?"

Viola didn't think much of Phil, perhaps because she was offended by his shaking, or perhaps because she assumed the man had nothing to offer the world. She turned around and glared at him.

"Let's not be stupid."

But Phil didn't think much of Viola either, not caring much for the obese state of her body. Phil had worked hard during his lifetime and saw Viola as just a lazy slob, content to be just that.

"Better stooped than stupid," Phil muttered under his breath.

Next to Viola, Eunice shook her head in agreement with her friend's comment, talcum powder rising from her hair as though she were dusting for tomato bugs.

"Why not let it alone?" Phil asked. "Why do anything at all?"

Everett, who had settled in a chair across the room from Phil, was surprised that the man showed any interest at all in the boundary dispute. It wasn't like Phil.

Reef Langley spoke, his white teeth gleaming under the lights.

"I kinda agree with Phil. What do we have to gain by opening a can of worms like this?"

That reference to a can of worms brought a reply from Flem Frederickson, who, as a fisherman, thought he'd better say something just because worms were mentioned in the conversation.

"I'd like to cut the line on this myself," Flem said, his Norwegian accent flowing. "But I'm sure you'd all agree that this is an opportunity we have here now if we'd only see it for what it is."

"Go on, Flem," Owen encouraged.

"It seems to me," Flem continued, "that if we was to bring Deke and Durham Petler into the town, they'd be under the same rules and understandings that we are under. Is that not right?"

Owen shot a look at Everett, who nodded his head.

"I would think you are correct," Owen said.

"Then that would mean also that what we can't do, they can't do, either. Right?"

Owen nodded once more, after another glance toward Everett.

Earl Shilling, quiet in the back, suddenly seized the opportunity to stand and speak.

"Correct me if I'm wrong, Sheriff," he began. "But isn't there a law against shooting guns off inside the city limits?"

Kevin M. Prochaska

9 Roller Coaster Road

It had been too much to hope for, Everett realized. He knew that someone in the crowd was bound to bring up the fact that shooting guns within the city limits was illegal. But they weren't the ones who would have to face the Petler brothers, and Everett knew, Deke and Durham weren't going to be happy when he told them about what the town had decided to do about their constant shooting. The group had voted to restore the town's boundary to the original location west of the Petler property, mainly because Earl Shilling had brought up the subject of guns. Now Deke and Durham would have to obey the law, and how the consequences of that action would tax Everett's ability as a lawman were yet to be seen. Thinking back to the meeting, Everett wondered if Phil Granger hadn't of been the most levelheaded of the bunch.

Everett sat in his office, thinking how much easier his life would be if the crowd would have voted to leave the sign where it was, and just let the Petlers alone. The brothers, after all, lived in their own mess, like pigs in mud, and hadn't bothered anyone much. Their mess was now married to Apology as part of the town. Everett thought people had been too quick to vote, pushed by their own emotions, at first fueled by the fiery tongues of Viola Vanderhoff and Eunice Boxliter, and later, by the gun issue. But Everett knew, over years of dealing with the small town logic, that if you can make someone else miserable, that's almost as good as making yourself happy. Only it was up to him to do the dirty work, with the town shielded behind his badge.

Everett recalled how, at the end of the meeting, all eyes turned toward him when Jacob Witt mentioned that he was glad he wasn't the one who had to give the news about no shooting to Deke and Durham.

Everett knew he'd have to give the Petler boys the bad news before too long, before they heard it from someone else in town. If the boys heard the scoop from somewhere other than him, Everett realized, God only knew how they'd react. But Everett had figured out a plan to soften the blow while fixing the problem that their father Angus had created thirty years before.

Twenty minutes later Everett headed west, passing through the quiet streets of Apology. The Petler place was separated from the main town by a large field, and adjacent to the field, on the slope of the road, stood the sign that read "Apology City Limits." Everett eased the patrol car next to the sign, pulling off the road onto the narrow shoulder. Exiting the car, he opened the trunk and reached down to pull out a pair of pliers. The two bolts holding the sign to the steel posts were already loose. Years of rattling back and forth in the wind had shaken the fastening nuts, and the sign had been replaced many times since Angus Petler had erected the first one. Everett unbolted the sign and threw it in the trunk of his car. Grabbing a hacksaw he cut off the steel post at ground level. Everett stood up, glancing toward the Petler house. He saw movement behind the kitchen window. At least one of the brothers was watching him, which was exactly what Everett wanted.

The patrol car rolled slowly by the Petler place as Everett scanned the ditch for the steel post that the surveyors had located in the ground. A dot of bright orange paint marked the spot and Everett stopped. He got out and opened the trunk once more, pulling a cylindrical driver and a brand new steel post from the trunk. Everett stood the new post up next to the survey marker and brought the driver head down hard on the top of the post. As the driver hammered the steel, a loud metallic clank escaped and echoed off the west side of the Petler house. Everett raised the driver and struck again, feeling with his other hand that the post was sinking into the soil. He drove the steel another three feet, threw the driver back into the trunk, and pulled out the sign and the two bolts. As he fastened the sign to the new post he looked toward the Petler house, and through the west window saw two heads watching his progress.

Everett decided not to stop at the Petler's place just yet. He'd give them a chance to mull on what they'd seen and think about the consequences involved. He made a U-turn and headed back into town.

As he drove through the downtown he spotted Phil Granger coming out of an alley, poking a cane in front of him for balance as he struggled along. Phil liked taking the alley because fewer people saw him, and he felt belittled because he was forced to walk with a cane.

Everett pulled up beside him.

"Morning, Phil."

Phil stopped and looked to his right.

"Well, morning to you, Everett. What are you doing up so early?"

"Just doing a little sheriff business."

Phil rubbed his hand across his cheek and pointed to Everett's cheek. Everett caught his reflection in the side mirror, seeing what Phil was trying to point out. He had a smudge of dirt on his face.

"Forget to wash this morning, did you?"

Everett rubbed the dirt off.

"No," he said. "Had to move the sign."

"Oh," Phil said, surprised. "So soon?"

"No use waiting."

"Did you tell Deke and Durham yet?"

"Not yet," Everett said. "But they know, I'm sure. I'm gonna give them a little time to chew on it before I stop by."

"Probably a good idea," Phil agreed. "You know how hot and cold those boys can be."

Phil glanced above Everett's head, to a distinct dent in the strip of chrome surrounding the windshield of the Pontiac.

"Never did get that fixed, did you?" he grinned.

"Never did," Everett replied, grinning. "But at least that rock didn't break the glass."

The teeny dent in the chrome was small but had a big impact on the town. For it hadn't been a flying rock that had dented the chrome above Everett's head. It had come from "The Ride" through Roller Coaster Road.

The roads around Apology were mainly straight and flat with land of the same topography, and pocketed with washboard gravel. Most roads ran north-south or east-west, and from the air, the roads divided the land into square checkerboards. Three anomalous roads, however, provided drivers with more challenging opportunities–the Pipe, the Duncan Curve, and Roller Coaster Road.

The Pipe was a ten-mile long piece of pavement east of Apology, where the blacktop from Apology ended, intersecting the Pipe at a T. Drag racers liked the road because its path was wide open, and drivers could spot Iowa Highway Patrol cars for two miles, giving them ample time to call off the race.

The Duncan Curve was a piece of gravel road running south of Apology. The washboard road contained two sharp turns, the first curving to the left and the second to the right. Over the years, the Curve, as it was called, had collected quite a few cars in its ditches, as all types and sizes of vehicles and drivers miscalculated the snaking road and paid for their mistakes abruptly.

Roller Coaster Road had been constructed on a series of three glacial hills cut and graveled north and west of Apology. Three rolling hills over a span of a mile and a half gave drivers the up-and-down thrill of a roller coaster ride as they sped over the loose gravel. As drivers approached the hills from the north, they'd gun the engine, racing into a small trough just before the first hill. As they crested the first hill, the car lifted, as if it were going to fly, and some drivers claimed that they got the front tires to actually leave the ground. As gravity brought the car to earth, it flew downhill, toward the second trough. The driver would accelerate, trying to work up enough speed to run through the trough and still maintain momentum as the car turned to climb the second hill. The smart drivers knew that at the bottom of the second hill the road was as rough as the corrugated ribs of a washboard. If a driver hit the ribs too hard, the tires would bounce, throwing the car into a sideways skid. On either side of the road, steep ditches, fifteen feet deep, waited, and had gobbled up many a car over the years.

An experienced driver could run through the hills of Roller Coaster Road at sixty-five miles an hour, if he could fight the steering wheel through the washboards. Some of the local teenagers, bragging, claimed to have run it even faster. Everett smiled when he heard them brag about how they'd rode the hills. For he knew that the best had done no more than seventy-five, and that was during the day. One dark night, Everett, fed up with all the bragging, had run the hills himself in the patrol car.

Phil Granger was riding with Everett that night, and only he and the full moon witnessed the outcome of that great ride.

"I heard some of the boys bragging," Phil said, his body shaking uncontrollably in the front seat of the patrol car.

Everett had picked the man up half an hour before, for he knew Phil could stand a little conversation and some time away from the loneliness of his house. Phil received few visitors because folks felt uncomfortable with being around a man who all of the sudden began to shake.

"About what, Phil?" Everett asked, as they drove cautiously along a gravel road north of town, headlights catching the eyes of animals hidden in the ditches.

"Oh, you know you those young bucks are," Phil said. "They were saying how they run the hills a few weeks ago at eighty."

"Eighty, huh?"

"That's right, Everett," Phil replied. "That's what they said."

They continued west, the patrol car rumbling as the tires rolled across the railroad tracks that cut diagonally through the gravel road.

"Who is 'they'?" Everett asked.

"The Lawler boys," Phil said.

He looked over at Everett, his head shaking in lights of the dashboard.

"And I don't think they're lyin'. They run the dirt track pretty much every Sunday at Renoir. And they don't have to lie about something like that."

Everett knew the Lawyer boys, Jim, Dewey, and Ben. They could turn a mean engine at the racetrack–that was for sure. When they weren't helping their dad in the fields, they spent most of their time stripping engines to hop up their cars for the track. Phil was right, Everett knew–they had no call to tell stories about the run through Roller Coaster Road.

"What else did they say, Phil?"

They had traveled three more miles, the moon resting on the little man's shoulder as he rode shotgun. Everett turned south.

"They said that if they ever made a run away from you, that Chevy of there's would leave this old Pontiac of yours standing still."

"That a fact?" Everett replied, looking straight into the night, his eyes fixed on something over the beam of his headlights.

Everett stopped the car and peered ahead. Phil looked through the dust of the windshield and felt the downward slope of the road. Everett flicked on the high beams to reveal the trough in the road, marking the northern approach to Roller Coaster Road.

"You ain't thinkin' about makin' your play through the hills, is you, Everett?"

"Why, Phil?" Everett asked. "Does that scare you?"

"Look at me," Phil replied. "How could you ever tell? I shake like I'm scared all the time, anyhow."

Everett revved the engine and the car shook in fury.

"They said eighty, huh?"

"All of eighty," Phil answered. "As much as they race, they ought the know how to read a needle."

Everett stared out the window, lost in thought.

"If it helps you make up your mind, Everett," Phil said at last, "I'm dead anyway. I just can't get my brain to shut down."

As if given approval, Everett gunned the engine once more, hard, and dropped the car into gear. The tires spun rapidly in the dirt, spewing gravel and dust fifty feet behind the car, where it fanned out like the tail of a gigantic rooster. The dull clunking sound of stones hitting metal rattled through the car as the momentum of the spinning tires drove gravel into the undercarriage. As the rubber bit into the road the patrol car surged forward into the darkness. Dust swirled high into the sky like smoke from a campfire, and Phil felt himself pinned back into the seat as the patrol car buried its nose in the first trough. The car lifted and rose upward over the first hill, and the men hung on, feeling the weightlessness as the front wheels lifted from the road. The wheels dropped hard, jarring the men, and Phil grabbed the door handle for support. He saw Everett's eyes focused on the second trough and the field of washboard ribs in the road below. As the car flew down the hill in the darkness, the speedometer hit sixty-five. Phil saw the ditch fly by, a bottomless pit, dark, like hell. The tires slammed against the washboard ribs, the vibrations pounding through the steel hull as rocks peppered the windshield through a swarm of angry dust. The men grimaced as the car swung sideways, Everett fighting to force the vehicle toward the middle of the road. As an inky darkness loomed before them, Phil felt the right tire bang hard against a rut, and luckily too, for the car changed direction, twisting away from the ditch. Everett straightened the car, veered toward the center of the road and, without hesitating, sped up. Phil knew the devil must have come out of the pit now, and had his foot on the gas. For this couldn't be Sheriff Everett Hiram driving like this.

About this time Phil was regretting the comment he'd made a few seconds ago about already being dead, for it appeared that Everett might be testing his words.

The car topped the crest of the second hill at ninety-seven miles an hour and all four tires lifted from the road. The car rose in the air like a horse at a steeplechase, and the tires dropped away from the car, legs reaching for the ground. Phil felt the weightlessness come fast this time and stay longer, his heart shooting like a fast elevator to the top of his rib cage. Just as quickly he felt a hard jar as the front bumper of the patrol car slammed into the gravel, followed by the bouncing of the wheels. The patrol car pounded violently, shaking the men. Phil found steel in Everett's eyes, and flashing back the dashboard lights, they fired with the eyes of the devil. At the third trough Everett fought the wheel once more and kept the car in the center of the road, his foot jamming hard on the gas.

As they approached the top of the final hill, the speedometer hit one hundred miles an hour. And still Everett pushed the Pontiac faster, while Phil sat in the dark, his face white with sheer terror.

A pair of eyes flashed in the darkness, and a deer, caught in the glare of the high beams, froze on the crest of the hill. The men spotted the animal, and with that split-second of notice, braced for impact. The deer's body rose in the air, a brown blur, directly in the path of the windshield. The instinctive leap saved the animal's life, and the only damage to the patrol car was a hoof mark in the chrome surrounding the windshield just above Everett's head. The patrol car crested the hill at one hundred thirteen miles an hour, churning up angry dust behind it. Everett slowed the car as the road turned level away from the hills.

"By God, Everett!" Phil shouted, shaking more than usual. "One-hundred thirteen miles an hour! On Rolly Coaster Road! What the hell were you thinking, man?"

The swirling dust they'd left behind now caught up with them, drifting past as Everett braked to a stop. The gray cloud enveloped the car, blocking out the moon and casting an eerie hue like some apocalyptic nightmare.

"You said you was dead already," Everett replied nonchalantly.

Within him, Everett swelled with a hidden pride. He let Phil think about what they'd done for a minute or so, and it finally dawned on Phil.

"By God, Everett!" Phil shouted once more, his voice now filled with pride peppered with astonishment. "One-hundred thirteen miles an hour! On Rolly Coaster Road! Lord Almighty, wait until this gets around town!"

"It won't get around town," Everett snapped, his face stone sober, "And you see to it that it doesn't."

"Why is that, Everett? I mean one-thirteen. No one's ever done that! Nobody!"

"And no one has done that," Everett said.

Everett looked toward Phil, a sternness in his eyes.

"See, Phil," he began, "Let me explain something to you. I'm the sheriff. And I'm supposed to be upholding the law around here. What would people think if they knew what we did here tonight?"

"Hell, they'd give us a medal, I suppose," Phil declared.

"They'd give me the boot, is what they'd give me," Everett shot back. "That's what I'd get, and that's what I'd deserve, too. So let's just keep it to ourselves, OK?"

"Whatever you say, Everett," Phil replied, a disappointment in his voice.

By the next morning, word of what was to become known as The Ride slowly began to circulate through town. Folks talked behind the sheriff's back, not quite knowing at first whether the whispered words coming from Phil Granger's mouth were true or not. But the word from veterinarian Taylor Cantrell, who'd inspected the ding in the chrome, was that the dent closely resembled the outline of a deer hoof. Voices soon filled with pride at the sheriff's accomplishment, for he'd quieted those who'd bragged about running the hills. The Ride was the subject of much conversation at Duffy's Tavern for several weeks following that moonlit night, at least when Everett wasn't in the establishment. And for a while Phil Granger was quite popular with the patrons not at all concerned with his sporadic shaking.

Of course, Everett never admitted what he'd done that night, for it might have meant the end of his sheriffing days in Apology. Folks asking about the dent were told about how a rock had flown up and hit the car. Everyone knew, but nobody knew. That's the way it was to be.

Two weeks later, on a Sunday afternoon, the Lawler boys, doing ninety, flew from Roller Coaster Road, burying the nose of their Chevy in the soft mud at the bottom of a small creek that paralleled the road for fifty yards. Dewey Lawler, the best driver of the three, was behind the wheel. Miraculously, the three brothers walked away from the wreck without a scratch. It was said that Everett could scarcely contain his smirk as Plit Bulter's wrecker strained to pull their hopped up Nova from the water.

Someone later noted that the Petler boys had a rooster that couldn't tell when to crow, but the town of Apology had one who didn't need to crow at all.

"Well, it's a just small ding," Phil noted, rubbing the dent in the chrome with his finger as he balanced his frail body with his cane.

It was, however, the biggest small ding Phil had ever seen.

Kevin M. Prochaska

10 The Law West of the Petlers

Owen Fuller's wish regarding the Petler property moving farther away from Apology hadn't been granted. The town, in actuality, had moved west toward them. And around noon Everett figured he'd better let the Petlers know that it had. As he pulled into the driveway Everett saw Deke and Durham sitting under a tree, looking at the new sign he had erected earlier in the day. Above their heads rabbit skins dangling from branches swung back and forth in a soft breeze.

"Morning boys," Everett greeted as he approached.

Everett was surprised when he saw the fence next to the driveway, for the gate that fell to the ground during his visit to disarm Durham had been hammered back in place. Everett could only assume that the boys had done some smart thinking about all the trouble one loose rooster had caused them, and didn't want to find out what unforeseen complications a whole flock running through downtown Apology could stir up. Everett opened the gate and stopped as their mangy dog crouched, daring him to move into the yard. Everett halted, staring the bared-fanged mutt down until the animal ceased its low growling and rose to slink away, tail curled upward between its legs. As Everett entered the yard, Deke got right to the point.

"You was up kinda early this mornin', Sheriff."

"Did I wake you?" Everett asked.

"Only half of us," Deke replied. "I had to shake Durham out."

"Well, you didn't need to," Durham shot back, yawning. "You just did."

"You clankin' on all that metal would've opened the eyes of the dead," Deke said, looking up at Everett. "What was you doing anyway, Sheriff, that couldn't have waited until a decent hour to get done?"

"Had some business to attend to," Everett began, "that involves you two directly."

"I must have missed somethin'," Durham said. "What did we do last night, anyway?"

"We were here," Deke answered, looking at Durham. "Remember?"

"I got some news for you boys," Everett continued. "Some good news, in fact. You two remember those surveyors that came by a few days ago?"

"Hey, we treated them real nice, Sheriff," Durham defended. "And left them alone. Just like you told us. I even gave them some fresh dill pickles."

Everett raised the flat of his hand toward Durham.

"I'm sure you did," he said. "But that's not what I'm here about. The surveyors found out during their work that the town boundary was out of kilter. The sign marking it was in the wrong spot. And that's what I was doing this morning. I put the sign where it was supposed to be all these years, right next to the old survey marker they found in the ground. That's where the town boundary is supposed to be."

"So that's what all the noise was about?" Deke asked. "Just fixin' a sign?"

"It's a little more complicated than that, boys," Everett explained. "You see, you guys made out real good."

Everett glanced above, noting the rabbit skins flapping above their heads.

"Because we found this important error out, your property is now inside the city limits of Apology. And that makes you citizens of the town."

Everett watched for a reaction as the two men stared at each other, wondering what this all meant.

"So what?" Durham said finally.

"I just thought you'd like to know," Everett said, "that the citizens of Apology voted last night to have you boys join us. Now, doesn't that make you feel good?"

"Last night?" Deke said, surprised. "When?"

"At the town meeting," Everett answered.

"What town meetin'?" Durham asked.

"The special town meeting," Everett explained. "Called on Saturday afternoon."

"Nobody told us anythin' about no meetin'," Deke said. "Why did they call a meetin' and not tell us?"

"I don't know," Everett replied. "But they voted to move the sign and it would have passed with or without you being there anyway."

"So they moved the sign," Durham said. "Big deal."

"It may be a bigger deal than you think," Everett explained. "For now you have to live by the rules of the town."

"Hell, we do that anyway," Deke defended.

"Well," Everett continued, "I'm afraid there's a few new rules you might have to get used to."

"Like what?" Deke asked.

"Guns," Everett said. "We may have to place some restrictions on your shooting out here all the time."

Durham stared at Deke, a look of bewilderment on his face.

"Wait a minute, Sheriff," Deke said, his voice rising. "You can't do that. You know we have to practice for our shootin' meets. We can't stop that."

"Yea," Durham added, "we've been doin' that for years. That's where we make our money."

"I know, boys, I know." Everett said. "And I'm trying to figure out a way to solve this. But you might catch some flack about it until I come up with something."

"Well if that's the way it's gonna be," Deke said, irritated, "I don't want to be part of this town."

"Me neither," Durham added. "Why don't you just run over and put that sign back where it was?"

"I wish it were that easy," Everett replied.

"That sign couldn't be in the ground that hard," Durham said. "Let me pull it out for you. I'm pretty strong."

"That's not what I meant," Everett explained. "The sign is not the problem."

"Well I think the town pulled somethin' on us last night," Deke said, anger in his voice. "And I'm not one bit happy that we weren't given a chance to speak our mind about it."

Everett saw that his approach in telling the boys how lucky they were now residents of the town was not working. It had been a bit of a long shot he had to admit, expecting the Petler brothers to just roll over and take it. For the Petlers were free spirits, and didn't like annoying changes, especially when they involved the kind of change that would create a burden to them.

"We want to talk to the mayor," Deke said.

His words surprised Everett, but the Petler brothers had a way of sometimes being unpredictable just when the sheriff thought he'd figured out their way of thinking.

"Owen Fuller?" Everett asked. "You want to talk to Owen about this?"

"I sure do," Deke said firmly. "In fact, I just out and out demand it."

"Me, too," Durham added.

Durham wasn't so sure what he was going to say to the mayor, but Deke seemed to be on a roll and there was no use slowing down the train now.

"Well, let's go find him then," Everett said.

"Don't you think we'd better at least wash up first?" Durham asked.

189

"No," Deke shot back. "Let's go dirty. That way he'll know how mad we really are about all this."

If they didn't wash up, Everett thought, the mayor might not know how mad they felt, but he'd know how bad they smelled.

"Ok, let's go then," Everett said. "I'll drive you up there myself."

"Think we ought to take Owen some pickles, Sheriff?" Durham asked.

"Let's hold off on the pickles right now," Everett replied. "OK?"

"Yea," Deke said, turning to Durham, "we don't want to be accused of trying to bribe anyone."

Bribing Owen with dill pickles wasn't why Everett told the boys to hold off–he'd just gotten the dill smell off his front seat and liked the strong lemon smell inside his car. And besides, Everett concluded, soldiers marching off battle shouldn't bring gifts to the enemy.

The trio soon found themselves backing out of the Petler's driveway, heading into Apology. They rode past the cornfield to their left and Everett grinned, knowing that the golden ears would soon be harvested, ruining the Sunday afternoon ritual for some of the good folks of the town until the corn rose high again next spring.

It was well known that Merle Oaken sold very little beer out of his grocery store during the course of the business week. The fact that selling beer in a grocery store was illegal in the state of Iowa in the first place put a big crimp in Merle's sales, but Merle stored a few cases of brew in the backroom of the grocery store anyway, for preferred customers, which meant anyone who could pay for it and keep their mouth shut. But the simple truth about this behind-the-counter business was, surprisingly, that high demand for this barley brew rather than a lack of sales contributed to Merle's dismal beer revenue. This dilemma made sense if one understood small town logic. It was OK to buy all the groceries one needed at Merle's Grocery Store, but for beer, proper etiquette dictated that this item be purchased in Renoir, the reason being, then no one knew how much you were buying. That way no one could tell how much you drank. For some reason, that secret was of paramount importance to everyone in town. It was a well-known fact that Doris Donahue left her empty beer cans upside down in the kitchen sink for a day or so, just to make sure every drop of beer drained out of the can. That way there'd be no tell tale smell left inside. Doris would bury the empty can deep inside a black plastic garbage bag so the garbage man would think it was a pop can if he happened to see it bulging through the bag full of trash.

A nagging fault with human beings is that they sometimes don't plan for unexpected events, like running out of beer on Sunday. And it helps to have a cornfield nearby, especially if it juts up against the northern border of a town whose grocer's back door faces the cornfield, and who's got a refrigerator full of beer stocked in his garage, destined for the backroom of a grocery store. Between June and October the corn grows tall and green, and the sharp blades of the corn leaves have cut many a body moving through the rows toward that back door. God, in his infinite wisdom, saw to it that the sun that makes the corn grow also brings thirst to a body. This tendency toward thirst, and its solution, seemed to apply especially on Sunday.

On some Sunday afternoons during the growing season Merle would sell more beer through the back door of his house than he would sell all week at the store. Most of the sales would be by phone, the interested party telling Merle that they wanted so much beer and would send one of their kids sneaking through the cornfield with the money to pick it up. And off the child would go to Merle's back door, sometimes carrying just a quarter for a single can of beer, but more often with a couple of dollars for a six pack. The fact that, technically, he was selling beer to a minor didn't seem to bother Merle, for he'd been assured that the beer would be turned over and consumed by an adult. Sending a child to pick up the beer accomplished two other things besides actually getting this refreshment. The child who walked the cornrows generally got a little money as reward for his service, and the consumer of the beer gathered no telltale cuts on his body from the sharp corn leaves. Officially, Sheriff Hiram wasn't privy to the Sunday business conducted from Merle's back porch during the summer months, even if he'd noticed the incriminating corn cuts on the face and arms of the young children of the town. But to be truthful, not much got by his lawman's eyes.

When the cornfield was harvested in the fall, the flow of Sunday beer sales stopped until the crop grew once more the following spring. And if the farmer happened to plant soybeans instead of corn, Merle sure seemed to get a lot of visitors on the back porch around sunset during those same summer Sundays.

"Smells like lemon in here," Deke said as the patrol car rolled past the cornfield to their left.

"No, that's dill," Durham argued. "Hell, you should know that smell by now, Deke."

Owen Fuller ran his insurance business out of a small office on Main Street, directly above Anita's Cafe. The office was spacious, and doubled as the mayor's office, saving the town money, as Bonnie was quick to remind people. Owen stored his insurance files in the office but he also kept a separate, smaller file for town business. He sat in his office at the moment, the warm sun comfortably heating the room. One floor below, the inviting smell of steaming green beans rose through the floorboards. As he worked, Owen heard the hard pounding of feet on the wooden steps leading upstairs to his door. He looked up to see Everett Hiram peering through a crack in the door.

"Come on in, Everett," he said, smiling.

The smile left his face abruptly as the Petler brothers followed the sheriff into the room. Their presence had been unexpected, but Owen knew why they were there.

"Got Deke and Durham Petler with me," Everett said, motioning to the brothers.

"So I see," Owen said cautiously.

"They'd like to talk to you, Owen, in your capacity as mayor."

"I haven't got but two chairs for you, boys," Owen replied. "But take a seat."

The brothers sat down, facing Owen. Everett leaned against a wall, making sure to position himself between the mayor and the Petler brothers. The sun caught the brass of his badge and light flashed across the room to the opposite wall as he moved back and forth.

"Everett tells me we're in town now," Deke began.

"That's right," Owen replied. "Actually, you have always been in town. We just didn't know about it until now."

"Well, what do we get out of it?" Deke asked.

Owen glanced at the sheriff.

"What do you get out of it?" Owen repeated. "What is it you want out of it?"

"We want to be able to shoot off our guns," Durham said. "That's the way we make our money."

"Yea," Deke added. "That's the only way we make our money."

Owen looked at Everett again.

"You can't take away our livelihood," Deke said. "If you do, I want the town to make up for our lost winnin's."

"Wait a minute," Owen said. "We can't do that. That's ridiculous. And anyway, how could we tell when you were supposed to win and when you were supposed to lose? That wouldn't work."

Owen turned to Everett.

"What do you think, Sheriff?"

Everett had his answer ready.

"They're right, Mayor," he explained. "That's the only way they make any money. They've been doing it for years. It doesn't seem right to just make them stop just because we moved a sign."

It wasn't the answer Owen wanted from his sheriff, but it's the answer he got.

"Yea, Mayor," Deke agreed. "That's our property and we've got a right to shoot out there. We need to practice for our shootin' meets."

"What do you think the town will say about all that shooting and noise?" Owen asked.

"Who cares?" Durham asked. "We've been out there for years. And that's a lot longer than we've been part of this town, that's for sure. We don't tell Earl Shilling how to cut hair or Merle Oaken how to sell groceries, so they shouldn't be tellin' us how to be makin' our livin', either."

"But they don't make all that racket, like you two do, with those guns of yours," Owen argued.

"Racket?" Deke shot back. "You want to talk racket? You know how much racket all those durn noisy tractors make a pullin' those wagons full of beans and corn to the elevator during fall? Rr-ruu-ruu-ruu-ruu-rr–on and on and on they go. They come a snortin' down the road like some damn monster on the prowl and at all hours of the day and night, mind you. Can't a body get no sleep between August and October and that's a fact. And nobody's complainin' about them farmers makin' a livin'. So what about that?"

Owen glanced toward Everett, as if looking for a reply from the town peacekeeper.

"They got a point," Everett said, taking the pressure off Owen. "You can't argue with their reasoning."

Owen sat for a moment, pondering.

"Well, do you boys think you can behave yourselves with those guns, now that you're in town?" he asked, speaking with authority.

"We'll behave ourselves," Deke assured him. "We just want to go on livin' like we have been. You won't even notice we're around."

"Let's see that you do," Owen warned. "I don't want to get getting any calls from the Ivy sisters, telling me about all the hell you're raising down at your end of town."

"You won't hear a peep out of them," Deke promised.

"OK, then," Owen said. "We'll at least give you a fair chance to start. And we'll see what happens then."

Everett left with the Petler boys, skeptical about how this agreement would all work out. Owen returned to his work, hoping that the alliance he had just forged with the Petler boys wouldn't return to haunt him.

"Why would the Ivy sisters give a hoot about what we do on our land, anyway?" Durham asked as Everett drove the brothers west along Main Street. "We don't even associate with those two. And we sure could care less about what they do."

"I don't really think Owen is concerned about Etta and Patsy complaining," Everett said. "He was just pulling up the first names that came to mind."

"I hope you're right," Durham said as he looked past Everett's profile to the Ivy house.

"You're probably right, Everett," Deke smirked as the patrol car rolled past the house. "Those two skinflint females are no more interested in what we do than they would be in openin' up a loan company."

Kevin M. Prochaska

11   Men of Duffy's

Duffy Macland wiped a damp rag across the face of the bar, more from habit than to clean away any spilled beer. Duffy owned the tavern for twelve years now, slowly building the quaint establishment into a flourishing business, garnering for his efforts a legion of loyal patrons from the town and surrounding farming community. After a ten-year stint in the United States Navy, Duffy had grown tired of never having any solid roots, but he appeared to have found the home he sought in the small town of Apology. A dozen years back he'd emptied the contents of his sea bag on the floor one last time, and the canvas bag now collected dust on a shelf in his garage. Rounded but muscular, Duffy always wore his T-shirts a little tight to remind rowdy strangers that he could back up what he said. A large anchor, with the words "United States Navy" below it was tattooed in inky blue on his right bicep, and moved when the sinewy muscles below the skin flexed. Duffy wore his brown hair crew cut short, a holdover from his Navy days, and mournful-looking eyes below an ample brow appeared to be just on the verge of crying, even though the man was comfortably content most of the time. He no longer missed the sting of the brisk sea winds on his face, the salt-filled air tearing his eyes. As he worked behind the bar, Duffy always kept an ear opened to the conversations taking place at one of the tables.

"How are the Petlers doing, now that they're part of the town, Everett?" Quizzy Boxliter asked as he sat at a table, holding a handful of cards.

Sitting in a circle with Quizzy and Everett, Lenny Bowman and Plit Butler also held cards.

"So far, so good," Everett replied. "But it's only been a few days. And they haven't been practicing much."

"Well, that's good," Lenny Bowman replied. "Let's hope it stays that way."

A skinny, average-looking man, Lenny's thin wisps of brown hair hung limply at a slant across his forehead. Lenny worked at the elevator in Apology and always had grain dust clinging to the extremely long hairs jutting from his nostrils. Behind Lenny's back older kids in town would tease the smaller kids, telling them that the man with the horns growing out of his nose was going to eat them.

Lenny took a lot of ribbing about his cat, which he called the Abaca, short for the Attack Cat of Abaca, whatever that meant. He'd bought the animal on a whim, finding it in a cardboard box outside of a grocery store in Lost Meadows. The nine-year old boy who'd owned the kitten was beside himself with glee when Lenny offered him a ten spot for the tiny animal. As Lenny walked away, cradling his new pet in his arms, the boy held the money up to the sun, trying to comprehend why anyone would give ten dollars for a free kitten.

Lenny used to brag about his cat, telling everyone what a good mouser Abaca had become since the cat's rescue from the cardboard box.

"That cat couldn't catch his breath," Tall George Himmel declared to Lenny one day as the two men stood watching Abaca curled up for one of his prolonged nap attacks.

Abaca did sleep a lot, curled up, his long, orange fur always disheveled. People were quick to point out the matted areas on the cat's fur, telling Lenny that the reason the fur was matted down was because mice took turns sleeping that nest of hair. It seemed that even the rodents knew Abaca was too lazy to get up and chase them away.

"We'll find out tonight, most likely," Everett said, watching Lenny. "The Petlers do their best hell raising on Friday nights."

Duffy's always smelled like smoke and stale beer. Years of cigar and cigarette smoke puffed over countless poker games under hanging lamps had saturated everything with the lingering odors of burned tobacco. Men with yellowed fingers would still sit at the poker tables on long winter evenings, joking with their neighbors as they tried to figure if their opponents were holding four queens or bluffing with a pair of three's. Duffy, seeing an opportunity to make a buck, began supplying free decks of cards a few years back, for serious card players remained at the tavern longer, drinking more beer, if the cards were snapping briskly in the shuffle. Men talked freely beneath the glare of dim bulbs, and the unwritten rule was that very little of what was said went back to the house when the men left the tavern. So, that being said, some of the conversations at times seemed to make no sense at all, unless one happened to be part of the talk when they began.

This night the game was poker. The deck was new, the cards snapping crisply like a springing mousetrap, and the talk ran freely.

"Do you have to blow that damn cigar smoke this way?" Everett complained to Quizzy. "I was hoping to wear this uniform at least one more day. I don't get no clothing allowance like those cops do in Renoir."

"You need to get yourself a wife, Everett," Quizzy replied. "Then you'd never have to worry about stuff like that."

Everett turned his head toward the Plit and Lenny.

"That's what I like about Quizzy's ideas," he explained. "He never really has a train of thought. What he comes up with is more like a caboose full of bad ideas."

"Women are OK," Lenny interjected, "if you handle them right. You just have to use the time tested Garden of Eden approach when you're dealing with them, that's all."

"I know there's got to be an answer in there somewhere," Everett said. "What's the punch line?"

"Oh, just a little something Adam learned–but just a tad too late," Lenny continued. "You see, when you're dealing with a woman, you'd best make sure you're butt's covered."

"Throw 'em, boys," Quizzy said, licking his thumb and pressing the digit against the back of the deck. "How many ya need?"

In the background the four men heard the muted sounds of Irk Hickenlooper arguing with another farmer about who owned the better tractor, a faint smell of fresh cow manure rising from the soles of Irk's work boots. A farmer knows his tractor like a cowboy knows his horse, and will defend it sometimes more vigorously than he would his own wife. After a few minutes of arguing tractors, the men found themselves at a deadlock, and the conversation inevitably turned to the weather and its consequences on their lives. The two men discussed the chance of isolated thunderstorms moving into the area during the next day or so and how long it would be before the storms would run their course.

"Damn," Lenny said, looking over at Irk and his friend, "I swear if those farmers didn't have the weather to talk about, they wouldn't have anything to say to one another at all."

"Hey, Everett, "Quizzy asked, nodding his head toward the two farmers, "You suppose they ever do?"

"Do I suppose they ever do what?" Everett asked.

"You know," Quizzy continued, "those isolated thunderstorms they're talking about over there–you suppose they ever get lonely?"

"Yuk, yuk," Everett answered, twisting his face. "And I do mean yuk."

Quizzy dealt the cards and the stakes were raised.

"I call," Plit said finally.

Plit and Lenny laid down their cards. Both men were holding a single pair.

"Someone pinch me," Quizzy said, laying down three kings. "I must be dreaming."

"My old daddy used to tell me that if you think you're dreaming, don't pinch yourself," Everett said smiling, laying down a full house of jacks and sevens. "Pinch the girl next to you. She'll let you know real fast."

Everett pulled the stack of bills and coins across the table as the door swung open. Olaf Clancy entered and pushed the door shut behind him. As Olaf walked, his leg caught on a chair and he stumbled, catching himself on the edge of the table next to where the men sat. Olaf stood above the card players, inhaling a whiff of Quizzy's cigar, and began coughing uncontrollably.

"Don't blow your eyes out there, Olaf," Duffy said from across the bar. "Need a shot to calm you down?"

He lifted a bottle of Wild Turkey from the bench behind him. Olaf coughed once more and stopped, waving Duffy away.

"You know what," Quizzy said. "It's kind of a strange thing about smoking. Someone told me once that if I was going to give it up, I'd have to give up cold turkey."

Quizzy took a deep puff and blew out the smoke.

"Well, I gave up cold turkey over ten years ago, but I'm still smoking these here cigars."

It was an old joke and everyone had heard it before. But they all laughed, as was the proper thing to do.

"What do you hear out of Deke and Durham, Everett?" Olaf asked.

"Not much–yet," Everett answered as Plit picked up the cards.

The men listened to the crisp snapping as they watched Plit shuffle the cards.

"Hey, Olaf," Quizzy said as Plit dealt, "we think Everett needs to find himself a wife. What do you think?"

Olaf surveyed the faces below him, hesitant to give an answer.

"I'm about the last person in this town you want to get advice from about a wife," he finally replied.

Olaf's remark drew a variety of expressions from the crowd, none of which were smiles, for the memory of Zelda was still upon their minds. But Olaf hadn't meant his reply to be funny, and they all knew it. The man had tried hard to make amends with the town, and the men who frequented Duffy's had never turned their back on Olaf when word of Zelda's demise got out. There was something about the whole thing that wasn't being told, they figured, for gentle Olaf Clancy was just not a killer, and the truth would somehow be made known to them in good time. Quizzy pulled the cigar from his mouth, rolling his tongue against the back of his teeth.

"Damn, I think I thust bit my thongue," he said, his speech slurred as he spoke.

"Ith that tho?" Lenny said, mimicking Quizzy. "You're supposed to smoke that thing, not eat it."

"Oh, are we speaking in our native tongue now, Quizzy?" Olaf said, anxious to get a shot in on someone.

Everett spoke up as he dropped two cards on the table and motioned across the table for more.

"That reminds me of a story I heard about this tribe in Africa. Seems they only had one letter in their entire alphabet."

"One letter?" Plit asked. "How could that be? How could they talk to each other?"

"I don't know," Everett said, a serious look on his face. "But I would guess that accentuation is everything."

The front door of Duffy's flew open suddenly. Old Duke charged in, shouting at the top of his voice.

"Shots fired from the Petler place, Everett! Lots of 'em!"

Kevin M. Prochaska

12 A Separate Peace

Everett was still irritated with Old Duke on Monday morning for pulling him away from his poker game, especially when things were just heating up. And it appeared to have been all for naught, for the Petler boys were behaving themselves. Oh, they were practicing all right, but for some reason this particular night, the sounds of their gunshots were echoing off something, magnifying the noise. Zippy Martin claimed the echoes were just a fluke caused by some atmospheric abnormality, but no one really knew for sure. All the echoing did was get Old Duke riled up and take Everett away from what, up until that point, had been a very financially rewarding poker game, not to mention a good time with the boys. Everett had staked his patrol car west of the Petler place for an hour that night, waiting for some sort of disturbance, but nothing had come. When he returned to Duffy's to try and extend his streak of luck, the poker game had broken up.

One good thing about Monday morning at Anita's Cafe was the smell of freshly baked cinnamon rolls dripping with thick white frosting. The sweet taste of the soft dough would help take Everett's mind off his interrupted poker winnings. As he opened the front door, the brass bells hanging from the top of the door dinged, letting everyone know someone was entering the cafe. Anita's greeted Everett warmly as the sheriff scanned the row of booths lining the left wall.

Anita Biningham owned and operated Anita's Cafe on Main Street, just a couple of doors west of the sheriff's office. Anita face was always rose-colored and cheerful, and she always wore a pink waitress dress when she worked. Unfortunately, she'd put on a little weight over the years, and her sides bulged slightly over her apron strings. But people said that just proved that the food cooking back in the kitchen was good. Anita's dirty blond hair was always tucked under some sort of hair-catching contraption, riding on the top of her head like an uneasy jockey. A few strands of rebellious hair would work their way loose during the day and Anita continually blew these annoying wisps out of the way as she took orders from her customers, speaking a million words a minute while she eyed everything going on at the next table. Anita was an expert at switching back and forth among the various conversations going on at any of the tables, always remembering just where she'd left off when she returned to each table to serve the food.

When the shop had originally opened many years ago, it had been a leather goods store. The smell of leather still came from the wood after a rain, when, some said, one could pick up the taste on their tongue, especially if the coffee was strong that particular day. The cafe was similar to hundreds of other small town Iowa establishments of the same sort, confined, lined on the walls with booths, and covered with tables on the open floor space. A lunch counter ran half the length of the right wall, where Anita and her help would busily work when the lunch crowds arrived from the bean fields during the summer. Groups of teenagers from Apology and the surrounding farms would descend on the cafe around noon each day, and like the swarms of locusts mentioned in the Good Book, would eat the place empty before going back under the hot, afternoon sun to face the long rows of beans, where the weeds attempted to camouflage themselves from the wrath of a well-aimed corn knife blade.

Anita prided herself in the home cooked meals she prepared, growing some of the vegetables in a large garden in back of her house. Anita knew there was nothing better than fresh-cooked vegetables to compliment a meat and potatoes entrée and satisfy the stomachs of hard-working farm hands. She baked her own desserts, mainly apple, rhubarb, and peach cobblers in gigantic pans, quickly gobbled up each noon hour.

The cafe opened for breakfast at 6:30 each morning, catering at that hour mainly to farmers who either had never married or farmers milking cows in the early morning chill, who had to rise early anyway. Everett sat at the counter, next to Irk Hickenlooper, who sipped on his third cup of coffee while telling his seventh story to anyone he could get to listen. As Everett ordered coffee and cinnamon roll, Irk finished his story and turned his attentions to the sheriff, asking Everett about what he thought about the weather. Everett listened to Irk talk, his mind wandering, and his eyes distracted by the chunky curves of Anita Biningham at work on the opposite side of the breakfast counter.

Everett left the cafe shortly after breakfast, his belly gratefully full, and his tongue still savoring the sweet taste of frosting mixed with cinnamon. The walk from Anita's to his office was short and Everett had already parked his car in its usual spot before going to breakfast. Everett unlocked the office door and entered, feeling a slight coolness in the air inside.

Two hours later Owen Fuller called, and Everett knew by the tone of the man's greeting that it wasn't a social call.

"I'm starting to get complaints about the Petlers, Sheriff," Owen said. "You're going to have to talk to them boys."

"Who's been complaining?" Everett demanded, rising to look out the front window, as if attempting to locate the complainant.

The sweet rolls warming his stomach began to churn.

"I can't tell you that, Sheriff," Owen said.

"Why not, Owen?"

"The party who phoned doesn't want anyone to know."

217

"Well, how am I going to do anything about this alleged problem if I don't know the specifics of the complaint?"

"They just told me that the Petler boys were being too noisy," Owen said. "That's all."

"Hell, Owen," Everett shot back. "I was out there just yesterday. Them boys weren't being any more noisy than they usually are. You know they're getting ready for a shooting competition over in Glanville in a couple of weeks. The last time they shot was a month ago, and I expect their winnings are almost gone. They're practicing because they need the money so badly."

"I understand that, Everett," Owen continued. "I truly do. But the rules have changed. The Petlers are now within the city limits and we have bent the rules for them because of what they do. But we have to think about the citizens of the town, especially those at the west end, who live closest to the boys. And Everett, by the way, there is one other thing."

"And what would that be?" Everett said.

"There is some talk that you're giving special favors to Deke and Durham. You know, turning your head and not looking as hard as you might."

Everett's face tightened.

"Now, Owen," he defended, "you, of all people, should know that's not true."

"I know it, Everett," Owen replied. "But do you?"

Without waiting for Everett to answer, Owen continued.

"Anyway, just to let you know that there is some validity in what I just said, the person filing the complaint contacted me, not you. That should tell you something."

"That they think I'm favoring the Petlers, right?" Everett asked.

"Read it as you like, Sheriff," Owen said. "I'm just passing along the complaint."

Everett hung up the phone, wondering who would have contacted Owen. It must have been someone at the west end of town, he concluded, for those people lived closer to the Pelters. It could have been Moog or Ellen Raymond possibly, or the Ivy sisters, or perhaps Doris Donahue. It wasn't likely to be Olaf Clancy, because Everett had run into the man in front of Duffy's recently and Olaf didn't have a bad word to say about anyone. Whoever the unknown person, a complaint had been filed, and Everett had to act. But it perturbed the sheriff that the call went to the mayor and not to him. It made him look bad.

Everett knew his only option was to speak to the Petlers directly, even though he felt they had done nothing wrong. He drove to the Petler place, knowing he would have to confront the boys, reluctant as he was to do so. They seemed surprised to see him.

"Come to get some more dills?" Durham said.

Everett worked his way past the flock of chickens that had approached him when he entered the yard. He'd made a motion with his hands, and by habit, the chickens thought he was throwing corn at them. The chickens should have been used to the ritual by now, for Deke and Durham pulled this trick on them often. The two brothers would throw out a few kernels of corn and the chickens would run in the direction the throw would take the corn, find it, and peck it from the dusty ground. When the corn was gone, the boys would pretend to throw more, and the chickens would run all over the yard, banging into each other as they searched the ground in vain for the nonexistent

food while Deke and Durham howled with delight at their stupidity.

Everett smiled.

"No, boys. I'm still enjoying the ones you gave me."

"Well, what can we do for you, Everett?" Deke asked.

There was no easy way to tell them except straight out, Everett

had concluded.

"Well, boys, I'm here to tell you that someone has registered a

complaint over you boys shooting your guns off so much. "

Durham grew angry.

"Who's complainin'?" he demanded.

"I don't know," Everett explained. "They didn't phone me. They

phoned the mayor."

"Hell, Everett," Deke said, "we're practicin' for a shootin' match

comin' up in two weeks. What do people expect us to do–point our

fingers and go bang-bang?"

Durham chuckled.

"I understand that," Everett continued. "But I'm caught between a

rock and a hard place with you fellows. Now that you're part of the town, people are more aware of your presence and more likely to complain."

"You mean the gossipers are runnin' loose, don't you, Everett?" Deke asked.

"They also have their concerns," Everett explained. "They just want to be assured that you two will behave yourselves with those guns."

"We do," Durham defended. "Hell, Everett, you know we're the best shots in the county. Ask anybody."

Everett didn't need to ask anyone. He'd shot against both of them a few months back–and had come in third.

"Remember, boys," he said, "the town is doing you a big favor here. You're not supposed to be shooting within the city limits. I stuck my neck out for you boys, and I would consider it a big favor if you'd work with me here."

"What do you want us to do, Everett?" Durham asked. "You just name it."

"What I'd like you to do for right now is just pick a time every day to practice. Try and make it about the same time so people can get used to it. Maybe that will work until I can find out who's the complaining. That way at least no one can say you're shooting all hours of the day and night. Can you boys do that for me?"

"Oh, we can do that easy," Deke said, a look of relief on his face. "I thought you was going to ask us to do somethin' hard."

"Yea," Durham added, "we can practice late in the afternoon everyday. It's cooler then and we still get to sleep in late."

"OK then," Everett said, satisfied. "If we all do what we're supposed to do, then everything should be fine."

Everett stopped by Owen's office, explaining the situation with the Petler boys and how the brothers had agreed to limit their practices sessions to the same time each day. If everyone knew that the boys were shooting at a designated hour, perhaps the calls to Owen would stop. Everett hoped the plan would settle things down, but Owen still wouldn't tell him who had complained so vigorously.

Everett checked up on the Petler boys over the next few days, and they appeared to be sticking to the rules he'd laid out. Everett hoped this would put an end to their problems with the town. They would compete in the shootout at Glanville and then stop practicing until they depleted their winnings. Then they'd gear up for the next competition. Everett often wondered why Deke and Durham didn't compete year round, at bigger competitions. The brothers seemed quite content to shoot only at local events, winning just enough money to feed themselves. The boys were deadly shooters, but never rose to the potential Everett knew they were capable of. On the other hand, Everett realized, in a world where people too often surrendered their souls to money, the Petlers chose to take only what they needed, as the Indians used to do with the land.

Of course, Everett thought grimly, look what happened to the Indians.

13   Duck Hunting With Merle and Rooney

Over the next two weeks the Petler boys banged away at the west end of Apology as the farmers picked the corn from their fields. The local dog pack avoided the place when they ran, each dog familiar with the sound of gunfire and its consequences. The Petlers wouldn't have shot at the dogs, but the pack weren't taking any chances. The dogs had been shot at lots of times, and many of them carried a bead or two of lead shot beneath their fur.

The pack knew what a pistol could do in the hands of a man. Everett had been forced to shoot one of their members one evening, and most of the dogs had been witness when it happened. The incident had been regrettable, but a dog caught in the glare of headlights sometimes freezes. If he's lucky, he's killed outright by force of the bumper. But if he's not, the pain of his yelping isn't pleasant, and a bullet does a faster job of mending than anything else. This particular task had been forced on Everett more than once.

Everett basked in his peace for the moment, shadowing the pack. What he could really use now was something relaxing, like duck hunting.

During the fall Everett enjoyed one of his favorite sports, and that was duck hunting. Down from the north, making their way to warmer climates for the winter flew mallards, teals, and wood ducks in small flocks. These flocks stopped to rest and feed themselves on the many small ponds and gravel pits around Apology, also landing on slow moving creeks flowing through the farm country.

Everett knew several good hunting spots, but one of his favorites was a secluded duck blind overlooking Fletcher's Creek. Everett's hunting blind was located three miles south of Apology, on a bend in the creek. The creek flowed south but bent sharply to the west near a half dozen ponds. The ponds had been created when road crews from Corwith County excavated the rich deposits of outwash gravel, and subsequently the pits had filled with water.

The blind sat on a rise over the west bank, at the inside of the bend, commanding an excellent view of this section of the creek. The water traveled more swiftly along the eastern edge of the creek, undercutting the bank as large sections of the unstable sediments collapsed into the river. As this cutting and collapse gradually shifted the creek bed to the east, fine-grained sands and silts built up on the western side as a series of elongate C-shaped sand bars beneath the slower moving water. The water ran deeper on the eastern, cutting side, but flowed shallow across the bars below Everett's duck blind. During dry seasons, the bars were sometimes exposed as isolated islands as the water level dropped.

The duck blind was ideally situated for several reasons. The small rise shielded the approach, allowing a hunter to sneak right up to the creek and peek over the bank unseen. This gave the hunter a first shot at any unwary ducks resting on the sand bars. When the first shot spooked the flock, the shooter was free to pick the ducks out of the air as they rose to take flight. If a shooter didn't find any ducks on the creek when he arrived, he just waited in the blind, and when the ducks approached to land, picked them off. And just west of the duck blind, an isolated pond afforded the shooter an additional opportunity if a flock attempted to set down on the waters of the gravel pit.

The blind was Everett's paradise, for its isolation allowed him to escape the duties of sheriffing. It was good medicine to spend some time alone, Everett had concluded many years ago, and the blind gave him just that chance. But as fate would have it, his plans for a relaxing duck hunting trip were about to get interesting

"Take me hunting, Everett," Merle Oaken said as Everett stopped by the grocery store after one of his visits to the Petler place, checking to make sure the boys were behaving.

"Hunting?" Everett replied. "You, Merle?"

"Sure, Everett," Merle said, confidence booming in his voice. "I got a brand spanking new sixteen gauge I wanna try out."

Everett hesitated.

"I generally like to hunt by myself, Merle" he said.

Everett had actually hunted with others before, but found their reckless behavior with guns dangerous, and didn't want to make the Renoir radio news as the sheriff who'd gotten shot in his own duck blind.

"Just once," Merle pressed.

"I don't know," Everett argued. "That blind is pretty small."

"I'll make due," Merle said. "I don't take up much room."

"Got a license?" Everett asked, hoping he didn't.

"Got it yesterday," Merle said.

"Got a duck stamp?"

Merle grinned.

"Got that, too."

The man was certainly persistent, Everett realized. He'd never thought of Merle as a hunter, but Everett had to admit that he didn't know all of the secrets about every person in town, and was thankful that he didn't.

"You sure you want to do this, Merle?"

"Really, Everett. I really want to hunt."

"OK, Merle," Everett said. "I'll take you once and we'll see how it goes. Be ready on Saturday. I'll pick you up at six o'clock. That's a.m. now. Early morning. Before sunrise."

Everett was hoping the early hour would dampen Merle's enthusiasm.

Two days later Everett's patrol car pulled up in front of Merle's house. Merle opened the front door, a bright hat made of orange vinyl crowning his head. Long furry flaps hanging over his ears looked like bookends, and he carried his shotgun recklessly, as if it were a rake. Rooney bounded past Merle as he headed toward the car, the muzzle of the gun pointing at the door.

"You might wanna lower that barrel, Merle," Everett warned.

Merle appeared unconcerned that the gun had been pointing at the sheriff's head. He opened the back door of the patrol car and tossed the shotgun and a box of shells on the floorboard. As Everett turned to watch, Rooney jumped through the open door and plopped down on the back seat. To Everett's surprise, Merle slammed the back door behind the dog and opened the front door. Merle saw down next to Everett, the orange side flaps of his hat dangling down against his ears.

"What's that dog doing in here, Merle?"

"That's the surprise I've been waiting to tell you about, Everett," Merle blurted, his eyes dancing. "I've trained Rooney to be a retriever. Isn't that great?"

Now if Everett didn't have much faith in Rooney as a guide dog, he had no faith at all in the mongrel as a retriever. Everett had witnessed the pair training many times, with Merle pulling Rooney reluctantly up the street with closed eyes as the man pretended to be blind. A guide dog was supposed to be in front of his master, not behind, and he was supposed to be leading, not being led. And if the dog couldn't get that through his head, how in the world was he going to switch careers and become a retriever? Everett had a feeling that this might turn into a long day, and his idea about getting some relaxation in the solitude of a duck blind might have just gone out the window. As they drove the gravel road south to the blind, Everett watched Rooney through the rear view mirror. The dog was excited, and big drops of frothy slobber dripped from his tongue onto Everett's clean back seat as the mutt enjoyed his ride.

Everett hid the car beneath some trees near the gravel pit and the two men and the dog tramped two hundred yards through the grass to the hill where the blind was located. Rooney was about as happy as he'd ever been. He was free from his leash and his master wasn't pestering him about this guide dog nonsense. Everett didn't say much when the dog bounded over the top of the blind and knocked one side down. Merle fixed the blind, relating to Everett how he had trained Rooney as a retriever.

"First thing I'd do if I were you," Everett advised, "is to get rid of that cap."

"My cap?" Merle asked. "Hell, it's brand new. I just brought at Rutland's Store yesterday."

"Was it the only color they had?" Everett asked.

"Oh, no," Merle answered. "They had lots of colors. But for some reason, this was the cheapest."

Merle also thought he'd got a bargain when he bought Rooney near the stockyards in Renoir, Everett reminded himself.

"Merle, you know if you keep that hat on your head, there's not a duck within twenty miles of here that is going to land near us today."

"Why not, Everett?" Merle asked. "The Lute brothers told me when I bought this hat that ducks was color blind."

"They may be color blind," Everett replied. "But they're not stupid. And if you want to test that sixteen gauge today, you'd better save that hat for deer hunting season."

The men waited for an hour, scanning the skies for approaching ducks. The few ducks that tried to land were scared away by Rooney's barking, and Merle finally had to rap the dog on the head with the butt of the sixteen gauge so he'd get the message to be quiet. When the ducks did start to come in Everett let Merle take the shots, but Merle, new to the hunting game, couldn't hit a thing.

"How many shells did you bring with you, Merle?" Everett finally asked.

"A whole box," Merle replied. "Don't worry, Everett. If I run out, I'll just borrow some of yours."

"That would be a little tough," Everett said. "You got a sixteen gauge. I shoot a twelve. My shells won't fit in your gun."

Merle checked his pocket.

"Well, I've got four shells left anyway. That might get me one."

"What are you using, Merle?"

"Shotgun shells."

"I know that," Everett said. "You using four shot?"

"Four shot?"

"Number four shot," Everett explained. "That's the size of the pellets."

"Pellets?"

Everett stuck out his hand.

"Let me see one of them shells."

Merle handed Everett one of the shells as Rooney watched the exchange, hoping food was involved somehow. For the dog was getting hungry.

"These are deer slugs," Everett said, shaking his head in disgust. "No wonder you can't hit nothing, Merle. These are for hunting deer. You might as well be trying to knock those ducks down with a rifle."

"Oh," Merle replied. "Well, that's all I got with me. I must have picked up the wrong shells when I bought my hat yesterday."

Everett was growing increasingly irritated with the man, but tried to control his frustration. As a lawman, he needed to.

"That's too bad," Merle said. "I really wanted to shoot down a duck."

"I'll tell you what, Merle," Everett said, handing the man his shotgun, "use my gun."

Merle looked surprised, but relieved as well. His face lit up.

"You sure, Everett?"

"Go ahead. As long as we're here you may as well see if you can knock one down."

Merle accepted the shotgun and the two hunkered down to wait.

"How many shells you got in here?" Merle asked.

"Three," Everett replied. "That should be enough."

As Everett spoke, a flock of twenty ducks flew over the treetops, coming from the north. Everett looked down at Rooney, giving the dog a look that Rooney knew was a warning to be quiet and not bark. Merle raised the gun and prepared to fire.

"Not yet," Everett whispered. "Let them come in."

Merle was anxious, but listened to the sheriff.

"They're coming in a 'V' formation," Everett said. "Let them fly right at us and sight on the lead duck."

This was good logic. Normally Everett would have sighted on the lead duck but would aim slightly ahead of the bird to compensate for the speed of flight. But Everett figured that was a little too complicated for a man who would bring deer slugs to a duck blind. If

Merle could sight on the lead duck and shoot, perhaps he might hit one of the ducks flying in formation behind the leader. As he glanced down at Merle's guide dog, Everett caught himself thinking that even a blind man ought to be able to pick off at least one duck out of that flock.

And that's pretty much what happened.

"Now!" Everett shouted. "Hit 'em now!"

Merle pulled the trigger and the muzzle exploded, the kick hurling Merle back against the side of the blind. Merle hadn't known to hold the larger-gauged shotgun tight in his hands and was caught off guard by the force of the blast. If Merle was surprised at the sound, Rooney was terrified when his master fell backward. Rooney jumped over the side of the blind and bolted toward the car.

"Get back here, dog!" Merle shouted.

"Look," Everett shouted, "you got one!"

Merle turned to see a large mallard drake dropping from the sky. The duck plummeted toward the creek and landed in an inch of water flowing across a sandbar.

"Rooney, get back here!" Merle yelled, turning to see the duck in the water.

"Look at the size of that duck," Everett said.

Everett had bagged many mallards from this blind and he could tell that this one was a large one. Merle left the blind and pulled Rooney back.

"Watch this now, Everett," Merle said excitedly. "You just watch this dog."

Merle bent down and looked the dog in the face.

"Remember what I taught you, boy," he said, aware that Everett was watching them.

Merle pulled the dog over to the creek bank and pointed to the duck floating on the water.

"You go in there and get that duck, boy."

Rooney looked at Everett with questioning eyes, and then at Merle, who was encouraging the animal to act by speaking right into the dog's face while nodding his head toward the duck. Rooney finally got the message and laid one paw out, pressing it into the soft sediments of the sandbar.

"Go get it, boy," Merle encouraged. "Go get it, big dog."

Rooney took a few more steps and stood above the duck. The dog turned his head back toward Merle, who opened his mouth and pointed his finger toward the inside, motioning for the dog to put the duck in its mouth. Rooney bent down and gingerly plucked the duck from the water. Everett walked down and stood beside Merle.

"Good boy," Merle said, smiling and looking back at Everett for approval. "Bring it here, boy."

As commanded, Rooney brought the duck over and dropped it on the ground in front of the two men.

"Look at the size of that duck," Everett said in awe.

Everett had downed a lot of mallard drakes over the years, but had never put one down that measured up to the size of this one.

"You ought to get that one stuffed, Merle," he said. "That's a trophy duck, if every I've seen one. Damn lucky for your first duck. Taylor Cantrell could mount that for you, no problem."

"Maybe I will," Merle replied.

But Merle's thoughts were on something else.

"Did you see that dog, Everett? Did you see him get that duck? I told you he could do it."

Merle was actually more relieved than pleased over Rooney's accomplishment, for he knew Everett had been skeptical all morning over the dog's abilities.

Everett picked up the duck, turning it in his hands.

"Look at this duck," he said, amazed. "Look at these feathers. This will look great stuffed and mounted."

Merle grabbed the duck from Everett's hands and heaved it back into the creek. He pointed toward it and shouted excitedly at Rooney.

"Go get it, boy. Go get it."

Rooney looked confused, but ventured back into the water to pick up the duck a second time. The duck was warm and Rooney could taste its blood on his tongue. Once again he laid the bird at the feet of his master.

"Good boy, Rooney. Good boy," Merle said, patting the dog on the head. "What do you think now, Everett? How about that dog, huh?"

If Rooney was trying hard to please his master, Merle was trying equally hard to impress Everett.

"Now, Everett," he said. "Watch this."

Merle picked up the duck once more, heaving with all his might toward the far shore. The duck soared in a high arc, plopping in the water halfway across the creek.

"Go get it, Rooney!" Merle shouted excitedly. "Go get it, big dog!"

Sometimes it's just smart to leave the poker table before the game breaks up, just to make sure you save at least some of your winnings. And, in hindsight, that's probably what Merle should have done before he sent Rooney into the waters of Fletcher's Creek to fetch the duck for the third time.

Rooney ventured out once more to do his master's bidding. The water on which the duck floated was a foot deep, but the bottom of the creek was sandy, and his large, flat feet held the dog firmly. Rooney, confused, looked back at his master and then to the duck.

"Pick it up, boy," Merle encouraged from the bank.

Rooney felt the warmth of the duck in his mouth once more, and tasted a little more of the fresh blood. He turned to face his master, a hunger burning in his stomach, and the primordial instincts of his ancestors reaching up toward him. If dogs do think, Rooney must have been doing some mental calculating about this time. It was as if his master didn't want the duck because he kept throwing it away. And to the dog's way of thinking, there was little sense in letting good meat go to waste. With that established in the dog's mind, Rooney let his instincts take over. As the two hunters watched from the bank, Rooney sat down in the middle of Fletcher's Creek and began to eat Merle's trophy mallard.

Merle, shocked at what he was seeing, reacted swiftly.

"Rooney!" he shouted. "You bring that duck back here!"

Rooney ripped out the breast of the duck with his powerful jaws, his attention focused on quelling his burning hunger. Merle ran to the edge of the water, shouting once more, louder.

"Rooney, damn you! Bring that duck here!"

By now a trail of duck feathers were beginning to float away from Rooney as the dog concentrated on the meal before him. Everett watched patches of feathers head south with the flow while Merle stood on the bank and shook his fist at the dog.

For a day or so after the hunt, Merle contemplated selling Rooney. Merle figured that a dog that couldn't do a simple thing like retrieve a duck would never handle all the responsibilities to be undertaken by a guide dog. Everett talked Merle out of it, telling the grocer that maybe Rooney just got confused when Merle tried to mix the two careers.

Merle sold his shotgun not long after that. But he kept the orange cap. Everett slipped out to the duck blind the afternoon following his adventure with Merle, telling his whereabouts only to Old Duke. In the silence of the isolated blind, Everett found the relaxation he had sought earlier. The sound of the Petler boys blasting away filtered through the air, music to Everett's ears after his adventure with Merle and Rooney.

14 Sugar Cubes and Tippy

Grain dust colored the air as the wind blew in spasms, yellow plant debris swirling above the pickers as across the length of Iowa, the corn harvest surged forward in full swing. The rich black topsoil rose also, stirred from the ground by the curved plow shears of farmers anxious to complete the fall plowing. The grain dust and soil mixed, the wind carrying the clouds into the streets of Apology. At the north end of town, one side of the street was lined with tractors pulling trailers full of grain, the drivers waiting with the patience of statutes to unload the year's crop at the grain elevator.

The Petler boys had done well at Glanville, winning first and second prize money in the pistol shoot. As Everett had predicted, Deke and Durham suspended their shooting, satisfied with their winnings for the moment, and a thankful quiet reigned over the west end of Apology. This peace made Owen Fuller happy, for the annoying complaints about the brothers shooting had ceased, and the happiness cascaded down to Everett, who didn't have to listen to the mayor griping.

The only person who didn't seem too happy appeared to be Old Duke, for when the surveyor's left town a few weeks before, the deputy no longer had any task which made him feel important, as keeping track of the survey progress had. But, Everett noted, that hadn't kept Old Duke awake during the day, worrying about it. His part-time deputy still found plenty of time for napping, much to the chagrin of Bonnie Fuller, who regularly walked past Everett's office to Owen's place of business. If she didn't always try so hard to peek in and see what was going on inside, Everett concluded, she wouldn't have to worry about seeing Old Duke napping at his desk nearly as much as she did.

Bonnie had walked past the window just that morning and had found Old Duke behind the desk, snoozing away as usual in Everett's chair. Everett snuck up behind Bonnie as she leaned over to peer through the glass, putting her hand over her forehead to cut the glare, as if she were a wagon train scout on the lookout for Indians. At least if she was going to snoop, she was going to get the full picture. Bonnie, surprised at being caught, expressed concern for the bandage on Old Duke's hand, hoping Everett missed the fact that she'd been caught with her own hand in the cookie jar, so to speak. Deputy Duke McCalley had been duly injured in the execution of the duties of his office, Everett told her in official language that sounded believable. Everett generally didn't pull out his book of fancy terms unless he really needed them, but now was just such a time. Everett asked Bonnie if she would kindly pass that information on to her husband, the mayor, as Bonnie excused herself, citing her need to be present at some fictitious function, and scurried off down the sidewalk.

Everett had told Bonnie a small lie, for Old Duke had no insurance of his own, and the stitches in his hand had cost more that he could afford to pay the doctor in Renoir out of his own pocket. Old Duke had caught his hand in something all right. But it had been in the mouth of his pet raccoon.

A few months back, during the spring, Old Duke had found a dead coon on the road near his house. The poor animal had been caught around midnight in mid-stride by the wrap-around bumper of a '55 Buick. The coon would normally have waited until the car passed before crossing the road, but she'd been distracted, chasing something. When Old Duke lifted the carcass from the road to fling it into the nearby ditch, he found the young coon that the mother had been pursuing, huddled beneath the cold body. Exposed to the night, and frightened by the death of his mother, the animal tried to make a break for the ditch as well, but Old Duke caught the baby and kept it. He called his new pet Tippy. Duke, lonely since the demise of wife Blanch, gave the coon the run of the house as he fed and cared for the animal.

As the raccoon grew, it gained weight rapidly and moved clumsily about the house at night, knocking things over. Everett wondered why Old Duke's office naps just kept getting longer and longer until he found out that his deputy was unable to get a decent night's sleep because Tippy kept rattling pans in the kitchen and raiding the cookie jar after the lights went out. Duke thought he had the problem solved when he began letting Tippy roam outside at night. Tippy would exit the kitchen window a little after sunset and scamper into the woods. That was OK with Duke, who thought Tippy was just playing with other coons and would eventually return to live with them after the coon figured out he was one of them.

Tippy was on the prowl all right, not with other coons as Old Duke thought, but creeping through the open windows of other houses around town. If a window screen were loose, Tippy wiggled through and began nosing around for food. People began calling Everett about goldfish being stolen from their fish tanks, or minor items being taken. It didn't take the sheriff long to figure out that Tippy was the poacher. A respectable burglar didn't steal little swimming fish or oatmeal raisin cookies. The night prowler even wore the attire of choice for his profession, for Tippy's eyes were framed by the black mask of a bandit.

"You're going to have to find a way to satisfy that coon, Duke," Everett warned. "Or someone some night is going to shoot him dead."

Duke, who'd had Tippy for five months now, didn't like the idea of losing his beloved pet that way. If Tippy chose to return to the woods, that was one thing, but to be lost to a bullet was another. Tippy was actually a very clever animal and could figure out all sorts of things. The coon's natural curiosity spurred it to experiment with mechanical doodads that animals generally weren't exposed to. The coon would unlatch kitchen cabinet doors, a task requiring skillful manipulation of its paws, and the animal's cleverness increased as the level of difficulty in prying the latch open increased. Tippy even stuck his paw through a tiny tear in a screen one evening and pulled the lock, prying the screen window open to steal some homemade blueberry muffins intended for breakfast the following morning. Another night the coon returned to Old Duke's house all decorated up with one of those long sticky, flypaper strips that hang from the ceiling by a tack. Duke had to rise from his bed and administer a thorough scrubbing to Tippy to remove the fly strip and the sticky, tar-like adhesive from the coon's fur. Everett was right, Old Duke concluded, as he fought to scrub the playful animal in the bathtub. Tippy needed something to do to keep him out of trouble.

That's when Duke came up with the idea of sugar cubes. Duke knew from watching Tippy that the coon had a habit of washing everything before he ate it. So, a week earlier, Old Duke began to hide sugar cubes around the house, making sure that Tippy didn't see that it was Duke that was putting them there. It didn't take Tippy long to discover the treats. Tippy sniffed them cautiously at first, rolling them up in his paws, and examining them like he was a crapshooter suspicious of loaded dice. Elated over his discovery, Tippy found more of the tiny white squares scattered around the house, and soon had half a dozen of them to play with. When the time came for him to eat one, Tippy waddled into the bathroom, where Old Duke kept four inches of water sitting in the tub at all times.

Coons love playing in water, and are finicky about washing their food before they eat it. Tippy plunged into the tub, sugar cube grasped tightly in his little paws. The coon lowered the cube into the water and began to scrub vigorously. Old Duke hid behind the bathroom door, watched through the crack. When Tippy pulled his paw to eat his treat, the cube was gone, dissolved in the water. The animal searched the bathtub, spinning around and around in the water as his paws groped the bottom. But the search proved to be fruitless–the sweet morsel of sugar had simply disappeared. Old Duke smiled approvingly, for he'd finally figured out something that would keep the coon busy.

Tippy found more cubes around the house, but each time he dropped them into the tub and attempted to wash them, the tiny squares of sweetness disappeared in his paws. Ten, then fifteen cubes were lost to the waters of the tub, with nothing to show for it.

Now it is a well-known fact that coons sometimes get impatient. It is also a well-known fact that coons get angry. But when a coon gets both impatient and angry, the dam that holds back the waters of consequence is surely destined to break.

Three days after Old Duke initiated his sugar cube trick, Tippy had found yet another one of the square morsels on the coffee table. As usual, the coon plunged into the tub and lost his sweet treat to the water. But about this time Duke's soft heart began to feel sympathy for Tippy, for the prank had been going on for a while, and the coon had nothing to show for all his efforts. As Tippy searched the water in the tub, Old Duke crawled into the bathroom on his hands and knees, keeping low so his pet would be unaware his presence. He clutched five sugar cubes in his closed fist as he crawled across the floor. Duke figured that if he dropped them all in at once, chance would dictate that Tippy have to find at least one of them intact and finally get to eat. Duke inched his hand up over the tub and began to slide the cubes down the edge of the tub.

Tippy heard the first cube plop in the water, and then the second. After three days of frustration, the coon finally spotted some of his missing treasures that had been lost beneath the water. But then Tippy spotted something else, a hand reaching down to steal his sugar cubes. The raccoon, frustrated by his futile attempts up to this point, saw victory in his grasp unless he did something about the thieving hand descending into the water to snatch his food. And what the coon did to protect his territory surprised the hell out of Old Duke. Tippy leaned across the tub and bit deep into Old Duke's hand, sinking his teeth into the meaty tissue across from the thumb.

Needless to say, this sharp pain came as a bit of a surprise to Duke, who was only trying to do the coon a favor while making amends for his prank. Duke shot from his horse stance next to the tub and jumped to his feet, pulling his hand from the tub. Tippy held fast to Duke's hand, and the added weight of the coon severely increased the pain of the bite. As Tippy rose into the air, the mechanics of physics forced its razor-sharp teeth to sink even deeper into Duke's flesh. Duke hopped around the room on his toes, a searing pain in his hand, swinging the raccoon around the bathroom like the man had hold of a furry bowling ball, and all the while twisting his arm, frantically trying to shake the animal loose. Tippy swung around the room, dancing the jig with Duke, jaws meting out justice to the hand of the sugar cube thief.

The coon finally opened its eyes and realized that it was biting on its owner. Releasing Duke's hand in mid-swing, the animal's momentum carried it across the bathroom, where it bounced off the side of the wicker clothes hamper, as if it were flying from a trampoline. Tippy bounced to the floor and scurried from the bathroom, dazed, and still not rewarded with the taste of a sugar cube.

The whole incident, from the time Tippy latched onto Duke until the coon went sailing into the clothes hamper had taken no more than five seconds, but had left a deep impression on Duke. Thirteen stitches had been required to close the coon's bite marks, and Everett had chewed Duke out up and down while he drove him to the hospital in Renoir, trying at the same time to contain his amusement. It's a good thing Blanch wasn't alive to see her house turned into a zoo, Everett told Old Duke. Or see her husband turned into a monkey by a raccoon.

Everett opened the door to his office and purposely slammed it as hard as he could. Hearing the sound, Old Duke bolted upright in the chair, exactly as the amused sheriff had planned. Old Duke banged his hand as he moved, and the renewed pain caused him to rub the injury.

"How's it feeling?" Everett asked.

"Better," Old Duke replied.

"That's good," Everett said. Did you fill out that form like I asked you to?"

Old Duke pulled a paper from the desk and handed it to Everett. Duke had written a lengthy account of his injury ordeal on the insurance form Everett had provided.

"Chasing a bank robber?" Everett asked incredulously as he read his deputy's words. "I swear, Duke, sometimes I just swear. Don't you know that the mayor's got to sign this? He knows you haven't been chasing any bank robbers. He might, on a slim chance, believe you if someone had happened to come along and actually robbed the bank. But as mayor, he'd probably know about a little thing like a bank robbery in Apology by this time, don't you think?"

He handed the man back the form.

"You're gonna have to think of a better lie if you want the town to pay for that stupid coon bite," Everett said.

Old Duke took the form back and coughed.

"Damn, that dust would choke the devil," Duke replied as he looked outside. "I'll think of something."

"I'm sure you will," Everett replied.

The front door opened and Irk Hickenlooper and Tiny Fremont entered the sheriff's office. Irk, as usual, wore loose overalls and chewed on a straw. Tiny's bulk blocked most of the sunlight attempting to squeeze through the doorway.

"Morning, Everett," Tiny greeted, noticing the bandage on Duke's hand. "Oh, Duke, what the happened to you?"

Duke hesitated, looking toward Everett.

"Old Duke got hurt helping some lady change a tire," Everett explained.

"What happened, Duke?" Tiny teased. "Did she get frisky and bite you?"

Duke looked at Everett, uneasy.

"Nothing like that," Everett said. "But he did get his hand pinched in the jack real bad. You know how shoddy some of them jacks are. You get them on an uneven road and wham–down they come."

"Sorry to hear that, Duke," Irk said. "Hope you'll mend OK."

"I feel much better now than I did when it happened," Duke replied.

What brings you boys here?" Everett asked. "Just being social?"

It was funny to see the two together again, for Irk had really been chafed at Tiny over the cow incident a while back. Tiny had gotten some milk, but Irk had lost his best dairy cow. But the two had reconciled, and even joked about it now. In a town as small as Apology, where people bumped into each other all the time, civility was forced upon them, at least in public. Away from each other, they were quite free to cut each other's character into ribbons if the urge arose.

"I'm always in the mood for sociability," Tiny said. "Just waiting for the party to start."

"But I'm afraid we've got some bad news for you," Irk added.

"Not that it's anything earthshaking," Tiny continued. "Kinda trivial, in fact. But something you might like to know."

"What's that?" Everett asked.

"Well, Everett," Irk said, "somebody's shot your brand new sign full of holes."

15 Catch a Falling Star

"It wasn't us, Everett," Deke said soberly as he stood in the back yard with Durham. "Hell, why would we do somethin' like that? In our own backyard?"

The two brothers faced the sheriff, their expressions clearly those of surprise.

"Yea," Durham defended, "what do you think we are, stupid?"

It was awfully tempting for Everett to say what was in his heart about the answer to that question, but he hadn't come to the Petler place to rate an intellectual quotient he already knew.

"Well, if you didn't do it," Everett continued, "who did?"

"I wouldn't know, Everett," Durham replied. "But I swear it wasn't us."

"Yea," Deke added, "we didn't know anythin' about it until you told us. I swear we didn't"

"How could you two not know?" Everett asked. "Your house only sits about a hundred feet from that sign."

"That's a curious revelation," Durham answered. "But it must have happened late last night. We was gone until about midnight. We took a drive over to Renoir for some beer and stayed over there a little longer than we should have."

Durham winked at Everett.

"Just spending some of our of our winnin's is all."

"Why don't we just go take a look out there?" Deke suggested.

"Good idea," Everett said.

The men walked west out of the main yard and through the ditch. Struggling up the steep slope they continued their walk onto the blacktop. Everett had driven by the sign a few minutes before, just to confirm what Irk and Tiny had told him. The three men stood before the sign, looking through the holes. There were seven neatly rounded marks, each about the size hole a paper punch would make. They could see the town through the bullet holes.

"Well, Everett," Durham said, rubbing a finger over one of the marks, "these are bullet holes all right. But as you can see, they're too small for our pistols."

"Yea, Deke added, "these were made by a twenty-two, sure as hell. And by a rifle, more than likely, I'd bet."

Everett had driven by the sign earlier but hadn't studied the damage closely, assuming the two brothers had fired the shots making the holes. He kicked himself now for not examining the evidence more thoroughly, realizing that he should have known better, and appearing less than professional in front of the boys was his punishment for his prejudgment. The holes were obviously much too small for the forty-fives the Petler brothers used. It had been this oversight that had caused him to falsely accuse the Petlers, and he felt foolish because of it.

"You sure you boys ain't got a smaller pistol around here somewhere?" he asked.

Deke let out a grunt of disgust, pointing to the bullet holes.

"What in the hell would we do with somethin' that teeny?" he sneered. "Why, I could pee harder than that thing hits. Even we got our pride, Everett. You know that."

"And like we said," Durham added. "We were gone last night until late. If someone was shootin' somethin' as teeny weeny as a twenty-two, maybe no one even heard it over the wind. You know, those little pop guns don't bang loud like their big brothers do."

"And, Sheriff," Deke said, "if we'd have shot that sign, we could've hit it from our back steps. The bullet holes would have been coming the other direction, from the east, not from the west like they are."

Deke was right; the bullets had been fired from the west. Whoever had fired the shots was aiming at the front of the sign where the town's name was painted in black on a white background. Each bullet had entered the front of the sign, leaving a neat hole, but upon exiting, had torn through the opposite side, leaving jagged teeth of metal in its wake.

"And we just won at Glanville," Durham said. "We got money and we got beer. Why on God's green earth would we want to make trouble for you?"

Everett thought their logic quite sound. In order to reap the misery of wealth one first had to taste the joys of poverty, and the Petlers had tasted that joy for weeks before they won at Glanville. He believed them.

"OK, boys," he assured them, "as far as I'm concerned, you two are in the clear."

"Whatcha gonna do?" Deke asked.

"Nothing," Everett said. "I expect some night up at Duffy's someone with a little too much drink will start talking. I'll find out then. Until then, I'll let the mayor know you two are clear as far as I'm concerned."

"Thanks, Everett," Durham said, grinning.

Everett turned to go, and then looked back with one final comment.

"You boys are doing real good as citizens of Apology. Thanks."

Everett felt good as he backed the Pontiac out of the driveway. He wasn't patronizing Deke and Durham by what he'd said about their conduct, regardless of what Owen Fuller sometimes thought. He was truly proud of them right now.

But who had shot the sign full of holes?

Everett drove through town and turned north on a side street. It was getting dark and the sheriff saw the first star of the evening shining through his windshield. The star hung high in the northern sky, alone. The sight of the star, and its singularity reminded Everett that he'd meant to stop by Phil Granger's place for some time. And the man's house happened to be a short distance ahead.

As he approached, Everett found Phil sitting on the porch, alone, like the star that shone directly above his head.

Phil Granger wanted to do just one thing before he passed on to his eternal reward. He had never officially told anyone about it because he knew everyone would laugh at him. For what he wanted to do had never, to Phil's knowledge, been accomplished by anyone. And the fact that if, by some remote chance, this thing had been done, the accomplishment wouldn't be told, for the doer would most certainly be dead. But that little technicality didn't bother Phil. To Phil's way of thinking, his body was already poisoned beyond repair by the pesticides coursing through his veins and permeating his skin, so he figured he didn't have much to lose anyway.

In his youth Phil had been an athlete, a star catcher on his high school baseball team. He'd gone on to play a short stint on a minor league team, but that life hadn't been it for him. He'd always been half a step behind or half a swing too late to make it any further as a professional ballplayer. Years later, his working days behind him, those memories of his playing days returned to him as he sat on his front porch alone at night, thinking, his body shaking from all the poisons he'd sprayed on pests over the years. Phil would gaze in awe at the lights in the sky above him–and one night the idea came to him.

If anyone ever wondered if the poisons had affected Phil's mind, this might have been the opportunity to prove that they had, if people had known what Phil was thinking. For the next night, and for most nights after that, Phil sat on his front porch, catcher's mitt close by, scanning the skies for the falling star he hoped would come blazing his way.

Weeks passed and most nights Phil would sit on the porch, waiting. People driving by his home began to notice Phil sitting alone with his old baseball glove, and worried about the man who appeared to have wandered so far into the past that it had become more of a reality to the man than was the present. But to a dying man, perhaps that's true.

Neighbors became so worried about Phil's peculiar behavior that they asked Everett to look in on him. Perhaps, they suggested to Everett, it was time to send Phil to a place that caters to those who have lost their capacity to think rationally. Everett did visit Phil, several nights in a row, and discussed baseball when the sheriff noticed the mitt covering Phil's right hand.

"What are you doing with that mitt out here anyway, Phil?" he teased, "Trying catch a falling star?"

Everett grinned at his friend, but the grinned swept from his face with Phil's next words.

"Yes, Everett," the man replied. "That's exactly what I'm going to do."

Everett was taken aback, for how does one reply a man who sits holding a catcher's mitt, waiting for a star to fall from the heavens? That's the stuff of childhood; the dreams of someone who doesn't know any better. Perhaps the neighbors were right, that the man's uncontrollable fits had finally shaken the common sense right out of his head.

"What are ya going to do with it if you catch it, Phil?"

Phil looked up at the sky once more, his head quaking. Everett sometimes wondered why Phil's head didn't shake completely off his shoulders and tumble to the ground when the fits raged so violently within.

"It's not important what I do with it, Sheriff," he answered. "It's just important that I do it."

"What if one never comes?"

"It'll come," Phil answered confidently. "Just look at that moon up there, would you? Look at all those holes put there by all those meteors over the years. They've hit every square inch of that place one time or another. And if they can do that there, they can do it down here. So I'm figuring it's just a matter of time when one comes my way."

Everett realized what Phil was telling him was true. But it was that long stretch of time over which those things occurred, millions of years, that Phil appeared to be ignoring.

"You know, I hear those things come down pretty fast," Everett warned. "And they're hotter-than-hell hot."

Phil seemed unfazed.

"That's why I got a catcher's mitt," he replied, pointing at the glove. "The leather's thicker than a regular glove. And I don't much care about how fast the damn thing's going–I once caught for Bob Feller. Now that was fire."

As Everett drove away later that night, the man remained seated, pounding a fist against the pocket of the worn mitt, his eyes turned toward the heavens above.

Spotting the man now as he eased the patrol car into his driveway, Everett wondered if Phil had even moved from the porch since that night they spoke of catching falling stars. For there Phil sat, mitt in hand, looking up at the night sky.

"I'm glad the trees are turning," Phil said as Everett climbed the steps. "I don't know if I've missed any meteors with all those leaves blocking my sight."

"I'm surprised you haven't cut that old tree down," Everett said, sitting down next to him. "It's damn near dead now."

Fragments of peeling bark, mixed with small branches broken from the tree during an August storm, lay scattered around the trunk. Phil studied the barren branches shivering against the sky, almost as if he were in a trance.

"Nah. Killed enough poor creatures in my life," he said finally. "It's gonna be a helluva thing to be remembered for. The guy who killed so he could live. Sounds like a damn mercenary."

"Well, don't feel too bad, Phil," Everett said. "If it ain't tacked on your tombstone, no one's gonna know nothing about it in a few years, anyway."

Phil changed the subject.

"Whatcha doin' out this way, anyhow, Everett?"

"Just come from the west end," Everett explained. "Checking on our newest citizens."

"The Petler boys?" Phil asked.

"That would be them," Everett answered.

"If this town had any sense, they'd have left those two guys alone."

"I'd hoped so, too," Everett said. "But so far the boys are doing OK, after they recovered from the shock of not having any say about being pulled into town."

"Well, what have they been up to?"

"Nothing bad," Everett answered. "They took first and second at the competition in Glanville last week. But then somebody shot holes in the town sign west of their place last night."

"Sounds like something Deke and Durham would do, just out of spite," Phil said.

His body shook uncontrollably for a moment and he grabbed his leg, attempting to stop the motion.

"Wish I had a smoke," he said, the shaking stopping.

Phil had been sitting in the heat of the sun most of the afternoon, and Everett could detect a faint smell of pesticide coming from his yellowed skin.

"The Petlers told me they didn't do it," Everett said, watching the lights of the town flicker on.

The grain dust hung in the air, and they could hear the sound of tractors pulling their loads as farmers continued to come in to Apology with their grain trailers full of corn. The elevator was lighted up like a Christmas tree and would be open as long as farmers continued to haul in grain, and that usually meant until long after midnight. Everett glanced down at Phil's lap, where the catcher's mitt rested. The leather, old and worn, had deep scratches along the length of the mitt.

"You having any luck with that putt?"

"I've always had lots of luck with this here putt," Phil answered. "Now if I could only get the sky to cooperate, I'd be in great shape."

The city park sat directly across the street from Phil's house, a block of trees and grass housing a row of three swings, a slide, and a merry-go-round. From Phil's vantage point, he could see everything going on at the park, even after sunset, for two lights shining from high wooden poles at opposite ends of the park dimly illuminated the entire area.

A silver flagpole rose from a concrete base in the center of the park, to a height of twenty feet, topped by a large chrome ball. The American Legion Post had erected the flagpole in memory of the veterans who'd fought in World War II and Korea. The town purchased a surplus World War II howitzer and cemented the cannon into the ground, muzzle pointed north. Children often perched on the barrel, charging forward on their imaginary steed as they rode to danger in their fantasies. Five years before, on Halloween night, a car full of teenagers from Lost Meadows hooked the howitzer to the rear of their car and attempted to drag the gun back to their town. The group succeeded only in yanking their rear bumper off, and in their haste to get away, managed to get the car stuck in the muddy rut created by their spinning tires.

Everett and Phil studied the howitzer across the road. The gun, though painted a dull Army brown, caught the light from the two poles, and the two men could see the outline clearly. The muffled roar of the tractors filled the air, and Everett thought about Deke Petler's comment to Owen Fuller about the noisy monsters running past their home as they made their way to the elevator. In the bushes around

Phil's house, and in the park, lightning bugs twinkled from the darkness, hovering, and turning out their lights, reappearing a few feet away.

"Sure is peaceful," Everett said, watching the tiny lights dancing.

"Enjoy your peace while you can, Everett," Phil cautioned. "Someone's gonna come along and stir things up with those Peter boys out there. You can just about bet the farm on that."

Phil was correct in his assumption, Everett realized. People might think the man was crazy for sitting out on his porch at night with a catcher's mitt, but Phil Granger knew the town rationale, and how this all was going to have to play itself out for some citizens to be satisfied.

"Don't worry too much about me, Phil," Everett grinned, winking at his friend. "For you're talking to a man who has survived a duck huntin' trip with the famous big game hunter, Merle Oaken."

Kevin M. Prochaska

16 A Catfish Too Far

"Any bites on your side of the boat, Everett?" Flem Frederickson asked, twisting a rebellious rod eye back into alignment on his fishing pole.

Everett pulled gently on his line, feeling his sinker slide smoothly across the sandy bottom of Tinker's lake, twenty feet below Flem's boat. Tinker's Lake comprised two hundred acres of serene blue water enclosed by tall oaks along most of the shoreline. The majestic oaks were deep into the magic of transforming their luscious green summer foliage to a fall cloak of reds and yellows. The chatter of squirrels could be heard as they scampered about, leaping from branch to branch, indifferent to the men occupying the floating island in the middle of the lake.

At the south end, the shambles of a cornfield ravaged by harvest butted against the shore. The once sturdy stalks had been snapped off at ground level by the sweeping onslaught of the monstrous corn picker pillaging the clustered seedlings each mothered plant had spent its brief lifetime nursing to fruition. Toward evening deer would venture onto this silent battlefield, feasting on casualties overlooked by the sword of the picker.

At the north end of the lake, a length of shoreline had been set aside for a small park thirty years before, and three red picnic tables stood out in stark contrast to the autumn colors now adorning the vegetation behind them.

The lake happened to be in the flat Iowa farmland because glaciers had swept through the area a short, ten thousand years before, eventually melting as the global climate warmed. As the glaciers receded, massive rivers of blue, iridescent melt water stormed through the ice field with a deafening roar, and tons of imprisoned rock debris captured in Canada tumbled from the ice to regenerate on the country limestone and shale. With the melting of the ice the pulverized stone that would become the rich Iowa soil was strewn on the face of the land, and with it, the carved depressions full of water, one of which would become Tinker's Lake. At its deepest point the bowl-shaped lake now held only forty feet of water.

The men were after catfish. The day broke cloudy, and the autumn air smelled fresh above the glassy waters of the lake. The flat surface stirred occasionally as the men inside shifted their weight after prolonged periods of sitting in one position. The hard wooden seats of Flem Frederickson's fourteen-foot fishing boat had little mercy on a man's back. The men fished near the middle of the lake, where Irk Hickenlooper's Studebaker had plunged through the ice four winters ago. The sunken car provided an excellent fishing location.

"How about you, George?" Flem asked.

George Himmel reeled in his line. His hook had been stripped of bait, as it had been most of the morning.

"All I'm gettin' is baby bullheads having a good ol' time feasting on my worms," George complained. "If they keep stealing my bait like they are, we're gonna run out by noon."

"Don't worry about bait," Flem assured the two men. "Edith went out last night and got me a bunch of nice fat crawlers."

Everett turned toward the men, disgusted.

"Hell, I can't even get Irk's Studebaker to bite," he complained.

Since the car had plunged to the bottom of the lake, many a fisherman had snagged a bumper or hooked a fender as they attempted to ease their bait to where the fish now congregated.

"Did that little filly of yours ever learn to cook, Flem?" George asked.

"Who cares if she can cook?" Flem replied, handing George a fat crawler. "Look at the size of these babies."

Flem really didn't give a flip if Edith could cook or not. He'd learned that by himself in his bachelor days and wasn't the least bit concerned about Edith's cooking abilities. But the fact that she was the best night crawler snagger in the state of Iowa is what he liked most about her.

"Doesn't make diddly to me one way or the other," George said, sticking the point of a barbed Eagle Claw hook through the squirming head of the crawler. "I eat good enough at my own home."

Tall George Himmel stood well over six foot, a skinny-looking fellow generally calm as a lamb. He lived two miles north of Apology on five acres of excellent ground he'd never even put a hoe to. His wife Mamie, a short, stern woman about a head shorter than George, was just about as skinny as George, but didn't look it because she was so short. When George and Mamie stood side by side they resembled the farm couple in Grant Wood's American Gothic painting, except Mamie was thinner than the woman in the portrait and George was taller and had more hair. Mamie's clothes were about as exciting as Stella Hissy's were, bland and shapeless. Mamie spent a good deal of time trying to keep George from getting into mischief, as he was prone to do when he mingled with some of the boys from Duffy's. When Mamie got angry at George, she had to tilt her head toward the sky so she can get a good shot at him with her voice. They had a young son named Harvey, but they called him Scrapper. Scrapper was born late in their union, after George and Mamie had been married for fifteen years. The boy was an only child, but well loved as one could imagine after such a drought.

George shifted his weight and let loose a long cast that arched high over the water, landing fifty feet from the boat. The heavy sinker hit the water with a loud "ploop" and immediately sank. The worm splashed on the surface and split in two at the point of the hook, the tail shooting off across the water where a bluegill hanging near the surface gratefully gobbled it down.

"Damn, Flem," George complained, moving his long legs around to ease the stiffness. "You just got to get yourself a bigger boat."

"My boat's plenty big," Flem defended. "Maybe you just need to get shorter legs, George. You don't really need those bony old stilts of yours. Just get 'em sawed off and get some wooden ones like Rinny Bitten had."

Rinny Bitten had been the caretaker at St. John's Cemetery east of town. The man had a wooden leg, and limped around the graveyard while he worked. After he died the undertaker discovered that Rinny had hollowed out the leg, concealing a whiskey bottle, and sneaking a pull or two as he worked among the headstones when he knew Father Coleman wasn't around to catch him.

"You'd like that wouldn't you?" George answered. "That way I'd be as short as you."

Flem wasn't a short man compared to most, but George stood a full six inches above him.

"George, if you'd shed about half a foot maybe for once, you two might see eye-to-eye on something," Everett teased.

"And I'd share my hidden bottle with you to boot," George grinned.

"Wonder what ever happened to Rinny's bottle?" Flem wondered aloud.

"I got it at home," Everett answered, "on my mantle. The undertaker gave it to me, I guess because Rinny had no one, and I was the sheriff."

Flem reached into a cooler for a sandwich.

"Whatcha eating there, Flem?" George asked.

"Oyster sandwich," Flem replied.

"Ick," George said, making a face. "Cold oysters and bread? What kind of food is that?"

"Well, what'd you bring?" Flem asked.

George reached into a sack and pulled out a glass bottle filled with pink pieces of meat.

"Pickled pig's feet," George said proudly. "Good when they're cold and better when they're warm."

Everett looked through the glass, making out the outline of individual pieces of pig feet covered with pitted skin. The treat looked as though it had been stolen from a biology lab.

"I believe I'd take the oysters," Flem said. "At least I don't have to chew on them."

Everett, listening to the men, grasped his rod tighter as he felt a bite. The line pulled taut as the end of the pole bent toward the water.

"Now who the hell is that, you suppose?" George asked, nodding his head to the west.

Flem and Everett turned toward the direction of George's nod and saw dust rising from the gravel road that led to the boat ramp. The car raising the dust pulled in next to Flem's truck.

"Hey," Flem said, "isn't that Old Duke's car?"

The fishermen were a good distance away from the ramp, but Everett recognized Old Duke's car. Duke had purchased the DeSoto from an unfortunate driver who'd rolled the car south of Apology one night when he'd missed the notoriously unforgiving Duncan Curve. The driver, an insurance salesman, was well versed on loopholes, and with a bit of creative paperwork, totaled the car out. He sold it to

Duke a day after Plit Bulter towed it to his garage. Plit hammered out the dents from the roof and replaced the smashed front windshield as a favor to Duke. The DeSoto wasn't the prettiest sight up close, but from a distance, the car looked fine.

Everett jerked hard on the line as the end of the pole bend toward the water.

"I got one!" he yelled, pulling back hard.

George and Flem turned to see Everett's reel spinning, the drag singing as line peeled from the spool.

"Get him, Everett!" George yelled. "My God, he's bending the pole right into the water."

The line cut through the water and Everett swung his legs around to face the opposite side of the boat as the fished moved below them.

"He's pulling the boat!" Flem yelled.

"You sure you ain't got a log?" George asked.

"That's no log," Flem said. "Logs don't pull up and down like that."

The fish swung the bow of the boat around to the west.

"Hey," George yelled, pointing. "It is Old Duke. And he's waving at us."

"Never mind that old fart," Everett said. "I got me a world class catfish here."

George waved back at Old Duke.

"Look at that old fool," Flem said. "He's got his feet in the water."

"He's yelling something at us," George said.

"Let him yell his fool head off," Everett replied. "Let me work on this here fish."

"He sure is waving awfully intense," Flem said. "Maybe I can make out what he's saying."

"He's getting his shoes all wet, too," George added. "Hope they're not new."

"I've never known Duke to own anything new," Everett said, fighting the fish. "So don't worry too much about that."

"Hey," he's waving a flag or something," Flem yelled. "Look."

Everett looked up from the pole.

"That's not a flag," he replied. "His bandage is coming off his hand."

"Bandage?" George asked. "How did Duke get hurt?"

"Stop waving your damn arms, Duke!" Everett yelled toward the shore as he shifted the pole. "You're gonna break those stitches."

"What's he yelling about, anyway?" George asked.

Flem cupped his hand to one ear as Old Duke placed his hands over his mouth like a megaphone. Duke yelled.

"Can't make it out," Flem answered. "You just keep working that fish, Everett. It's a helluva big one if it can turn this boat around."

"Hey, look," George said. "Look at Old Duke wading out into the water."

Duke was indeed moving into deeper water, trying to keep his bandaged hand dry and his body balanced as he slid his feet along.

"I hope he's not stupid enough to try and swim out here," Flem groaned. "That's all we'd need while we're trying to bring this big cat in, to have to stop and save the guy from drowning."

"Well, he's up to his knees now," George said.

"Look," Flem said, "he's yelling again."

Old Duke hands cupped around his mouth, the end of the bandage dangling from his hand.

"Can you make out what he's saying yet?" Everett asked. "Man, this big guy doesn't want to give me back any of this line."

"I hear him now," George replied. "He's asking 'Whatcha got?'"

George cupped his hands to his mouth and yelled at Old Duke.

"A big catfish! It's a whopper!"

"He didn't hear you," Flem said. "See."

Old Duke waded out a little deeper into Tinker's Lake, the water now to the middle of his thighs.

"Whatcha got?" the men in the boat heard Duke yell.

"Can't that old coot hear anything?" George asked.

He screamed back toward the shore.

"A big cat! Holy Hannah! Everett's got a big catfish on!"

"How ya doin, Everett?" Flem asked.

"I got him hooked good," Everett replied, concentrating on the line knifing the water in front of him, "but he ain't giving up no line. None at all."

"He's a big one then," Flem said. "That's for sure. Thirty pounds or better, I'm guessing. Keep on him."

Flem reached over and touched the drag on Everett's reel, turning the dial half a notch.

"Here," he said. "We'll tighten the drag a little bit. That'll wear him down. He's in open water and we'll just have to follow him wherever he goes."

"He's pulling us toward Old Duke," George said. "And, look, Duke is still yelling at us."

"A big cat!" Flem yelled at Duke. "My God, are you deaf, man?"

"Go baby, go!" Everett yelled as the drag zinged, the fish pulling a foot of line off the spool with one tremendous yank.

"Man," Flem said with awe, "he's gotta be a big one. I just tightened the drag and he's still taking line like that. Keep on him, Everett. They're aren't many like him in this lake."

"I don't know which is gonna happen first," George said, swinging his head back and forth between Everett and Old Duke, "the fish coming out of the water or Old Duke going in."

"The fish is still pulling us toward him," Flem said. "What a fish! Everett, you lucky bastard."

"What's he yelling now?" Everett asked, watching Duke.

"You just keep that fish hanging," Flem instructed. "Let Duke fend for himself."

"A big cat!" Flem screamed, pointing toward Everett's bent pole. "A huge cat!"

"Wait," George said, "Hold on. I think I can make out what he's saying now."

He turned toward them, shocked.

"He's not saying 'Whatcha got?'"

"Well, what in the hell is he trying to say then?" Everett asked.

George continued to look toward shore, where Old Duke was standing in water above his waist.

"He's saying, 'The mayor's been shot.'"

17 The Mayor Gets Shot – Somewhere

Everett jerked his head around as he heard George's words.

"The mayor's been shot?" he repeated, surprised. "You sure you heard that right, George? Ask him again. You know how Duke likes to get attention."

Everett looked back at the pole and pulled hard, the muscles in his forearms bulging against his rolled up sleeves.

"Hey, he's giving back a little now," Everett said, cranking the spool three full turns.

"Don't get too anxious there, Everett," Flem cautioned. "He only gave you back about eight inches or so. There's plenty more line out there."

"What did you say?" George yelled to Old Duke.

They were closer to the shore now, for the catfish had pulled them to the west.

"The mayor's been shot!" Duke shouted toward the boat.

They were near enough to Duke now so they all could hear the man's words.

"No mistakin' that," George said. "The mayor's been shot. That's what he's saying."

Flem watched Everett's pole bend in fury, the end plunging beneath the water.

"Owen picked a hell of a time to get shot," Flem said. "That fish ain't near being tired out."

"Yell over there and ask Duke how bad it is," Everett told George.

George cupped his hands.

"How bad?" George yelled.

His words echoed from a humongous glacial boulder rising from the water near the edge of the cornfield.

"In the heart!" Old Duke yelled back. "He's been shot in the heart."

"God Almighty!" Everett exclaimed.

Everett looked toward Flem.

"That fish has got ten, maybe fifteen minutes of fight left in him, Everett," he said.

Everett looked down at the water, knowing there was just one thing he could do.

"You want to bring him in, Flem?" he asked.

Flem waved him off, shaking his head.

"I don't catch fish someone else hooked," he replied. "No dignified fisherman pulls second-hand fish."

Everett was grateful for Flem's answer. It just didn't seem right to turn over his pole to someone else.

"Gimme your knife then, Flem."

Flem handed Everett his buck knife, and as George and Flem watched, Everett reluctantly cut the line. The pole sprung back as loose black line disappeared beneath the boat.

"Didn't even get to see him," George complained.

Flem fired up the motor and the bow soon nosed onto the sandy beach next to the boat ramp. Duke met them at the shoreline, his pants and shoes thoroughly soaked with water. The fishermen crawled over the side of the boat as Duke rewrapped the loosened bandage back around his hand.

"What the hell happened?" Everett asked.

"You know as much as I know," Duke said. "Bonnie Fuller called me about fifteen minutes ago saying Owen had been shot in the heart, and that you'd better come over quick."

"Me?" Everett exclaimed. "She doesn't need me. She needs an ambulance. And right damn now. Why didn't she call one of the men on the volunteer fire department? We got a rescue unit that we never use sitting in the firehouse."

"Hey, I'm just the message boy," Duke defended. "Don't be yelling at me."

"Well, let's get going," Everett said. "Get that DeSoto cranked up."

Everett turned to Flem.

"I'll get my stuff later," he said, nodding toward the boat.

"OK," Flem answered somberly.

Flem wanted to tell Everett that it was too bad about losing the fish, but this wasn't the time.

Everett jumped into the shotgun side of Duke's car and the two rode the ten miles back into Apology. Water dripped from Duke's pants and onto the floorboard all the way into town, carving little rivulets in the carpet of dust on the floorboard. As they entered the town from the east, Everett recalled the night Flem had driven this same route from Tinker's Lake, pulling his boat in the dark of a rainstorm, and how he'd made news all over town the next morning by destroying the town's only traffic light.

Old Duke turned the DeSoto into the driveway of the Fuller home. Bull, Fuller and Arnold were playing on the front porch, taking turns jumping up and down on the small trampoline Bonnie had purchased as an alternative to the boys jumping up and down on her couch. Everett climbed the front steps and walked past the boys, sensing by their gleefulness that the boys were unaware of Owen's tragic plight. Bonnie was probably waiting inside, Everett guessed, and he would have to be the one to break the unfortunate news to Owen's sons. Everett opened the screen door, with Old Duke close behind, his drenched pants leaving trails of water with each step. As Everett stood in the entryway, he thought he detected a whiff of burnt gunpowder.

They found Bonnie in the parlor to their right. The woman was hunched over, her attention focused on something hidden from their view. When Bonnie heard the front door close, she stood up and moved to one side. Owen Fuller sat on a chair, red-faced with anger, holding a cotton swab to a spot on his forearm. Everett turned to Old Duke, frowning.

"I thought you told me he was shot in the heart," Everett said.

Old Duke pointed to Bonnie.

"That's what she said over the phone," Duke defended. "He got shot in the heart."

"I said no such thing," Bonnie spat back indignantly. "I said he got shot in the *arm*."

Duke threw a sheepish glance at Everett.

"Are you *sure* you didn't say heart?" Duke asked.

"Why in the hell would I say heart?" she retorted. "Don't you think I know the difference between a heart and an arm. Anyway, if he got shot in the heart, he'd be dead. Does he look dead to you?"

"Well, no," Duke admitted. "But he does look kinda blotchy."

"What the heck happened, Owen?" Everett said, hurling a disgusted look toward Old Duke.

Old Duke knew the look was coming because, once again, he'd gotten the story wrong. Duke kept his eyes on Owen, who was watching water from Duke's pants dripping on the floor.

"Durham Petler shot me," Owen said, angrily.

"Durham Petler shot you? What for?" Everett asked. "What's he got against you?"

"He didn't want to give up his gun," Owen explained. "I was coming into town this morning from the west and spotted Durham walking in the ditch with his pistol. He shot me when I tried to take it from him."

"Why would you try to take Durham's pistol, Owen?" Everett asked.

"To stop him from shooting holes in the town sign."

"He was shooting holes in the sign, was he?" Everett asked.

"Yes," Owen replied gruffly, "a lot of them. And when I told him to give me the gun, he refused."

"Did you see him shooting holes in the sign?" Everett asked.

"No," Owen answered, raising the cloth on his arm to reveal a mark on his skin. "But he'd already put a dozen holes in there by the time I caught him. The sign is ruined. And when I called for his gun, he shot me. So I want him arrested for attempted murder, battery, and anything else you can get him on."

"Wait a minute, Owen," Everett cautioned. "Let's sort things out a bit first."

"Sort things out!" Bonnie screamed. "We're wasting time here. Hell, Durham's probably over at that lowdown Olaf Clancy's place right now, having coffee. First he shoots up the town, and now he takes pot shots at my Owen. Who's he gonna take a shot at next, Sheriff?"

Everett held up his hand to cut Bonnie off.

"In the first place, that sign wasn't shot up this morning. It's been shot up for a day or so. And I already talked to the Petler boys and they tell me they didn't do it."

"And you believed them?" Owen asked incredulously.

"No reason not to," Everett replied. "The gun that tore up that sign was a twenty-two. And they got too much pride to use something that small. They use forty-fives."

Everett knew Old Duke was listening with interest, for the sheriff hadn't told his deputy all the details regarding the sign incident yet, and that fact probably was chafing the man about now. As deputy Old Duke figured it was his duty to know everything the sheriff knew, but Everett sometimes held information from him. There were some things the boys at Duffy's would have to wait in due course to find out.

"Well, that still doesn't give him the right to take a shot at me, Sheriff," Owen answered. "I want Durham Petler brought in. I want his gun confiscated, and I want him brought to justice. I knew something like this was gonna happen eventually. And it's just damn lucky I'm still alive, I'm telling you. You go find him now."

"You need to see the doc in Renoir?" Everett asked.

Owen pulled the cotton swab away, revealing a red mark across his forearm, and surrounded by black.

"Hell, that's not even a decent graze," Old Duke said.

"You just shut up, Duke," Bonnie barked. "You don't even know the proper parts of the human body."

"Well, let's get to going then, Duke," Everett said, seeing no need for further discussion. "Let's go get Durham."

Old Duke hesitated, as if thinking. Which was just what he was doing.

"I gotta go have Plit look at this car engine first," Old Duke said finally, pointing to his car outside. "Something's knockin' under there and I don't want to blow the motor."

Everett was continually amazed at his deputy's ability to avoid anything possibly dangerous by swapping out something trivial. Having Duke around was like taking a baby to a gunfight, in that more attention had to be given to the baby than worrying about the cowboy packing a pistol at the other end of the street.

"Drop me off at my house, then, Duke," Everett said, as they exited the mayor's house, Bull Fuller eyeing the pair suspiciously from a lawn chair. "I can change into my sheriff's clothes and get the patrol car."

In his bedroom a few minutes later Everett glanced at his reflection in the mirror. His fishing clothes hung comfortably from his body, a reminder that an hour before he had cut the line on the biggest catfish he had ever hooked, or might ever hook, in his life.

Everett drove to the Petler place alone, torn by feeling as he approached the graveled driveway. He wore a sidearm, as a lawman he always did, but he hoped the piece would remain holstered. He knew the character of Durham Petler well enough, and would trust his lawman's instinct before second judging the man.

"He's hidin' in the cellar, Everett," Deke Petler said, standing on the back porch. "Crouched behind the pickle barrel. Don't' hurt him, Everett. He's scared."

If Deke had been expecting the sheriff's visit, Durham had been terrified, for the man was trying hard to hide. Everett bent down, peering through the open storm door that led down to the cellar. Although the pickle barrel was large, Everett could see Durham's foot poking out.

"Come on out of there, Durham!" Everett yelled angrily. "I see your foot."

"He didn't mean to do it, Everett," Deke defended.

"Let me talk with Durham about this, Deke, OK?" Everett replied.

Durham's head popped up from behind the barrel and he stood up. He climbed up the cellar steps slowly, his hands in the air.

"Don't shoot, Everett," he said. "I ain't got no gun."

"Durham, get the hell up here," Everett answered. "I got no reason to shoot you. You got a gun on you?"

"No-o, no-o Everett," he stuttered. "My gun's next to the pickle barrel."

"Well, get back down those steps and bring it on up," Everett demanded.

Everett stood in the open, his hands on his hips as he spoke. Durham retreated to the cellar and returned with the pistol, a waft of dill smell following him up.

"Now, Durham," he began," why don't you tell me what kind of silly assness went on out here this morning between you and the mayor."

"You're not gonna believe me over him anyway, are you?" Durham asked. "He's your precious mayor, after all."

"You let me worry about what I think," Everett said. "Just tell me what went on. And I want the truth the first time around."

Everett held out his hand and Durham surrendered his pistol. Everett sniffed the barrel. The acrid smell of burned gunpowder told him that the gun had been fired recently. Everett examining the gun, turning the cylinder to find one shell had been fired.

"It's been fired, Everett, sure it has," Durham said. "I'll not deny that."

"And the bullet that left this gun?"

"Hit the mayor," Durham replied. "Is he OK?"

"Owen's just got a scratch across the forearm," Everett explained. "More like a burn than a wound, actually."

"That fakin' old snake," Durham said, anger rising in his voice. "You'd a thought he'd been hit in the stomach the way he was hoppin' around out there in that ditch. I thought he was hurt real bad. Scared the bejeebers out of me at first."

"That's still no excuse for shooting anyone," Everett scolded. "Especially someone who's as good a shot as you are."

"But Durham didn't shoot the mayor, Everett," Deke protested. "He's innocent."

"I thought I told you to butt out, Deke," Everett warned. "This is between Durham and the law."

"But he's right," Durham said. "I didn't shoot the mayor."

Everett looked at Deke.

"So then you did it?"

"Not me, Everett. I was in the house when all this happened."

"Well, if you didn't shoot him," Everett said, turning first to Durham and then to Deke, "and you didn't shoot him, then just who in the hell did shoot him then? He says you were shooting up the sign and he tried to stop you by asking for your gun. And then you shot him."

"That's not how it was at all, Everett," Durham explained. "Sure, I was over by the sign when he drove by. And I had my pistol with me, I'm not denyin' that. But all I was doin' was walkin' back from doin' some asparagus huntin' along that line fence across the road. I didn't think I'd find any–it's all gone to seed–but I thought maybe I'd get lucky and find a couple of healthy stalks. Didn't find none at all worth cuttin'. I was just walkin' in the ditch, goin' back to the house, when Owen stopped his car and got out. Then he just up and starts cussin' me out for shootin' holes in the sign. Wouldn't listen to me at all when I told him I didn't do it. Called me a liar and asked me if I took him for a fool. Then that brassy old coot up and told me to hand over my gun."

"Well, then what happened?" Everett asked.

"I asked him why he wanted my gun if I wasn't doing anythin' wrong," Durham replied.

"And then?"

"Then he looked at the sign again and told me he was goin' to tell you."

"Then?"

"Then I told him you already knew about the sign and that you knew we didn't shoot it up."

"And?"

"Then he asked me again if I took him for a fool and grabbed for my gun."

"Then it went off in your hand?"

"Not right then. I reared back and lost my balance when I stepped on a rock. I was surprised that somebody would be fool enough to grab a loaded gun by the muzzle. As I fell, Owen jerked the gun out of my hand, and as I hit the ground, I heard the gun go off. And then I saw Owen drop the gun and start hoppin' around like a crazed rabbit."

"So the gun was out of your hand completely when it went off?" Everett asked. "Is that your official story?"

"That's just the plain ol' truth, Everett, believe it or not. But one other thing. When he grabbed the gun he reached across the barrel with his hand and grabbed the cylinder to pull."

"And so?"

Well, didn't you say Owen had more of a burn mark than a wound?" Durham asked. "And when he yanked the gun from my hand, don't you see how his fingers could have slipped around that cylinder and caught that trigger below?"

Everett tried to visualize what the man was saying, and how the events leading up to the shooting could have occurred.

"Can I show you what I mean, Sheriff?" Durham offered.

Everett handed the man back his pistol.

"Like this," Durham said, folding Everett's forearm across the barrel and placing the sheriff's hand across the cylinder. "You see, if you yank it like this, your fingers drop to the trigger. And if you ain't being careful you can shoot the gun yourself. And the bullet would whiz right along your forearm, just like it must have done with Owen. And it would leave somethin' more like a powder burn than anything else."

Everett listened to Durham's explanation. What the man said made sense.

"One other thing, Everett," he added. "I was less than three feet away from Owen when I was holdin' the pistol."

Durham hesitated, looking into Everett's eyes.

"You know as well as I do, Everett, that at that range, I couldn't miss."

"You still gonna take him in, Everett?" Deke asked.

"Just as a precaution," Everett answered. "Let me just take him up to my office so I can be seen bringing him in at least. For the record, Durham, what you say makes sense. I don't know why the mayor would try to disarm you, though. That's not his job, and if he was trying to take away your gun, that was a pretty stupid way to do it. Now let's go to my office."

Durham fell in behind Everett, silent as a lamb. He smelled of dill and felt a little foolish because he had hidden in the cellar like a coward. He should have known better, he realized. Sheriff Everett Hiram was a fair man who would judge him as he would any other man.

Everett drove the man uptown to his office, talking with him as if nothing had occurred. In that short ride, Durham relaxed, relieved because Everett's involvement now meant at least one sane head was working in the town of Apology. The men spoke good-naturedly, and Everett got the feeling that Durham, indeed, was telling the truth.

18 A Town On Fire

Father Coleman's sermon the following Sunday focused on the virtue of restraint. Being a priest, he, naturally, wasn't privy to the normal channels where the really juicy gossip flowed, but instead had to settle for the drippings. But Father John was aware of a foul stench that hung over his flock, for he'd heard about the recent confrontation between Owen Fuller and Durham Petler. It was the smell of strife.

"'Tis an ill wind that blows around us sometimes, friends," he said, his Irish brogue strong through the crackling of the microphone. "Let us not forget that in all men God put in a fine shakin' o' good, but then men themselves got to lettin' in some bad in their own right. The Good Book directs us all to love our neighbor and to forgive. The Good Book tells us to get along. The Good Lord didn't say the path was easy, friends. He only offered that the prize at the end of the road would be worth the walk. And that'll be the truth I'm telling yea. So me final words as I speak to you yea today would be to be kind to one another."

Those words, duly noted by the congregation, were, unfortunately, just as quickly forgotten. The following evening a town meeting was held to address the problem of the Petler boys and their guns. Bonnie Fuller worked the phone after Sunday Mass, all afternoon, massing her forces for the meeting hall. She aligned herself with Viola Vanderhoff, Stella Hissy, and Amy Flanigan. Of course, Bonnie had Owen on her side as well. Word had gotten out about the shooting, and speculation on whether or not Durham's errant shot had been intentional had been the topic of discussion for days now.

Everett leaned against the wall, watching the town's residents fill the meeting hall. This was to be an interesting gathering, and Everett saw folks present who normally didn't give a flip about any kind of business discussed by the town council. Everyone in town seemed to be there. Moog and Ellen Raymond, Jim Hissy, and Quizzy and Eunice Boxliter were bunched together in a section toward the middle. Olaf Clancy and Phil Granger sat in the same row, but on the chairs at opposite ends. Plit Butler was there, carrying an ample amount of auto grease and dirt under his fingernails. Earl Shilling and the Ivy sisters sat near the front, speaking in hushed voices. Clustered in a circle at the back of the room stood Zippy Martin, Bert Kestral, Irk Hickenlooper, and Flem Frederickson. Sitting in the back row, listening to the conversation was Everett's trusty deputy, Old Duke. Two seats to his left sat Jacob Witt, smatters of white paint dotting his cheeks. Sprinkled around the room in isolated groups sat many other of the town's residents.

Owen opened the meeting precisely at seven-thirty. Everett noticed a gigantic bandage woven around Owen's arm, greatly exaggerating the significance of the bullet wound. Even from the back of the room, no one could miss the glaring patch of white, and Everett figured that's exactly what Bonnie wanted when she placed the dressing on Owen's arm twenty minutes before. The mayor had no intention of mentioning the shooting incident–everyone already knew–but the oversized bandage would serve as a vivid reminder. Owen cleared his throat and got right to the point.

"I want to thank you good people of Apology for coming out tonight," he began. "Most of you know the main item on our agenda tonight, and that is the issue of firing weapons within the city limits. As you all know, up until a few weeks ago, the town banned all gunfire inside the city limits. We, as a responsible governing body, felt it was very dangerous to our residents and brought an undue amount of noise to the town. Our citizens shouldn't have to tolerate this kind of danger and noise."

Owen threw a glance at Everett, intending to remind the sheriff that it had been he who'd argued for the Petler's right to shoot after the boundary error was uncovered.

"As you all know, the town boundary has been moved about two hundred fifty feet to the west as a result of a recent survey, and the Petler boys are now within our city. In our attempt to be fair to all parties we granted the brothers permission to continue their activities, with the understanding that they would behave—"

The side door opened with a long, ghostly creak and all heads turned to find Deke and Durham Petler entering the meeting hall. The brothers stood eyeing the crowd for a moment and then turned to stare at Owen. The room filled with silence as the boys found seats in a hole in the crowd of filled chairs. Owen continued.

"It has been the law in this town for over fifteen years," he said, reading from the town's bylaws, "'that no guns will be fired within the borders of the town.'"

Owen looked across the crowd when he finished, stopping at the Petlers.

"I didn't make this law," he said, "but I'm ready to enforce it if you citizens will let me."

Deke Petler stood up.

"Wait a minute Mayor. We ain't done nothin' to be ashamed of. We ain't broken no law. We were shootin' a long time before we was part of the town."

Stella Hissy spoke.

"You was always a part of the town. Your dad was just so blamed cheap he didn't want to pay his taxes and moved the sign to get out of it."

"I don't know nothin' about that," Deke defended. "And you leave my poor dad out of this. He's gone to his Maker and it's fool talk to churn up lies about the dead."

Durham rose from the crowd.

"Yea," he said. "That wasn't our doin', even if it is true. All we want to do is shoot our guns. That's our livin'."

"You make too much noise out there," Amy Flanigan scolded. "Your guns are noisy and they scare people. You two are a hornet's nest hanging over our heads. And we're gonna walk outside one day and get stung bad."

Etta Ivy raised her hand.

"You don't have to do that now, Etta," Owen said. "This isn't the school house."

"I must say," Etta said in a soft voice, addressing the Petlers, "that I am greatly disturbed by all that banging down there. Couldn't you boys just shoot a little slower?"

"We shoot as slow as we can," Durham explained, surprised by her comment. "I don't see what difference shooting slower would make."

"Why can't you two go out to the gravel pit and shoot?" Moog Raymond suggested. "It's outside the city limits and no one can hear you out there."

"Why don't you go out to the gravel pit and live?" Durham replied, looking around. "You're the ones who're inconveniencin' us."

"That's just the kind of cooperation we've been getting from these guys," Bonnie Fuller said, standing and turning to face the crowd. "We've bent over backwards to help them. Welcomed them as residents of Apology. Bent our laws for them. Put up with their noisy guns and drinking. And for all those gestures of goodness, their response was to shoot up our new town sign and try to gun down my husband, your mayor."

Everett straightened up and stood away from the wall as Durham made a move toward Bonnie.

"See," Bonnie said, pointing a finger to drive home her words. "Now, in the absence of a gun, they want to resort to fighting."

Everett stopped Durham, staring coldly into his eyes.

"Sit down, Durham," he commanded quietly. "You're not helping yourself any by showing anger."

Everett could feel the sparks from Durham's eyes, for the man was fighting for his very way of life. Earl Shilling stood to speak.

"We've got no choice," he began. "I personally have nothing against either Deke or Durham Petler, and everybody here knows that. But this has gone on long enough. If the law says no firing guns in town, then let's enforce it, for the good of everyone."

"Wait a minute," Deke said, his voice rising. "We didn't have any say in whether we wanted to be in the town in the first place. And now you're gonna take away our right to shoot. What about our good? That's not fair. I ain't gonna obey."

"Me neither," Durham added. "We're gonna shoot whether you like it or not."

"The hell you will," Owen said sternly, staring forcefully at the two men and then turning toward Everett. "The law is very clear on this point. If we hear any shooting coming from down there, you two will be arrested and jailed."

"So what?" Durham asked. "A few days in jail. Big deal. I've been in jail plenty of times. I eat my best meals there."

"Yea, Mayor," Deke added. "You're just still mad because you shot yourself with Durham's gun and you won't admit it."

Owen face flushed, turning to a deep red.

"That's got nothing to do with anything," he huffed. "At least I wasn't running up the middle of Main Street shooting at a rooster I couldn't hit, like I was Wyatt Earp or something."

"Oh, sure, one bad day," Durham answered. "Hang that over my head, why don't ya?"

"And you boys are forgetting one more important thing," Owen said. "You boys owe thirty years back taxes on your property to the town of Apology. You behave yourselves or I *will* take the necessary steps to collect that money. That would mean selling your property right out from underneath you. And if you don't straighten yourselves up, I will do so, believe me."

In the front row, Bonnie Fuller, Viola Vanderhoff, and Amy Flanigan smirked at Owen's words.

"Do you two have any idea how much money you owe?" Owen asked.

Durham looked at Deke, and then at Everett. Everett was just as surprised by this turn of events as the Petlers were, for the mayor hadn't discussed the subject of the Petler's back taxes with him at all. Everett stared at Bonnie and found the woman watching him, as though she already knew what Owen had intended to say. The back taxes had been Bonnie's idea–Everett could see it in her eyes.

"How are we gonna pay back anythin'?" Deke asked. "If you take away our only way of makin' money?"

"Find some honest work, boys," Owen said. "You're going to have to someday. And it might as well start now."

Owen turned to Everett, clasping his hands firmly while they rested on the table.

"As of right now, Sheriff, there are to be no guns fired in the town of Apology. Period. By anyone. That's the law. No exceptions. If it happens, you will immediately take their guns and lock them up. Is that understood?"

Bonnie had put the screws to Owen, Everett realized. Perhaps this was her way of getting back at him for all the times Everett had made her look silly when he'd caught her spying through his office window at Old Duke. But the Petlers were the ones who were going to have to pay now. Owen had stated clearly what was to be done, and in front of everyone in town, so there would be no questions about it later.

Kevin M. Prochaska

19   A Bunch of Bull

Durham Petler held the pistol high, both hands clutching the handgrip, and slowly brought the muzzle down, sighting on a small target pinned to the wall of the gravel pit. He cocked the hammer, checked his alignment again, and fired. The bullet whistled true, striking the crudely sketched human head dead center between the eyes. Sand burst from the hole in the paper, dripping down over the words "Owen Fuller" printed below the head.

"Hey, I got the mayor," Durham said gleefully.

Three other pictures hung across the face of the wall, all saturated with bullet holes. The names "Bonnie Fuller" "Amy Flanigan", and "Viola Vanderhoff" were printed below a crude caricature of each

317

woman. Sand sifted through bullet holes as a soft breeze tempted the papers to flee their confinement.

The boys continued to shoot as the sheriff's car stopped behind them. Everett got out and walked over to where they stood. Fifty paces beyond Deke and Durham, Everett spotted the bullet-riddled targets.

"You boys feeling better now?" he asked.

"Oh, we're feeling lots better, Sheriff," Deke answered, managing a grin. "This time Durham didn't miss Owen."

Everett found that the paper sketch of Owen contained five neat bullet holes, centered on the forehead.

"It's a good thing you boys aren't much for holding grudges," he said, surveying the neat holes in the four targets.

"Believe me, Everett," Deke replied. "Don't think we didn't contemplate it. Not shootin' anyone that is, but some other things."

"Shootin' out tires would've been nice," Durham said.

"Well, I'm glad you didn't," Everett replied. "Or I'd a had to take you in. That's just what some of them wanted. Believe me boys, this isn't the way I'd have liked the hand to be played out–you know that.

But those are the cards that were dealt when the deck was shuffled. I had no idea Owen was going to do what he did."

"What are you gonna do?" Durham asked. "We just get looked down at. We never had a chance in there the other night."

Durham raised his pistol, aiming at the sketch of Viola Vanderhoff. The boys had drawn her fat face filling up the entire sheet of paper, puffing out her cheeks and furrowing her eyebrows like an angry bull. He fired, stitching an additional hole in a line already over her eyebrow.

"Fat old trouble maker," Durham said. "There she was, sittin' right in the middle of that bunch of old hens."

"Yea," Deke added. "I wish Irk's bull would've finished the job on her when he had the chance. And I wished I'd been there to see it."

Deke grinned. Everett knew that Deke was referring to Viola's unfortunate run in with Looper.

Farmers around Apology are proud of the animals they raise, and take even greater pride when they find a really truly unique one. Some men are prone to show their manhood by the size of their pickup trucks, and some show it by the quality of their herd. If a man can do both, he is truly the toast of Duffy's Tavern.

Irk Hickenlooper knew he had a prize bull when he started getting calls about studding. It seemed that the calves produced by his bull were exceptional and other farmers in the area soon wanted a piece of the action. Irk had named the huge black bull Looper, and was often teased about the fact that he had given the bull part of his own name. Some of Irk's farmer friends would chide him, imitating Irk's wife Neva and saying "Oh, Irk, why can't you be more like your bull?"

Irk soon found that his bull was a real cash cow. Farmers would drive from all over, pulling trailers containing fertile cows to Irk's farm. Soon the demand was so great for Looper's stud skills that Irk figured he'd have to come up with a better way to make money off his bull. Irk met with Taylor Cantrell, the veterinarian, and the two came up with a simple solution. The problem was that Looper had a lot of product to give away, but he could only service one cow at a time. And that bottleneck was slowing up the money machine. If Looper's product could be divvied up more evenly, Looper could do a better job of spreading the love around, so to speak. And, although Taylor had only seen pictures of it in trade magazines, he and Irk built the solution to the love deficiency.

The solution consisted of an oversized wooden sawhorse with a brown cowhide thrown over the top of it. This gave the contraption the look of a cow, but didn't do a whole lot to ignite Looper into the amorous equation. To coax the bull into action, Taylor ordered a special, scented oil to rub on the back end of the cowhide. The words on the label guaranteed that the scent of the oil would send any bull into reproductive fourth gear. Taylor called his creation the Wooden Wonder, and it succeeded beyond their wildest dreams. After getting a whiff of the special oil on the cowhide, Looper could have cared less if Taylor's Wooden Wonder was made of steel–he was going to drill it regardless. Looper would mount the contraption two or three times a week after Taylor applied the special oil, and Irk would collect his winnings as he hid beneath the cowhide with a special glass receptacle. This love potion was then divvied up among several cows, garnering Irk much more revenue than the one-shot method ever could.

And that was all well and good until Irk's wife Neva decided to have a rummage sale.

Now it is an unwritten law pretty much all around the world that if you go to a rummage sale and snoop around the day before and nobody finds out, it's OK to do so, as long as no money is exchanged prematurely. But if you get caught beating your neighbor out of something they wouldn't have probably bought anyway, then you're no better than a lowdown wolf sneaking into the sheep pen.

The day before the rummage sale, Viola Vanderhoff arrived at the Hickenlooper farm, looking for the best bargains before anyone else found them. The rotund Viola parked her car in the shade of a tree and waddled over to the chicken house next the barn, where the flyer advertised the sale was to be held.

Irk and Neva had driven into Apology on some errands, leaving Viola free to rummage through the sale items at her leisure. As Viola peered through the open door of the chicken house, she saw two rows of tables shoved against the walls on either side of the door. The tables extended the length of the building, and were covered with sale items. The spectacle before Viola was just like it would've been if she'd been in Alaska during the gold rush and pulled up a pan brimming with gold. She began walking along the open space between the tables, poking and prodding through all the items Irk's wife had dragged home from the many rummage sales she'd been to over the years.

As is the way with the curious ritual of the rummage sale, most items that are for sale owe their origins to somebody else's storage room, and most purchases go right back into storage, except that they're now packed away in someone else's garage. So, as Viola examined the paraphernalia set up in Irk's chicken house, she witnessed the end results of generations of their migratory wanderings. She stayed there for half an hour, noting where items she wanted were located, so she could get to them quickly when the sale opened the following day.

At the far end of the shed a second door opened to an area back of the barn. It came to Viola's mind that Irk might have set up another table in the sunny spot on the other side of the door. It was an old rummage sale trick–divide the crowd so no one could see everywhere at once. This tactic had been known to drive the hard core busybodies to distraction, especially if they had to turn a corner and look two directions at once. Not wanting to miss anything, Viola stepped outside into the sunlight. Lo and behold, there stood another table.

She was disappointed with the items she found. A couple clear glass jars shaped like bowling pins and a small bottle of perfume sat together on the table. Next to the table, a cowhide had been spread over some sort of wooden frame, giving it the appearance of a tent. Viola glanced curiously at the cowhide. The hide was unique and might be something worth owning, she thought. The small bottle of perfume caught her eye and she picked it up, unscrewed the lid, and took a sniff. Although not a connoisseur of perfume, Viola dabbed a bit on her fingers, rubbing it along her wrist and behind her ear. She sniffed her wrist, her face protesting at the smell. Putting the bottle back on the table, her attention focused on the cowhide.

Unknown to Viola, the wire over the gate to Looper's pen had come unhooked, and about this time the gate creaked open. Looper caught a whiff of his favorite scent, splashed liberally behind Viola's ear. Perhaps it was because Looper had a bit of Flem Fredrickson's poor eyesight; or perhaps it was because Viola was wearing a brown dress and was about the size of a cow; or perhaps because the woman had rubbed so much oil on her that the next event happened. As Viola stood beside the cowhide, petting it with her hand, Looper wandered up behind her. The bull, smelling the oil, must have thought he was in hog heaven as he stood behind this fertile half-acre tract of femininity. Viola, unaware that she was fast becoming the object of Looper's amorous attentions, continued to examine the hide, wondering where she would put it when she brought it home.

Viola suddenly felt a tremendous weight pressing down on her shoulders. Although she was an immense woman, Viola's knees buckled under the weight bearing down on her. She looked at her right shoulder, grabbing the object with her hand. Viola discovered a large bull hoof pressed down on each of her shoulders. As if that weren't a big enough surprise, Viola looked above her to see the enormous black head of a bull. Looper's face stared down at her, almost as if he were smiling. Looper, finding this ample display of femininity on his territory was serious about taking this mama cow to the barn dance.

The way the story was told later around Duffy's Tavern between bouts of laughter was, that when Irk and his wife pulled in the driveway, Viola was rounding the corner of the barn with Looper close behind, literally, sort of like the two were trying to form a conga line. Viola was desperately trying to free herself from the grip of the bull's hooves pressing down her, but Looper was determined that he was going to get his dancing done. Looper had failed before while in the throes of the conga, but never when the smell was so strong.

Viola was a strong woman, but not very fast. And as her legs began to fail her, she shook the bull off. Looper jumped on her shoulders once more, two-stepping in time with her movement. Irk watched as Viola twisted, knocking the bull off her shoulders again. She turned to face the bull, attempting to administer a right cross as the bull slammed down on his front hooves. Viola missed, lost her balance, and fell backwards. As her rear end shook the ground, Viola instinctively threw her hands out behind her. Her legs spread wide apart in front of her, and her dress covered them like a parachute.

When Viola looked up, she found Looper studying her. Confused by what was going on, the bull still had the look of want in his eyes.

He lowered his head to sniff Viola, but by this time, the woman had had enough. Viola pulled one of her arms from the dirt, swung it back as far as it would go, and launched it at the bull. She hit him in the nose, square between the mushy flesh of his bottomless nostrils. The blow sent Looper reeling backwards, dazed.

Most cows didn't usually resist much when Looper offered his services. And none of them ever tried to run away. Once in a while one of them would try to extend the conga time with him, but never had one hit him in the nose. He didn't need this, Looper must have thought. There's plenty of others heading my way, sister. As if to say, "OK, it's your loss," Looper snorted and trotted away.

Viola never made the rummage sale the next day, complaining about the heat, when actually the weather was comfortably warm. The word from the chiropractor in Renoir was that Viola had a slipped disk from a fall at her house. Perhaps it was just as well she stayed away from the sale that day. Whenever her name was brought up, someone in the crowd would go, "Moo-oo-oo." Then someone else, looking at some item, would look up and say "Moo-oo-oo." After a few more moos, the crowd would break out laughing.

"Well, don't be too hard on Viola, boys," Everett said, watching Owen Fuller's bullet-riddled sketch drop from the wall of the pit. "She's been a plump one all her life and that just makes her easy to influence, you know, wanting to be liked and all that. Bonnie just got ol' Viola tucked under her wing. I'm sure, deep down inside, she's a good person."

"With all that weight she's a packin'," Deke grinned, "anythin' about her's gonna be deep inside–all that sirloin, I mean."

"At least we got a place to practice," Durham said. "That's somethin' anyway."

"Even if it ain't the best circumstance," Deke added. "I hope it don't affect our shootin'."

Everett continued to watch the boys shoot, filling the remaining pictures so full of holes they fell from the pit wall, the flimsy paper dancing across the ground to land in the pond created where excavating shovels had penetrated the water table as they scooped up gravel.

"When's your next meet?" Everett asked.

"Three weeks," Deke answered. "The Thanksgiving Day Shoot in Fair River. And we plan on being ready."

20   A Deal With Lost Meadows

"I had to do it, Everett," Owen explained, a tint of remorse in his voice. "I had too much pressure from the town. You know that."

"I hope that's all it was," Everett replied, remembering the look Bonnie had given him during the town meeting a few nights before.

The two men stood outside the door of the sheriff's office. Everett had been leaving his office and met the mayor walking along Main Street, on his way to Anita's Cafe for coffee. Neither man felt ready to speak with the other just yet, for there had been friction between them over how to handle the Petler boys. But having bumped into one another, they now engaged in conversation.

"Well, at least it's been quiet at the west end," Owen observed. "Wonder what they're up to, anyhow?"

"Nothing," Everett answered. "They've been shootin' at the gravel pit south of town since you put the ban into play. Got a match in three weeks at Fair River."

"Thanksgiving?"

"That's' right," Everett answered. "That one's worth some big money. It's the biggest money shoot of the year for the boys, and if they win it, that cash will tide them over for the winter. Hope they'll be ready, having to practice with all that sand blowing up around them."

Everett hadn't meant for his comment to be taken as a slam toward Owen, but as he thought about his words, he wasn't the least bit sorry for saying them.

"Wish them luck for me," Owen said. "Really, I mean it."

In his mind Everett saw Owen's crude drawing pinned to the wall of the gravel pit, sand sifting through bullet holes in the mayor's forehead.

"Oh, I'm pretty sure you've been in their thoughts, Owen."

Owen turned, walked a step, and looked back.

"Thanksgiving," he said. "Isn't that about when we buried Grumpy Donahue?"

"That's right," Everett replied. "That we did."

"Good old Grumpy," Owens said. "Quite a piece of work he was."

Grumpy Donahue had been an recluse in the waning years of his life, choosing to spent time only with wife Doris within the walls of their home on Main Street. Some said that it was only when Grumpy finally died that Doris really began to live, for she took control of the small fortune the miserly banker had spent his lifetime squirreling away.

"That he was," Everett agreed.

The two men parted, Everett now forgetting why he'd left the office in the first place. He returned, wondering where Old Duke was hiding this time of day. Owen Fuller might do well to think about Grumpy's plight, Everett thought, and why it pays to give everyone a fair shake. Even if their name was Petler.

Everett stood near his desk, remembering now what he had meant to do before he'd run into the mayor. He drove west of town and removed the bullet-riddled sign from the post. He erected a brand new, freshly painted sign, light bouncing from the glossy letters of the words "Apology City Limits."

Plit Butler heard the lifters chattering as a pickup truck pulled alongside the gas pumps the following day, a tail of blue smoke spewing from the exhaust pipe. Poking his head from beneath the hood of the car he was in the process of repairing, the mechanic spotted his next paying customer.

"Fill her up, Plit," Deke Petler said, easing from the seat of truck as Plit sauntered toward the gas pumps. "The old girl is about bone dry."

Plit rubbed the grease from his hands only as much as he felt was necessary to complete the task of filling the man's gas tank. Plit was used to working filthy—he, in fact, loved it. Working in the confines of his parts-strewn garage, often baking beneath the hot summer sun, Plit got pretty dirty, and downright rank by the end of the day. For a while Plit had a girl friend over at Eagle Nest, but because of the strong, locker room odor permeating Plit's body after working in the hot garage each day, she had opted not to continue their relationship. Plit was crushed.

"But I'll shower you with gifts," he had begged.

"I'd just wish you'd shower," had been her snubbing reply as the phone abruptly clicked dead against Plit's ear.

But Plit recovered from the breakup rather quickly, for a better love had shown up at his doorstep, in the guise of a Ford Fairlane desperately need of a complete engine overhaul.

"Sounds good," Plit said to Deke. "How's the oil? She's clattering."

"You can check her," Deke answered. "But it should be OK."

Plit started the gas running and popped the hood.

"You need to change this oil once in a while," he told Deke, showing him the dipstick. "This is a real nice shade of black, but it doesn't do much for the health of the motor. That's why those lifters are chattering so bad."

"I don't care," Deke replied. "This old girl don't go very far–just to Renoir and to the shootin' meets. She gets us there and gets us back. And that's all she needs to do."

The black oil in his engine looked to Deke like dirty STP, the thick, syrupy oil additive people put in their motors to make them last longer. To Deke's way of thinking, that fancy STP stuff was nothing more than used oil, thickened by age and wear. So naturally, to spend money on something he already had in his oil pan was stupid, was his contention.

"OK," Plit said. "But you might think about changing the oil real soon. Winter's coming in a month or so and she's gonna be hard to crank up in the mornings with oil like this in the engine. I can put in a lighter weight oil and make it easier to start for you."

"We'll see," Deke said. "Maybe later."

A second vehicle pulled up on the opposite side of the pumps, a slick sounding engine compared to the racket coming from under Deke's truck. The unseen driver shut off the engine and got out.

"Good morning, fellows," the man greeted, slamming the door behind him. "Can you fill me up, Plit?"

Neal Rider was a man of medium height, but stocky. His eyes darted around nervously as he surveyed the area around him, as if he were on the lookout for a sniper. Some said that Neal's roving eyes told a good bit about the general character of the man, and that was, that he wasn't too be trusted far. The man's brown hair had a waxy

335

butch cut that looked like an upside down hard-bristled scrub brush. A wisp of breeze attempting to blow through the hair found the going tough, for the greasy cream that forced the hair to stand up also prevented it from being moved by something so weak as the wind.

"No problem, Neal," Plit replied. "You just passing through today?"

"Yep," the man answered. "Regular, Plit?"

"No problem," Plit said, grabbing the second hose and turning the crank on the pump.

The man studied Deke, in the process of scrapping a dried wad of smashed bug off the side mirror with his fingernail.

"Didn't I see you shoot over in Glanville a while back?"

"You did," Deke said proudly, holding up his finger to blow the bug off. "Me and my brother shot there."

"You boys won, didn't you?"

"First and second place prize money," Deke answered proudly.

"That's good. Where you gonna shoot next?"

"Well, Fair River, of course," Deke replied, as if the man should know. "The Thanksgiving Day shoot."

"That'll be a big one," Neal said, "lots of people watching."

"Maybe," Deke said. "Don't pay much attention to the crowd. It's the money we're after. And it's the biggest purse of the year."

"Well, hope you win then," Neal said. "That kind of money will sure keep your sponsor happy."

Deke looked toward Plit, puzzled, and then back at the man.

"Sponsor," Neal explained. "You know, the business that pays your expenses."

"Hey, now wait a minute," Deke said, irritated, "nobody buys us off."

The man held his hand up, smiling.

"I didn't mean that," he said. "I'm talking about the person who sponsors you, you know, who makes sure you have enough money so you can compete. Buys your equipment and bullets and stuff like that."

Deke looked puzzled

"We buy all our own stuff," he explained. "Always have."

The man extended his arm, offering a handshake to Deke.

"Well, let me introduce myself then," he began, pumping Deke's hand up and down. "I'm Neal Rider and I own the Lost Meadows Tavern, you know, in Lost Meadows. And your name is?"

"Deke Petler."

"That's right," Neal answered. "I should have remembered from the meet at Glanville. And your brother is–"

"Durham."

"That's right. Durham. Well, Mr. Petler, how would you like to not have to pay all those expenses for the upcoming meet at Fair River? How would you like to shoot for all that money at Fair River and not have to pay a cent to be there?"

Plit listened intently as the men talked, the gas humming through the hoses in the background.

"All my expenses?"

"All of them. And all of Durham's, too, of course."

Deke rubbed his chin, not knowing what to think of the man's proposition.

"Why would you be wantin' do that for us?"

"I want to sponsor you," Neal explained. "I'll purchase all the ammunition you need to practice, and I'll pay your entrance fees as well. In fact, I'll even pay for your gasoline, beginning with this tank full right here. What do you say?"

"You just want some of the prize money, right?" Deke asked. "That's it, ain't it?"

"No, I don't. Any prize money you win will be yours. I want just one little thing from you."

"What's that?"

"I want you each to wear sponsor shirts with the name of my tavern on the back, so people can see that I sponsored you. It would be a real nice shirt, all embroidered and everything. And I want to put your trophies on display in my tavern for a couple of months, and then I'll let you have them back. That's all I want."

"And you'll buy everything we need?"

"Whatever you need."

"And we get to keep the prize money?"

"You're the ones that earned it. Why would I want it?"

Plit pulled the hoses out of the gas tank openings as both pumps clinked off.

"Let me talk with my brother," Deke said. "But you might just have yourself a deal."

"By the way," Neal asked. "Where do you boys practice, anyway?"

Deke glanced at Plit.

"At a gravel pit south of town," Deke replied.

"Interesting."

"We used to practice right off of our back porch," Deke explained. "But the town made us stop. Said we were too dangerous."

Neal smelled opportunity.

"So the town of Apology thought two of the best shooters in the State of Iowa didn't know what they were doing? You need to shoot for Lost Meadows, then, Deke. We'll treat you better than your own next-door neighbors do, I'll guarantee you that. Seems to me that the town of Apology don't appreciate the kind of celebrities they have right under their own noses."

21   Not Too Hasty With That Deal

At Duffy's that night, Irk Hickenlooper was in the middle of telling a story. Sitting around the table with Irk, Zippy Martin, Everett, Taylor Cantrell, and Old Duke listened intently to the man's words.

"So this woman went to the doctor in Renoir, you see," Irk explained. 'These pills you gave me aren't working, Doc,' she said. 'You told me they're supposed to kick in four hours after I take them, but I'm still feeling really bad.' Now this woman had been pestering the poor doctor for years about one ailment or another, they tell me, and she was nigh on to driving him to distraction. And once, she'd even threatened to find a new doctor if he couldn't find anything wrong with her."

"So what happened?" Zippy Martin asked.

"Well, the doctor was pretty fed up with the woman by now. 'Let me see that bottle, Mira,' he says to her. And then he reads the bottle and says, 'No wonder your medicine's not working, Mira. See, right here, plain as day on this bottle–it says they're made in California.' 'So what?' she says. 'Well, Mira,' he explains, 'you gotta realize that California is two hours behind us. That means your gonna have to give these pills six hours to work, not four.'"

Irk looked around the group and grinned.

"You know, she went home and the doc never heard another word from her about being sick."

The men laughed as the story ended. The front door opened and Plit Butler entered the tavern.

"Hey Plit," Taylor greeted. "You all done for the night?"

Plit ordered a beer from Duffy and joined the crowd.

"Just got new plugs in Moog's car," he said. "Got her purring like a kitten."

"I'll bring my Pontiac in for a tune up in a day or so," Everett said. "It's running kinda sluggish. Slow on getting up to speed."

"Yea," Zippy teased, "Everett's got to keep his patrol car hopped up for the bad guys."

Plit sat down.

"Speaking of bad guys," he began, "guess who stopped in to see me this morning?"

"Father John?" Taylor kidded.

"No," Plit replied. "You know he's no bad guy."

"Well, who then?" Taylor probed.

"Deke Petler," Plit said. "That's who."

"So what?" Old Duke asked, figuring that was a snappy comeback no one would question.

"Nothing," Plit said. "Nothing at all."

"If you've got something to tell us, Plit," Everett said, "then spit it out."

Plit looked at his beer bottle and back to the men surrounding him.

"And who do you think pulled up as I was filling Deke's tank?"

"I bet it was Owen," Zippy said, leaning in and swiveling his neck slowly around the table. "And they had a gunfight right there at the pumps. Bad Deke against Dead-Eye Owen, right?"

"You can go ahead and make fun if you want," Plit explained. "Or listen to what I have to tell you."

"Tell us, then, Plit," Everett encouraged, reading the man's body language.

"Neal Rider pulled up to the station to fill up. And him and Deke started to talk. And you'll never guess what about."

"Who's Neal Rider?" Old Duke asked.

"Owns the Lost Meadows Tavern," Plit explained. "And he offered Deke a deal this morning."

"What kind of deal?" Everett asked.

The sheriff knew Plit's explanation had to be heading somewhere or the mechanic wouldn't be trying so hard to get the story out.

"Get this," Plit explained. "Neal Rider offered to sponsor Deke and Durham at the Fair River Turkey Shoot in three weeks."

"That's it?" Taylor asked. "That's the story?"

"Who cares?" Zippy added. "No skin off my back where they shoot who they shoot for."

"Don't make no difference to me, either, I guess," Plit responded. "Just thought you might like to know."

Plit had gotten the word early in the morning and had done a great deal of thinking about the conversation between Deke and Neal as he'd worked on cars all day. The others were hearing it fresh, and Plit knew that the consequences of that chance meeting would dawn on them, as it had on him.

Earl Shilling entered the tavern, smelling like the tonic waters that permeated the air in his barbershop. His hair gleamed in the dim light from the oily tonic he'd splashy liberally upon his scalp two hours before. Several black combs and a pencil jutted haphazardly from his breast pocket. Everett pointed to the man's pocket.

"You expecting to do a little business in here tonight, Earl?"

Earl glanced down, surprised.

"I guess I was in such a hurry to get out of there I forget to unload the shop," he grinned.

Earl motioned to Duffy and the bartender pushed a beer his way.

"Hey, Earl," Taylor said. "Guess what's going on with the Petler boys?"

"Surprise me," Earl answered, taking a swig.

"Plit here says the Petler boys are getting a sponsor. Someone's actually gonna pay them to shoot."

Earl remained silent, thinking.

"Who'd have thought anyone would pay those two yahoos anything," Zippy said.

"Somebody's going to sponsor Deke and Durham?" Earl asked.

"Yea," Zippy answered. "Isn't that a hoot?"

"Maybe they'll move to Lost Meadows," Duffy said from behind the bar. "I'd hate to be the person who bought that place of theirs. Would take a year to clean up that mess."

Duffy generally didn't say much when the men talked. He'd pretty much heard it all over the years and was content just to listen most of the time. But he could sense something was stirring, just by the way the conversation was heading.

"Then we'd be done with them," Old Duke added.

"Would we want to be done with them?" Everett asked.

347

His answer surprised everyone, with the exception of Plit Butler.

"What do you mean, Everett?" Taylor asked.

"I'd like to know that myself," Earl added. "I'd also like to know what kind of a deal Lost Meadows cut with the Petlers to get them to go over there."

"I can tell you that easy," Plit explained. "Neal Rider told Deke that he would pay all his expenses–ammo, entrance fees, and even gas to get to the meets if the boys would shoot for him."

"And what does Neal get out of the deal?" Earl continued.

"He only asked the Petler boys for one thing. He is going to provide them shirts with the logo of Lost Meadows Tavern on the back."

"That's it?" Irk asked. "He sure doesn't want much."

"He's not even asking for a cut of the winnings," Plit continued. "He told Deke they could have it all the money they win. And he wants to put Deke and Durham's trophies on display in his tavern if they win."

"If they win?" Everett asked. "Sure they're gonna win. Who's gonna beat them?"

"So they're gonna put the Deke and Durham's brass where everyone can see it?" Earl asked, his tone one of concern.

"I'm sure that's the reason," Everett answered.

"Hey, Duffy," Duke joked. "Why didn't you offer them a deal like that?"

Duffy rolled his eyes as he wiped dry a freshly washed beer glass.

"Perhaps," Everett said seriously, "he should have."

All eyes turned toward the sheriff.

"I think I'm inclined to agree with you about that, Sheriff," Earl said.

"Hey, I was just kidding," Duke explained.

"I can see the gears going round and round in your head, Everett," Taylor said. "What are you thinking?"

Everett glanced toward Plit and Earl.

"You two already have it figured out, don't you?" he asked. "I can tell by looking at you."

"Figured?" Irk asked. "What's to figure?"

"Well, Irk," Everett began, "let's just think on this. Where do Deke and Durham live?"

"Just outside town," Irk replied.

"Wrong," Everett shot back. "In town. Remember?"

"OK," Irk admitted reluctantly. "In town then."

"And what town is that?"

"Why, Apology, of course."

"Now," Everett went on, "where is the Lost Meadows Tavern located?"

"I got that one," Duke exclaimed, as if he were some school kid who'd just figured out the answer to the teacher's question. "It's in Lost Meadows."

"Very perceptive, Duke," Earl said.

Duke missed Earl's barb.

"Why thanks," he replied, delighted with Earl's perceived compliment.

Earl looked at Everett.

"So, what we have is two of the best shooters in the state, who've we've had in this town for twenty years, are going to shoot for some other town," Earl continued, "rather than the town they live in."

"So?" Irk asked.

"So?" Earl answered. "Don't you see what's going to happen?"

"We'll be the laughing stock of the county," Everett said. "Earl's right. If the town of Apology can't even keep two of the best shooters in the state from jumping ship, we're a pretty poor lot."

"It's never come up before," Taylor said. "Deke and Durham have never had sponsors as long as they've been shooting. It just wasn't important to them."

"Well," Everett replied. "Maybe nobody ever asked. But maybe somebody should have thought about it before now–me included. We've just taken them for granted, I guess, because they've always been around. But somebody sure thinks they're important now. And they've snatched the boys right out from underneath us. And to Lost Meadows, no less. You guys remember all the teasing we took from that Lost Meadows crowd about our traffic light moving around every two weeks? Remember how they made fun of our town?"

"I about poked one of those Lost Meadows boys in the snout over that," Duke said.

Coming from cowardly Duke, those words didn't carry a whole lot of weight, but the idea was good, anyway. Everett continued.

"Just imagine how much guff this town is going to take if the Petler boys, who live right in the town of Apology, show up at the Fair River Turkey Shoot wearing shirts with 'Lost Meadows Tavern' on their backs. What will people say about that, you suppose?"

He let his words sink in.

"Why, I don't think I like that idea at all," Irk said. "No, not one bit, I don't."

"And if the Petler boys win the shoot," Everett said, "their trophies will be on display at the tavern in Lost Meadows. Can you imagine what the talk will be about every night? I'll tell you what it will be–how the town of Apology is a bunch of dumb clucks, no smarter than the Petler's rooster who crows at dusk instead of dawn. And as long as those trophies sit there, we're gonna be eating crow, looking the fool."

"Well," Duffy said from the other side of the bar, "maybe I can sponsor the boys. I should have, I supposed, offered before this. But like you guys said, the subject just never came up."

"What makes you think you can convince them to come over to you?" Everett asked.

"Because they're part of the town," Duffy explained. "They owe us first."

"I'm not so sure they do," Everett said. "The town has always looked at them boys as something less than the rest of us. And now, don't forget, we just passed a law that said they can't shoot in town. They're out shooting in the gravel pit and they're madder than hell about it. I can tell you that the Petler boys aren't in the mood to hear this town's offer, or any other thing the town has to say to them. And I can't say I blame them."

Everett knew he had the crowd listening.

"They're gonna shoot for Lost Meadows. Unless we do something about it."

"Wait a minute," Irk said. "They can't do that. They'd be traitors to the town if they did."

"So what?" Everett shot back. "As far as they're concerned, the town has turned their backs on them. So who's the traitor?"

"Well, we just can't roll over and let that Lost Meadows bunch steal our shooters away," Taylor lamented. "Let's get them back— whatever it takes."

"What about Owen Fuller?" Everett asked. "He railroaded them out of here, remember. And he's got the final say."

"Damn him," Zippy said, disgusted. "That Owen."

"It wasn't Owen by himself," Earl reminded them. "We all had a part in what happened."

"Well, what's it gonna take to get them back?" Duffy asked.

Everett sipped his beer, the gears already whirling around in his head.

"Let me talk to the boys," he offered. "They'll listen to me."

"Are you sure?" Irk asked.

"Judiciously," Everett smiled, sipping froth as the plan formed.

22   Dead Pheasants in the Ditch

The new tires on the Pontiac were well broken in as they rolled over the dirt road that led from the main road and into the gravel pit south of Apology. Everett felt the gentle mushing below his tires as the sugary sand compressed under the weight of the steel and rubber. To Everett's right sat Bert Kestral, a dead pheasant flopped across his lap. The red ring around the bird's neck contrasted sharply with the gold and brown plumage adorning the remainder of the bird's body, and resting silently on Bert's blue jeans, one would have concluded that the bird was just sleeping.

Everett spotted Deke Petler's old Chevy truck parked near the pit wall, and the brothers were blasting away at targets. The boys were so concentrated on their shooting that they failed to hear the sheriff's car approach or the men getting out. Bert held the pheasant low, half-hidden behind his right leg as he walked, the bird's head dragging in the sand as Everett and he approached the shooters.

"How's the shootin', boys?" Everett yelled over the noise of the gunfire.

The men continued to fire, each taking a shot while the other watched where the bullet hit the target.

"I say, how's the shootin'?" Everett asked, his voice rising.

Deke shot at one of the ringed targets, the bullet hitting dead center. Hearing Everett's voice, he turned around.

"Hi, Everett," he replied, grinning as he eyeballed Bert. "We're gonna whip their pants off at Fair River. I can just feel it."

"Yea," Durham said, shifting his weight to his all-toed foot, "we ain't missin' nothing.'"

"That's real good news to hear, boys," Everett answered. "Mighty good news."

"Hey Bert," Deke asked, "what're you doin' out here? And what'd ya doin' with that there bird?"

"What's Bert doing here?" Everett asked. "Why I'm just giving Bert a ride out today 'cause his car's at Plit's. You see, Bert works for the county, and this here gravel pit is county property. You two did know that, didn't you?"

"Well, I never much thought about who owned it," Durham replied. "It's just always been here."

"It's OK to be here, ain't it Everett?" Deke asked. "I mean, it was you who told us we could. Remember?"

Everett raised his hand, motioning for calm.

"I did," he said. "And you certainly have done nothing wrong under the law. But, as with all things well planned, a problem has arisen which concerns you both."

"And what's that?" Durham asked suspiciously. "The neighbors complainin' again?"

"No, no complaints," Everett answered. "None at all."

Everett turned to Bert.

"Why don't you tell them, Bert?"

Bert lifted the dead pheasant, its wings unfolding as he grasped the legs firmly.

"We've been finding these along the roads lately," Bert said. "Lots of them."

"Dead like that?" Deke asked.

"Just like that," Bert replied.

"I bet some farmer's been sprayin' something to kill 'em," Durham suggested. "You know how them farmers like to spray stuff on everythin'. Hell, ain't a day goes by around here where you don't see a cloud of somethin' poison coming from a sprayer."

"I agree with you there, Durham," Everett said. "But this bird didn't die from any poison spray or anything like that. He died from a bullet."

"Well, it's not us," Durham defended. "We ain't shootin' no pheasants. We get blamed for enough stuff that goes on around here. This time we're innocent as lambs."

"Hell, no bullet killed that bird anyhow," Deke said. "There ain't a mark on him."

"There's no marks on him," Everett agreed. "That is correct. But it was a bullet that killed him, sure as the moon is yellow. And it was one of yours, I'm afraid."

"I'm tellin' ya, sheriff," Deke argued, "it ain't one of ours. We ain't been shootin' any pheasants. We're after the money at Fair River. And that's all."

"Yea," Durham added. "Besides, we got plenty of birds at home to butcher. If we wanted poultry, we'd just chase down one of our own and whack its head off and chuck it in the grease pan."

Durham was correct in that regard. The boys had a healthy flock of chickens that'd been stuffing themselves full of corn and fat grasshoppers all summer. But, to Everett's recollection, the only time the sheriff had seen either of the boys trying to run down a chicken was a few weeks before, when Durham chased their rooster down Main Street, lighting the fuse to the predicament in which the boys now found themselves.

"We wouldn't waste our time shootin' a pheasant in the ditch," Durham added. "And huntin' that way ain't sportin' anyway."

Durham looked at Deke, who nodded his head in approval of his brother's words.

"I'm afraid that it's your bullet that killed this bird," Bert insisted. "And I can prove it."

Bert took a knife from his pocket and flopped the pheasant on its back, resting the body on his palm. Holding the bird firmly, he plunged the blade into the soft organs below the rib cage. Slicing toward the tail, Bert opened a three-inch slit and removed the blade. He inserted two fingers, fishing around inside the bird's guts.

"I feel something," Bert said, continuing to probe while glancing at Everett.

He pulled out his bloody fingers, holding an equally bloody bullet.

"Here it is," he said. "Just like I thought. See."

He handed the bullet to Deke, who stood there flabbergasted.

Deke rubbed red clots away from the surface of the bullet, exposing a lump of distorted brass and lead. Examining the metal, Deke could easy tell that the bullet had been fired.

"It's a forty-five slug, right?" Bert asked.

Deke handed the bullet to Durham, who rolled it over and over in his palm.

"It's a forty-five slug," Deke said soberly, looking at Everett. "But honest to God, Everett, I swear I never shot that bird."

"We never said you did," Everett replied calmly. "And nobody's accusing you, either. The fact is, boys, nobody shot this bird."

"Nobody?" Durham exclaimed. "Well, that just don't make sense. If nobody shot this bird, then how did he get this slug in him then?"

Everett glanced at Bert and then back to the brothers.

"He ate it," Everett answered.

"Ate it?" Deke asked, shocked. "What do you mean he ate it? I don't understand."

Bert pointed to the wall of the pit.

"Your bullets," he explained. "In the wall over there. They're eating them."

Deke looked at Durham. The two broke up, howling with laughter.

"You really had us fooled, you two," Deke said, a broad grin splitting his face. "Pheasants eatin' bullets from the gravel pit. What a hoot."

"Yea," Durham added. "What'd they do, Everett, get a step ladder and crawl up the wall so they could get high enough to eat them bullets stuck in the sand up there?"

"Maybe they're just tryin' to get their daily iron," Deke grinned. "You really had us goin', Everett."

The brothers stopped grinning when Everett's face remained serious.

"Oh, come on, Everett," Deke said, his tone curt. "The joke's out."

"I think you'd better hear Bert out," Everett cautioned.

"I'm loadin' gravel out of this pit at least twice a month," Bert explained. "I spread it all over the roads around this part of the county, trying to keep all those washboards roads smoothed out. A few days ago I noticed a dead pheasant in the ditch. Didn't think much about it–come across them all the time. Then I noticed another one, and pretty soon some more. Twenty pheasants in all, I counted in my travels. Dead. No marks on the bodies. And what's more, I found them within a two-mile radius of this gravel pit. So I took three of them to Taylor Cantrell's veterinarian's office. He cut them open and found bullets in every one of them. Bullets from your guns."

"Well, I'll be dogged," Deke said.

"How else would a bullet get inside a pheasant without showing a wound on him?" Everett asked. "And you said yourself, Deke, there ain't no bullet marks on him."

"You two have been shooting hundreds of bullets into the gravel over the last few weeks and Bert's been spreading it all over the roads," Everett explained. "The pheasants run those roads at night lookin' for food and find those bullets on the road. Probably think they're June bugs or something like that in the dark. They swallow them and then die. God only knows how many of these poor dead pheasants are in the ditches around Apology."

"Well, what are we gonna do, Everett?" Durham asked. "We gotta practice. You know Fair River is the biggest money match of the year."

"I know that boys," Everett answered. "But, I'm afraid I'm gonna have to put the pit off limits to you boys until we figure something out. For the sake of the birds."

"What!" Deke screamed. "I don't believe this. First the town kicked us out and now you're doin' the same thing."

"It's not that I want to, boys," Everett explained. "It's that I have to."

"Wait a minute," Durham cut in. "You don't have any jurisdiction out here on county property, Sheriff."

Everett was momentarily stunned by his comment. Not only did the man make sense, but Durham actually had to stop and think before he expressed those few words of intelligence. This was unusual for the quick-firing Durham, but Everett recovered nicely.

"Well, I hate to have to do this," Everett replied, "but I'm just gonna have to declare martial law then."

"You can't do that," Durham said. "You're a sheriff, not a marshal. So you can't be declarin' that."

"Under the laws of the State of Iowa," Everett explained, "a marshal and a sheriff are about the same thing. I'm the sheriff and that's just another word for marshal, so I guess I can declare martial law just about anytime I feel like it. And as far as not having any say so in the matter, I can quote you some juris prudence that would provide habeas corpus for any judicious preponderance that would relegate to grand jury irrelevance."

"Whoooeee!" Durham exclaimed. "I didn't think you knew all that fancy law stuff, Everett."

Deke slapped Durham on the arm.

"What do you mean, 'Whoooeee,'" Deke scolded. "We're gettin' 'whoooeed' right out of our shootin' place, nitwit."

Deke turned to Everett.

"Well, Everett," he said, "I suppose everyone'll be happy now that we can't practice no place. And we'll probably starve to death come winter."

"Not so fast," Everett cautioned. "Not only have I got you a place to practice, I have other good news for you boys. How would you boys like to got back to shooting at your own place again?"

"Would we?" Durham exclaimed. "Does a pig like rolling in cow droppin's?"

23   Everett's Plan Unfolds

Everett stood in Owen Fuller's office, explaining his proposal to the mayor, careful not to reveal that he'd already approached the Petler brothers with an offer to let them back into town. But Owen's place of business hadn't been Everett's first stop after leaving the gravel pit. He'd visited Taylor Cantrell first.

"No, no, and no," Owen said, pounding a fist on his desk as he looked up at the sheriff. "There is no way I'm going to let those two yahoos start shooting up our town again, even if it's back on their own property. I'm disappointed with you, Everett. You're the sheriff and bound to uphold the law. I thought I made it unquestionably clear about the town's decision to ban gunplay inside the city limits."

Owen pulled a notebook from his desk and opened it to the handwritten notes of the recent town meeting.

"See here, Everett," he pointed. "It's all here, written right down. It's all in this record book. Now, let me just quote you directly from the words of that record."

And that's just what Owen did–quoting the words exactly as they were written down. Everett, aware from past experiences that words supposedly carved in stone were, in reality, written on paper, and could be blown one way or another, like a kite in the wind.

"Ah, yes," Everett replied. "The record book."

Owen patted the open pages with his hand.

"It's a done deal," he said. "There is just too much emotion over this."

"There is emotion," Everett agreed. "But now it's over something else. Something that involves the town's honor."

"What kind of nonsense are you talking about, Sheriff?" Owen demanded. "I hope this isn't one of your stunts."

"Hear me out, Owen," Everett said calmly. "I just found out a very important piece of information which you might like to know. That's all."

"Well, what is it?"

Everett explained how the Petler boys had been approached by Neal Rider and how the man wanted them to shoot for the Lost Meadows Tavern, and how it would make the town of Apology look bad if two of their own sons wouldn't even support the town in which they lived.

"I really can't see that it's that big a deal," Owen grumbled. "Let them shoot for Lost Meadows. See if I care."

The conversation was interrupted as the phone on Owen's desk rang. Owen picked up the receiver, lifting a wait-a-minute finger to Everett.

"Excuse me," he said. "It might be a customer."

By the shrill voice blaring through the receiver Everett knew that the person on the other end of the line wasn't the least bit interested in buying insurance.

"Ho-old ho-ld up, Bonnie," Owen stuttered, "slow down."

Owen covered the mouthpiece with his hand, looking up at Everett.

"These damn fool women around here. Gonna give me a heart condition, I swear."

Everett could hear Bonnie's excited voice. Just as he knew she would be. Owen continued to listen.

"Maggie Rider?" Owen asked. "From Lost Meadows. She did? What?"

Owen glanced at Everett, and stared down to the words firmly penned in his record book.

"Well, it was your idea," Owen defended.

Everett knew how the conversation was going, even though he couldn't hear Bonnie's words. At Duffy's Tavern Owen used to brag to the men about Bonnie, saying how the only thing that could replace a good wife was a bad husband. Everett wondered how Owen felt about that comment at this particular moment.

"But–that would be impossible," Owen stammered. "Why–we'd all look like fools–I'd look like a fool."

Everett could make out Bonnie's words now, her voice rising through the line.

"Well, damn it, Owen," she shouted "We can't have Maggie Rider and all those hussies from Lost Meadows sticking it to us again. By the way, she reminded me about your damn stoplight fiasco. And if those old biddies get way this time, we'll never hear the end of it."

"What do you want me to do about it?" Owen asked.

"I'd rather eat a day's worth of pride than swallow a year's helping of crow," Bonnie said firmly.

"What about Viola and the others?"

"You let me handle them," she said, her tone changing to one of purpose. "When I get through telling them about all the things those old hens from Lost Meadows are saying, that won't be a problem, I can assure you."

Owen glanced up at Everett, aware that the sheriff was watching him.

"I'll take it under advisement," he said. "Have to go now."

Owen hung up the phone and clasped his hands together, resting them on the record book.

"That was Bonnie," he said. "It seems that the wife of the man who made the offer to the Petler boys is starting to spread the word about their new shooters and how Lost Meadows stole them right out from under the stupid citizens of Apology. She called Bonnie to rub it in. Now Bonnie's all mad and she's going to start calling everyone in town to try and get the Petler boys to shoot for Apology."

Owen lowered his head.

"What a mess," he said, disgusted. "I just can't win here."

"Want me to see what I can do?" Everett offered.

Owen took a deep breath.

"If you can," he said. "But I don't think it will do much good. Remember all those people at the meeting the other night who wanted the Petler's heads. They were pretty set against the boys."

"Believe me, Owen," Everett said, "they can get on their high horses all they want, but when the pride of the town is at stake you can pretty much bank on these people to do the right thing. And that is to get the Petlers to shoot for us."

"Would they?"

"I think I can convince them to shoot for Duffy's Tavern," Everett explained. "That's almost like they're shooting for the town."

"What would it take?"

Everett looked hard at Owen.

"Like I already suggested when I walked in here, you're gonna have to rescind that shooting ban, Owen" he said. "Let the boys shoot back on their own property. That'll go a long way with them. Anyway, what have you got to lose now?"

"I know it's not going to be that easy," Owen replied. "What about all that stuff Lost Meadows Tavern offered them?"

"Duffy's Tavern will match it," Everett said. "I already spoke with Duffy about it. Everything that Lost Meadows was going to give the Petlers, Duffy's Tavern will offer."

"Think they'll buy it?"

"We can see," Everett said, the questioning tone of his voice exaggerated, more to fool Owen that to register concern.

Armed with the mayor's blessing, Everett saw that his plan was going as he'd hoped. There were, of course, no dead pheasants lining the ditches of Corwith County. Taylor Cantrell, Bert Kestral, and

Everett had come up with the pheasant idea, hatching the plan as a way to stop the Petler boys from shooting in the gravel pit without raising any suspicion in their minds. Everett recovered a forty-five slug from an oak log he'd shot, and with Taylor's help, rammed the deformed bullet down the dead pheasant's throat with a gun-cleaning rod. When Bert cut the bullet from the bird's stomach as the brothers watched, the evidence had been sound enough to convince Deke and Durham of the legitimacy of the dead pheasant story Bert was telling them. Deke and Durham accepted as gospel Everett's insistence that they either find another location to practice or continue to take the lives of innocent birds, something they wouldn't do. Everett, his plan moving forward nicely, told the boys that he could arrange for them to resume their practices on their property, but to hold off shooting until he could convince the mayor.

With the Petlers satisfied about being able resume shooting at home, Everett tackled the problem of convincing bull-headed Owen Fuller to let them. Like the great generals of the Civil War, Everett decided the best way to move against Owen would be with a flanking attack. A frontal assault might well end up as verbal duel between

Owen and him, and Everett wanted to avoid that confrontation, if possible.

Taylor Cantrell was a pretty fair singer, but he also had one other talent necessary for the success of Everett's plan. The veterinarian also did voice impersonations, regularly performing at Duffy's or at social gatherings held in the basement of St. John's Church. So when Taylor, disguising his voice as Maggie Rider, telephoned Bonnie Fuller, he laid it on pretty thick, first reminding Bonnie about the town's traveling stoplight, then moving on with barely a breath in between, rubbing salt in the wound about how the Petler boys were deserting Apology for Lost Meadows.

"Haw-haw-haw," Taylor's coarse imitation crowed from the telephone wires, the high-pitched tone reddening Bonnie Fuller's ears as her fingernails dug into her thigh. "Haw-haw-haw. Wait until this gets out."

Bonnie, enraged, telephoned Owen as Everett visited the mayor's office, just as the sheriff's plan called for. And now, with Owen's blessing, Everett could proceed with the next stage of his plan.

As Owen sat in his office, totally unaware of the duping, Everett drove west toward the Petler property, grinning like the Cheshire cat. Owen pulled a white handkerchief from his pocket, wiping blue smudges from where his hands had rested on the inky, carved-in-stone words of the town council's record book. His ears still ringing from Bonnie's phone tirade, Owen inadvertently wiped sweat from his brow, leaving small spots of blue on his forehead.

Ah, record books, Everett reminded himself as he drove, recalling Owen's clasped hands resting on the hard and fast words dictated into history during the town council meeting meant to seal the fate of the Petler brothers. What a wonderful idea.

24 We Owe Who What?

Everett was continually amazed at what a great invention the telephone was, and especially appreciative of how it had elevated the science of gossiping to the speed of light. No more than two hours after Taylor Cantrell phoned Bonnie Fuller, stoking her fire under the pretext of being Maggie Rider, Everett could almost see the telephone lines lining the streets of Apology jumping up and down as phones rang off walls, passing along the most recent bit of news. With all activity, Everett thought, it was a wonder that the crows could keep their feet wrapped around the wires as they looked down at the town from their perch. Or it might have been that the birds were just keeping their toes warm with all the heated discussion passing through.

After Bonnie gave Owen his earful, she immediately called Viola Vanderhoff, riling her up about the taunting call from Maggie Rider. Just to make sure the job was done right, Bonnie threw a little extra in about how Maggie had made snide remarks about Viola's weight, which wasn't true, but served to get Viola' fire lit. As Bonnie continued to pass the news to others, phoning Amy Flanigan next, Viola called Anita's Cafe, taking the shotgun approach. Anita Biningham took the call, relaying the information to the three tables of customers who happened to be in the restaurant at the time, and who in turn passed the news on when they left the cafe. With one phone call Viola scattered the news like the spread of number six shot from the mouth of a twelve gauge, much more efficiently than the single bullets Bonnie fired by calling one person at a time. The scoop was all over town in less than three hours. The nice windfall about all the activity for Owen Fuller's peace of mind was that the mayor didn't have to convene an additional town meeting to seek permission for the Petler boys to resume their shooting activity within Apology's borders. It was strongly urged by the proud residents of Apology that the Petlers be allowed back into the flock. Everett, delighted with the news, visited the Petler place.

"OK, boys," Everett said as he walked from the car to the back steps where Deke and Durham waited. "You can go ahead and start shooting again, just like I promised. And both the mayor and his wife send their regards to you."

"All right, Everett," Deke said. "What's the catch?"

"The catch?" Everett asked innocently. "You think there's a catch?"

"Yea," Deke repeated. "The catch. Let's have it. Why the sudden change of heart by the town? Especially by Owen and Bonnie Fuller? They were ready to string us from a light pole a few days ago."

"You two are too smart for me," Everett said. "So I might as well tell you. Remember back at the gravel pit when I told you I had some good new for you? Besides getting your shooting location back, that is."

"Yes," Durham asked suspiciously, "And just what would that be, Everett?"

Everett paused, grinning.

"Since you're back in the good graces of the town," he said, "you're gonna get to shoot for us. For Apology. Ain't that wonderful?"

"No. No, we ain't," Deke responded without hesitation. "We're shootin' for Lost Meadows Tavern. We made a deal with them. And a promise is a promise."

"But Duffy wants you to shoot for his tavern," Everett explained. "He's gonna give you everything that Lost Meadows offered you."

"Duffy!" Durham roared. "That no account weasel. He kicked us out of his bar a year ago and told us not to come back."

"Now, that's not quite right, Durham," Everett defended. "You gotta eventually pay for the beer you drink and you boys were getting pretty far behind. Remember?"

"Well, he didn't have to kick us out over that," Durham continued. "We would have paid eventually. You know that, Everett."

"Duffy knew you'd pay, fellows, "Everett explained. "Like you said, Deke, a promise is a promise. But if you recall, Duffy didn't kick you out for the money you owed him. He knows you're good for it. But, Durham, I don't care how intoxicated you get, you can't stand on top of the bar and pee in your beer glass. That ain't right."

Durham hesitated, thinking.

"Hell, Everett, I only peed a little. He made it out like the damn world was comin' to an end."

"I know that, Durham. But those two ladies who caught the backsplash two stools down were the ones who complained. Don't blame Duffy. He had to do something."

"Just the same, Everett," Deke cut in, "we're shootin' for Lost Meadows. They already bought the gas that's in my truck out there."

"Just pay it back," Everett urged.

"Don't have no money to pay it back with," Deke said. "That's why the Fair River shoot's so important. We need the dough."

"Duffy will pay it back then," Everett answered.

"But I gave my word to Neal Rider," Deke insisted. "And besides, after what they said about us at the town meetin', why should we stand up for anything that has to do with this town?"

"You know how riled some people get," Everett said. "Some of these old hens don't have anything to cackle about so they just squawk about the first thing that comes along. Just like those birds over there."

Everett nodded to a group of chickens near the fence, pecking away at bugs in the grass. One of the hens plucked a fat grasshopper from between two rocks and held it up high, little green legs kicking frantically. The other hens spied the prize and began chasing her, trying to steal away the meal. Off they ran, the flock trying to catch up to the hen carrying the grasshopper so one lucky chicken could snatch it from the owner's beak at a dead run.

"Nah, Everett," Deke said, "not this time. We're through runnin' with the chickens. We're goin' with Lost Meadows."

"Well, I hate to hear that, boys," Everett said, a discouragement in his tone. "But I can understand. I sure can."

He turned to leave, checking himself.

"Oh, by the way, I have something for you from Duffy. You two are so full of good news that I almost hate to give this to you."

Everett handed Deke a yellow slip of paper.

"What is it?" Durham asked, looking over Deke's shoulder.

"It's a bill!" Deke replied, incredulously. "For beer we drank at Duffy's–over a year ago! Why that dirty–"

"And Duffy wants to sponsor us?" Durham interrupted. "And he gives us a bill like this? What is he–crazy?"

Deke crumpled the paper into a tight ball and hurled it violently toward the flock of chickens. As the ball bounced on the ground, it rolled among them, and the flock abandoned their assault on the chicken holding the grasshopper, enthusiastically attacking the yellow wad, thinking they'd hit the mother lode of corn kernels. As the chickens crowded in a circle, surrounding the paper, the wad, pecked dozens of times, jumped among the hens as though it were some sort of strange animal, new to the farm country. The flock, wised-up by their futile pecking, turned en masse to Deke, shooting the man a dirty-chicken-look because they now knew the truth about the fake corn kernel. Undaunted by this setback, however, the chickens turned their attentions elsewhere, resuming their hunt for the lucky flockmate holding the prize grasshopper.

"I'm not paying this!" Deke shouted, watching the chickens scattering.

"You don't have to," Everett said calmly. "Duffy says if you'll shoot for him, he'll forgive the debt. It's that simple."

"Big deal," Durham huffed. "I should have piddled on his bar longer–a lot longer."

"Go tell Duffy to stuff it," Deke said.

Everett stood up straight, looking the men in the eye.

"If that's the way you want it, boys," he said firmly, "I'm afraid I'm gonna have to ask for your guns."

"What!" Deke shouted. "Our guns! What do our guns have to do with anythin', Sheriff?"

"Understand gentlemen, that I'm merely an instrument of the law here," Everett explained. "Sometimes I have to act, regardless of my personal feelings toward people. You saw the bill Duffy made out to you. You know you owe him–you have for more than a year. And you've made no attempt to pay him. You know he's been real patient with you, because deep down, he knows you're his friends. But he's tired of waiting and he wants his money. So I need your guns."

"You're gonna give Duffy our guns?" Durham asked.

"No," Everett replied. "He has no use for them. I'm going to take them to the pawnshop in Renoir, the one near the hardware store. Might get twenty bucks or so out of them."

Deke ran his hand through his hair, flabbergasted.

"Twenty bucks! You know how much those pistols are worth, Everett? Apiece? And you just want to up and sell them like second-hand lamps at a rummage sale?"

"Like I said, Deke," Everett pressed, "I'm merely doing my job here. I've got no stake in this other than upholding the law, and I sorely do not want to do this. Twenty bucks won't cover the debt, but it might calm Duffy down. But I wouldn't worry too much, fellows. You can buy the pistols back after you win at Fair River."

"If they're still there," Durham shot back. "And how are we supposed to win any money at Fair River so we can get our guns back when we don't have any guns to practice with so we can win any money in the first place?"

"You do have a bit of a problem there," Everett answered. "I can see that."

The brothers eyed each other.

"Like I said," Everett continued, "Duffy will forgive the debt if you shoot for him. Like I said, I've got no stake in all this, but if I were you, I'd take him up on his offer. You'll get the same things from him that Lost Meadows Tavern would have given you– including keeping your winnings. And come on now, wouldn't it make you feel better to shoot for your own town? Remember, boys, if Deke wouldn't have run into Neal Rider *by accident* at Plit's gas station, do you suppose you'd have a sponsor at all?"

Everett launched his final missile.

"After all, Lost Meadows didn't come looking for you, did they? But Apology did."

25   A Visit to the Ladies Club

"Hot damn," Taylor Cantrell grinned. "You did it, Everett. You really did."

The word was out all over town about how the Petler boys changed their minds and agreed to shoot for Duffy's Tavern. In essence, they were now shooting for the town of Apology. When word of the agreement reached Bonnie Fuller, she immediately phoned Maggie Rider in Lost Meadows, giving her the business about how the worm had turned. Maggie, unaware of any of the events unfolding in Apology, contacted husband Neal at the Lost Meadows Tavern to tell him of the strange phone call she had received from the wife of the mayor of Apology. Needless to say, this bit of information enraged Mr. Rider, for he had bragged in his tavern all week how he'd usurped the town of Apology, and his patrons had been having a good laugh about it. He now played the fool, and he knew it, for the Petler brothers had not told him of their decision to pull out of the agreement, and he was caught flatfooted. Neal Rider, regarding himself as a man of prominence in Lost Meadows, and not taking kindly to treachery, was seething. But in the town of Apology the uniform of the day was a beaming smile, and the news of the Petler brothers return to the fold was even the subject of much of the talk during the monthly luncheon of the Ladies Club.

The town of Apology had a Ladies Club, comprised of a dozen or so of the more affluent members of the community, affluence being measured by comparison to economics within the city limits. That is to say, there wasn't much competition. Stella Hissy and Bonnie Fuller headed up the group, arranging for the social functions to be held on the first Tuesday of every month, mostly card playing and lots of tongue wagging, followed by a specialty dessert. Once in a while a new arrival in town would apply for membership. This would set off a wave of excitement in the club, followed by a flurry of activity because a formal initiation of the candidate needed to be held.

On this occasion, newcomer Shirley Lebo, having just moved to Apology from Renoir, had applied for membership to the Ladies Club. Since her arrival in town a few weeks prior, the woman had heard lots of harsh talk about the notorious Petler brothers and their antics, and how they were a blight on the honor of the town. Not being entrenched in the Apology rumor mill just yet because she was new in town, Shirley was interesting in knowing why all of the sudden these same Petler boys were the town heroes, for this quick turnaround of attitude was a bit confusing to her.

Shirley thought of herself as someone who could add a bit of refinement to the Ladies Club, for after all, she had lived in the big city of Renoir, population 42,507, and was therefore, a worldly woman. The woman, slim and bubbly, anxiously wanted to get her name known, and was invited to attend the next meeting of the Ladies Club at Stella Hissy's home. Stella worked all morning, preparing a delicious custard dessert for the club members, and when the warm yellow liquid was ready, she poured it in a cake pan and set it to cool on a windowsill and then turned her attention to setting out the china and silver. The sweet smell of custard lifted into the air, and Everett caught a whiff of it as he drove by the house in his patrol car, on his way to the Petler place.

By coincidence Doris Donahue's sixteen-year old niece Katie was in town for a visit. There was nothing special about Katie other than she was the prettiest sight to hit Apology since Reef Langley's teeth were scrubbed clean in Sheriff Hiram's jail cell. Katie was growing to womanhood, with blond hair and a pretty smile that attracted the young bucks to her like a bear to honey. An hour before the start of the Ladies Club meeting, one of the three Lawler brothers, Jim, drove along Main Street in his souped up Chevy, slowing down to get an eyeful of young Katie Donahue. Katie happened to be walking on the sidewalk near Stella's opened window, where the custard had just been placed. The Lawler boy had done his homework–Katie's favorite colors were red and yellow, and those colors now comprised the flames he'd applied to the lower fenders just behind the front wheels of the car. A fresh coat of wax made the bright colors sparkle, the light catching Katie's eye.

Now the boy knew right away that Katie had taken a liking to the car. He stopped and struck up a conversation, and things appeared to be going real well until it began to sprinkle. The boy invited Katie into the car, out of the rain, but the big city girl from Renoir was much too sly to be taken in by a trick so shallow.

As the boy continued to coax the girl into his car, a rather long garter snake slithered across the wet pavement, in the direction of Stella Hissy's house. The snake crossed the road, hesitating behind the rear tire of the boy's car. The boy, knowing that he'd gotten about as far as he was going to get that day, tried one last trick to impress young Katie. As he pulled away he gunned the engine. The rear tires spun rapidly on the wet pavement, and the unfortunate snake was caught in the spinning tire. The momentum sent the snake sailing through the air, plopping into the center of Stella Hissy' warm custard. The dazed snake slowly sank to the bottom of the pan. Stella, noticing the rain, removed the pan of custard from the windowsill and set it on the kitchen counter, shaking cinnamon powder on top of the dessert. The custard continued to cool, erasing all evidence of the event that had just taken place. Stella continued to work, laying out all her best doilies and hiding Jim's pipe stand. Even the inside of the toilet tank got a cleaning, for there was always the chance someone just might look in there. After the custard finished cooling, Stella

placed the dessert next to her good china on the dining room table.

At two o'clock the members of the Ladies Club began to arrive,

and ten minutes later Shirley Lebo knocked on Stella Hissy's front

door.

"Why, Miss Lebo," Stella greeted, opening the door, "it's so kind

of you to come."

"I am so glad to be invited," Shirley replied. "And pray tell me,

what is that absolutely divine aroma I smell?"

The meeting was cordial and everybody welcomed Shirley and

tried to make her feel at home. The group played bridge for a while,

and as they talked, each of the members attempted to size the woman

up without being too obvious regarding their intentions, of which

Shirley was already well aware. Shirley turned the conversation to the

Petler boys, inquiring about them. Now the Bible mentions tongues of

fire among its many blessed words, but the Lord probably wasn't

referring to the many tongues in Stella Hissy's dining room, firing off

all that talk about what rough-hewn characters the Petlers were, but

how they were actually good people, loyal to their community because they were going to represent Apology in the Thanksgiving Day Shoot at Fair River. When the talk of the brothers slowed, Stella figured it was a good time to serve dessert, and the group gathered around the table. The freshly made custard was placed in front of their newest member.

"Miss Lebo," Stella said, handing the woman a knife from her silver set, "as your first duty as a member of the Apology Ladies Club, will you do us the honor of cutting the first piece of custard?"

"I will be more than honored," Shirley Lebo answered. "You have all been so nice to me."

With that the woman bent over the pan and slid the point of the knife into the custard. The knife bumped against the bottom of the pan, waking the snake. As Shirley attempted to slice the custard the snake's head shot straight up from the bottom of the pan, the body rising upward about a foot. Shirley, eyeball to eyeball with a snake covered with yellow custard dripping from its head, reared back, her belt catching on Stella Hissy's expensive family heirloom lace tablecloth. Shirley's chair fell backwards, her belt tearing a large hole in the tablecloth. As the back of Shirley's chair banged against the hardwood floor, Stella screamed, grabbing for her stack of good china. She had high hopes of rescuing it until the snake jumped into Bonnie Fuller's lap, trying to hide from all the ruckus by slithering into Bonnie's dress pocket. As the slimy yellow mass wiggled across her body, Bonnie shot up from her seat, furiously slapping her at her lap. Bonnie rammed into Stella, already off balance with an armful of china, and knocked Stella off her chair, where she went crashing to the hardwood floor. As she felt herself going down, Stella futilely attempted to regain her balance by grabbing onto Neva Hickenlooper's shoulder, but missed, pulling Neva's purple-tinted wig from her head. Neva's hands immediately shot up to cover her head, for beneath the wig Neva's graying hair was held haphazardly in place by a thick nest of black bobby pins. Neva had been helping Irk in the barn earlier and losing track of time, hadn't had time to properly get ready for the meeting. As the china plates crashed to the floor, breaking into dozens of pieces, Neva's wig dropped on the snake as the creature wriggled from Bonnie Fuller's lap.

The dust settled on the affluent members of the Ladies Club, with Stella Hissy pasted to the floor, surrounded by hundreds of pieces of broken china, and Neva Hickenlooper standing next to her, hands pressed against her head, face fire red with embarrassment. Bonnie Fuller's face turned ashen, as around her, other members froze rigid with shock, most notably, Shirley Lebo, who still clutched the knife in her hand. About the last thing anyone remembers from that particular club meeting was the sight of purple wig winding its way toward the kitchen doorway, leaving in its wake a trail of slimy yellow S's.

Katie Donahue left Apology the next day, her visit with Aunt Doris complete. Shirley Lebo, not near as bubbly now as she'd been upon arrival in Apology, moved back to Renoir hard on Katie's heels, sending her brother to fetch her things. Everett, who'd been called to come down and shoot the snake, recovered Neva Hickenlooper's purple wig on the floor of Stella Hissy's kitchen.

It was decided that the Ladies Club would meet at Bonnie Fuller's house next, and Bonnie agreed to serve Swanson's pies.

The snake was never found, and the only genuine good to come out of the meeting, that is, before all the excitement commenced, was a general feeling of what a wonderful thing Deke and Durham were doing for the town of Apology.

26 Walnut Launching and Stolen Guns

"OK, boys," Everett said sternly, "I don't want this to happen again. You might have hurt poor Phil here with all your tomfoolery."

As Everett spoke, he stared down menacingly at the three Fuller boys, with Phil Granger watching from his porch.

Everett visited the Granger house early, after getting a call from Phil the evening before. Everett knocked on Phil's door as his first order of business, and Phil explained the problem vexing him. Phil had been perched on his front porch a few nights before, facing the park, when he'd heard a pop like a small gun going off. As he looked around, Phil's eyes beheld a truly heavenly sight, a fiery orange glow arcing in the sky toward him. His meteor, the one he'd waited so patiently for, had finally appeared. Phil braced himself as the projectile hurled toward him, lifting his catcher's mitt to snatch the prize from the darkness. Down it came, straight toward him, like a messenger from the Almighty Himself. Phil held up the mitt to intercept the celestial rocket, turning his face away. He felt a disappointingly small thump in the pocket of his mitt, with no more force than a June bug hitting a bug zapper. Phil heard a hard rattling sound of as he cautiously opened his ball glove. The glove was empty, prompting Phil to search the porch floor. He found the object near the front door, and reached down to pick it up. Expecting the object to be hell hot from the friction of the ride, he was surprised to discover it was as cold as a December gravestone.

Laughter coming from the park caught his attention, and Phil looked up to see the Fuller boys–Arnold, Bull, and Fuller, watching him. Bull held the open end of a long metal pipe whose opposite end was planted in the ground. Phil studied the object and discovered that what he'd thought was a meteor was a walnut, sprayed with fluorescent orange paint. It dawned on Phil what the boys had done. The boys had jammed one end of the hollow pipe into the grass, at a slant, and pointed it at Phil's house like a cannon. They dropped several lighted firecrackers down the pipe, twisting the fuses together so they'd all explode at the same time. Then they dropped the walnut in on top the firecrackers. When the firecracker exploded, the walnut flew from the pipe, hurling toward Phil's porch in one rather amazing display of marksmanship.

The prank hadn't concerned Phil very much until the boys repeated it several nights in a row. Sometimes the walnuts would come raining down in groups of two or three. It bothered Phil that the explosions were getting louder as the boys, growing more daring, dropped four or five firecrackers into the pipe at one time. The force at which the projectiles were slamming into Phil's porch increased to the point where the man felt threatened. When one of the walnuts cracked a window, Phil had no choice but to phone Everett.

Everett, hearing the story, summoned the boys to Phil's house. He knew the boys weren't dangerous criminals, but at least one, Arnold was worth watching. Arnold was somewhat vengeful, as Everett witnessed one Sunday, with an incident involving Zippy Martin.

A few days prior to that particular Sunday Mass, mailman Zippy had put the run on Arnold when he'd caught the boy defacing a mailbox. Arnold said he didn't do it, but Zippy knew otherwise, and that frosted Arnold. The boy served Mass the following Sunday and one of his duties was to hold the palette for Father Coleman as the good priest distributed communion. The palette resembled a gigantic brass lollipop, held below the chin of each receiver to catch the communion host if it somehow fell. As Father Coleman worked his way along the line, Everett saw Arnold hold a finger under his nose, pretending to stave off a sneeze. With this ploy working, the boy began rubbing the edge of the communion palette back and forth across Zippy' throat. The fake sneeze made the rubbing look coincidental, and there wasn't much Zippy could do as Arnold sawed away at the mailman's oversized Adam's apple with the sharp edge of the palette for those few seconds. Zippy tried to look Arnold in the eye but the boy ignored his stare. What all that rubbing did was give Zippy an uncontrollable bout of coughing, holding up the whole communion line until he stopped. To Arnold, making Zippy have a coughing bout in front of everybody in church had just been topping on the cake.

"I know you boys was just having fun," Everett said. "But you broke Phil's window."

401

"We're sorry, Sheriff," Bull said apologetically.

"Well, don't tell me," Everett said, pointing, "tell Phil."

The boys poured apology after apology on Phil, saying how sorry they were and how they hoped Phil wouldn't hold it against them because they were really swell kids at heart.

"You gonna tell our dad?" Arnold asked Everett.

"No, I'm not," Everett answered, seeing a look of relief lighting the boys' faces. "But you can imagine what your dad would say, him being the mayor and all."

"Thanks, Sheriff," Fuller said, relieved. "We were just having fun, that's all."

Fuller always seemed just a bit angry, Everett had noticed over the years, compared to the other two brothers. Perhaps this trait came from teasing by his schoolmates because his name was Fuller Fuller. But Fuller had been Bonnie's father's Christian name, and it wasn't her fault, Bonnie figured, that she'd married a man whose last name was the same as her father's first name.

"You got anymore of those fireworks left?" Everett asked.

The boys looked at one another, hesitating.

"Gosh, I don't know, Sheriff," Arnold answered. "But we'll check when we get home and get back with you."

Everett winked at Phil. He knew they would hightail it and wouldn't be back.

"Well, you boys be careful," he cautioned. "I knew a boy who shot walnuts at a fellow once and put out his eye."

Everett looked at Phil, trying to contain his grin.

"And I hear tell that that boy still locked away in the jail Renoir somewhere–in the basement–you know–where the dungeons are."

The boys waited, feeling awkward. They wanted to leave but didn't know how. Everett made it easy for them.

"Now git," he said, waving his hand.

The boys shot away, running full speed toward the park. They were halfway across the street when Old Duke drove by, honking his horn at them. The deputy pulled into Phil's driveway, behind the patrol car. Everett walked to the front of Duke's car, his arms raised.

"Don't tell me!" Everett shouted, "Owen Fuller's been shot in the heart again."

Duke ignored the remark.

"Nothing so dramatic," Duke said. "But we got gun problems again, Everett."

"The Petlers?" Everett asked, his voice now serious.

"Afraid so."

"Where?"

"Their place, of course," Duke replied, surprised.

"I'm on my way," Everett answered.

Everett followed Old Duke to the west end of town and into the Petler driveway. What kind of complaint had been filed against the boys this time, Everett wondered? He'd thought he'd covered all the bases and that everything should be peaceful by now. As he shut off his engine, Deke and Durham ran from the house and through the gate, poking their heads through the window of Everett's car door, looking like two ostriches in heat.

"We've been robbed, Sheriff!" Durham exclaimed.

Everett was stunned. Robberies didn't happen in Apology.

"How much money did they get?" he asked.

"Money!" Deke shouted. "Hell, Everett, you know we ain't' got no money. They got something worse."

Everett studied the frantic looks on their faces as Old Duke walked up behind them. He glanced at Duke, remembering how he'd teased his deputy a few minutes before when he thought he'd be dealing with some simple problem like disturbing the peace.

"They got our guns!" Durham shouted, his face contorted in agony.

"Your guns?" Everett asked, surveying their faces. "Did they take anything else?"

Durham pulled his head back.

"Ain't that enough?" he answered. "That's like taking our checkbook."

"Let me get out," Everett said, waving the boys away from the door. "Let's go see."

Everett and Duke followed the brothers to the back entrance to the house. Everett examined the door.

"No forcible entry, by the look of it," he observed. "No scratches or pry marks that I can see. Nothing."

"Hell, the thing wasn't even locked," Deke explained. "We lost the key about a year and a half ago."

"We think it dropped in the dog dish," Durham explained, pointing to a round plastic bowl on the ground. "And the dog swallowed it. I dug through his crap for a week but never did find it. Anyway, we don't lock the house anymore 'cause we ain't got no key."

Everett looked past the brothers, watching the Petler dog wagging its tail. Most of the time the dog stayed in his doghouse, content to lie on the cool dirt floor until feeding time unless some stranger with a tasty leg ventured onto the property. But as the men crowded around the door, the dog sensed that feeding time might be earlier on this day.

"Get back," Durham ordered, looking meanly at the dog.

With that the dog retreated back to the safety of his house, his tail bent to the ground. Duke, who'd momentarily disappeared, returned, munching a dill pickle.

"Now we got two thieves, I see," Deke said.

"Just checking the cellar," Duke replied calmly. "Say, these are good."

"You can just finish that pickle out here, Duke," Everett said. "Let me check inside with the boys."

Duke entered the house, aware that he hadn't been inside the place for over two years. The dead fly that had been smeared across the front of the refrigerator door by the blow of a swatter last time he visited was still there, drying nicely among some advertising magnets. A stack of food-encrusted dishes filled the kitchen sink, the white porcelain sink rimmed by a brown coat of stain from the iron-bearing well water stagnating among the dishes. From what Everett could see around him, the entire kitchen was in a state of turmoil, and the general smell of needin'-cleanin' permeated the room.

"Where did you keep the guns?" Everett asked, running a finger along the dust covering the stove.

"In here," Deke answered, motioning.

Everett followed. In a small room off the kitchen, Deke pointed to a table filled with trophies and ribbons. The sheer number of awards sitting on the table surprised Everett. If only Owen Fuller could see this, Everett thought, it might convince the mayor that his decision to let the boys resume their shooting in town had been a wise move.

"There," Deke pointed as Durham stood beside him. "We kept them right on the table under that towel."

The towel now rested on the floor beneath the table. Everett reached to pick it up. The cloth smelled of gun oil.

"Who could have done this?" Durham asked angrily. "What kind of a lowlife would steal a shooter's gun?"

27 A Brotherhood of Heroes

The call went out from Everett's office to help hunt down the dirty, lowdown skunks who had stolen the two pistols from the Petler's house. A reward poster was tacked to the front door of Duffy's Tavern, with someone adding "DEAD OR ALIVE" in red magic marker below the $200 reward printed in big black letters.

Everett half-heartedly checked around town but his lawman's instincts told him that Apology wasn't the place to look for his thieves. With burly Duffy in the car, the two drove to Lost Meadows and confronted Neal Rider, the owner of the Lost Meadows Tavern. Though he knew little about the man, Everett's intuition told him the tavern owner was the man he sought. Abandoned by the Petler brothers, and embarrassed in front of the patrons who frequented the

Lost Meadows Tavern, Neal Rider had a strong motive to take some sort of action. Neal swore up and down that he knew nothing about the robbery, but with no proof to continue the investigation, Duffy paid the man back for the gasoline in Deke's tank and Everett and Duffy returned to Apology. But the man's body language made Everett even more suspicious that Neal Rider was their culprit.

"I still think it was him that done it," Everett told Duffy in confidence. "But until the guns are found, or until some witness comes forward, I can't do much. But don't tell the Petlers that I suspect Neal Rider. They're pretty hot right now and might try to handle it their own way. And I don't want that happening."

"What are we gonna do now, Everett?" Durham moaned when Everett reported to the boys that his search had come up empty. "Look at the fix we're in."

Several citizens town attempted to solve the problem created by the missing guns. No one could afford to put up the kind of cash necessary to replace the Petler pistols. The expense was just too great for that type of firearm, and two pistols, in fact, were needed. Offers came in from others to loan the boys guns, but in Iowa, most of the firearms were shotguns, with an occasional rifle collecting dust in a garage. There was nothing else available in the community except a flare gun someone had brought home from Korea. Everett's pistol was the only gun of any quality, and he wasn't about to loan that out to anyone.

Two days later Everett stopped at Duffy's in the early afternoon, just by happenstance. The tavern appeared empty.

"Anybody here?" Everett shouted.

He heard a noise from the back room as something dropped hard on the floor. Everett instinctively went for his gun, grabbing the pistol butt as he crouched.

"Be right with you!" Duffy shouted, poking his head through a doorway.

Everett eased his hand off the gun butt and stood up.

"Oh, hi, Everett," Duffy greeted cheerfully. "You're just the person I want to see. Let me clean up back here and then I'll be right out."

Duffy lifted a finger toward Everett.

"Now don't go away."

Everett looked past the doorway as Duffy disappeared inside. The floor was littered with odds and ends tumbling from three shelves that had collapsed like dominoes when Duffy tried to balance his body against them. In spite of the mess, Duffy found what he had been searching for. He reemerged from the backroom, carrying a flat, wooden box.

"You ain't gonna believe what I got, Everett" he said, grinning.

"If you were to ask me, I'd say it looks like you've found somebody's silver place setting," Everett guessed.

"Better than that," Duffy answered, opening the lid on the chest to reveal its contents. "Much better."

Everett, expecting to see neat rows of silver eating utensils, was amazed by what the chest actually held. Resting on a lining of red felt were two pistols.

"Dueling pistols," Duffy grinned. "Replicas, at least."

Everett pulled one of the weapons from the chest, the gun leaving an impression where it had rested. The pistol was a replica all right, with a heavy dark barrel and a smooth shiny finish on the dark wood of the grip.

"It breaks open like a double-barrel shotgun," Duffy said, pointing to the hinge in front of the trigger.

"A single shot?" Everett asked.

"Both of them," Duffy replied. "They're a set, identical. And they work."

"Where'd they come from?" Everett asked.

"I've had them for ten years, I bet," Duffy answered. "Got them at a farm sale, stuck in with a bunch of tools. The owner had died and the daughter was in from California, trying to liquidate everything fast. I was more interested in the sanders and routers than these. I had no use for them so I just stored them away. Just thought about them now and found them."

"And I suppose you want to loan them to the Petlers?"

"Why not? They're good guns."

"Their guns are six-shooters," Everett explained, "not single shots."

"Well," Duffy argued, "their six-shooters have come up amongst the missing. So they ain't practicing with anything, are they? Is there any reason why they can't use these until their own guns are found? At least to practice with?"

Everett studied the weapon, breaking open the gun he held. Peering down the barrel he spied the second pistol resting in the box.

"You say these work?"

"Not only do they work, but they're forty-fives."

"Hmm," Everett said. "Same caliber as the Petlers use. I guess it wouldn't hurt to ask them. At least the boys will know we're trying to help them out."

Everett accepted the chest and drove to the Petler place. The sheriff made a big fanfare out of opening the chest, getting the brothers excited about what mysterious secret lay inside. When he finally opened the lid the pistols glistened against the backdrop of red felt, like booty in a treasure chest.

"Wowwee!" Durham shouted. "Look at those guns. Boy, do they shine."

Deke, more skeptical, picked one up.

"Hey, these only shoot one bullet. They ain't no good to us, Everett."

"Oh, but they're so pretty," Durham said.

"Well, how many bullets can you shoot at once, Deke?" Everett asked.

"Only one," he replied. "But we shoot a bunch of bullets at one of those meets."

"Well, can't you practice with these, at least?" Everett asked.

"Yea, can't we?" Durham asked. "These sure are pretty guns."

Durham hadn't shot in a three days. Not only was he enthralled by the pistol's beauty, he was also anxious to shoot.

"They're forty-fives," Everett said. "Same caliber as you boys use."

He handed the second gun to Deke, who examined it, balancing it in his hand.

"Kinda clumsy at first, but it feels OK, I guess," he said finally. "I might get used to it."

"Got a shell?" Everett asked.

"Always," Durham said, pulling a bullet from the pocket of his blue jeans.

"Why don't you see how this thing shoots then?" Everett asked. "Before you make a judgment."

"Guess it wouldn't hurt," Deke answered.

Not waiting for his brother, Durham broke open his pistol and shoved home a shell.

"See that leaf on the end of that oak limb," Everett pointed. "Try hitting that."

Durham aimed the weapon where Everett indicated, steadying his hand.

"You gonna shoot that gun or let the birds perch on it?" Deke asked.

"Never you mind, Deke," Durham answered. "Just checking the wind direction."

The muzzle exploded and the leaf flew from the tree as the bullet split the stem holding it to the branch.

"Not a bad shot, Durham," Everett said. "What do you think?"

"Not a bad shot, he says," Durham answered. "That was a hell of a shot. I think I could get used to this. And real quick."

"Well, Deke, what do you think?" Everett asked, encouragingly.

"I suppose we could use them," Deke finally said. "But it'd only be for practice. You gotta find our guns before the Turkey Shoot at Fair River."

"I'll see what I can do," Everett replied. "But you boys just keep on practicing. Like we said, Duffy will foot the bill for your ammo, so don't worry about your expenses. Just worry about your shooting."

As Everett pulled away from the property he noted that Deke had loaded his gun and was busy firing at a tin can fifty feet away.

"It's music to my ears," Owen Fuller told Everett as the slow, methodical sound of gunfire returned to the west end of Apology.

What Owen more likely meant, Everett figured, was that the mayor would just as soon hear the Petler's guns than Bonnie's incessant ranting again.

A week before the Thanksgiving Day Shoot, Deke and Durham focused intently on their marksmanship. The pair learned to aim, fire, break down, and reload their weapons with the smoothness of a machine. The reloading part had been annoying to the boys at first, but they had overcome the extra step through patience and practice. The boys picked up a natural rhythm in the process, their love of the gun overcoming all obstacles. Some residents of the town commented that the gunfire wasn't all that bad because the boys shot very slowly and methodically. The gunfire sounded less menacing than when the pair would act like they were at the OK Corral, blasting twelve shells in a matter of ten seconds, and then repeat the same procedure over and over again.

Two days before the shoot, Everett visited the boys with the news.

"You're gonna have to shoot with those," he said. "Because whoever has your pistols has not been caught."

The Petlers, having practiced with their new guns, brimmed with confidence.

"OK," Deke said. "We'll shoot with these. But we want to own them. We want to go to the shoot holding our own weapons. Then we'll go to Fair River for the town."

Everett could see their point. He had his own weapon at his side, purchased with his own money. It was a point of pride, not to be obliging to anyone. That was all right with Duffy, who'd gotten the guns free when he'd purchased some tools at a sale ten years earlier.

"Tell them they can have the guns," he told Everett. "But only if they win at Fair River. They don't mean much to me but it might make them a little more hungry."

The Petlers had done all right. Not only did they get ammo, shirts, gas money, and entrance fee taken care of by Duffy, but they now owned the guns if they won at Fair River. Lost Meadows never offered that kind of deal, or anything close.

On Thanksgiving Day most of the town of Apology watched at Fair River as Deke Petler, wearing the embroidered words "DUFFY'S TAVERN, APOLOGY IOWA" across his back, hit center target on forty-nine of fifty shots, shooting and reloading with a rhythm never seen before at the meet. Durham, wearing a shirt identical to Deke's, did better, blasting fifty out of fifty centers for the only perfect shoot of the meet. The prize money and guns were theirs as the citizens of the town gathered round to celebrate their new heroes.

At Duffy's that night, an intoxicated Durham stood on the bar and peed in his beer glass, prompting Everett to drive him home. During the ride home, Durham, through slurred words, told Everett how he hoped winter would hurry up and pass, and how he would use the prize money to buy a new six-shooter in the spring.

28 Winter Time

The starkness of winter has a way of cleansing the land, in a much different way than any warm spring rain can do. For while the snow of winter and the rain of spring bring something very physical, the winter adds something spiritual as well. The snows seem to filter off some of the meanness in people, decreasing the amount of collective orneriness available for distribution. Perhaps the falling white powder reminds people of a purity they should be seeking throughout their lifetime, because it is a fact that fewer crimes are committed during the winter months. Gentle winds shift the fallen snow over the vast horizon of empty fields laid bare by the harvest, the white blanket in sharp contrast with the black soil sprouting through the whiteness, the very soil of nurture now the crop until spring. In this contrast between snow and soil, Mother Nature reminds all that, in her world, there are few areas of gray. Those are inventions man has chosen to make.

During the winter months the town of Apology pretty much just buttons up its coat and waits out the weather. The winter is a busy time for Bert Kestral, plowing the snow and salting the blacktop and gravel roads while occasionally pulling cars from ditches. The town council hibernates, going through the motions of government, but really accomplishing nothing. The three Fuller boys and Scrapper Himmel spend a lot of time on Jasper Knob, a small but prominent rise of land near the town's northwestern border, just right for sledding. A small pond at the base of the knob turns to ice, offering a smooth surface for sliding. The smooth frames of Bonnie Fuller's kitchen chairs are made of chromed aluminum, and when Owen and Bonnie are away, Arnold, Bull, and Fuller drag the chairs to the top of Jasper Knob and ride them down the hill as sleds, returning them to the kitchen before their parents return to find out.

The gravel pit, Everett's duck blind, and the fields around Apology rest idly during winter, trapped motionless until the coming of spring thaws the hourglass of time once more. Fletcher's Creek freezes over, except where the water flows swiftest, and occasionally a late arriving duck finds that water. The creek turns clear as murky sediments drop from the slower moving water to lie in slumber in the creek bed until the spring floods wake them with violent churning.

The Petler boys retire to the warmth of their homes, opening a window once or twice a day to throw corn to the waiting chickens. If the boys forget to close the storm cellar door before the first snow hits, it remains open all winter, and the brine left in the pickle barrel freezes, spoiling any dills left inside. Everett Hiram keeps sheriffing, happy that his town is more subdued during these months.

Some folks celebrate winter by enjoying outdoor sports. Doris Donahue enjoys sports, too. But watching is what she does mostly, peering between the slit in her front room curtains, like a baby peeking through the womb to catch its first glimpse of the world outside.

After Grumpy died, Doris was pretty lonely that first year, and she'd sit in the front room, watching every little thing that happened outside her window. What she soon found out was, that even to a new widow, the action outside was pretty thin. Sometimes the only person

Doris talked to all day was Zippy Martin as he delivered the mail, and even he shied away after a few weeks, thinking that the new widow might be taking a fancy toward him. In reality Doris just wanted a few words with anyone who happened along. Zippy's misinterpretation of the widow's intentions made the rounds at Duffy's for a while, unduly tainting the women's reputation. But God, in His greater glory, was looking out for Doris. After a few weeks of ribbing by the boys about how the widow Doris was sweet on him, Zippy regretted that he'd brought up the matter to the patrons at the tavern, for his red ears were now completing penance for his sin of slander.

The only thing that seemed to bring delight to Doris was the children who passed by her house as they returned home from school each day. The trouble was, they passed too quickly, leaving Doris longing for more of the youthful gaiety they brought to her heart.

Grumpy had died in late November, and by January, his estate had settled, leaving Doris with more money than she would ever need. Perhaps it was with this knowledge that Doris devised a plan to keep children lingering in front of her house a little longer.

One cold night in late January Doris left her house, carrying a pitcher of water, heading for a shallow depression next to the sidewalk in front of her house. Doris brushed the snow away and filled the depression with clear water, and then pulled a dollar from the pocket of her coat. She pressed the money to the bottom of the depression and left. During the night the water froze.

Doris waited for the children the next afternoon, peeking through the curtains as she always did. She spotted them approaching the ice pond she'd created the night before, hoping they'd look down. They did, discovering the dollar bill trapped in the ice. Doris watched them pointing down, and knew by their movements that they were excited about their find. At first they looked around suspiciously, almost as if they'd done something wrong, but their excitement soon overcame their caution. The children began to kick at the ice, but his approach proved fruitless

One of the boys found a stick and began poking at the ice, only to have the wood break before any progress was made. Doris watched from behind her slit, overjoyed at the events taking place. Watching the children, it dawned on her that the happiness she now felt was partially the result of Grumpy's tightwad ways. Grumpy would never have offered a dollar to anyone unless he received something in return. The boy who'd broken the stick took one of the shorter pieces and attempted to pry the entire block of ice from the ground. After numerous attempts her grew frustrated and gave up.

A small girl approached the ice, holding a large rock in her hand. The rest of the kids tried to steal the prize from her, but she resisted, keeping the rock above her head. The group surrounded the small pond, as if a treasure chest lay buried below them. The only barrier standing between them and the candy counter at Merle's Grocery was two inches of ice. The girl lifted the rock high and then dropped it on the ice. The force of the stone cracked the face of the ice and a second attempt shattered the ice into pieces. Doris clapped her hands with delight as the children cheered their success. Prying the bill from the bottom of the depression, a boy held the prize high, a jagged chunk of ice still clinging to one edge of the dollar. Chattering with excitement, the group headed toward downtown. Merle's Grocery would see some serious candy buying on this day, and Doris's heart leapt once more as the children returned with chocolate lips to reclaim the schoolbooks they'd abandoned in the snow.

So far during the winter months following Grumpy's death the children had found dollar bills on three occasions, but apparently hadn't caught on to Doris' game yet. Grumpy had often reminded Doris to make a dollar stretch, and Doris, in clear conscience, thought it was money well spent.

The confinement of winter brings creativity in many forms, which is what got the Dwivel-Othoco billboard tiff going over fifty years before. And some things just don't change much as the years roll by. And that's true in Apology, too, during these purification months. Some winters seem longer than others, and because of this, a seemingly small incident can mushroom into something much more interesting, like it did one night with Tall George Himmel.

It all started over which freezes faster, hot water or cold water. At Duffy's Tavern one Friday night in early January, that particular subject had come up. A heated discussion began about anti-freeze and the theory behind it and why it had to be mixed with water in the first place. As it always happened with this sort of situation, two sides formed, and the conversation grew more heated as the night wore on. One side argued that cold water would freeze faster because it was already cold, so all it had to do was freeze. But the other side argued that hot water froze faster because it took as much energy to cool the water down as it did to freeze it. And once it was cooled down it just naturally froze. So, about two hours later, twelve men stood in the alley behind Duffy's, beer bottles in hand, their eyes fixed on two cake pans full of water. As they waited, they discussed all sorts of other important things that came to mind, such as how cold their toes were getting.

No one remembers how the argument was resolved, or even if it ever was. It is known that Tall George arrived home very late that evening, and Mamie was waiting for him. Tall George couldn't recall who gave him the ride home, but he does remember someone telling him to kiss Mamie for them in a specific, but unmentioned part of her anatomy.

"Hi, sweety," George began happily as Mamie walked onto the front porch, "You know, I'm supposed to kiss you where the sun don't—"

Kevin M. Prochaska

That is about as far as he got with that request. About the time George hit the front porch, Mamie lit into him like pigs at a slopping trough, informing him that it was two in the morning and he stunk like a brewery. George tried to defend himself, but he admitted, he'd had a beer or so and some pickled pigs feet to boot. A smart man would have kept quiet, knowing that the whole affair would have blown over by the morning. But instead George found himself tangled in a shouting match with Mamie under the light of a full moon of a January sky. Yelling's not a bad thing, but when the normally mild-mannered George got mad, he did something he usually didn't do—he swore.

About fifty feet from the front porch sat a watering trough made from a wooden barrel sawed in half. The trough sat beneath a tall pole, and on top of the pole a bright light illuminated the property at night. One of many kinds of animals that drank from the trough included George's dog, who'd ambled onto the property one day as a young pup. As common practice in this part of the country, people who didn't want their cats or dogs just drove by someone's farm and let the animals go, knowing that they'll wander into a home. That's how George happened to own the young pup he'd named Bomber.

George had always wanted a hunting dog and saw no reason why this young puppy wouldn't do. So, as the puppy grew, George began to train it to hunt. Everything went along fine at first, but Bomber was just a puppy and wanted to play rather than participate in this strange game with its stringent set of rules. George grew frustrated as Bomber grew, then angry after five months of stupid dog training. And when George got angry he swore. One day, George, fed up with what he felt was the young dog's just plain stubbornness, grabbed the animal by the nape of the neck and tossed it into the water trough. The dog plunged beneath the surface of the water.

"You dumb bastard!" he shouted, as the dog's head popped up like the periscope of a submarine. "You dumb bastard!"

Over the next few weeks, George, increasingly frustrated with the animal's inability to learn, continued to pitch the dog into the trough after any minor infraction during training. Each time the man found failure with Bomber, the animal sailed through the air and into the water as George swore at it in mid-launch. But the animal actually did learn something with George's new approach to training. After a while all George would have to do was yell "You dumb bastard!" and the dog would run to the trough and jump into the water. That was good in a way, for the dog eventually got too big for George to throw, and the fact that Bomber would volunteer to make a hole in the water by himself made the whole process a lot easier on George's back. It also gave George something to show visitors when they came to the house–the jumping swear dog–except, of course, he could never show Father Coleman.

Now as George stood arguing with Mamie that night, he swore, using some of those very words he had used while attempting to train Bomber. He wasn't calling Mamie those words, mind you, but just blurting out general information to the sky above. The dog, older and wiser now, heeded George's command, and without hesitation ran over and jumped into the water trough, as the animal had been taught. A small geyser exploding into the sky escaped George's notice as he stood trying to extol his virtues to Mamie. Bomber bounded back out of the trough, dazed from diving through a layer of ice crusting the water. The dog shivered in the cold, satisfied that he had been obedient to his master's wish. George, in the midst of a heated debate with Mamie, failed to notice Bomber, who waited for some sort of well-done sign.

As the discussion got a little more intense, George swore once more, and then again, marking his profanities with the precision-like timing of a cuckoo clock. The second time the dog plunged, the animal found the going easier, for the thin crust of ice he'd crashed through during his first dive was now a mish-mash of floating puzzle pieces. Each time George swore Bomber jumped into the trough and right back out again. George swore many times over the next ten minutes as he proclaimed his innocence to Mamie and the Iowa sky.

Finally convinced that her husband had learned his lesson, which is the only thing she had really wanted in the first place, Mamie stopped harping at him, instructing George that he was not to come home this late again. Mamie pecked George lightly on the cheek and stepped into the house without another word, leaving the man alone on the front porch, exhausted and bewildered by this abrupt ending. It was only then that George spotted Bomber, lying on his back in the snow, panting for all it was worth, a cold, frosty mist rising above him. Shards of ice clung to the dog's rapidly freezing fur. Bomber, surviving his marathon training session, was spent.

"What's wrong with you, you dumb bastard?" George spat at the dog.

Bomber, hearing the command one more time, struggled to his feet and galloped to the water trough, plunging into the icy water as George, oblivious to his dog's action, staggered inside.

The next morning George took Bomber to Renoir and let it go by the stockyards, where, three months later, Merle Oaken unknowingly purchased the dog to train as a guide dog, calling him Rooney. That might have explained why it didn't bother the dog to sit in the flowing waters of Fletcher's Creek later, eating a trophy mallard, as Merle Oaken shouted obscenities at him–kinda like Tall George used to do.

29   The Spring of Discontent

The spring arrived, bringing two crises to the town as the last isolated patches of muddied snow sought in vain to hide from the dawning of a warmer sun. The first crisis was rather small, and corrected rather easily, as it had planned to be. The second would require a little more effort.

The previous fall Irk Hickenlooper had taken control of the large piece of farmland that bordered Apology to the north, casually mentioning a few weeks before the planting season that he was going to put soybeans into the field instead of corn. This bit of news raised the hackles of some of the townsfolk, who were hoping that the field would sprout corn, the reason being, of course, that they could send their kids through the cornrows to buy beer on Sunday from Merle

Oaken's back door. Irk had the last laugh, finally letting people know that he'd been pulling their leg and had planned to plant corn all along. Unfortunately for Irk, his reputation underwent various shades of defamation from those whose backs ached from toting cases of beer down steep, cramped steps, stockpiling their favorite beverage in cellars while the womenfolk were away. Now, to their dismay, all that work was to be for naught because the corn would be there and they were free to purchase their beer via the Cornrow Express anyway. For a population whose modus operandi was to wait until tomorrow to do something if don't need to be done today, this farsightedness proved a total waste of time and money.

The second crisis erupted when the Petler boys announced at Duffy's their intent to resume practice with their single-shots, and with their winnings purchase new six-shot repeaters. The boys had planned to use the money they'd won at Fair River the prior fall, but their nest egg had been squandered on a multitude of vices during the darkness of the winter months. To the citizens of Apology, who had reveled in the glory honey the Petler boys won for the town in November, the memories had, unfortunately, grown stale. However

437

traitorous that would appear to an outsider, the town had gotten used to the silence the winter had brought to the west end, and it was only natural that the fickleness of the human animal would rise up to ask the age old question, "What have you done for me today?"

"Why do they need new guns?" Viola Vanderhoff wailed. "Those dang six-shooters raise too much ruckus."

"I know they stood for the town," Amy Flanigan stated. "But a good citizen should do the right thing just because they're a good citizen."

"I paid them Petler boys plenty," Duffy complained. "And Durham still peed on my bar."

This Brutus-like affection of the townsfolk toward their Caesars of November had played itself out on more than one occasion during the history of Apology, with different players and reasons each time, though the turnaround time in this case seemed to be cutting it a little close to the memory bone. The first town meeting of the year was called.

"I can't see why the Petlers can't go on using those guns they have," Bonnie Fuller moaned. "They make half as much noise."

Bonnie had a point. The Petlers could only fire one bullet at a time, she argued, not six. That was tolerable at least, for it cut down on the number of bullets fired, over a longer period of time, and reduced the irritating noise of the rapidly chattering six-shooter. Once again the town council ruled about what kind of rules would govern the discharge of guns within the borders.

"It is the opinion of the town council," Owen Fuller explained to the crowd at the meeting that night, "that the town of Apology will limit firearm discharge to those weapons capable of holding only one bullet. No exceptions will be considered nor given."

With that, Owen pounded the table with a gavel as heads nodded in agreement. Everett was called on once more to enforce this order, his first duty being to notify the brothers of the new law.

"But we shot for the town just four months ago," Durham said, bewildered. "What about that?"

"I know," Everett explained. "But they just want you to continue with what you were doing. It will cut down on the noise, that's all. Use the singles, boys. They work–you found that out at Fair River, didn't you?"

439

The boys couldn't disagree with the sheriff–they'd won solidly with Duffy's pistols. And, Everett explained, they didn't have any guns to shoot with anyway except the ones they now held.

"Spend your winnings somewhere else," Everett told them. "You have guns already. You don't need any more."

The boys agreed, and everything seemed right with the town. Farmers on tractors pulling disks or plows hit the fields, raising swarming dust clouds as the warmer weather sucked the final beads of moisture from the soil. Not far behind came the planters, dropping corn and soybean seeds in symmetrical lines, each farmer trying to outdo the other with the perfection of straight-as-an-arrow rows. Once again the spring brought forth order as crops sprang from the soil in regimented uniformity.

One night a dark figure crept from this order and onto the Petler property, hurling a gigantic chunk of raw steak toward the dog as he opened the gate. The dog greedily accepted the two pounds of bloody meat and obligingly let the intruder pass unhindered. A little past sunrise, Durham stepped out onto the back porch and tripped on a hard lump sitting on the top step, his butt landing squarely in the dog's food dish. When he recovered, he summoned Deke to show him what he'd found.

BLAM-BLAM-BLAM-BLAM. BLAM-BLAM-BLAM-BLAM.

Everett answered Bonnie Fuller's call.

"Them Petler boys have got a hold of some new guns, Sheriff!" she yelled over the phone, "and are over there breaking the law. I can hear that racket clear up here."

Disgusted by the news, Everett immediately visited the Petlers. He found them as Bonnie had said, blasting away at paper targets with six-shooters.

"I thought you boys was going to use the single shots," Everett said. "Where in the hell did you get the money to buy new guns, anyway?"

"But Everett," Durham replied excitedly, "look. See what we got. Our pistols are back."

"Yea," Deke said. "They showed up this morning, sitting on the back porch."

"They did?" Everett asked.

"Yep," Durham said happily. "Like manna from heaven. I guess whoever took them finally got guilty."

"Sounds kinda strange to me," Everett said. "Why would someone risk getting caught to return something they stole? Something they could have sold?"

"Beats me," Deke said. "But I'm glad they did."

"They won't do you much good," Everett warned. "Remember the new law about single shot pistols only?"

"You're not gonna really enforce that, are you, Everett?" Deke asked.

"It's not that I want to boys, you know that. It's that I have to. And besides, you boys agreed to abide by that law."

"Well sure, Everett," Durham replied. "But that's when we only had single shots. Things has changed now. Our guns is back."

Everett didn't like the new law or much care for the fickleness of the town toward their heroes of the previous fall. He didn't like having to enforce the new law, either. But in another way he did–it would make his job easier and convince the tongue waggers that he didn't favor anyone.

"I tell you what you can do," Everett suggested to Deke and Durham, as they continued to talk beneath a large tree on the Petler property. "Why don't you practice with the single shots and fire off the six-shooters at the meets? That sounds fair, don't it? That way everybody will be happy and things won't get messy. Understand me, boys?"

Everett's suggestion that the boys practice with the single shots at their house and use their own six-shooters at the meets seemed to work. Deke and Durham admitted that was a pretty darn good idea, and with this new policy in place, there would be no mess to clean up at all. It was a win-win situation for everyone involved, and everyone appeared to be appeased by the plan.

Just a week before their first shooting meet of the year, Deke and Durham visited a sporting goods store in Renoir, purchasing ammunition, where they chanced to meet Horace J. Tallmite, gun enthusiast. Horace was a small man, but came across as loud and bully-like, sounding like a politician when he spoke. Horace wore round, wire-rimmed glasses, the intent of which was to make him look more intelligent. There was nothing special about Horace that would normally attract the Petler boys to him, but they found themselves talking guns to the man, and about their practicing restraints with the town of Apology. Horace took a keen interest in this particular part of the conversation, for he was a lawyer, five years graduated from Drake Law School, he told the boys. Horace smelled a strong case of injustice in the air, and with his lawyer lingo, told the boys that they could go ahead and shoot whenever they wanted on their own property. The law couldn't do a thing, he told them. Assured up by the smooth talking attorney, Deke and Durham did just that, blasting away with righteousness.

"Whatta ya arrestin' us for, Everett?" Durham asked as Everett cuffed him.

"You know darn well what for," Everett explained gruffly. "We had a deal all worked out with you two. That you two yahoos agreed to, I might add."

"But somebody told us that you couldn't do that," Deke moaned as Everett guided the man's red head below the roof of the patrol car as he took them into custody.

"I don't know who told you that," Everett shot back, "but I'm just upholding the law that you boys agreed to abide by."

Just as Horace J. Tallmite had planned, the Petler boys went to jail. But surprisingly, the boys made bail and were soon free.

"What the hell is this?" Owen Fuller screamed, flashing some papers at Everett.

Everett studied the papers.

"We're being sued," Everett said, "it looks like. By the Petler brothers."

"Sued for what?" Owen roared.

"Denying them their constitutional right to bear arms, I guess," Everett replied. "If I'm reading this paper correctly."

"Well, you just go down there and tell them boys to quit this foolishness," Owen instructed. "Tell them they can eat that paper for lunch."

Everett visited the Petler place as he was told. There he found an unfamiliar car in the driveway and a spectacled stranger in the back yard.

"Hi, Everett," Durham grinned.

445

Everett glanced at the stranger seated in the lawn chair beneath the shade tree.

"What's this all about boys?" Everett asked, waving the legal papers.

The stranger stood, extending his hand.

"Let me introduce myself, Sheriff Hiram," he said. "I'm Horace J. Tallmite, and I'll be representing Deke and Durham Petler in their upcoming lawsuit against the town of Apology."

The man wore a strong cologne that reminded Everett of the inside of a cathouse, even though Everett had never darkened the door of such an establishment.

"I'm afraid I'll have to ask you not to talk to my clients, Sheriff," Horace instructed, "unless in the presence of the town's attorney and myself."

"What's in it for this Tallmite guy?" Owen asked, when Everett reported back. "He's got to know the Petlers have no money to pay him. Maybe when he realizes that, he'll head back to Des Moines and leave us run our town as we see fit."

If the town thought this incident a small matter, their eyes were opened the following day when a news truck pulled up and parked just beneath the water tower. A reporter from a TV station in Des Moines, alerted by a call from Horace Tallmite, visited the town, accompanied by a news crew. Horace explained when he'd telephoned the station that the Petler plight would make a nice human-interest story, of two innocent victims trying to make an honest living, being harassed by a town government bent on seeing to their failure. A few minutes after the camera crew had set up under the water tower, Horace arrived, the Petler brothers in tow.

The reporter stood in front of a camera, a breeze stirring his sandy hair, and began to speak.

"Leslie Lemming, reporting for Channel Six News Rural Rover, where we bring you interesting stories of small town life here in Iowa. I'm here in Apology, in southern Corwith County, reporting on a story of interest to all you gun lovers out there. I'm standing directly below the town's water tower, and as you can see by the big black letters on the tower above me, someone is obviously in need of a spelling lesson. Now it seems that two residents of the town, brothers

447

Deke and Durham Petler, are taking the town of Apology to court over the issue of guns. The town says it's OK to have a gun, but they just want to control the noise and the number of bullets being fired. So they have put restrictions on the brothers, who compete as pistol shooters for their livelihood. The town has told the Petler boys they can only shoot single shot pistols within the city limits, a law the brothers contend violates their constitutional rights."

The reporter motioned for the three men to come forward. Deke and Durham faced the camera, Durham grinning like a cat, while Deke was obviously uneasy. Horace stood next to them, exuding the confidence of a campaigning politician who's just gotten word that his opponent has dropped dead of a heart attack.

The reporter continued.

"These two men are Deke and Durham Petler, residents of Apology, who maintain that they are being unfairly treated by the town because of the way they make their livelihood. And this is their attorney, Mr. Horace J. Tallmite, who has filed suit at the Corwith County courthouse in Renoir for the Petlers, against the town of

Apology, seeking to overturn what he insists is an unconstitutional act by the town. How do you see this going, Mr. Tallmite?"

"I actually don't see the case taking very long to hear," Horace replied, looking into the camera. "The town of Apology is obviously in the wrong here and they know it. This is just one more case of big brother attempting to impinge on the rights of citizens who have done absolutely nothing wrong. And I intend to see to it that justice speaks for these gentlemen. The United States Constitution is very clear on the right to bear arms, and I find it very ironic that a town whose very laws are rooted under the flag of democracy would seek to deprive anyone of their constitutional rights."

The reporter held the mike under Durham.

"What do you say to that, Mr. Petler?"

Durham held his hand up, waving as he grinned.

"I'd just like to say hi to my Aunt Ruth in Lost Meadows–"

Horace put his hand over the mike and pulled it away from Durham.

"As you can see," Horace explained, "the man is quite confused by all this legal entanglement that the town of Apology has thrust upon him."

Horace looked into the camera once more.

"All Mr. Petler wants is to do is to be allowed to exercise his constitutional rights, just like everyone in this country wants."

The reported regained the mike, pulling it away from the attorney.

"And now we go to Howie Sternbergen, at the Corwith County Courthouse in Renoir."

They watched a monitor in the back of the van as a face appeared on its screen.

"Yes, Leslie, as you can see behind me, I'm standing in front of the Corwith County courthouse in Renoir, about twenty miles from you, where this confrontation between the Petler brothers and the town of Apology will be played out. Judge Claudius Einpapple, the most experienced judge in Corwith County, has agreed to hear the case."

"Howie, do you have any feel as to how this trial will go," Leslie asked. "I mean, is there any legal substance to what the town has done?"

"From what my sources tell me, Leslie, this well may be a precedent-setting case, pitting an individual's clearly stated constitutional rights against a community's assertion that they be allowed not to take away that right, but to restrict it for the good of the majority."

"Damn them Petlers!" Owen shouted as he watched the newscast with Everett. "And damn that sweet-talking two-suited lawyer of theirs. What a dirty rotten trick to pull."

What Owen was referring to was the fact that, when the news truck was under the water tower preparing their story, the town had not yet received any official notification whatsoever of the upcoming trial. Horace Tallmite had surged ahead with his plan, unbeknownst to the town. The town council had discussed the issue at length, but concluded that the incident would just blow over, as these things always did in a small community. Feuding citizens had made threats in the past, but they'd always been just threats, and eventually the issue had been resolved. The problem in this particular case was that one extra ingredient had been added to the cake mix, and that ingredient happened to be Horace J. Tallmite, who had no intention of making this crisis easy for anyone.

Viola Vanderhoff phoned Moog Raymond, one of the town council members, berating the group for their failure to act on correcting the misspelling on the water tower.

"See what happens when we don't fix something," she lectured. "Did you see our water tower on the news, held up to ridicule for everyone in the State of Iowa to see? I bet all those big city folks think we're nothing but country hicks now."

"We ain't even got a town attorney," Owen moaned.

Any kind of simple task resembling legal work, like taxes or building permits, had always been handled by Owen.

"Well, looks like we're gonna need one now," Everett said.

Everett's lawman's intuition told him that this legal storm rising over the town might well kick up a bigger tempest than even Olaf Clancy's trial had. And it was all because Horace J. Tallmite appeared to want it that way.

"You know we're gonna have to get a lawyer to represent the town," Everett said.

"You already said that once," Owen snorted. "But who?"

"What about Norman Ludlow?" Everett asked.

"Norman Ludlow," Owen replied. "He's retired. I can't even get him to work on any business for the town. Not even building permits. If he would, I wouldn't have to do some of this stuff. And now you think he's gonna defend us in court?"

"Well, I can get him," Everett declared.

One thing consistent regarding Sheriff Everett Hiram–when he wanted something done, he generally made it happen. And his conscience was clear about employing whatever kind of shady trick it required to make it happen.

Sixty-four year old Norman Ludlow possessed the mental faculties of a man half his age. Norman's immaculately groomed white hair and slightly rotund midsection bestowed upon the man the distinguished look of an elderly statesman. His face shined in the light, the baby pink skin free of blemish. Norman put one in mind of a Southern gentleman often seen on TV shows, grandfatherly, and slow and deliberate when he had something to say. Norman had been retired for three years and had no yearning to practice law anymore, as shown by his refusal to help the town of Apology with even the smallest of matters. Norman lived at the east end of Apology and was rarely seen in public, preferring to stay close to home. The attorney spent a great deal of time alone in his private study, reading books about history, a subject dear to his heart. When Everett arrived to visit, he found Norman in his library.

"I'm sorry, Sheriff," Norman replied politely as he sat amidst a pile of books, wearing a comfortable-looking red and black checkered flannel shirt. "I've made it quite clear that I am retired and don't wish to practice law any further."

"That's probably good, in a way," Everett answered.

"And why would that be?"

Everett went on to explain the Petler's attorney's assessment of Apology; that from what he'd seen since arriving in town, no one within a five mile radius knew what the hell was going on most of the time, and how its citizens were just small town boys trying to play a big city game. Of course, Everett used some liberal interpretation in relaying the man's words to Norman.

"He said what?" Norman asked, sitting up in his chair.

"Horace Tallmite said it," Everett fibbed. "He also said that the lawyers coming out of Drake now are better educated than those that came out of there forty years ago. Said that the only reason Drake put them out on the streets back then, even though they knew better, was that the laws were simpler and anybody would have been able to understand them. Tallmite said that lawyers nowadays have to be more intelligent and savvy when they showed up in the courtroom."

Horace hadn't mentioned a word about Drake Law School, but Everett knew that Norman, like Tallmite, had graduated from that esteemed institution.

"Well, I suppose Horace Tallmite is entitled to his opinion, just like everyone else," Norman said.

"He also mentioned your name specifically, as proof of what he said," Everett lied again. "Said some old goat like you couldn't even get a pro bono offer these days."

"He did, did he?" Norman asked, a glint of fire forming his eyes.

"Well, he probably didn't mean you as an old goat, Norman. Maybe he was just talking about–all old goats in general."

With that salvo, Norman made his decision. Everett may have cut the line on the biggest catfish of his life at Tinker's Lake, but the crafty sheriff had just reeled in an attorney for the town. It was to be Norman P. Ludlow squaring off against Horace J. Tallmite at the Corwith County courthouse in Renoir, in the case of *Deke and Durham Petler vs the Municipality of Apology, Iowa.*

30   The Sweet Scent of Liberty

The spring had been pleasant, the April rains falling on the fields warmer than usual, greedily sucked into the pores of the waiting soil. This cleansing had a dark side however, as Sheriff Everett Hiram had been forced to arrest the Petler brothers on two more occasions for violation of the gun law. Everett made sure to act cordially as he hauled them away, lest the conniving Horace J. Tallmite find opportunity to levy some sort of police brutality charge his way. Everett explained each time he arrested he brothers that it was nothing personal, just the law, and he harbored no ill will against them. Most residents sided with the town, content that the town council was duly exercising its rights by implementing the modified gun law. A few east-enders, however, shielded from the noise by distance, remained aloof.

The trial began on a beautiful day in early May, in the oak-adorned courtroom in Renoir. That such a grand old building served as the site for settling the petty squabbles of the human animal seemed almost a shame, for the building was a magnificent tribute to the beauty man could contribute to the world when he set his mind to it. Native Iowa limestone, cut and shaped to build the outside walls, had been quarried from a site several miles away, and every squared stone was unique unto itself, with individual imperfections of earth's distant past frozen in each limestone block.

In front of the courthouse, large limestone steps led visitors inside, the steps partially covered by a white portico extending along the full length of the steps. Four stately white columns resting on the top step supported the weight of the portico roof. A fresh coat of paint had been applied to each column by order of Judge Claudius Einpapple, and the grounds nearby had been trimmed and meticulously manicured. Flowers had been planted where no flowers had grown before and not a weed was to be found on the property.

The trial attracted news media people from several larger cities in Iowa, and at least one national gun magazine sent a representative to sit with the audience filtering into the courtroom.

The courtroom always carried the faint smell of mildew, the aftermath of a rain-spewing tornado that ripped off half the roof fifty years before, drenching the plaster and wood lath in the walls. Oak panels installed over the tornado-ravaged walls had been designed to hide the damage, and had, but a dank odor continued to seep through the wood. The smell wasn't bad, kind of sweet in fact, and gave people a memory to savor later.

The room where the trial was to be held was arranged in typical courtroom fashion, with rows of audience chairs toward the back, divided evenly by an aisle down the middle. A wooden railing separated the audience from the trial stage, where opposing parties resided at their respective tables. The judge's bench faced the room, elevated like a king's throne. The jury box, situated on the right side, held thirteen chairs arranged in two rows, with a wooden railing isolating the jury.

The courtroom was comfortably filled, but not overcrowded, with body heat staving off the morning chill until the early afternoon sun burst through the tall windows on the west side. The jury, a fashion designer's nightmare, arrived and sat waiting for the judge to emerge from his chamber. At the table in front of the jury box sat Horace Tallmite, speaking to Deke and Durham Petler in a hushed voice.

"Don't worry about all this hype," Horace assured them. "The law is clearly on your side here. This all will be over soon. And then you can get back to your shooting."

Across from them Norman Ludlow sat, with Everett and Owen seated behind him in the front row. Many of the residents of Apology were also in the crowd, including Moog Raymond, Evander Carlson, and Bonnie Fuller.

Everett scanned the room, catching Durham Petler's attention. Durham waved his hand and grinned.

"Hi Everett," he mouthed, when he was sure Horace wasn't watching.

"What is that fool doing?" Owen asked. "Doesn't he know he's on the opposing side?"

461

"What I think," Everett answered, "is that those two boys are just part of the sideshow and they don't know it. Horace Tallmite is here to be the ringmaster. He's got something else on his mind, other than the welfare of Deke and Durham. You can bet on that."

Judge Claudius Einpapple entered the room, and true to the protocols rendered to a man of his stature, the crowd rose, hailing the god of judicial dispensation. Claudius was known to be a fair man, though slow in making decisions. His black robe gave him the distinguished look of academia, as if he were about to make the commencement address at a University of Iowa graduation. His head, surrounded by a nest of wiry brown hair, made him look a bit like a mad scientist, but curiously contributed to the relaxed appearance the judge generally exhibited, whether genuine or not.

Claudius got right to the case, explaining to the jury what their duties were, and instructing the two attorneys to present their opening statements. Norman Ludlow opened, directing his remarks to the jury. Grandfatherly, and with voice betraying little emotion, Norman laid out the town's argument in a business-like manner.

"It is the right," he began, running his hand along the rail in front of the jury box as he walked, "no, I must insist, it is the duty of government to ensure the safety of its citizens. In doing so, a government must take upon itself the authority to pass laws, unpopular as they may be to some, so the majority may benefit. We don't seek, and never have sought, to deny any individual the right to bear arms. That was never our intent. But a government's duty must ensure that the rights of others are not compromised in the process."

Norman stood at the end of the rail, facing the jury.

"We will prove during the course of this trial that the town of Apology acted prudently and within their rights when they restricted the loud and dangerous gunplay of Deke and Durham Petler. The town was within its rights trying to protect the citizens of Apology, including her children, from dangers the town had experienced time and time again."

When Norman completed his opening statements, Horace stood up. Horace walked toward the rail and stood before the jury, not saying a word. He pulled a roll of masking tape from his pocket, and in grand display, ripped a long strip. He held the tape up to his eyes for a moment, studying it, and then slapped it over his mouth. Horace walked along the rail in front of the jury, looking each juror in the eye. Turning away from them, he walked in front of the crowd, looking down at Owen and Everett. Horace returned to the jury, grabbing one end of the strip and violently ripped it from his mouth. He breathed deeply as the tape pulled free, his chest heaving as he raised his hands.

"What you have seen, ladies and gentlemen, is a demonstration of how the town of Apology would handle the constitutional right of free speech, if someone were to dare disagree with town policy."

Horace took another deep breath, his chest with puffing in grandiose gesture as he cupped his upturned palms. His nose flared, sucking in air with all the energy of a blacksmith's bellows.

"But I smell the sweet scent of liberty," he said, shaking a forefinger in the air.

"That bastard," Owen whispered. "Show off."

Norman turned, looking behind him at the mayor. Horace continued.

"You say not? Not in America? That free speech is something guaranteed to everyone, even criminals in this country? That's what I thought just a few short months ago–that our freedoms were sacred, guarded, and carved in stone like this grand old building in which we now are gathered."

He turned to Norman.

"Could a town pass a law making it a crime to speak freely? Well, the town of Apology seems to think so. For in trampling on the sacredness of one constitutional right, they have opened up all our God-given rights to attack, rights that our forefathers fought and died for on the hallowed grounds of Lexington and Concord. If someone could take away one right, like the town of Apology has done to my clients, why not just take them all away, one precious right at a time, until there's nothing left to take at all? Bleeding our fundamental liberties right from our very being. Then we'd be right back where we started two hundred years ago, wouldn't we? That is the crux of this case, my friends, and that is why we must not allow this injustice to go unpunished. Let us send a clear message to the town of Apology, and moreover, to the country."

465

Horace raised his hands once more, palms exposed to the ceiling as he addressed the jury.

'I say, let the bells of liberty continue to ring over this great nation of ours."

His opening statement completed, Horace sat down next to Deke and Durham.

"What a crock of dog doo-doo," Owen said, shaking his head.

"He certainly has a way with words," Everett said. "That was quite a performance."

As a lawman, Everett had experience with the inner workings of a courtroom, and knew that jurisprudence often boiled down to ten percent law and ninety percent acting. He'd heard similar ravings of injustice before, meant to cloud the truth, the flowery patriotism designed to take people's minds off the real reason they were there in the first place.

"Mr. Ludlow, would you kindly call your first witness?" Judge Einpapple asked.

"I call Owen Fuller to the stand," Norman replied.

Owen took the stand and explained the circumstances leading up the enactment of the gun law, beginning with Durham Petler's episode of rooster hunting down Main Street. Owen stated how dangerous this stunt had been, and how bullets had come raining down over the town that day as Durham, drunk, endangered the lives of the citizens. Owen told of the recent survey at the west end of town and how the town's borders had moved to the west, bringing the Petler brothers into the city limits.

Horace Tallmite cross-examined, questioning Owen's comment about Durham's condition as he hunted the rooster.

"So, Mayor Fuller," Horace began, "you confronted Durham Petler on Main Street during the shooting incident with the rooster?"

"No," Owen replied. "I didn't see any of it. Sheriff Hiram told me about it."

"You didn't see any of it," Horace asked, amazed. "So, what you're telling me is just hearsay? You were never really there at all?"

Owen looked toward Everett.

"That's right."

"Well," Horace continued, "what you're tell me is that you didn't see any of these alleged actions purportedly performed by Durham Petler being done. Isn't that right?"

"I didn't see Durham that day, no," Owen admitted, "but I heard about them."

"So if you didn't see Durham, how did you know he was drunk, like it has been alleged that he was?"

"Sheriff Hiram told me later," Owen said.

Owen could offer no proof that Durham had been drunk at the time, only the word of the sheriff. Horace dwelled several minutes on the hearsay issue, making sure that most of what Owen had heard from Everett was thrown out. Horace pressed on, attacking the town's logic regarding moving the boundary.

"So you hog-tied the Petler brothers into becoming citizens of the town!" Horace roared. "When they didn't want to be, didn't ask to be, and were quite content to be outside of town, where they could practice their shooting without any interference from anyone."

Horace continued his questioning, grilling Owen about the shooting incident in the ditch.

"So when you tried to take away Durham's hand gun, without any authority whatsoever to do so I might add, you ended up shooting yourself," Horace explained. "Isn't that right?"

"Not exactly."

Everett knew what the next words would be, for he'd been there before.

"Just answer the question, Mayor Fuller," Horace continued. "Better yet, let me put the question another way. And remember, Mayor, you're under oath. Did Durham Petler shoot you that morning?"

Owen grimaced, then answered sheepishly.

"No."

Horace looked around the room.

"And were the two of you alone in the ditch at the time?"

"Yes," Owen answered.

"So, then," Horace pressed. "If Durham didn't shoot you, then you must have shot yourself."

Owen, his face red as a plump beet, was excused from the witness stand as the room filled with laughter.

Over the next two days, Norman called several witnesses for the town, including the surveyors who'd found the boundary error. Norman did this to prove to the jury that the town had not conspired against the brothers–the boundary error had been a mistake for thirty years, one that needed correcting. Horace thundered back, railing the town fathers for running an incompetent government that didn't even know its own borders and looking for a scapegoat for past misdeeds.

Viola Vanderhoff, Amy Flanigan, and Bonnie Fuller testified for the town, each telling the same story, how the constant gunfire and drunken behavior of the Petler boys had endangered the citizens. Once again, Horace fought back, asking the jury to strike as hearsay all remarks about the Petler brothers being drunk, for no one had offered any proof that this was so.

"Just how many citizens of Apology have the dangerous Petler boys shot, anyway?" Horace asked Viola.

Viola, fidgeting in a witness chair too small for her immense frame, hesitated, and then replied.

"None."

"I'm sorry," Horace apologized, cupping a hand to his ear, "could you say that a little louder for the jury?"

"None," Viola repeated. "They haven't shot anyone."

Horace turned to face the jury, obviously happy with Viola's remark.

"'None,' she said. None."

Horace noted some jurors shifting in their seats, a sign that they were interested.

"So, Mrs. Vanderhoff, what you're trying to tell me is that you have no proof that the boys were drunk when they were shooting, and that these so-called hoodlums haven't hurt a hair on anyone–ever. Would that just about sum it up?"

"Durham shot Owen Fuller," she answered.

"I ask the court to strike that last comment," Horace said quickly. "Nothing of the sort has ever been proven."

"Granted," Judge Einpapple replied. "I'll ask the jury to please disregard the witness' last statement."

Horace turned again to Viola.

"So neither of the Petler boys have ever shot anyone, correct, Mrs. Vanderhoff?"

Viola, her face reddening, answered.

"No."

"No what?"

"No. They've never shot anyone."

A murmur rose from the crowd. Everett glanced to his left, across the aisle, as Viola left the witness stand. Scribbling furiously, the man representing the gun magazine had filled several sheets of paper during Viola's testimony.

Olaf Clancy took the stand, very comfortable in his role, for the last time he'd been at the courthouse he'd been in the hot seat, charged with murdering his wife. Olaf even greeted Claudius Einpapple, the same judge who'd presided over his trial almost three years ago. Norman guided Olaf as the man told the crowd how he'd met up with Everett on Main Street the day Durham shot up the town, and how the sheriff and he had walked to the Petler place to confront the brothers.

"In your opinion, Mr. Clancy," Norman asked, "do you think that Durham Pelter was drunk the day he chased his rooster up Main Street, shooting at it?"

"I think he was," Olaf answered. "His eyes were wild and he smelled like a distillery."

"Anything else?" Norman asked.

"Yea," Olaf replied. "Something even more damning."

"And what would that be?"

"He missed the rooster," Olaf answered.

The crowd chuckled with delight. Olaf went on to explain how Everett had taken Durham's gun away, but had given it back later, cleaned and oiled.

"Did you feel threatened by the Petlers when you went on the property" Horace asked when his turn came to cross-examine.

"No," Olaf replied.

Olaf was going to add that he didn't feel threatened because he'd made sure he stood behind the sheriff so wouldn't get shot by a bullet, stray or otherwise. But that response was not included in a yes or no answer.

Moog Raymond took the stand, retelling the story he'd told in Shilling's Barbershop the day following Durham's rooster hunt along Main Street, a story that added little substance to anything. Although Moog had seen the entire scene unfold from his second story window, he could only speculate on the state of Durham's sobriety.

Everett took the stand.

The sheriff laid out his story, telling how he'd found the brass shell casings on the street as Durham chased the rooster through the cornfield, and how Durham Petler had come back to the house scratched up and smelling of liquor. Norman Ludlow was trying to build a case against the Petlers as less than responsible citizens who could use some control, but Norman had been thwarted in his attempts thus far by Horace, who, through vigorous objections had successfully turned back all attempts to portray the brothers as irresponsible drunks. Everett told of the night after the boys had won the Turkey Shoot at Fair River, how he'd taken Durham home after he'd jumped on Duffy's bar and peed in his own beer glass.

"Would you say that this was the action of a sober man, Sheriff?" Norman asked.

"No," Everett answered, looking at Durham. "Not really."

"Would you say then, as an experienced lawman who has dealt with this kind of behavior in a number of situations, that Durham Petler was drunk then?"

"Yes," Everett answered. "I would."

"Have you received other complaints about the activities of Deke and Durham Petler?"

"I have."

"Specifically?"

"I have been called on numerous occasions to the Petler's residence after receiving complaints from citizens of the town. As Viola Vanderhoff, Amy Flanigan, and others have already testified, the gunfire has been noisy, coming at all hours of the day and night, and has disrupted the peace and quiet, particularly to the west end. I have repeatedly asked the brothers to tone it down."

"And what steps did you take, Sheriff?" Norman continued.

"I took no action at all, as long as they boys stayed outside the town limits. But that all changed when the boundary mistake was found and the Petler property became part of the town. I had to make sure the boys behaved themselves and abided by the rules of the town."

Norman completed his questioning and Horace stepped to the witness stand to confront Everett. He turned, moving toward the jury.

"So Durham Petler peed in a beer glass," he said grinning, walking along the rail in front of the jury with his hands raised like a preacher, "like some helpless college kid at a fraternity party."

He turned toward Everett and pounded on the front of the witness box.

"So I take it peeing in a beer glass must be a felony in this part of Iowa."

Everett remained silent, hearing a few snickers in the crowd.

"Tell me, Sheriff, what Durham Petler was doing the night he committed this heinous crime of peeing in his beer glass."

"Celebrating his win at Fair River," Everett answered. "He and Deke both shot well."

"And who were they shooting for?" Horace asked.

"Sponsors, you mean?" Everett asked.

"Exactly. Who fronted them the money for the shoot?"

"Duffy's Tavern sponsored them," Everett answered.

"Duffy's Tavern," Horace repeated. "Very interesting. And where is Duffy's Tavern located?"

Everett knew this question was going to be asked.

"It's in Apology."

"In Apology?" Horace asked incredulously, shouting the town's name while clutching his chest with one hand. "You mean the town with no guns?"

Horace turned and picked up a square of cloth from the table, opening it to show the jury and then turning to the crowd. Horace held the blue denim shirt Durham had worn at the Fair River match the previous fall.

"Read these words to me, Sheriff, if you would be so kind," Horace requested, showing Everett the back of the shirt.

"DUFFY'S TAVERN, APOLOGY, IOWA," Everett said.

"Tell me, Sheriff," Horace asked, "just which of these bold words contain the larger letters on this shirt–the name of the town or the name of the tavern?"

"They're the same size," Everett answered, reading the words on the shirt again.

"The same size, Sheriff," Horace said, shaking the shirt in front of him like a matador's cape. "The same size and of the same importance. Meaning that these boys were representing the town of Apology just as much as the tavern. In actuality, Sheriff Hiram, weren't the boys really shooting for the town of Apology? And when the town of Apology was through with them, when the boys had won the glory for the town, the town shed them like the skin from a snake, even though the town of Apology had gone to great lengths to steal the brothers away from the rival town of Lost Meadows, who'd earlier offered to pay the Petler brothers to shoot for them. Was the town of Apology thinking of its own safety then, Sheriff?"

Everett knew the twisting ways of the witness stand, and was aware that these kinds of questions were all a part of the show. But there was little he could do about the specifics of words muddied in their real meaning by the constraints of a mere yes or no. It was more often a matter of what was left unsaid than what was said that got the point across in a courtroom. Luckily, Horace's last question had been for show only, requiring no answer at all. Everett knew that the question was one for the jury to chew on, and not meant to bring a response from him, as sheriff.

Durham Petler was called to the stand to give his story. Durham told of how he and Deke had been happy, earning their livelihood from shooting competitions, and how they had done quite well at their trade for years. Horace had all their trophies and ribbons wheeled into the courtroom on several carts, impressing the jury with the sheer number of awards the brothers had collected.

"How long have you been shooting?" Horace asked.

"As long as I can remember," Durham answered. "Over twenty-five years, I guess."

"Twenty-five years," Horace said, putting his hand to his heart in amazement. "You mean to say that, for twenty-five years, you've been endangering the lives of all these citizens and only just now the town of Apology has gotten around to doing anything about it?"

Durham shook his head.

"I guess."

"My," Horace smirked, "and I thought my calendar was full."

Everett watched smiles appear on several of the jurors as well as many faces in the crowd.

"So you and your brother Deke were minding your own business, making a living on your own property, and not bothering anybody until the town annexed your property into their borders. Isn't that about right, Mr. Petler?"

"Yes," Durham answered, looking uneasy.

He faced his neighbors, looking out at a crowd that represented a cross section of the town of Apology.

"Tell me, Mr. Petler," Horace asked, "just how did you happen to end up shooting for the town of Apology at the Fair River Turkey Shoot last fall?"

Durham pointed to Everett, grinning.

"That's easy," he said. "Everett–I mean Sheriff Hiram, recruited me."

A murmur rose from the crowd, rippling through the room.

"The *sheriff* recruited you," Horace repeated. "That's very interesting. Please, do go on."

"Yea," Durham continued. "He came to me and talked me out of shooting for Lost Meadows. They'd offered to pay for both me and Deke, our expenses, that is. Said that we owed our loyalty to the town of Apology, not Lost Meadows."

"Very interesting. Then what did you do?"

Durham glanced at Everett.

"We told him we'd do it."

"After you agreed to shoot for Apology," Horace asked, "what happened?"

"Some lowdown thief stole our guns, that's what happened."

"So you had no guns."

"No, we had guns."

"I thought you said your guns were stolen," Horace said.

"I did," Durham replied. "And they were. But Everett got us new ones."

"You mean Sheriff Hiram, the same man who later arrested you on three occasions for illegally shooting inside the city limits? *He* gave you guns?"

"That's right. He gave us the single shot pistols we used to win the meet at Fair River last Thanksgiving."

"So at that time," Horace said, "the sheriff had no problem whatsoever with your ability to shoot or your responsible behavior with weapons. Can I assume this is true?"

Durham seemed puzzled.

"I guess so," he replied. "After all, he gave us the guns."

31   Run Rabbit Run

"Hey, Everett," Durham greeted during a thirty minute recess called by Judge Einpapple, "this is real exciting, ain't it?"

Everett and Durham stood on the steps on the Corwith County courthouse, breathing in the cool air of the day. It's just a game to Durham, Everett thought, as he studied the man. It must be refreshing to view the world such simplistic colors as black and white, as Durham did. Back in the courtroom those colors mixed, as word smithing and procedural duels turned every minute detail into clouds of gray. Durham seemed to be comfortably unaware of this.

Norman Ludlow took over after the break. His first question surprised everyone.

"Mr. Petler," he began bluntly, "how many shots do you think it would take you to hit a rabbit?"

Durham looked across the crowd, his pistol-pride reaching out past those few shreds of intelligent thought buried somewhere inside his head. For these were the very folks who had watched him shoot at Fair River.

"That's a stupid question," Durham replied. "Everyone here knows that it only takes me one shot to kill a rabbit."

"So you always hit your target with the first shot, Durham" Norman said, grinning as he patted Durham's hand.

Durham, drawn in by the man's friendly response, lowered his guard.

"Yea," he grinned, "unless I've been drinkin'– "

Durham, caught, tried to check his response as he watched Horace cringe.

"Thinkin'," he said, fidgeting with embarrassment. "I meant thinkin'."

"Well," Norman pressed, smiling, "Do you sometimes both think *and* drink when you're shooting?"

Durham glanced toward Judge Einpapple.

"Maybe," he replied.

"It's a yes or no response he's looking for," Judge Einpapple said. "Give him one or the other."

"Yes," Durham answered. "Sometimes a little nip helps me shoot better. Settles me down, you know."

"So that's why you drank at Duffy's the night after the shoot at Fair River," Norman said. "So you could make sure to hit the rim of your beer glass when you stood on the bar?"

A few chuckles rose from the audience.

"Oh, now you're embarrassin' me," Durham said sheepishly.

"Anyway, you say, when you're not drinking, that you can hit a rabbit with the first shot. Is that correct?"

"Damn straight," Durham said. "Me and Deke both can do it. "

"And never miss?"

"And never miss."

"And how often do you hunt rabbits?"

Horace Tallmite interrupted.

"Your Honor," he complained loudly, "I'm very glad that Mr. Ludlow is interested in the hunting habits of Mr. Petler. But what has this got to do with what we're here for?"

"Mr. Ludlow?" Judge Einpapple asked. "Care to explain?"

"If your honor will allow me," Norman explained, "I will shortly make that known. Just one or two more questions on the subject, please."

Horace shrugged, as the judge nodded for Norman to continue.

"So you always get your rabbit on the first shot," Norman said. "Tell me, Mr. Petler, how many rabbits do you and your brother shoot during a hunt?"

"Why, just one," Durham answered, as though Norman should already know. "Our dad taught us to be like the Indians and not waste things. And Deke and me can only eat one rabbit between us. We like our game fresh, so we don't freeze our kills. So we only take one when we hunt."

Norman smiled.

"So I take it that you don't take kindly to those hunters carrying five shells in those pump shotguns they hunt with?"

"Amateurs," Durham said disgustedly. "Rank amateurs. Almost heathens. Anybody can hit a target with three foot of spread."

"So you shoot the rabbit, with one bullet," Norman said. "And eat it fresh."

"Yes, that's about it."

Well, I guess I only have one other question for you right now, Mr. Petler," Norman said slowly, "and that is this. Why then do you need six bullets in your gun–"

Norman hesitated for a moment before continuing, making sure the jury was paying attention.

"–when one bullet will do the job?"

Durham seemed stunned.

"Oh, you're not sure about that first shot, are you, Durham?"

Durham looked toward Horace.

"You need those other five bullets, don't you, Durham? Come on now, tell the truth."

Everett leaned forward in his seat, seeing Owen doing the same.

"Oh, now I see–it's pretty easy to be cocky when you've got five shells to back you up if you miss, Durham. Right?"

Norman turned, facing the jury as he spoke his next words.

"Maybe you aren't the crack shot you brag yourself up to be, Durham? Maybe you're just–lucky."

Durham stood, angered.

"The hell with you, Norman," he shouted. "You know I don't need the other five bullets in that gun."

One could almost hear a rush of air as Horace's butt puckered at Durham's comment.

"Which is precisely my point," Norman replied, turning back to the jury.

"Sit down, Mr. Petler," Judge Einpapple ordered.

As Durham sat back down, Norman turned away from him and addressed the jury, well aware that the crowd was listening just as intently.

"Should a rabbit be punished for outrunning a shooter fair and square? Come on, let's make it a sport, if we are truly going to be sportsmen. You've got six bullets in that gun, Mr. Petler–that's six chances. Hell, the rabbit's only got four feet to run away with."

Norman turned to face Durham, the crowd smirking at his remark.

"Tell me truthfully, Mr. Petler, why you think you need to have all those six big old bullets in your big old gun just to hunt down a poor little old defenseless rabbit who only has four legs to run away from you? To accomplish the same thing that you yourself have repeatedly stated that you could do with just one bullet anyway."

Norman could tell that the jury was intrigued, waiting for Durham's reply. Durham, trapped by his own cocky words, uttered the only reply that made sense to him.

"I don't."

32 A Shot Heard 'Round

The trial had become the focus of several newspapers across the state, and especially enticing for anyone having relatives living in or around Apology. Several more newspaper reporters had shown up in the courtroom, scribbling notes as fast as they could, and then hunting for an open phone to call in their story. Phones were ringing in Apology, too, with callers, mostly relatives from outside, saying that they had seen so and so on the news last night, wearing such and such an outfit, and wondering who that was sitting next to them in the courtroom.

The following day Deke took the stand, repeating much of the same story that Durham told the day before. Horace, aware of Durham's damaging testimony about needing only one bullet, a comment adding validity to Apology's case, sought to lessen the damage.

"This trial isn't about hunting rabbits," Horace explained. "It's about killing snakes–snakes that hide in the grass, pretending to be friends, until they got what they want from you. Then they strike with venomous fangs and take what is rightfully yours, just as the town of Apology did with Deke and Durham Petler."

Horace pulled out the patriotic flag as he spoke to Deke.

"You know, Deke," he said, "we're beginning to send a lot of our boys over to help out that little bitty country in Southeast Asia right now. To fight for this country and defend its principles of freedom. To defend the very Constitution itself. What do you think our brave American fighting men would say if we were to send them over there to defend the very roots of democracy with only one little bullet in their gun?"

"Oh, I don't think they'd like that at all," Deke said.

"Our boys wouldn't get much accomplished now, would they?" Horace asked. "In their fight for liberty."

"No, sir," Deke answered. "I don't think they would."

"You're damned right they wouldn't," Horace said.

"Quite a little flag waver for someone who I'm sure has never spent a day defending this country in uniform," Owen whispered to Everett. "Hope he drowns in his own hypocritical words."

"Just like a rat in a rain barrel," Everett replied.

"Horace does put you in mind of a rat," Owen said, watching Horace working the jury. "He's got everything a rat's got except a long tail and whiskers. I just wonder what kind of cheese this particular rat is hunting for?"

The closing arguments came two days later, following a cleansing rain that washed the dust off the petals of the newly planted flowers in front of the courthouse. Horace Tallmite led off, facing the jury, a stern look upon his face. He pulled two bullets from his coat pocket and held them up high, one in each hand. The brass casings gleamed under the courtroom lights.

"Ladies and gentlemen of the jury," he began, "I have a question for you."

He held up the bullet in his left hand, level with his eyes, and shook it vigorously.

"Suppose I held this bullet here about this far off the floor. And then I took this other bullet and put it in a gun. And then I fired that bullet through that window over there until it ran out of steam and landed on the ground. But at the exact moment I shot that gun, I also let this other bullet drop to the floor. The distance to the floor is about five feet. The distance the other bullet would have to travel before its energy was expended would be over half a mile. Now, my question is, which bullet would hit the ground first?"

Horace looked at the bullet in his left hand and then to the floor.

"Not a very long way to go, is it?" he asked, raising his eyebrows. "Especially since the second bullet has all that distance to cover before it drops to the ground. The answer seems obvious, doesn't it?"

He held the bullets together in one hand again, pointing at them with his free hand.

"Like you, I would also think, at first, that the bullet dropped from my hand would hit the ground before the bullet shot from the gun would. But, in reality, ladies and gentlemen, both projectiles freed from confinement would hit the ground at the exact same moment."

He turned toward Owen and Everett.

"Perhaps this trial has boiled down to just something that simple, a case of distance and direction. A distance of two hundred and fifty feet along a little traveled road, an error that the town of Apology didn't think important until a survey revealed it to them. And, did I say direction? Perhaps the word I should use is misdirection. You want to talk about how far things will go? You want to talk about misdirection? What we have here is a small town, quite content with the behavior of two of its citizen for years, and then suddenly, the town changes direction, trying to force its laws on two innocent people who didn't even want to be a part of the town in the first place. It was OK for my clients to shoot whatever way they chose when they weren't part of the town, but once they were *forced* to become part of the town the good citizens of Apology caught a bad case of self-righteousness. This, of course, was done for the town's own narrow-minded benefit, and no other purpose. And on the way, the town fathers trampled on the rights of these two gentlemen. It is strange that the town of Apology, up until the time of the annexation of the Petler property, had a rather ambiguous gun law, and merely passed an additional law, knowing that this single shot provision would impact only two people–Deke and Durham Petler. In doing so, the town was well aware that this action would deprive the brothers of their only source of income, leaving them destitute and unable to fulfill their economic responsibilities to their creditors."

"Give me a break," Owen Fuller grumbled, keeping his comment hushed enough to be heard only by Norman Ludlow seated in front of him.

Horace continued.

"This trial, ladies and gentlemen, has the potential for far-reaching consequences, its impact reaching far beyond the walls of this courthouse. As I have clearly stated before, our Constitutional rights should be held as sacred to each citizen, and are not to be trifled with for the benefit of any small, misguided group touting their own agenda. Our basic rights are our life, and any attempt at stifling these treasures would be a slap in the face to those who have fought so bravely to win them for us. If we take away the right to bear arms, we might as well take away all our precious rights guaranteed under the Constitution."

Horace put his hands on his waist, hooking his thumbs on the inside of his belt. He began dancing around the room, his feet sweeping lightly across the floor, as if they were a broom. He spoke his next words rhythmically, moving his head side to side, as if trying to touch his shoulders with his ears.

"We take away this and we take away that and who in God's name will then bell the cat?"

He stopped abruptly, stood frozen for a moment, and stared at the crowd.

"Who will bell the cat?" he roared, slamming the edge of one hand into the palm of the other as he repeated the words. "Who–will–bell–the–cat?"

He paused, giving them time to absorb his words.

"For if we give away the precious rights, we might as well be mice, at the mercy of any stray cat that comes along."

He walked along the railing in front of the jury, shaking the bullets in one hand.

"So it comes down to this, ladies and gentlemen of the jury–are we going to be mice or men about this issue?"

Horace gave the jury a hard look and returned to his table. Owen tapped Norman on the shoulder.

"I hope you've got something good prepared," Owen said. "Horace has got that jury eating out of his hand with that bleeding heart act of his."

Norman stood up and faced the jury, his finger to his lips, thinking.

"My, I'm glad I'm not a mouse," he said, smiling as he threw a glance toward Horace. "Or a rat, either, for that matter."

He heard a chuckle from the audience. He addressed the twelve waiting faces.

"So am I to understand that the town of Apology is self-righteous? Is that what I heard? A town that has sent its sons to war time after time in defense of democracy–*every* war, from the Civil War to Korea, I might add–is now attempting to thwart those very liberties for which they fought? Is that the essence of Apology? I think not, ladies and gentlemen. That just doesn't make sense."

Norman halted for a moment, gathering his thoughts, and knowing that the jury waited for his words.

"A town that merely seeks to ensure the safety of all its citizens is misdirected? Is that what I heard? A town that gave two of its most unruly citizens chance after chance to clean up their act has no heart? A town that tried bringing these two citizens into the circle of rational thinking time and time again is now accused of undue cruelty? A town that bent over backwards to provide both monetary and moral support when these valued citizens had none is selfish? Ladies and gentlemen of the jury, does that sound like a community of self-righteous and self-centered people to you? It certainly doesn't to me. Having lived in Apology many years myself, and I have always been proud to be a part of this town, ladies and gentlemen, but today I feel especially honored to call myself a citizen of Apology and stand proudly with these good people."

Norman searched across the faces in the crowd, knowing the jury would do the same. He noted the pride in the eyes of his fellow townsfolk, and was aware that his shoulders bore the weight of the town's honor. His next words were important, and he knew it.

"I agree completely with Mr. Tallmite's earlier statement that this case isn't about rabbits or snakes," he said, reaching across the table to pick up a thick book. "That is true."

Horace turned to Durham, brimming with satisfaction. Norman held the book up so the audience could see.

"I do a lot of reading," he said. "And last night I was reading this."

Norman waved the book above his head, moving it in an arc as he showed it to the courtroom.

"A history book," he said. "It's tough to hide the truth held within these pages."

He hesitated.

"Though some have tried."

He opened the book.

"Let's see," he said, thumbing through the pages, "If my memory serves me correctly, I believe Mr. Tallmite earlier in this trial brought up the subject of Lexington and Concord. Funny he should bring them up, especially for this trial, since from those two towns erupted an important test of liberty one April day in 1775, and from which would bear the fruit of a great nation. Small towns, I believe, weren't they? With small ideas? Oh, and I guess if their ideas are small, then we can assume that the people who thought these ideas up were also small-minded, is that not right, also? Small-minded? Interesting, is it not? These ruffians from Lexington and Concord sound a bit like the small-minded folks from Apology. After all, when you get right down to it, they both seek the same thing–the right to govern themselves as they see fit. And if those ideals are small-minded, as Mr. Tallmite has been purporting for the town of Apology throughout the course of this trial, then perhaps we could all benefit from being so intellectually inclined."

Norman scanned the faces of the jury, knowing by each questioning expression that he had their attention.

What do you say we test Mr. Tallmite's rationale with a little history lesson of our own?"

Norman nodded his head toward a man in the back of the room. The ceiling lights dimmed as fife music began to play through a speaker, slowly at first, then livelier. A drum joined in, matching the tempo of the fife. Every person in the room immediately recognized the sound of the music as the Revolutionary War song "Yankee Doodle Dandy." Bits of the lyrics, dormant in their memories, rose through the blur of time. Norman Ludlow knew the words of the first verse by heart, for he'd reviewed them the night before.

Father and I went down to camp, along with Captain Gooding, and there we saw some men and boys as thick as hasty pudding.

On the wall next to Judge Einpapple a patch of light two feet square appeared, and a cartoon began to roll. Three animated Revolutionary War soldiers marched toward the crowd, carrying their wounds proudly as a tattered Old Glory fluttered in the breeze above their heads. One soldier wore a bloody bandage over his head as he played the fife with zeal. A second, wearing a bandage on his arm, banged on a drum. The middle soldier carried the tattered battle flag on a staff above his head, the cloth fluttering in a breeze. The music continued, the soldiers marching toward the crowd as the chorus played.

Yankee Doodle, keep it up, Yankee Doodle Dandy. Mind the music and the step and with the girls be handy.

Plit Butler joined the chorus of music, whistling the notes.

503

Wh-wh-wh-wh-wh-wh-wh, wh-wh-wh-wh-wh-wh, wh-wh-wh-wh-wh-wh-wh, wh-wh-wh-wh-wh-wh-wh.

Others followed Plit's lead, whistling in tune with the fife. Moog Raymond tapped a finger on his knee, keeping time as he whistled along.

If Judge Einpapple was confused by the events taking place in his courtroom, what happened next stunned him.

The double doors in the rear of the courtroom opened and two guards entered, struggling with a large bale of hay. The men carried the bale to the front and set it below one of the tall windows on the left side of the room. The guards stood the bale up and returned to the back of the room. A wooden board hung from the twine that held the bale together. The wood had been painted white, and in large black letters, the word "TYRANNY" had been crudely painted on the face of the board. The cartoon rolling on the wall next to Judge Einpapple froze, the image of the three marching soldiers in the frame now like a portrait.

The music grew louder, the banging of the drum drowning out the fife.

Yankee Doodle, keep it up, Yankee Doodle Dandy. Mind the music and the step, and with the girls be handy.

More of the crowd picked up the melody, including three jurors, and the courtroom filled with the whistling of the old Revolutionary War melody.

Wh-wh-wh-wh-wh-wh-wh, wh-wh-wh-wh-wh-wh, wh-wh-wh-wh-wh-wh-wh, wh-wh-wh-wh-wh-wh-wh.

The music abruptly stopped, and the whistling died out. The portrait on the wall went dark. The room grew silent as dozens of heads searched around, pondering what was coming next. The people in the back row stirred, focusing on the double doors behind them. Other rows, curious, followed their example.

Old Duke appeared in the doorway, framed by the dark oak. Everett was shocked to find his deputy dressed in the uniform of a Continental soldier. A white-tailed wig covered Duke's head, above which rested a three-cornered hat. A blue Revolutionary War era uniform coat dangled from the deputy's scraggly body, giving him the look of a half-starved soldier. Duke clutched an old Revolutionary War musket tightly in his hands, his eyes fixed straight ahead. A drum roll signaled him to step out into the room, and Old Duke moved stiffly forward with graceful rhythm, timing his steps to the beat of the drum as he marched up the aisle. The fife started once more, playing the melody to "Yankee Doodle Dandy."

Everett had never seen Old Duke look so serious, his face almost stone. The crowd was mesmerized by the man's presence as he marched in full uniform past the rows of chairs. When Old Duke reached the front of the courtroom, Norman stepped aside to let him march by.

"You want to see where small town ideas can lead you?" Norman shouted over the sound of the fife and drum.

Old Duke stopped and raised the musket to his shoulder, pointing the muzzle toward the bale. An umbrella of sunlight poured through the window where Duke had stopped. He peered over the heavy barrel, sighting on the wooden sign. Duke pulled back the hammer, the metallic cocking sound magnified in the pin-drop silence. Duke froze like a statue, the muzzle of the gun wavering. The crowd stared at him, waiting in their own trance, and unaware that each of them even drew breath. The drumming increased, suspenseful, then ceased, leaving the room in silence.

"You want to see an exercise in small town rights?" Norman roared.

Old Duke, bathed in the light from the window, fired the weapon. The flint sparked and touched off the powder in the barrel. The crowd jumped en masse at the thunder exploding into the room. A dragon's flame spewed from the mouth of the barrel, followed by a swirling cloud of blue smoke. As Old Duke disappeared into the billowing cloud, the musket ball shattered the board, the word "TYRANNY" splintering into fragments of wood that flew violently in all directions. Judge Claudius Einpapple, mouth open wide, raised a gavel. It too, froze in the air.

"Where'd he go?" someone shouted.

Bodies leaned forward, and eyes strained, as if expecting to find that Duke had disappeared into the pages of the history book from where he had come. When the sun cut through the smoke a few seconds later, Old Duke reappeared through the blue haze, rigid as a rock, still poised in his shooting stance. Bits of wood lay scattered on the floor.

Norman held the history book above his head.

"Small ideas?" he shouted. "Narrow-minded thinking? Do you really think so? It's all these pages what small towns can do. And look what happened after that first shot was fired."

He pointed to Old Duke.

"And guess what they used to fire the shot heard 'round the world?"

Norman held up a gray musket ball.

"One bullet," he said. "One single bullet. That's all those boys had. Each one of them. That's what they started this country with."

He glanced toward Horace.

"And as Mr. Tallmite has already so eloquently stated, 'by those who fought so bravely to win.' A narrow-minded idea of liberty from a small town whose guns held *just one bullet.*"

The crowd erupted, jumping to their feet as they roared their approval of Norman's final words. Moog Raymond hugged Amy Flanigan tightly, much to the chagrin of Ellen. Plit Butler, caught up in the emotion, attempted to hug Viola Vanderhoff, but could only make it halfway around her body. Jacob Witt and Evander Carlson high-fived with Earl Shilling and Quizzy Boxliter, the four jumping around like a bunch of drunks who'd just gotten all their DWI charges dropped. Irk Hickenlooper, Olaf Clancy, and a dozen others danced in the aisle as Judge Einpapple pounded furiously on his gavel, shouting for order in a vain attempt to squelch the circus his courtroom had become.

Whatever pettiness waited back in Apology was forgotten for the moment, for all had been united by the power of Norman Ludlow's words. The music to the old war song played loudly over the courtroom din. Several news reporters sprang to their feet, falling over each other as they raced to phone their editors, not waiting to hear the final verdict. Horace Tallmite sprang to his feet also, shouting words of anger at Norman Ludlow. Norman merely smiled, waving the musket ball in front of Horace's red face. Old Duke lowered his musket and walked past Everett as he left the courtroom through the commotion.

"Looky, Everett," he grinned, opening his hand. "Norman gave me twenty bucks."

Epilogue   The Town's Still Here

Horace Tallmite appealed the case to federal court, where the verdict from Corwith County was quickly overturned. For somewhere buried in that mishmash of fancy legal dialog, the federal court ruled that the Constitution was a might murky in regard to the specifics of gun laws, and therefore, it was just best not to try and fix anything when the case rested solely on the assumption that something only *might* need fixing. Most residents of Apology, scrutinizing the government's decision, felt that the deck had been stacked against them before the federal trial had ever begun. The federal courts would never admit that the government could ever make a mistake about anything to do with the Constitution, whether they knew it was wrong or not, was the general feeling around town. Durham Petler, ecstatic over the victory in federal court, accidentally shot off his remaining big toe during a bout of jubilant celebration. Now Durham doesn't limp near as bad anymore, for his feet are in balance. Unfortunately, that tidbit of good news did little for brother Deke's piece of mind, for when Durham pulled the trigger to launch that bullet into his own toe, he was wearing Deke's brand spanking new two hundred dollar Texas cowhide boots.

There was, however, no accidental shooting involved late one night in the town of Lost Meadows shortly after the conclusion the Corwith County trial. Patrons drinking comfortably at the Lost Meadows Tavern were hurled to the floor by the sharp crack of two single gunshots, fired simultaneously by unknown persons across the street, who fled the scene without being identified. The bullets shattered the huge plate glass window at the entrance of the establishment, each projectile boring its way into the expensive painting of a female belly dancer Neal Rider had recently imported from the Far East and proudly hung over the bar. As the bewildered patrons stood back up among the shattered plate glass and spilled beer, they were amazed to discover the eyes of the dancer had been shot out dead center to the pupil. The morale of the story appeared to be–be careful whose guns you're stealing.

The Petler case has been squeezed in with a bunch of others like it from around the country and pushed to Washington D.C., where the United States Supreme Court will hear it, they say. People say that this will be the end all this gun mess, one way or another, once The Court of the Land finishes hashing through the issue. They say it wouldn't take long to sort out, but you know those fellows in Washington. This is, after all, 1966. How long could it possibly take to straighten out a few simple gun laws?

Horace J. Tallmite got what he wanted–a big trial with a lot of publicity. If a man was ever born to bask in the glow of an audience, Horace is that man; and he's enjoying every minute of those golden rays of sunshine. Horace has sold his story several times already, mostly to the gun magazines and whatnot that supported him as the avid champion of the besieged gun owner. Horace has also announced that he will run for a seat in the Iowa Senate. This was the cheese Owen Fuller had wondered about during the Petler trial.

Back in Apology things are returning to normal, that being a relative term. People have softened a bit toward Olaf Clancy, for the Petler trial made Olaf's look like a jaywalking stunt through a cemetery. The summer was relaxing, with a lot of kids making good money running through the cornrows for beer on Sunday. Luckily for Merle Oaken it was a hot summer, so lots of trips were necessary. Old Duke, his hand healed from Tippy's bite, finally took the raccoon out and let him loose in the woods, but you can just about bet the farm that Duke hasn't seen the last of that particular varmint.

Phil Granger keeps his catcher's putt well oiled, still searching the sky at night for his meteor to fall, and will probably do so until they find him stone cold stiff on his porch one morning. Flem Fredrickson remains happy as a clam, getting all the worms he needs from wife Edith's nightly knee excursions into the wet grass out back of the house.

Every once in a while Everett tries his luck at Tinker's Lake, knowing his monstrous catfish still lurks in the waters near Irk Hickenlooper's Studebaker, munching on bullheads. On his last trip out, Flem Frederickson swears he felt a bump beneath the hull of his fishing boat, hard enough to rock the boat. Flem says that when he bent to look over the side, he spotted a long black stretch of fishing line moving through the water, ending in a swirl twenty feet away. Flem figures it was Everett's catfish, telling Flem to pass the word on to Everett that the battle wasn't over just because the line had been cut. But then, Flem was alone at the time, and he's got bad eyes.

Merle Oaken, still hoping to make a guide dog out of Rooney, now attaches horse blinders to the dog's head when they train, the reason for this still unknown. Merle was a bit disgruntled the first time Rooney wore his new eye gear, for a stranger slowed down to inform Merle that the old nag he was dragging behind had to be about the butt ugliest Shetland pony the man had ever put his eyes on.

Owen Fuller continues to be the mayor of Apology, however, Norman Ludlow is now doing the town's legal work, pro bono. The Petler trial showed Norman that, since he lived in the town he might as well participate with the population, for being a recluse delving into ancient history books all day wasn't near as exciting as diving into the muck of the human experience happening right outside his own front door.

And if you're careful and happen to be watching the Donahue house on any given afternoon, you can still catch Doris peeking out the slit between the front room curtains, although Doris has learned that, with a bit of eyeball straining, she can find out just about as much by poking her nose through a two-inch slit as through a four-incher. Jacob Witt don't mind it a bit, though. He gets to fix the curtain runners when they get to sticking from all that use.

The town howitzer got a new paint job this past summer, and that's an interesting story in and of itself. For the big gun had been left abandoned in the park for years, paint peeling from its magnificent steel barrel, but so low on the town council's "To Do" list that it was always left on the last page, ignored. Nobody seemed to care about the big gun that had once barked in fury at the Japanese during those tumultuous war years when the very fate of the human race lay in the balance. That irritated Everett immensely, for the gun had been put in the park in tribute to all those boys who'd fought in World War II and Korea, and it was as if folks had forgotten about what those brave men had done to keep the world free. But as luck would have it, the gun's refurbishing was a nice piece of fallout from the Petler affair.

After the Petler trial ended and things began to settle down a bit, Everett remembered the burned gunpowder he thought he'd smelled in the hallway when Duke and he arrived at the Fuller house the day Owen got shot. At first Everett had sloughed it off as his imagination, but later his lawman's intuition put two and two together. Whether the mayor knew or not, it had been his three sons who'd shot the holes in the sign west of the Petler place, sparking their father's confrontation with Durham Petler. The trio had snuck the rifle out of the house, taking turns firing at the new sign late one afternoon, making sure not to be seen. Everett tricked the boys into revealing this fact when he nonchalantly asked them if they knew of anyone who had a twenty-two rifle for sale. Before Arnold or Bull could stop him, Fuller admitted that his father had just such a rifle stored in the front hallway, but that it wasn't for sale. With a bit of bluffing Everett wrangled a confession from the boys, and from there, it was all downhill. If the boys would perform some community service work around town, Everett told them, their dad would never have to know that he'd been the victim of his own sons' prank, a piece of information sure to anger him, and the boys would never have to suffer the consequences of their father finding out that his sons were budding criminals. And as the three boys worked at the city park for over a week, stripping and repainting the town's howitzer a lovely shade of Army brown, Phil Granger contently watched their activity from his front porch, all the time cracking walnuts and digging out the sweet meat inside. Owen, unaware of the deal struck between Everett and his sons, pranced around town later, bragging about what fine young citizens his three boys had grown to be by volunteering to help clean up the park.

The town's name is still misspelled on the water tower, but if the town council can ever agree on a color for the new letters, that might eventually change. But pretty much everybody agrees that the painter they hire this time will be from Iowa and not one of those shanty Swedes from Minnesota. But not many people seem to be pushing for the fix too hard, for it gives the good citizens something to talk about during those dry spells when words are coming slow at Shilling's Barbershop or Duffy's Tavern. After all, Apology's water tower did make the news coming out of Des Moines when the Petler ruckus broke, and that's something even the big town of Renoir has never has done.

And speaking of news, a piece of bad news hit the town a few weeks back, downright distressing those who love the thrill of the ride. The word from Bert Kestral is that the county has decided to iron out that bumpy Roller Coaster Road, to flatten out those hills everyone loves to run up and down. Since word got out, that road has been busier than the Interstate 35 most nights, with everybody getting in their last rides before the dozers show up. Hell, things are getting so interesting out there now that they're even setting up barbeque grills and selling hot dogs. The number to beat running the hills, however, is still one-one-three, set by Sheriff Everett Hiram one full moon night, and the bets are heavy that the record will be standing long after they pull the plug on the roller coaster.

The Petler boys, fed up with the legal mess they'd created, and isolated by all the restraints righteous brings with it, *volunteered* to practice with their single shot pistols, and are back in favor with the town, where the pair are quite welcome to quaff at Duffy's–if they promise not to pee on the bar. People say Durham couldn't afford another victory celebration anyway, for he has no more big toes left to shoot off.

Perhaps, when it all shook out, the Petlers were, ironically, the big winners from the ruckus they stirred in Apology by the moving of the boundary sign. Deke and Durham finally figured out what everybody else in town already knew when the door to Duffy's opened to welcome them back once more, and that is, long after the lawyers and politicians have gone their separate ways, Apology will hold onto its own.

About The Author

Native Iowan Kevin Prochaska has returned to his roots, bringing with him an odd assortment of characters in *A Shot Heard 'Round*. A graduate of the University of Northern Iowa and Western Michigan University, he worked first as a petroleum geologist in the oil fields of South Texas, and later, throughout the United States and Europe in the environmental industry. The product of a small Iowa town, he is the tenth child from a family of thirteen offspring, and many of the stories in the book owe their origin to childhood events. An author of numerous technical documents, *A Shot Heard 'Round* is his first foray into the literary scene.

Printed in the United States
1162500001B/76-168